THE BLACK LIZARD ANTHOLOGY OF CRIME FICTION

EDITED WITH AN INTRODUCTION BY EDWARD GORMAN

BLACK LIZARD BOOKS • 1987

ACKNOWLEDGMENTS

INTRODUCTION Copyright ©1987 by Edward Gorman.

THE USED Copyright ©1987 by Loren D. Estleman.

A COLD FOGGY DAY first appeared in ELLERY QUEEN'S MYSTERY MAGAZINE, copyright by Bill Pronzini 1978.

SWAMP SEARCH first appeared in MURDER, July 1957, copyright renewed 1985 by Harry Whittington.

TAKE CARE OF YOURSELF first appeared in MURDER, July 1957, copyright renewed 1985 by William Campbell Gault.

A MATTER OF ETHICS is an original story and appears here for the first time. Copyright ©1987 by Robert J. Randisi.

TOUGH first appeared in MIKE SHAYNE'S MYSTERY MAGAZINE, November, 1980 and is copyright 1980 by John Lutz.

THIS WORLD, THEN THE FIREWORKS first appeared in a limited edition of THE KILLERS INSIDE HIM. It is copyright 1980 by Alberta Thompson and has been edited and somewhat revised for publication by Max Allan Collins.

SOFT MONKEY Copyright ©1987 by The Kilimanjaro Corporation. All rights reserved.

YELLOW GAL by Dennis Lynds first appeared in NEW WORLD WRITING, copyright 1957 by the New American Library.

SCRAP is an original story, and appears here for the first time. Copyright ©1987 by Max Allan Collins.

SET 'EM UP, JOE is an original story and appears here for the first time. Copyright ©1987 by Barbara Beman.

SHUT THE FINAL DOOR first appeared in ALCHEMY AND ACADEME edited by Anne McCaffrey. This version copyright ©1976 by Joe Hensley.

DEATH AND THE DANCING SHADOWS first appeared in MIKE SHAYNE'S MYSTERY MAGAZINE March, 1980. It is copyright 1980 by James Reasoner.

A KILLER IN THE DARK by Robert Edmond Alter is copyright 1963 by H.S.D. Publications. Reprinted by permission of the author's estate and agent, Larry Sternig.

PERCHANCE TO DREAM by Michael Seidman first appeared in MYSTERY, March, 1981. It is copyright 1981 by Michael Seidman.

HORN MAN by Clark Howard first appeared in ELLERY QUEEN'S MYSTERY MAGAZINE. It is copyright 1980 by Clark Howard.

SHOOTING MATCH by Wayne Dundee first appeared in HARDBOILED and is copyright 1985 by Wayne Dundee.

THE PIT is an original story and appears here for the first time. Copyright ©1987 by Joe R. Lansdale.

TURN AWAY is an original story and appears here for the first time. Copyright ©1987 by Edward Gorman.

THE SECOND COMING by Joe Gores first appeared in ADAM and is copyright 1966 by Joe Gores.

ISBN 0-88739-039-0
Library of Congress Catalogue Card No. 86-72053
Typography by QuadraType, San Francisco
All rights reserved. Printed in the U.S.A.

TABLE OF CONTENTS

INTRODUCTION   vii
    Edward Gorman

THE USED   1
    Loren D. Estleman

A COLD FOGGY DAY   17
    Bill Pronzini

SWAMP SEARCH   25
    Harry Whittington

TAKE CARE OF YOURSELF   41
    William Campbell Gault

A MATTER OF ETHICS   63
    Robert J. Randisi

TOUGH   81
    John Lutz

THIS WORLD, THEN THE FIREWORKS   93
    Jim Thompson

SOFT MONKEY   135
    Harlan Ellison

YELLOW GAL   149
    Dennis Lynds

SCRAP   161
    Max Allan Collins

SET 'EM UP, JOE   175
    Barbara Beman

SHUT THE FINAL DOOR   183
    Joe L. Hensley

DEATH AND THE DANCING SHADOWS   191
    James Reasoner

A KILLER IN THE DARK   215
    Robert Edmond Alter

PERCHANCE TO DREAM   229
    Michael Seidman

HORN MAN   247
    Clark Howard

SHOOTING MATCH   261
    Wayne Dundee

THE PIT   297
    Joe R. Lansdale

TURN AWAY   313
    Edward Gorman

THE SECOND COMING   325
    Joe Gores

INTRODUCTION

Edward Gorman

I still remember buying it. I could hardly forget. It packed the same charge of anxiety as purchasing one's first teenage beer.

The woman behind the counter of the place—then called Horak's, now called The Neighborhood Tavern—peered down at me and said, "Pretty racy stuff, isn't it?"

Or at least I think that's what she said.

Whatever formulation of syllables she used, the point was this: I was a fourteen year old Catholic school boy in a working class Irish-Czech neighborhood and this just wasn't the sort of thing kids my age were supposed to be buying.

But I would not be dissuaded. I put down my quarter and a penny for tax and she took it.

Buying condoms could not have been much more intimidating, not with the baggage of disapproval that accompanied my purchase.

Outside, shut of the woman, I got my first good glimpse of it there in the new spring sunshine.

The cover, designed by the masterful Mitchell Hooks,

Edward Gorman *is the author of four recent suspense novels:* ROUGH CUT, NEW IMPROVED MURDER, MURDER IN THE WINGS, *and* MURDER STRAIGHT UP. *He is the executive editor of* Mystery Scene *magazine, as well as an author in the fields of horror and historical fiction. Mr. Gorman lives in Cedar Rapids, Iowa.*

depicted one of his wild but forlorn red-heads submissive at the feet of a hood with a .45 in his hand. The coloration was extraordinary even by Hooks' standards: purple, black, a burnished red for her hair, and even a patch of white behind her to make her blouse and hair more startling. The title was in yellow, as was the medallion in the upper right hand that would virtually change my life.

Gold Medal book number 663 was DEATH TAKES THE BUS by Lionel White.

This was the first of probably twenty novels I read by White. While nobody would accuse him of being a great stylist, he was a great, deft plotter (I think Donald Westlake made the same point somewhere) and his "Bus" ride certainly proved it.

I can't define exactly what drew me to the book. The sex, such as it was, was great; so was the violence. It seemed, unlike the books I'd read up till then, real. More like the street-gang violence I'd come to know personally, and less like the heroic stuff of cowboy movies.

But ultimately it was White's people that made me start roaming the second-hand stores for more of the man's books. None of his innocents were quite innocent and none of his hoods were entirely bad. And none of them had many answers. Life was a curse, White seemed to be saying, and no matter what you did, you never got out with much of anything resembling dignity or meaning. A year later, when I discovered Hemingway, I found some of the same themes, and while Hemingway was the greater artist, of course, it was easier for me to identify with White's people. They hung out in grubby bus stations and prowled grey streets, much as I did. Not even the romance of war saved them.

That was my first Gold Medal book.

Within a month I probably owned fifty of the damn things, mostly bought used for a nickel each. I lined them up along my bedroom window. They all had yellow spines with black type and the Gold Medal medallion at the bottom. I even got my cousin, Terry Butler, to read them. On the basis of their wisdom, and a few other suspicions, we came to the early conclusion that life was a sinkhole and that these guys knew it. They didn't pretty up that fact and could even, once in a nasty while, rub your face in it.

Among the Gold Medal writers were David Goodis, whose

bleakness remains unsurpassed in crime fiction; Bruno Fischer, whose heroes were always confused and frightened men; Charles Williams, who saw most forms of love as little more than a set-up for betrayal; Vin Packer, who seemed to speak with equal authority about the gutter and the country club; Wade Miller, whose DEVIL MAY CARE is as harrowing a novel as any GM ever published; Gil Brewer, who was into jailbait as an expression of masochism; Stephen Marlowe and his somber detective Chester Drum, who was a somewhat existential version of Mike Hammer; Peter Rabe, whose books were so rife with Catholic guilt that it was like overhearing somebody else's Confession; Day Keene, who, when he was on, could outplot Christie and give you Los Angeles almost as well as Raymond himself; and John McPartland, who read like a failed Steinbeck and who died, far, far too young right after hitting it big (and well) with a perfect snapshot of life in a housing development, NO DOWN PAYMENT. (Watch for the movie adaption which still shows up on cable; good stuff.)

Marcus Aurelius and Celine had nothing on these guys in the despair department. (The exceptions were the gorgeous confections of Richard S. Prather, whose ALWAYS LEAVE 'EM DYING is still one of the most shrewdly plotted mysteries I've ever read. Not to mention the funniest.)

What I didn't know at the time was that much of these men's work derived from Hammett, Chandler, and James M. Cain—or some complex combination thereof. But it's too easy to dismiss the best of the GM writers as simply derivative. And wrong, too.

They filled in the details about life in the '50s the way no other group of writers did. For the most part—and again I make reference here to the best of them—they wrote about the people and places I knew. The taverns. The barbershops. The whores. The pathetic, scared little men. The predators.

Only recently have I realized that people such as Vin Packer came not from crime fiction but from the realists and naturalists such as the vastly undervalued John O'Hara. Presumably the GM writers were good as they were because at least one editor there was equally good at his task, the legendary Knox Burger, whose editorial years deserve an essay of their own.

One writer remains to be mentioned, a man who also came

more from realistic fiction than from the suspense field, the best GM writer of them all, John D. MacDonald. Where do you begin lauding John D.? Do you talk about APRIL EVIL or THE CROSSROADS or THE NEON JUNGLE? Do you quote THE DECEIVERS or THE BEACH GIRLS?

(I surrender; I've just spent twenty minutes skimming half a dozen MacDonalds and there's so much to quote, I can't quote anything. I will say only that anybody who wants to write mysteries should buy a copy of DEAD, LOW TIDE and memorize it. It is without flaw and filled with sensational observation about America circa 1953.)

So why am I telling you all this? Because, if you know what I consider holy, this anthology will make more sense to you.

While the authors and styles here are diverse, every one of them could fit into a book of GM stories. Indeed, at least two of them, Harry Whittington and William Campbell Gault, were GM authors (well, ok, technically, Gault published Crest Originals, GM's sister-line: look up his SWEET WILD WENCH) and virtually everybody included could easily have written a GM. (If time travel were actually possible, I know that's just what Max Collins and I would do; travel back there, buy us a Royal, and start work immediately.)

They told the truth, and if for most of them it was a modest truth, it was nonetheless a valid truth, and one that pertained to most of our mothers and fathers and sisters and brothers. And ourselves.

It is too bad so many good novels die during their time. Go to a library sale and thumb through some of the books that get tossed and forgotten. You encounter occasional brilliance in them and wish they had been allowed at least some small form of transcendence. (Thank God for the Black Lizard Books series, which is bringing many of these works back into print.)

What you're about to read, at least from my point of view, is a tribute to all of the GM writers who taught a whole generation of us not only the tricks of writing but a few tricks about living as well. These are the kinds of stories you found in those beautifully packaged and profane old books. I hope you enjoy them.

THE BLACK LIZARD ANTHOLOGY OF CRIME FICTION

THE USED

Loren D. Estleman

"*B*ut I never been to Iowa!" Murch protested.

His visitor sighed. "Of course not. No one has. That's why we're sending you there."

Slouched in the worn leather armchair in the office Murch kept at home, Adamson looked more like a high school basketball player than a federal agent. He had baby-fat features without a breath of whisker and collar-length sandy hair and wore faded Levi's with a tweed jacket too short in the sleeves and a paisley tie at three-quarter mast. His voice was changing, for God's sake. This slight bulge under his left arm might have been a sandwich from home.

Murch paced, coming to a stop at the basement window. His lawn needed mowing. Thought of it awakened the bursitis in his left shoulder. "What'll I do there? Don't they raise wheat or something like that? What's a wheat farmer need with a bookkeeper?"

"You won't be a bookkeeper. I explained all this before." The agent sat up, resting his forearms on his bony knees. "In return

*Though barely in his thirties, **Loren D. Estleman** has distinguished himself as a writer of both first-rate detective fiction and first-rate western fiction. His literary voice resonates with a real toughness you rarely find in "tough guy" writers. Estleman, who can also be the gentlest of stylists, isn't bluffing. His Amos Walker books already form a major body of private eye work.*

for your testimony regarding illegal contributions made by your employer to the campaigns of Congressmen Disdale and Reicher and Senator Van Horn, the Justice Department promises immunity from prosecution. You will also be provided with protection during the trial, and afterwards a new identity and relocation to Iowa. When you get there, you'll find a job waiting for you selling hardware, courtesy of Uncle Sam."

"What the hell do I know about hardware? My business is with numbers."

"An accounting position seemed inadvisable on the off chance Redman's people traced you west. They'd never think of looking for you behind a sales counter."

"You said he wouldn't be able to trace me!" Murch swung around.

Adamson's lips pursed, lending him the appearance of a teenage Cupid. "I won't lie and say it hasn't happened. But in those cases there were big Syndicate operations involved, with plenty of capital to spend. Jules Redman is light cargo by comparison. It's the senator and the congressmen we want, but we have to knock him down to get to them."

"What's the matter, they turn you down?"

The agent looked at him blankly.

Murch had to smile. "Come on, I ain't been in this line eighteen years I don't see how it jerks. Maybe these guys been giving your agency a hard time on appropriations, or—" He broke off, his face brightening further. "Say, didn't I read where this Van Horn is asking for an investigation into clandestine operations? Yeah, and maybe the others support him. So you sniff around till something stinks and then tell them if they play ball you'll scratch sand over it. Only they don't feel like playing, so now you go for the jugular. Am I close?"

"I'm just a field operative, Mr. Murch. I leave politics to politicians." But the grudging respect in the agent's tone was enlightening.

"What happens if I decide not to testify?"

"Then you'll be wearing your numbers on your shirt. For three counts of conspiracy to bribe a member of the United States Congress."

They were watching each other when the doorbell rang upstairs. Murch jumped.

"That'll be your escort," Adamson suggested. "I've arranged for a room at a motel in the suburbs. The local police are lending a couple of plainclothesmen to stay there with you until the trial Monday. It's up to you whether I ask them to take you to jail instead."

"One room?" The bookkeeper's lip curled.

"There's an economy move on in Washington." Adamson got out of the chair and stood waiting. The doorbell sounded again.

"I want a color TV in the room," said Murch. "Tell your boss no color TV, no deal."

The agent didn't smile. "I'll tell him." He went up to answer the door.

He shared a frame bungalow between the railroad and the river with a detective sergeant named Kirdy and his relief, a lean, chinless officer who watched football all day with the sound turned down and a transistor radio in his lap tuned in to the races. Kirdy looked bigger than he was. Though his head barely reached the bridge of Murch's nose, he took a Size 46 jacket and had to turn sideways to clear his shoulders through doorways. He had kind eyes set incongruously in a slab of granite. No Chin never spoke except to warn his charge away from windows. Kirdy's conversation centered around his granddaughter, a blond tyke of whom he had a wallet full of photos. The bathroom was heated only intermittently by an electric baseboard unit and the building shuddered whenever a train went past. But Murch had his color TV.

At half-past ten Monday morning, he was escorted into court by Adamson and another agent who looked like a rock musician. Jules Redman sat at the defense table with his attorney. Murch's employer was small and dark, with an old-time gunfighter's handlebar moustache and glossy black hair combed over a bald spot. Their gazes met while the bookkeeper was being sworn in, and from then until recess was called at noon Redman's tan eyes remained on the man in the witness chair.

Charles Anthony Murch—his full name felt strange on his tongue when the court officer asked him for it—was on the stand two days. His testimony was complicated, having to do with dates and transactions made through dummy corporations, and he consulted his notebook often while jurors stifled yawns and the spectators in the gallery fidgeted and inspected their finger-nails. After adjournment the first day, the witness was whisked along a circuitous route to a hotel near the airport, where Kirdy and his partner awaited their duty. On the way Adamson was talkative and in good spirits. Already he spoke of how his agency would proceed against the congressmen and Senator Van Horn after Redman was convicted. Murch was silent, remembering his employer's eyes.

The defense attorney, white-haired and grandfatherly behind a pair of half-glasses, kept his seat during cross-examination the next morning, reading from a computer printout sheet on the table in front of him while the government's case slowly fell to pieces. Murch had thought that his dismissal from that contracting firm upstate was off the books, and he was surprised to learn that someone had penetrated his double-entry system at the insurance company he had left in Chicago. Based on this record, the lawyer accused the bookkeeper of entering the so-called campaign donations into Redman's ledger to cover his own thefts. The jurors' faces were unreadable, but as the imputation continued Murch saw the corners of the defendant's moustache lift slightly and watched Adamson's eyes growing dull in the gallery.

The jury was out twenty-two hours, a state record for that kind of case. Jules Redman was found guilty of resisting arrest reduced from assaulting a police officer (he had lost his temper and knocked down a detective during an unsuccessful search of his office for evidence) and was acquitted on three counts of bribery. He was fined a hundred dollars.

Adamson was out the door on the reporters' scurrying heels. Murch hurried to catch up.

"You just don't live right, Charlie."

The bookkeeper held up at the hissed comment. Redman's diminutive frame slid past him in the aisle and was swallowed up by a crowd of well-wishers gathered near the door.

The agent kept a twelve-by-ten cubicle in the federal building two floors up from the courtroom where Redman had been set free. When Murch burst in, Adamson was slumped behind a gray steel desk deep in conversation with his rock musician partner.

"We *had* a deal," corrected the agent, after Murch's blurted interruption. His colleague stood by brushing his long hair out of his eyes. "It was made in good faith. We gave you a chance to volunteer any information from your past that might put our case in jeopardy. You didn't take advantage of it, and now we're all treading water in the toilet."

"How was I to know they was gonna dig up that stuff about those other two jobs? You investigated me. *You* didn't find nothing." The ex-witness' hands made wet marks on the desk top.

"Our methods aren't Redman's. It takes longer to subpoena personnel files than it does to screw a magnum into a clerk's ear and say gimme. Now I know why he didn't try to take you out before the trial." He paused. "Is there anything else?"

"Damn right there's something else! You promised me Iowa, win or lose."

Adamson reached inside his jacket and extracted a long narrow folder like the airlines used to put tickets in. Murch's heart leaped. He was reaching for the folder when the agent tore it in half. He put the pieces together and tore them. Again, and then he let the bits flutter to the desk.

For a numb moment the bookkeeper goggled at the scraps. Then he lunged, grasping Adamson's lapels in both hands and lifting. "Redman's a killer!" He shook him. The agent clawed at his wrists, but Murch's fingers were strong from years spent cramped around pencils and the handles of adding machines. Adamson's right hand went for his underarm holster. Meanwhile his partner got Murch in a bearhug and pulled. The front of the captive agent's coat tore away in his hands.

Adamson's chest heaved. He gestured with his revolver. "Get him the hell out of here." His voice cracked.

Murch struggled, but his right arm was yanked behind him and twisted. Pain shot through his shoulder. He went along, whimpering. Shoved out into the corridor, he had to run to catch his balance and slammed into the opposite wall, knocking a memo off a bulletin board. The door exploded shut.

A group of well-dressed men standing nearby stopped talking to look at him. He realized that he was still holding pieces of Adamson's jacket. He let them fall, brushed back his thinning hair with a shaky hand, adjusted his suit, and moved off down the corridor.

Redman and his lawyer were being interviewed on the

courthouse steps by a television crew. Murch gave them a wide berth on his way down. He overheard his employer telling the reporters he was leaving tomorrow morning for a week's vacation in Jamaica. Ice formed in the bookkeeper's stomach. Redman was giving himself an alibi for when Murch's body turned up.

Anyway, he had eighteen hours' grace. He decided to write off the stuff he had left back at the hotel and took a cab to his house on the west side. For years he had kept two thousand dollars in cash there in case he needed a getaway stake in a hurry. By the time he had his key in the front lock he was already breathing easier; Redman's men wouldn't try anything until their boss was out of the country, and a couple of grand could get a man a long way in eighteen hours.

His house had been ransacked.

They had overlooked nothing. They had torn up the rugs, pulled apart the sofa and easy chairs and slit open the cushions, taken pictures down from the walls and dismantled the frames, removed the back panel from the TV set, dumped out the flour and sugar canisters in the kitchen. Even the plates had been unscrewed from the wall switches. The orange juice can in which he had kept the rolled bills in the freezing compartment of the refrigerator lay empty on the linoleum.

The sheer cold logic of the operation dizzied Murch. Even after they had found the money they had gone on to make sure there were no other caches. His office alone, its contents smeared out into the passage that led to the stairs, would have taken hours to reduce to its present condition. The search had to have started well before the verdict was in, perhaps even as early as the weekend he had spent in that suburban motel. Redman had been so confident of victory he had moved to cut off the bookkeeper's escape while the trial was still in progress.

He couldn't stay there. Probably he was already being watched, and the longer he remained the greater his chances grew of being kept prisoner in his own home until the word came down to eliminate him. He stepped outside. The street was quiet except for some noisy kids playing basketball in a neighbor's driveway and the snort of a power mower farther down the block. He started walking toward the corner.

Toward the bank. They'd taken his passbook too, but he had

better than six thousand in his account and he could borrow against that. Buy a used car or hop a plane. Maybe even go to Jamaica, stretch out on the beach next to Redman and wait for his reaction. He smiled at that. Confidence warmed him, like whiskey in a cold belly. He mounted the bank portico, grasped the handle on the glass door. And froze.

He was alerted by the one reading a bank pamphlet in a chair near the door. There were no lines at the tellers' cages and no reason to wait. He spotted the other standing at the writing table, pretending to be making out a deposit slip. Their eyes wandered the lobby from time to time, casually. Murch didn't recognize their faces, but he knew the type; early thirties, jackets tailored to avoid telltale bulges. He reversed directions, moving slowly to keep from drawing attention. His heart started up again when he cleared the plate glass.

It was quarter to five, too late to reach another branch before closing, and even if he did he knew what would be waiting for him. He knew they had no intention of molesting him unless he tried to borrow money. They were running him like hounds, keeping him within range while they waited for the go-ahead. He was on a short tether with Redman on the other end.

But a man who juggled figures the way Murch did had more angles than the Pentagon. He hailed a cruising cab and gave the driver Bart Morgan's address on Whitaker.

Morgan's laundromat was twice as big as the room in back where the real business was conducted, with a narrow office between to prevent the ringing of the telephones from reaching the housewives washing their husbands' socks out front. Murch found the proprietor there counting change at the card table he used for a desk. Muscular but running to fat, Morgan had crewcut steel-gray hair and wore hornrimmed glasses with a hearing aid built into one bow. His head grew straight out of his T-shirt.

"How they running, Bart?"

"They need fixing." He reached across the stacked coins to shake Murch's hand.

"I meant the horses, not the machines."

"So did I."

They laughed. When they were through, Murch said, "I need money, Bart."

"I figured that." The proprietor's eyes dropped to the table.

"You caught me short, Charlie. I got bit hard on the last three at the Downs Saturday."

"I don't need much, just enough to get out of the city."

"I'm strapped. I wish to hell I wasn't but I am." He removed a quarter from one stack and placed it atop another. "You know I'd do it if I could but I can't."

The bookkeeper seized his wrist gently. "You owe me, Bart. If I didn't lend you four big ones when the Dodgers took the Series, you'd be part of an off-ramp somewhere by now."

"I paid back every cent."

"It ain't the money, it's the doing what's needed."

Morgan avoided his friend's eyes.

"Redman's goons been here, ain't they?" Murch was accusing.

Their gazes met for an instant, then Morgan's dropped again. "I got a wife and a kid that can't stay out of trouble." He spoke quietly. "What they gonna do I don't come home some night, or the next or the next?"

"You and me are friends."

"You got no right to say that." The proprietor's face grew red. "You got no right to come in here and ask me to put my chin on the block."

Murch tightened his grip. "If you don't give it to me I'll take it."

"I don't think so." Morgan leaned back, exposing a curved black rubber grip pressing into his paunch above the waistband of his pants.

Murch said, "You'd do Redman's job for him?"

"I'll do what I got to to live, same as you."

Telephones jangled in back, all but drowned out by the whooshing of the machines out front. The bookkeeper cast away his friend's wrist. "Tell your wife and kid Charlie said goodbye." He went out, leaving the door open behind him.

"You got no right, Charlie."

Murch kept moving. Morgan stood up, shouting to be heard over the racket of the front-loaders. "You should of come to me before you went running to the feds! I'd of give you the odds!"

His visitor was on the street.

Dusk was gathering when he left the home of his fourth and last friend in the city. His afflicted shoulder, inflamed by the humid weather and the rough treatment he had received at Adamson's office, throbbed like an aching tooth. His hands were empty. Like Bart Morgan, Gordy Sharp and Ed Zimmer pleaded temporary poverty, Zimmer stepping out onto the porch to talk while his family remained inside. There was no answer at Henry Arbogast's, yet Murch swore he had seen a light go off in one of the windows on his way up the walk.

Which left Liz.

He counted the money in his wallet. Forty-two dollars. He had spent almost thirty on cabs, leaving himself with just enough for a room for the night if he failed to get shed of the city. Liz was living in the old place two miles uptown. He sighed, put away the billfold and planted the first sore foot on concrete.

Night crept out of the shadowed alleys to crouch beyond the pale rings cast by the street lights. He avoided them, taking his comfort in the invisibility darkness lent him. Twice he halted, breathing shallowly, when cars crawled along the curb going in his direction, then he resumed walking as they turned down side streets and picked up speed. His imagination flourished in the absence of light.

The soles of his feet were sending sharp pains splintering through his ankles by the time the reached the brickfront apartment house and mounted the simpering stairs to the fourth floor. Outside 4-C he leaned against the wall while his breathing slowed and his face cooled. Straightening, he raised his fist, paused, and knocked gently.

A steel chain prevented the door from opening beyond the width of her face. Her features were dark against the light behind her, sharper than before, the skin creased under her eyes and at the corners of her mouth. Her black hair was streaked in mouse-color and needed combing. She had aged considerably.

"I knew you'd show up," she snapped, cutting his greeting in half. "I heard all about the verdict on the Six O'Clock News. You want money."

"I'm lonesome, Liz. I just want to talk." He'd forgotten how quick she was. But he had always been able to soften her up in the past.

"You never talked all the time we was married unless you wanted something. I can't help you, Charlie." She started to close the door.

He leaned on it. His bad shoulder howled in outrage. "Liz,

you're my last stop. They got all the other holes plugged." He told her about Adamson's broken promise, about the bank and his friends. "Redman'll kill me just to make an example."

She said, "And you're surprised?"

"What's that supposed to mean?" He controlled his anger with an effort. That had always been her chief weapon, her instinct for the raw nerve.

"There's two kinds in this world, the ones that use and the ones that get used." Her face was completely in shadow now, unreadable. "Guys like Redman and Adamson squeeze all the good out of guys like you and then throw you away. That's the real reason I divorced you, Charlie. You was headed for the junkpile the day you was born. I just didn't want to be there to see it."

"Christ, Liz, I'm talking about my life!"

"Me too. Just a second." She withdrew, leaving the door open.

He felt the old warmth returning. Same old Liz: Deliver a lecture, then turn around and come through after all. It was like enduring a sermon at the Perpetual Mission in return for a hot meal and a roof for the night.

"Here." Returning, she thrust a fistful of something through the opening. He reached for it eagerly. His fingers closed on cold steel.

He recoiled, tried to give back the object, but she'd dropped her hand. "You nuts?" he demanded. "I ain't fired a gun since the army!"

"It's all I got to give you. Don't let them find out where it came from."

"What good's it against a dozen men with guns?"

"No good, the way you're thinking. I wait tables in Redman's neighborhood, I hear things. He likes blowtorches. Don't let them burn you alive, Charlie."

He was still staring, holding the .38 revolver like a handful of popcorn, when she shut the door. The lock snapped with a noise like jaws closing.

It was a clear night. The Budweiser sign in the window of the corner bar might have been cut with an engraving tool out of orange neon. Someone gasped when he emerged from the apartment building. A woman in evening dress hurried past on a man's arm, her face tight and pale in the light coming out through the glass door, one brown eye rolling back at Murch. He'd forgotten about the gun. He put it away.

His subsequent pounding had failed to get Liz to open her door. If he'd wanted a weapon he'd have gotten it himself; the city bristled with unregistered iron. He fingered the unfamiliar thing in his pocket, wondering where to go next. His eyes came to the bright sign in the bar window.

Blood surged in his ears. Murch's robberies had all been from company treasuries, not people, his weapons figures in ledgers. Demanding money for lives required a steady hand and the will to carry out the threat. It was too raw for him, too much like crime. He started walking away from the bar. His footsteps slowed halfway down the block and stopped twenty feet short of the opposite corner. The pedestrian signal changed twice while the was standing there. He turned around and retraced his steps. He was squeezing the concealed revolver so hard his knuckles ached.

The establishment was quiet for that time of the evening, deserted but for a young bartender in a red apron standing at the cash register. The jukebox was silent. As Murch approached, the employee turned unnaturally bright eyes on him. The light from the beer advertisement reflecting off the bar's cherrywood finish flushed the young man's face. "Sorry, friend, we're—"

Murch aired the .38. His hand shook.

The bartender smiled weakly.

"This ain't no joke! Get 'em up!" He tried to make his voice tough. It came out high and ragged.

Slowly the young man raised his hands. He was still smiling. You're out of luck, friend."

Murch told him to shut up and open the cash register drawer. He obeyed. It was empty.

"Someone beat you to it," explained the bartender. "Two guys with shotguns came in an hour ago, shook down the customers and cleaned me out. Didn't even leave enough to open up with in the morning. You just missed the cops."

His smile burned. Murch's finger tightened on the trigger and the expression was gone. The bookkeeper backed away, bumped into a table. The gun almost went off. He turned and stumbled toward the door. He tugged at the handle; it didn't budge. The sign said PUSH. He shoved his way through to the street. Inside, the bartender was dialing the telephone.

The night air stung Murch's face, and he realized there were tears on his cheeks. His thoughts fluttered wildly. He caught them and sorted them into piles with the discipline of one trained to work with assets and debits. Redman couldn't have known he would pick this particular place to rob, even had he suspected the bookkeeper's desperation would make him choose that course. Blind luck had decided whom to favor, and as usual it wasn't Charlie Murch.

A distant siren awakened him to practicalities. Soon he would be a fugitive from the law as well as from Redman; he wasn't cold enough to go back and kill the bartender to keep him from giving the police his description. He pocketed the gun and ran.

His breath was sawing in his throat two blocks later when he spotted a cab stopped at a light. He sprinted across to it, tore open the back door, and threw himself into a seat riddled with cigarette burns.

"Off duty, bud," announced the driver, hanging a puffy, stubbled face over the back of his seat. "Oil light's on. I'm on my way back to the garage to see what's wrong."

There was no protective panel between the seats. His passenger thrust the handgun in his face and thumbed back the hammer.

The driver sighed heavily. "All I got's twelve bucks and change. I ain't picked up a fare yet."

He was probably lying, but the light was green and Murch didn't want to be arrested arguing with a cabbie. "Just drive."

They passed a prowl car on its way toward the bar, its siren gulping, its lights flashing. Murch fought the urge to duck, hiding the gun instead. The county lock-up was full of men who would ice him just to get in good with Redman.

He got an idea that frightened him. He tried pushing it away, but it kept coming back.

"Mister, my engine's overheating."

Murch glanced up. The cab was making clunking noises. The warning light on the dash glowed angry red. They had gone nine blocks. "All right, pull over."

The driver spun the wheel. As he rolled to a stop next to the curb the motor coughed, shuddered and died. Steam rolled out from under the hood.

"Start counting." The passenger reached across the front seat and tore the microphone free of the two-way radio. "Don't get out till you reach a thousand. If you do, you won't have the time to be sorry you did. You'll be dead." He slid out and slammed the door on six.

He caught another cab four blocks over, this time without having to use force. It was a twenty-dollar ride out to the posh residential district where Jules Redman lived. He tipped the cabbie five dollars. He had no more use for money.

The house was a brick ranchstyle in a quiet cul-de-sac studded with shade trees. Murch found the hike to the front door effortless; for the first time in hours he was without pain. On the step he took a deep breath, let half of it out and rang the bell. He took out the gun. Waited.

After a lifetime the door was opened by a very tall young man in a tan jacket custom made to contain his enormous chest. This was Randolph, Redman's favorite bodyguard. His eyes flickered when he recognized the visitor. A hand darted inside his jacket.

The reports were very loud. Murch fired a split-second ahead of Randolph, shattering his sternum and throwing off his aim so that the second bullet entered the bookkeeper's left thigh. He had never been shot before; it was oddly sensationless, like the first time he had had sex. The bodyguard crumpled.

Murch stepped across him. He could feel the hot blood on his leg, nothing else. Just then Redman appeared in an open doorway beyond the staircase. When he saw Murch he froze. He was wearing a maroon velour robe over pajamas and his feet were in slippers.

The bookkeeper was motionless as well. What now? He hadn't expected to get this far. He had shot Randolph in self-defense; he couldn't kill a man in cold blood, not even this one, not even when that was the fate he had planned for Murch.

Redman understood. He smiled under his moustache. "Like I said before, Charlie, you just don't live right."

Another large man came hurtling through a side door, towed by an automatic pistol. He was older than Randolph and wore neither jacket nor necktie, his empty underarm holster exposed.

This was the other bodyguard, Ted. He held up before the sight that met his eyes.

"Kill him," Redman told Ted calmly.

Murch's bullet splintered one of the steps in the staircase. He'd aimed at the banister, but that was close enough. "Next one goes between your boss's eyes" he informed the bodyguard.

Ted laid his gun on the floor and backed away from it, raising his hands.

The bookkeeper felt no triumph. He wondered if it was fear that was making him numb or if he just didn't care. To Redman: "Over here."

Redman hesitated. Murch cocked the revolver. The racketeer approached cautiously.

"Pick that up." Murch indicated Randolph's gun lying where he had dropped it when he fell. "Slow," he added, as Redman stooped to obey.

He accepted the firearm between the thumb and forefinger of his free hand and dropped it carefully into a pocket to avoid smearing the fingerprints. To Ted: "Get the car."

Murch was waiting in front with his hostage when the bodyguard drove the Cadillac out of the garage. "Okay, get out," he told Ted.

He made Redman get behind the wheel and climbed in on the passenger's side. "Start driving. I'll tell you what turns to make." He spoke through clenched teeth. His leg was starting to ache and he was feeling light-headed from the blood loss.

The bodyguard watched them until they reached the end of the driveway. Then he swung around and sprinted back inside.

"He'll be on the phone to the others in two seconds," jeered Redman. "How far you think you'll get before you bleed out?"

"Turn right," Murch directed.

The big car took the bumps well. Even so, each one was like a red-hot knife being twisted in the bookkeeper's thigh. He made himself as comfortable as possible without taking his eyes off the driver, the revolver resting in his lap with his hand on the butt. He welcomed Redman's taunts. They distracted him from his pain, kept his mind off the drowsiness welling up inside him like warm water filling a tub. He wasn't so far from content.

The dead bodyguard would take explaining. But a paraffin test would reveal that he'd fired a weapon recently, and the gun in Murch's pocket was likely registered to Randolph. Redman's prints on the butt and the fact that Randolph worked for him, together with the bullet in Murch's leg and a clear motive in his testimony in the bribery trial, would put his old boss inside for a long time for attempted murder. "Left here."

The lights of the 14th Precinct were visible down the block. Detective Sergeant Kirdy's precinct, the home of the proud grandfather who had protected Murch during the trial. Murch told Redman to stop the car. It felt good to give him that last order. Charlie Murch had stopped being one of the used.

He recognized Kirdy's blocky shape descending the front steps as he was following Redman out the driver's side and called to him. The sergeant shielded his eyes with one hand against the glare of the headlamps, squinted at the two figures coming toward him, one limping, the other in a bathrobe being pushed out ahead. He drew his magnum from his belt holster. Murch gestured to show friendship. The noise the policeman's gun made was deafening, but Murch never heard it.

"That was quick thinking, Sergeant." Hands in the pockets of his robe, Redman looked down at his late captor's body spreadeagled in the gutter. A crowd was gathering.

"We got the squeal on your kidnaping a few minutes ago," Kirdy said. "I was just heading out there when you two showed."

"You ought to make lieutenant for this."

The sergeant's kind eyes glistened. "That'd be great, Mr. Redman. The wife and kids been after me for years to get off the street."

"You will if there's any justice. How's that pretty granddaughter of yours, by the way?"

A COLD FOGGY DAY

Bill Pronzini

*T*he two men stepped off the Boston-to-San Francisco plane at two o'clock on a cold foggy afternoon in February. The younger of the two by several years had sand-colored hair and a small birthmark on his right cheek; the older man had flat gray eyes and heavy black brows. Both wore topcoats and carried small overnight bags.

They walked through the terminal and down to one of the rental-car agencies on the lower level. The older man paid for the rental of a late-model sedan. When they stepped outside, the wind was blowing and the wall of fog eddied in gray waves across the airport complex. The younger man thrust his hands deep into the pockets of his topcoat as they crossed to the lot where the rental cars were kept. He could not remember when he had been quite so cold.

A boy in a white uniform brought their car around. The older man took the wheel. As he pulled the car out of the lot, the younger man said, "Turn the heater on, will you, Harry? I'm freezing in here."

Given the number of books he's published (well over twenty-five) and the number of accolades he's received (from The Private Eye Writers of America to The New York Times*), it seems foolish to say that* **Bill Pronzini** *awaits major discovery. Yet he does. His "Nameless" series is one of the three most important private eye series of the past two decades, but it is rarely recognized as such. One senses and hopes that Pronzini will soon, and at last, find his reputation matched by popular recognition.*

Harry put on the heater. Warm air rushed against their feet, but it would be a long while before it was warm enough to suit the younger man. He sat blowing on his hands. "Is it always this cold out here?" he asked.

"It's not cold," Harry said.

"Well, I'm freezing."

"It's just the fog, Vince. You're not used to it."

"There's six inches of snow in Boston," Vince said. "Ice on the streets thick enough to skate on. But I'm damned if it's as cold as it is out here."

"You have to get used to it."

"I don't think I *could* get used to it," Vince said. "It cuts through you like a knife."

"The sun comes out around noon most days and burns off the fog," Harry said. "San Francisco has the mildest winters you've ever seen."

The younger man didn't say anything more. He didn't want to argue with Harry; this was Harry's home town. How could you argue with a man about his home town?

When they reached San Francisco, 20 minutes later, Harry drove a roundabout route to their hotel. It was an old but elegant place on Telegraph Hill, and the windows in their room had a panoramic view of the bay. Even with the fog, you could see the Golden Gate Bridge and the Bay Bridge and Alcatraz Island. Harry pointed out each of them.

But Vince was still cold and he said he wanted to take a hot shower. He stood under a steaming spray for ten minutes. When he came out again, Harry was still standing at the windows.

"Look at that view," Harry said, "Isn't that some view?"

"Sure," Vince agreed. "Some view."

"San Francisco is a beautiful city, Vince. It's the most beautiful city in the world."

"Then why did you ever leave it? Why did you come to Boston? You don't seem too happy there."

"Ambition," Harry said. "I had a chance to move up and I took it. But it's been a long time, Vince."

"You could always move back here."

"I'm going to do that," Harry said. "Now that I'm home again, I know I don't want to live anywhere else. I tell you, this is the most beautiful city anywhere on this earth."

Vince was silent. He wished Harry wouldn't keep talking about how beautiful San Francisco was. Vince liked Boston; it was his town just as San Francisco was Harry's. But Vince couldn't see talking about it all the time, the way Harry had ever since they'd left Boston this morning. Not that Vince would say anything about it. Harry had been around a long time and Vince was just a new man. He didn't know Harry that well— had only worked with him a few times; but everybody said you could learn a lot from him. And Vince wanted to learn.

That was not the only reason he wouldn't say anything about it. Vince knew why Harry was talking so much about San Francisco. It was to keep his mind off the job they had come here to do. Still, it probably wasn't doing him much good, or Vince any good either. They only way to take both their minds off the job was to get it done.

"When are we going after him, Harry?" Vince said.

"Tonight."

"Why not now?"

"Because I say so. We'll wait until tonight."

"Listen, Harry—"

"We're doing this my way, remember?" Harry said. "That was the agreement. *My* way."

"All right," Vince said, but he was beginning to feel more and more nervous about this whole thing with Dominic DiLucci. He wished it was over and finished with and he was back in Boston with his wife. Away from Harry.

After a while Harry suggested they go out to Fisherman's Wharf and get something to eat. Vince wasn't hungry and he didn't want to go to Fisherman's Wharf; all he wanted to do was to get the job over and done with. But Harry insisted, so he gave in. It was better to humor Harry than to complicate things by arguing with him.

They took a cable car to Fisherman's Wharf and walked around there for a time, in the fog and the chill wind. Vince was almost numb by the time Harry picked out a restaurant, but Harry didn't seem to be affected by the weather at all. He didn't even have his topcoat buttoned.

Harry sat by the window in the restaurant, not eating much, looking out at the fishing boats moored in the Wharf basin. He had his face close to the glass, like a kid.

Vince watched him and thought: he's stalling. Well, Vince could understand that, but understanding it didn't make it any easier. He said finally, "Harry, it's after seven. There's no sense in putting it off any longer."

Harry sighed. "I guess you're right."

"Sure I am."

"All right," Harry said.

He wanted to take the cable car back to their hotel, but Vince said it was too cold riding on one of those things. So they caught a taxi, and then picked up their rental car. Vince turned on the heater himself this time, as high as it would go.

Once they had turned out of the hotel garage, Vince said, "Where is he, Harry? You can tell me that now."

"Down the coast. Outside Pacifica."

"How far is that?"

"About twenty miles."

"Suppose he's not there?"

"He'll be there."

"I don't see how you can be so sure."

"He'll be there," Harry said.

"He could be in Mexico by now."

"He's not in Mexico," Harry said. "He's in a little cabin outside Pacifica."

Vince shrugged and decided not to press the point. This was Harry's show; he himself was along only as a back-up.

Harry drove them out to Golden Gate Park and through it and eventually onto the Coast Highway, identifying landmarks that were half hidden in fog. Vince didn't pay much attention; he was trying to forget his own nervousness by thinking about his wife back in Boston.

It took them almost an hour to get where they were going. Harry drove through Pacifica and beyond it several miles. Then he turned right, toward the ocean, onto a narrow dirt road that wound steadily upward through gnarled cypress and eucalyptus trees. That's what Harry said they were anyway. There was fog here too, thick and gray and roiling. Vince could almost feel the coldness of it, as if it were seeping into the car through the vents.

They passed several cabins, most of them dark, a couple with warm yellow light showing at the windows. Harry turned onto another road, pitted and dark, and after a few hundred yards they rounded a bend. Vince could see another cabin then. It was small and dark, perched on the edge of a cliff that fell away to the ocean. But the water was hidden by the thick fog.

Harry parked the car near the front door of the cabin. He shut off the engine and the headlights.

Vince said, "I don't see any lights."

"That doesn't mean anything."

"It doesn't look like he's here."

"He'll be here."

Vince didn't say anything. He didn't see how Harry could know with that much certainty that Dominic DiLucci was going to be here. You just didn't know anybody that well.

They left the warmth of the car. The wind was sharp and stinging, blowing across the top of the bluff from the sea. Vince shivered.

Harry knocked on the cabin door and they stood waiting. And after a few moments the door opened and a thin man with haunted eyes looked out. He was dressed in rumpled slacks and a white shirt that was soiled around the collar. He hadn't shaved in several days.

The man stood looking at Harry and didn't seem surprised to see him. At length he said, "Hello, Harry."

"Hello, Dom," Harry said.

They continued to look at each other. Dominic DiLucci said, "Well, it's cold out there." His voice was calm, controlled, but empty, as if there was no emotion left inside him. "Why don't you come in?"

They entered the cabin. A fire glowed on a brick hearth against one wall. Dom switched on a small lamp in the front room, and Vince saw that the furniture there was old and over-stuffed, a man's furniture. He stood apart from the other two men, thinking that Harry had been right all along and that it wouldn't be long before the job was finished. But for some reason that didn't make him feel any less nervous. Or any less cold.

Harry said, "You don't seem surprised to see me, Dom."

"Surprised?" Dom said. "No, I'm not surprised. Nothing can surprise me any more."

"It's been a long time. You haven't changed much."

"Haven't I?" Dom said, and smiled a cold humorless smile.

"No," Harry said. "You came here. I knew you would. You always came here when you were troubled, when you wanted to get away from something."

Dominic DiLucci was silent.

Harry said, "Why did you do it, Dom?"

"Why? Because of Trudy, that's why."

"I don't follow that. I thought she'd left you, run off with somebody from Los Angeles."

"She did. But I love her, Harry, and I wanted her back. I thought I could buy her back with the money. I thought if I got in touch with her and told her I had a hundred thousand dollars, she'd come back and we could go off to Brazil or someplace."

"But she didn't come back, did she?"

"No. She called me a fool and a loser on the phone and hung up on me. I didn't know what to do then. The money didn't mean much without Trudy; nothing means much without her. Maybe I wanted to be caught after that, maybe that's why I stayed around here. And maybe you figured that out about me along with everything else."

"That's right," Harry said. "Trudy was right, too, you know. You *are* a fool and a loser, Dom."

"Is that all you have to say?"

"What do you want me to say?"

"Nothing, I guess. It's about what I expected from you. You have no feelings, Harry. There's nothing inside of you and there never was or will be."

Dom rubbed a hand across his face, and the hand was trembling. Harry just watched him. Vince watched him too, and he thought that Dominic DiLucci was about ready to crack; he was trying to bring it off as if he were in perfect control of himself, but he was ready to crack.

Vince said, "We'd better get going."

Dom glanced at him, the first time he had looked at him since they'd come inside. It didn't seem to matter to him who Vince was. "Yes," he said. "I suppose we'd better."

"Where's the money?" Harry asked him.

"In the bedroom. In a suitcase in the closet."

Vince went into the bedroom, found the suitcase, and looked inside. Then he closed it and came out into the front room again. Harry and Dom were no longer looking at each other.

They went outside and got into the rental car. Harry took the wheel again. Vince sat in the rear seat with Dominic DiLucci.

They drove back down to the Coast Highway and turned north toward San Francisco. They rode in silence. Vince was still cold, but he could feel perspiration under his arms. He glanced over at Dom beside him, sitting there with his hands trembling in his lap. From then on he kept his eyes on Harry.

When they came into San Francisco, Harry drove them up a winding avenue that led to the top of Twin Peaks. The fog had lifted somewhat, and from up there you could see the lights of the city strung out like misty beads along the bay.

As soon as the lights came into view Harry leaned forward, staring intently through the windshield. "Look at those lights," he said. "Magnificent. Isn't that the most magnificent sight you ever saw, Vince?"

And Vince understood then. All at once, in one stinging bite of perception, he understood the truth.

After Dominic DiLucci had stolen the $100,000 from the investment firm where he worked, Harry had told the San Francisco police that he didn't know where Dom could be. But then he had gone to the head of the big insurance company where he and Vince were both claims investigators—the same insurance company that handled the policy on Dom's investment firm—and had told the Chief that maybe he did have an idea where Dom was but hadn't said anything to the police because he wanted to come out here himself, wanted to bring Dom in himself. Dom wasn't dangerous, he said; there wouldn't be any trouble.

The Chief hadn't liked the idea much, but he wanted the $100,000 recovered. So he had paid Harry's way to San Francisco, and Vince's way with him as a back-up man. Both Vince and the Chief had figured they knew why Harry wanted to come himself. But they had been wrong. Dead-wrong.

Harry DiLucci was still staring out at the lights of San Francisco. And he was smiling.

What kind of man are you? Vince thought. What kind of man sits there with his own brother in the back seat, on the way to jail and ready to crack—his own brother—and looks out at the lights of a city and smiles?

Vince shivered. This time it had nothing to do with the cold.

SWAMP SEARCH

Harry Whittington

I noticed the blue-gray Caddy on my road, but had no time to watch it twist and bounce the twenty miles through Everglades sawgrass, palmetto and slash pine from the Tamiami trail to my place.

I'd been out all morning in the helicopter hunting for strays and just as I glimpsed the Caddy, I saw one of my Santa Gertrudis heifers caught in a bog. Lose a cow in that ooze, you never see her again. I needed every cow I had, every penny I could earn on my farm. I was in hock, even paying for the 'copter on installments.

I engaged the pedals, the wings rotated slowly and I hovered over the bawling cow. The pinch-rig I'd made was an ice-tong affair of steel and leather I let down on my cable.

"Take it easy, baby," I told the cow. "You're too valuable to lose in that goo."

The cable winched down, I closed the pincher about her belly and started upward. The sucking noise of the ooze and bawling of the cow rose above the revving of my motor.

Harry Whittington is, by any measure, a professional writer's professional. By his own admission he has written more than one hundred books in every category from nurse romance to western. What is remarkable about Whittington is that, no matter the job at hand, he brings to it integrity and gritty style. In the fifties he was hailed as "King of the Paperbacks." And what paperbacks they were—tight, dramatic, colorful, suspenseful. Many of them are permanent additions to the literature of crime fiction.

I let the heifer swing a moment to impress her, then set her down in high grass, cussed her once for luck, reeled in my line and peeled off toward the house where the Caddy was parked in the yard.

She was sitting in the Caddy looking around when I walked toward her. What she saw was bare sand yard without even a slash pine growing in it, brown frame house of four rooms and porch, coal-oil lamps and outhouse. Rugged, but beautiful to me. It had belonged to my folks. They'd died while I was in a Chinese prison camp. It got so this lonely place was what I'd dreamed of coming back to.

"How'd you get this far off the trail?" I said. "My road is hard to find."

She got out of the car, smiled. Except for her shape she wasn't terrific; wavy brown hair, deep-set brown eyes and squared chin. "Not as hard to find as your house. I had a ball getting here—the car scraped between the ruts."

"It's been dry or you'd never have made it."

"I'd have made it." Something about her voice made me look at her again, closer.

Her gaze touched my helicopter, and didn't move on. She smiled again. "You Jim Norton?"

I nodded and she said, still watching the 'copter, "I'm Celia Carmic . . . Mrs. Curt Carmic."

Carmic. I stared. The whole state had been alerted in a search for Curt Carmic. He had crashed in his private plane on an Everglades hunting trip. After a week of intensive searching, the Coast Guard had abandoned him as dead.

I invited her up on the porch. "I'm sorry about your husband, Mrs. Carmic."

"Yes." She shook her head as though still unable to believe it. She made a wad of her handkerchief. "Curt and I were—very happy, Mr. Norton. He was—well, several years older than I, but he was a vital man, had the world in his hand." Her head tilted. "I don't say Curt didn't have enemies. Every strong man does."

Her eyes were moist, her voice sounded full of tears. She told me about Carmic. She glossed over the way he got a discharge from the Marines in 1943, but said that from 1945 he'd had great success, headed two companies making parts for the Korean police action, Carmic Defrosters.

"Curt was due in Washington on the Monday following his trip. They were investigating his war profits. Curt was ill at this injustice, his doctor told him to rest. His idea of rest was a week-end hunting trip in the Everglades. But more than anything, Mr. Norton, he wanted to come back and clear his name." Her chin quivered. "I can't believe Curt is dead."

I didn't know what to say. All I wanted down here was peace, and a chance to make a living my way. I'd been in the world she talked about. I'd had it.

"They searched for Curt for a week. I know they were thorough and didn't find a trace. I can't give up. Can you understand that, Mr. Norton? I've got to find him. That's why I came to you."

I waited, not knowing why I didn't want to get mixed up in this thing. She said, "I'll give you a thousand dollars—and pay all expenses if you'll help me search for him."

I had plenty of use for a thousand dollars. I couldn't buy the picture she painted of Curt Carmic. Him I never knew, but I knew his Defrosters and there was a good reason for that Senate inquiry. Still, no man would take to the Everglades even to escape a government investigation.

"How long would you want to search?"

"Until we find him." She paced my porch. "I'll pay the thousand dollars for anything up to ten days. After that—" she spread her hands, left that unfinished. Tensely she watched me until I nodded. She cried then. She stood rigid and tears ran down her cheeks.

•   •   •

The rest of the day we studied flight plans and maps. She had all the information she could get on the Everglades and the weather.

I tried to shrug off the feeling of wrong that persisted. Any profiteer who'd sell Carmic Defrosters to his country should have been investigated and any woman who'd lived ten years with him should know that. Yet she spoke of him as though he were saintly. I reminded myself it didn't matter, it was a thousand dollars to me, but the nagging sense of emptiness stayed.

We set up the first flight pattern, figured mileage, weather and gas capacity and set for seven the next morning. When the time was set, Celia Carmic became a different woman.

First she'd been the bereaved wife, then the cold general over map briefing and weather data. At supper she chatted about her life in Washington. She ate delicately—like a she-wolf with a Vassar education. I'd never met anyone like her; I had to smile.

"Why are you laughing at me?"

I fumbled my fork. "I'm not laughing."

She stopped eating, touched her lips with a paper napkin. "How old are you, Jim?"

I remembered the war years, the prison. "I'll be a hundred next April."

"I'd say twenty-three."

"Say whatever you like."

She looked around. "No girl to share all this?"

I shook my head. "The kind that would share this I wouldn't want. And the other kind—" I stopped. I suddenly knew the only kind of woman I'd ever wanted. We just looked at each other. . . . "I can't afford what I want," I said.

"What would you do to be able to afford her?"

"Anything."

"Sure?"

"Anything at all."

"You might be held to that," she said. "And soon."

About five A.M. I heard something stir in the house and jumped out of bed. Sleep-drugged, I staggered across the room. I reached the guest room door before I remembered Celia was there.

I stopped in the doorway, fully awake, realizing I was in my undershorts; it was too hot to sleep in anything more.

She was fully dressed, white shirt, jodphurs, gleaming boots. She had a handful of maps and weather data. "Sorry I wakened you, Jim. I couldn't sleep any more. I'm too anxious to get started."

I mumbled something and backed off. She let her eyes prowl over me and then walked out into the front room leaving me gaping after her. Where was the bereaved wife? Where were those unshed tears?

From that moment there was a sick emptiness in my stomach. But the second the flight started, she was all business.

She sat with the flight pattern mapped on her lap. After I filled all gas tanks at the Lewiston Airport, she watched compass and mileage indicator until we reached the lines marking our first pattern. Coldly serious, she read that country minutely with field glasses.

She never took five, never relaxed. This land was huge bolts of scorched brown, ribboned by black strings of water. Heron took flight, I pointed out a wildcat. Nothing down there but silence and heat waves.

We made our circle, reached the end of the flight pattern. She sat back, dropped the binoculars. Red circles encased her eyes. "We know they're not in there."

"We'll take the second pattern tomorrow."

She seemed to have lost interest. She was watching me again from the corner of her eyes. I set the 'copter down in the yard.

"Think I could learn to handle a windmill, Jim?"

"It's not easy. But I could teach you."

She looked thoughtful.

After supper she wanted a drink to celebrate the end of our first flight. All I had was a few cans of warm beer. We drank that. She laughed and talked, teasing me about being a farmer stuck away from the world. Suddenly for no reason we stopped laughing and we stopped talking.

Crickets and frogs screeched outside the windows. It was so quiet I heard mosquitoes frantic against the screens.

I tried not to stare at her, but I couldn't keep my gaze off her. I asked if she were sleepy. She said no. We sat for a long time and listened to the crickets. That night I didn't sleep much. . . .

•   •   •

Next morning I was out of bed and dressed hours ahead of Celia. I fixed breakfast but not even the odors of coffee and eggs wakened her. I let her sleep. I didn't trust myself in that room. I remembered why she was here—a husband lost in the swamp. I had to keep remembering that.

At a quarter of seven she came out, voice angry. "Why didn't you wake me up?"

I stared at her, knowing how I'd fought to keep out of that room. "Why didn't you bring an alarm clock?"

We stood tense across the table. Then she smiled and looked very pleased about something. . . .

We'd been flying about three hours and suddenly Celia grabbed my arm. An electric charge went through me at her touch. Maybe you don't know what it is to want like that. I was sick, wanting just two things: never to find her husband and to have money so I could afford Celia Carmic.

She pointed to something glittering. I engaged the pedals, idled off the engine and we settled in a cleared space six inches above water.

She scrambled out of the plane, ran through muck and sawgrass. I plodded after her. When I reached her, she was swearing, words she shouldn't even have known.

Somebody had cut open a five gallon oil can, tossed it beside the creek. She followed me back to the 'copter.

We retraced and she was silent, did not even mention learning to handle the 'copter. We set down in the yard about four and she walked silently into the house.

After supper she discovered the old wind-up phonograph in the front room. She played an ancient record. *"Sweet—Stay As Sweet As You Are."* She wound it, played it again.

"Reminds me of you," she said. "Sweet and innocent."

I remembered her disappointment this afternoon when she thought we'd found a sign of her husband. This was a different woman.

"Come on, Jim, dance with me."

"I don't dance."

"I'll teach you." She came over, took my hands. Hers were like ice. I stood up. She came into my arms, moved closer. Her hands slid up my back. . . .

I wanted to sleep through next morning. It was good burying my face in the warm fragrance of her hair. But when I thought about the flight, I thought about her husband. I didn't like that.

I pulled her closer. She went taut. "No, Jim. We're going to search." She pulled away, eyes hard. "We're going to search all day. Everyday."

In the plane, I felt her nearness, I could smell her. All day she kept binoculars fixed on that changeless land.

"We're not staying out long enough," she said.

My voice was hard. "We'll look as long as you like. That doesn't keep me from hoping we—don't find him."

Her fingers closed on my arm. "Don't say that, Jim. Pray we do find him."

How could she do that, turn her emotions off and on? I could not forget last night; for her it had never happened. She loved her husband. She came to me. It didn't make my kind of sense. I clammed up.

We reached the end of the pattern. She dropped the glasses, rings deep about her eyes. But when she dropped the binoculars, she dropped the search. Now her brown eyes sought something else. "How long, Jim, before we get home?"

Her voice was breathless. I went empty. Her hand gripped me. "It's too far. Hurry."

I tried to hurry but they never built enough speed in a flying windmill for us. I set the 'copter down in the yard, killed the engine. We ran across the yard. That was when I saw the car tire tracks.

I stopped. The tracks came in from the road. "Somebody's been here." I sounded like Papa Bear.

Celia frowned, but pulled me toward the house. "Probably some salesman."

Footprints in the sand led around the house, paused at every window. "Persistent." I said.

For no reason I could explain, I felt that old sense of wrong mixed with unexplained fear. "I'll take the 'copter. Maybe I can catch him before he gets back to the Trail."

"Don't be a fool." She pressed against me. "I've waited all day. You're not chasing down some salesman. You're not going to leave me tonight."

I didn't, either. . . .

•   •   •

Next morning I woke up thinking about those tire tracks and footprints. Too many things were unexplained, wrong. I fixed breakfast but didn't eat anything. Celia ate like a plowman.

I followed the flight pattern but my mind wasn't on it. Celia never relaxed. We'd not found one encouraging sign, yet she never mentioned quitting. One thing was now certain. She was compelled by something stronger than that love she'd talked about the first day. Did she love Carmic at all? She never discussed him outside the 'copter. She never worried about the hell he endured if he were alive in that swamp country. All she did was glue her gaze to that ground.

When we returned, I searched first for new tire tracks. There was none. I couldn't say why, but I felt no better.

Celia pretended disinterest, but she looked for them, too.

After supper, she started the phonograph. It blared but only intensified the silence. She toppled into my lap. "It's too quiet, doll. I'm a big city girl. The Embassy—F Street. Got to have excitement. Where you going to take me?"

I smelled the warm fragrance at the nape of her neck. "I know where I want to take you."

"There's a juke joint about a mile down the Tamiami Trail from your road."

"Twenty miles. Nickel juke. Ten cent beer and mud farmers."

"That's where I want to go."

I looked at her squared chin, didn't even bother to argue.

She drove recklessly on the twisting roadway, parked beside the Seminole Inn. An anaemic neon glowed fitfully. There were gas pumps out front, motel cottages in the rear. Inside was boot-scarred bar, small dance space, unpainted tables, candles in beer cans, booths. There were half a dozen customers. We sat at a table, ordered beer. She seemed to have forgotten her husband, so I tried to.

A man sat alone at the end of the bar near the juke. I didn't pay any attention to him at first. I noticed he was pretty-boy handsome, with a golden, sculptured profile, thin mouth.

We'd been there about ten minutes before I realized he was watching every move we made. Every time I looked up, his eyes would go flat and he'd stare beyond me.

"You know that character?" I said to Celia.

"Who?" She said it too carelessly. There weren't that many people in there. I got that old empty feeling.

"Handsome," I said. "The blond god over there. He must know you, he's staring at you."

Celia looked dutifully. Her eyes met Handsome's for an instant. I saw something flicker in his flat eyes—something green like jealousy, red like hatred. It flashed and was gone. He looked at his beer.

"I'm sure I never saw him before," Celia said. "Want to dance?"

What I wanted was to hit somebody or something. If she knew the guy, why didn't she say so? I had to be sure. I excused myself, went through the door marked "His'n."

From inside I watched Celia. She got up after a moment, walked over to the juke. Handsome swung around at the bar as I'd known he would.

For a moment I was ill. I pressed my ear against the pine paneling, trying to hear what they said. Celia punched coins into the juke. "Stay away." Her voice was a sharp whisper.

"I've got to see you."

"You can't. I told you you couldn't."

"You're crossing me—" The blaring music drowned his words. I washed my face, rinsed out my mouth, staring at my reflection in the dirty window.

I was silent driving home. Celia laughed, teased, called me a baby. She slid over close, laid her head on my shoulder. It was a gray night, strung with stars and full of wrong.

"I wish you'd teach me to run the 'copter, Jim."

I felt pebbles in my throat. I wanted her to tell me the truth, but by now I knew better. I wouldn't waste my breath. "You couldn't take your eyes away from those binoculars long enough to learn."

She sighed. "That's right. That's most important, isn't it?"

I didn't say anything. It didn't seem important at all.

When we got back next afternoon from the fifth flight pattern, I saw the new tracks. "Well, he was back again," I said.

She took it big. "Somebody is trying to sell you something."

"That's God's truth."

"—and just can't believe you're gone so much." She met my gaze evenly when she said that and didn't even blush.

We ate supper silently. Afterwards she marked out the next flight pattern. I didn't even bother to look at it. I told myself I was going to bed alone. I didn't. She had me all clobbered, but I wanted her worse than ever.

•   •   •

The next morning we took off as usual. I asked her to explain the prowler.

She said it must be a neighbor of mine, or a salesman.

I shook my head. "Don't give me that. I have no neighbors. A salesman would travel that road once, maybe; never twice."

She shrugged. "It's your country."

"It's your boyfriend," I told her.

"My boyfriend!" She laughed. I let her laugh. She got tired and stopped, cold.

"I heard you two at the juke." My voice was as tired and empty as I felt.

Her eyes flickered.

"Why not level with me, Celia? What are you looking for? What do you want?"

She stared out at the horizon. She bit her lip and closed her eyes tight, but didn't speak. My heart hurt against my ribs. I wanted her to be something she wasn't and never would be.

I wanted her and hated her, and wondered what she was really here for.

We reached the beginning of the flight pattern, the same parched pepper grass, same tufted pines and endless silence. This was the next to the last day. I heard her sigh; she placed the binoculars against her eyes. After a moment, she removed them, wiped her tears. "I love you, Jim."

"Sure you do."

"I didn't mean to, I didn't even consider it. But—you don't know what it means to me to find Curt." She sank her fingers into my arm. "You won't be sorry, Jim."

"I'm already sorry. I went nuts when you walked on my place. All I've thought about was having you—and I couldn't afford you, even if I could overlook the rest of it."

"We've got to find him." She turned back, put glasses to her eyes. "And we will."

Time slipped away. And miles. I was about to make the circle, but she told me to go on a bit further. Then I heard her catch her breath, but I'd already seen it. You don't need field glasses to see smoke in that flat wasteland. She dropped the binoculars, looked at me, face rigid.

She touched my arm, then her fingers were clinging to me. "We've found him, we've found Curt."

"Sure," I said. "Didn't you know we would?"

I set the plane down near the black river. We saw the man standing beside the smudge fire. He was alone. Celia and I got out of the 'copter and went toward him.

He wasn't dirty, ragged or bearded—his face wasn't swollen with mosquito poisoning—the way it should be with a man lost in the Everglades. He'd built himself a hut of a parachute, sheltered by rude ribs made of pine limbs. I looked around. There was no sign of the plane.

I congratulated him under my breath. He was a smart guy, all right. He had survived. He had been ready. He'd had a parachute. What had happened to the plane—or what had been made to happen to it—I'd never know. Neither would anyone else. Sixty feet under, in the Gulf, no doubt.

"Well, baby," he was saying to Celia, "I see you finally made it." His voice was angry.

She snarled back at him. "I came as soon as I—could."

"Well thanks." His gaze raked me and his mouth twisted. "Not bad," he said. "Not bad at all."

She said, "I had to wait for the air forces to call off the search. I had to get a pilot."

His brow tilted. "Yes, I see you got a nice young one. Another in your long list? Is this what delayed you until the last day, Celia?"

"We did the best we could, Curt." Her breath was sharp. "Did you have sense enough to save the money along with yourself?"

Carmic laughed. "Well, your grief hasn't changed you, pet. You've still got to have money, haven't you?" He glanced at me. "My wife has some kind of complex—maybe it's an allergy— she can't stand poverty. She was born in it and she scratched her way out. God help anybody who stands in her way. My dear little wife. Never wanted anything but old money and new men."

Celia said, "Your exile didn't improve your disposition."

"Nothing will improve my disposition except a long rest in Rio."

She shrugged. "Where is the money? I'm ready to get out of here."

Carmic laughed, reached up inside his parachute hut. He pulled down a bulging brief case. I didn't have to see inside. I knew what was there—what Celia had been looking for—all the cash and negotiable securities he'd managed to get his hands on—his profits from Carmic Detectives.

"Well, baby, it's finally working. Just the way we planned. I wish you hadn't brought a 'copter. I'm not sure I can handle it."

I went cold. The nightmare was complete, I saw all they'd planned. Carmic disappeared, destroyed his plane. Celia searched for him and was lost in the search. That must be Handsome's part in this—to make sure the authorities wrote her off as well as her husband. Then much later two very rich people would turn up in Rio—and live happily ever after. I wasn't sure where that left Handsome, how much he was getting out of this.

But I saw where that left me. The river looked cold and black. I wouldn't be lonely—the alligators would keep me company. What was murder when Carmic faced prison and his wife faced poverty? It had been a well-planned if desperate gamble—but the odds hadn't been as long as they seemed.

Carmic pawed in the brief case. I saw the gleam of green bills, the black of an automatic. He said, "We'll take care of your boyfriend and then we'll get out of here."

"Curt." Celia's voice was deadly.

We both faced her, moving in slow motion.

"Curt," she said again. "You're not going anywhere. You were lost in a plane crash. Remember? We couldn't find you. I'm sorry, Curt. But I'm not sure I'd like Rio. Why should I run? I can go back to Washington—the rich widow of a martyred hero."

We both stared at the .25 automatic she'd taken from her shirt. A woman's weapon. She'd had it all the time. She'd saved it for this.

Curt's mouth dropped. His eyes widened, hurt and sick. Maybe no man can ever believe the woman he trusts will cross him. It was like that with Carmic. He stared at the gun in her hand and still didn't believe it. He looked in her eyes and saw it all there, and still doubted it. It was clear enough. She wasn't going to run the rest of her life. She didn't have to run. She could have his money and a life even better than she'd ever had. In her eyes he saw that had been her secret plan all along, no matter what lies she'd told him.

"You think you'll have her?" he said to me. "You think you'll be different than the hotel clerks and the band leader and football heroes on Saturday night—" he was almost crying, the poor dope. "But you won't be different—they've got to be new. They've—"

The little gun in Celia's hand made a popping sound in the silence. It popped again. She didn't miss. He was too big a target and she was too close.

Curt stopped talking and he stopped breathing as he crumpled to the ground where he would stop living. I heeled around suddenly and grabbed Celia's wrist. I twisted hard. She didn't fight and she didn't cry out. She folded a little at the knees, bit her lip. She dropped the gun. I picked it up, thrust it in my pocket.

She stared at me. "I had to kill him, Jim. Don't you see? He was in the way. I love you and he was in the way. It's all right. Everybody thought he was dead—and now he really is. There's a quarter of a million dollars there, Jim. A quarter of a million! It's all ours. He didn't steal it—not all at once—nobody can ever claim it. He accumulated it, as steadily and as quickly as he could. There was some suspicion, but nothing they can prove. It's ours, Jim! Didn't you say you wanted money enough so you could afford me? We've got it now. We'll be rich. Richer than any dream you every had."

"You killed him. Murdered him."

"You don't know. How he has beaten me, insulted me, hurt and degraded me. He was a beast, Jim. He deserved to die." She shook, her shoulders sagging and she looked as if she might fall. I steadied her.

Her arms went around me, her trembling mouth found mine. She was sobbing then and I felt her warmth, her animal-like warmth against me. "Let's get home, Jim," she cried softly. "Let's get home."

I couldn't forget her husband's body, but there was nothing I could do for him. Not now, not here.

•   •   •

Celia didn't speak all the way back. She sat with the satchel of money between her feet.

I didn't say anything. There wasn't anything more to say.

That little .25 had said it all back there on the black and bottomless river in the unchartered glades, into which the 'gators would have pulled Curt Carmic by now.

I thought about the way I had wanted money enough so I could afford Celia, and there it was—the money and Celia. But would I have come back, would she have let me come back if she could have handled a 'copter? If I had taught her, would I be doing the dead man's float beside her husband?

I set the plane down in the front yard. Handsome's car was baking in the sun beside Celia's Caddy.

I helped her out of the 'copter. I managed to hide what I felt. I tried to remember back to when she'd come here that first day. I couldn't make it. I was cold. In the blazing sun, it was ten below.

We reached the steps. We went in. The door slammed behind us, hard. Handsome had a gun in his hand. I stared at him. Then at her. I got it. *They* had what they wanted now.

"Stay right where you are," he said to me.

"Do I have a choice?" I asked him. "Now take it easy with that thing . . ."

Celia would be happy with him, him and Curt's money. They could buy the world. I was all that stood between them and freedom with that quarter million.

Handsome nodded at the satchel in Celia's hand. His mouth broke into a smile. "You found Curt." It was a statement. He dampened his lips. "You got the money."

Celia must have nodded. I wasn't looking at her. I was watching him, and that gun.

He jerked his head toward the Caddy. "Get Norton's gun, Ce. Take it and get into the car. I'll follow in mine, as soon as I've taken care of Hayseed here."

She didn't look at me. She went around behind me. She held the satchel in one hand—that previous, bloody satchel. With her hand he felt my pockets for the guns, mine and the one she'd used on Curt.

I felt lighter without the guns, and helpless. I sweated, wishing I could sucker Handsome near enough to jump him. I'd give him odds, I'd let him have the first shot. Celia had not moved from behind me.

"All right, Celia," he said. "Get away from him—get out to the car."

"No. I'm sorry. We can't get away with killing him. We'd have to run. Hide. Always. If you'd had the guts or brains to learn how to handle a 'copter, like I wanted, it might have been different. But no. I'm sorry, but I'm not going to run and have to hide forever."

She stepped away from me. It sounded like a cannon. I swear I felt the burn of it, my ear drum felt as though it were bursting.

The surprise and horror in Handsome's face were deeper even than Curt's had been. All the hours he must have spent planning the way it would be . . . and now he, too, was in her way. She'd knocked him out of her life, because I'd stepped into it.

He looked as though somebody had hit him in the chest and left a dirty brown stain on his shirt. He rocked backward under the impact of the bullet but his knees buckled first and he toppled forward and fell slowly down to the floor.

I didn't move. I stared at him, knowing he was dead. I didn't have to touch him. His gun lay on the ground at my feet. I didn't touch it either.

Celia's voice seemed to be coming at me from across the widest everglades. I could hardly hear her.

"You'll say you shot him, Jim. It'll look better that way. He was prowling and you shot him. He really was prowling, wasn't he? They won't even hold you. Then we'll meet, in Rio—anywhere. But we won't have to stay, Jim. We can come back, live on the west coast or in the northwest. Anywhere, in fact. Jim, it'll be like you wanted!"

Like I wanted. I'd told her I'd do anything to have her and she'd dealt me in. Her hand was double-murder and she was making me her partner. I heard her that first night saying *You might be held to that. And soon.*

I was hearing Curt Carmic asking if I thought I'd have her, if I thought I'd be different than all the other men she'd had. Old men and new money . . .

I was Number One on her hit parade now. I'd won the jackpot—the quarter million dollars and Celia—because I'd owned a 'copter, and was six-two and rugged and had fallen in love with her. But six months from now, a year? I felt Handsome looking up at me, sightlessly, and was sorry for him.

Who will be next, Celia? What man will you want tomorrow,

next week, next year? How will I get it, Celia, when I'm the one who stands in your way?

She was staring at me, lips parted, breathing hard, reading my thoughts, the questions in my eyes. "You don't love me," she whispered softly. "You're like the rest of them. Just talk. I killed for you—and you're afraid of me. You'll turn me in, won't you? You'll tell them. All this money—and you'd tell them." Her voice rose, was almost a shriek.

I lunged as the gun came up in her hand. I grabbed her right wrist; the satchel flew out of her left hand. I twisted hard.

She fought at the trigger, and never fought me at all. Her arm went limp and I heard the gun blast between us, rocking the very earth. For a moment she quivered as though in a spasm and then she relaxed all over. I held her to keep her from falling. But it could do no good. She was falling away from me.

I let her down gently. She was no good, a killer. Mad, maybe, for all I knew. But all the same, my eyes blurred as I got into my car to go for the sheriff.

TAKE CARE
OF YOURSELF

William Campbell Gault

I finally caught up to her around eleven o'clock in a bar just off Windward Avenue. Windward Avenue is in Venice and Venice is not what you would call the high-rent district in the Los Angeles area.

A juke box was doling out the nasal complaints of a hillbilly songstress and most of the men at the bar looked like they worked with their hands. At the far end of the bar from the doorway, Angela Ladugo was sitting in front of what appeared to be a double martini.

The Ladugo name is a big one in this county, going way back to the Spanish land grants. Angela seemed to have inherited her looks from mama's side of the family, which was mostly English.

I paused for a moment in the doorway and she looked up and her gaze met mine and I thought for a moment she smiled. But I could have been wrong; her face was stiff and her eyes were glazed.

The bartender, a big and ugly man, looked at me appraisingly and then his gaze shifted to Miss Ladugo and he frowned. A

William Campbell Gault *wrote the best private eye novel of his generation,* DON'T CRY FOR ME. *He followed it up with at least half a dozen others that were also major novels, and he continues to write today in a style that manages to be both contemporary and timeless. More than anything else, Gault has one writerly quality you can't learn, fake or steal—his own voice. Nobody ever wrote with his particular cadences and insights and only fools would try.*

couple of the workingmen looked over at me and back at their glasses of beer.

There was an empty stool next to Angela; I headed toward it. The bartender watched me every step of the way and when I finally parked, he was standing at our end, studying me carefully.

I met his gaze blandly. "Bourbon and water."

"Sure thing," he said.

"New around here, are you?"

"Where's *here*—Venice?"

"Right."

Before I could answer, Angela said, "Don't hit him yet, Bugsy. Maybe he's a customer."

I looked over at her, but she was looking straight ahead. I looked back at the bartender. "I'm not following the plot. Is this a private bar?"

He shook his head. "Are you a private cop?"

I nodded.

He nodded, too, toward the door. "Beat it."

"Easy now," I said. "I'm not just *any* private cop. You could phone Sergeant Nystrom over at the Venice Station. Do you know him?"

"I know him."

"Ask him about me, about Joe Puma. He'll give you a good word on me."

"Beat it," he said again.

Angela Ladugo sighed heavily. "Relax, Bugsy. Papa would only send another one. At least this one looks—washed."

The big man looked between us and went over to get my whiskey. I brought out a package of cigarettes and offered her one.

"No, thank you," she said in the deliberate, carefully enunciated speech of the civilized drunk on the brink of the pit.

"Do you come here for color, Miss Ladugo?" I asked quietly, casually.

She frowned and said distinctly, "No. For sanctuary."

The bartender brought my bourbon and water. "That'll be two bucks."

He was beginning to annoy me. I said, "Kind of steep here, aren't you?"

"I guess. Two bucks, *cash*."

"Drink it yourself," I told him. "Ready to go, Miss Ladugo?"

"No." she said. "Bugsy, you're being difficult. The man's only doing his job."

"What kind of men do that kind of job?" he asked contemptuously.

A silence. Briefly, I considered my professional decorum. And then I gave Bugsy my blankest stare and said evenly, "Maybe you've got some kind of local reputation as a tough guy, mister, but frankly I never heard of you. And I don't like your insolence."

The men along the bar were giving us their attention now. A bleached blonde in one of the booths started to giggle nervously. The juke box gave us *Sixteen Tons*.

Angela sighed again and said quietly, "I'm ready to go. I'll see you later, Bugsy. I'll be back."

"Don't go if you don't want to," he said.

She put a hand carefully on the bar and even more carefully slid off the stool. "Let's go, Mr. —"

"Puma," I supplied. "My arm, Miss Ladugo?"

"Thank you, no. I can manage."

She was close enough for me to smell her perfume, for me to see that her transparently fair skin and fine hair were flawless. She couldn't have been on the booze for long.

Outside, the night air was chilly and damp.

"Now, I'll take your arm," she said. "Where's your car?"

"This way. About a block. Are you all right?"

A wino came lurching across the street, narrowly missed being hit by a passing car. From the bar behind us, came the shrill lament of another ridge-running canary.

"I'm all right," Miss Ladugo said. "I'm—navigable."

"You're not going to be sick, are you?"

"Not if you don't talk about it, I'm not. Where did Papa find you?"

"I was recommended by a mutual acquaintance. Would you like some coffee?"

"If we can go to a place that isn't too clattery. Isn't Bugsy wonderful? He's so loyal."

"Most merchants are loyal to good accounts, Miss Ladugo. Just another half block, now."

She stopped walking. "Don't patronize me. I'm *not* an alcoholic, Mr.—Panther, or whatever it is."

"Puma," I said. "I didn't mean to sound condescending, but you must admit you're very drunk."

"Puma," she said. "That's a strange name. What kind of name is that?"

"Italian," I told her. "Just a little bit, now, just a few steps."

"You're simpering, Mr. Puma. Don't simper."

I opened the door of my car on the curb side and helped her in. The flivver started with a cough and I swung in a U turn, heading for Santa Monica.

Nothing from her. In a few minutes I smelled tobacco and looked over to see her smoking. I asked, "Zuky's joint all right?"

"I suppose." A pause. "No. Take me home. I'll send someone for my car."

"Your car—" I said. "I didn't think about that. I should have left mine and driven yours. I guess I live closer to Venice than you do."

"In that case, why don't we go to *your* house for a cup of coffee?"

"It isn't a house; it's an apartment, Miss Ladugo. And my landlord frowns on my bringing beautiful women there."

"Am I beautiful?"

I thought she moved closer. "You know you are," I said. "All beautiful women know it."

Now, I felt her move closer. I said, "And you're drunk and you don't want to hate yourself in the morning. So why don't you open that window on your side and get some cold, fresh air?"

A chuckle and her voice was husky. "You mustn't give me a rejection complex." Another pause. "You—"

"Quit it," I shot back at her.

Her breathing was suddenly harsh. "You bastard. I'm *Spanish*, understand. Spanish and English. And the Spanish goes back to before this was even a state."

"I know," I said. "I just don't like to be sworn at. Are you sure you don't want to go to Zuky's?"

Her voice was soft again. "I'll go to Zuky's. I—I didn't mean what I said. I—In bars like Bugsy's, a lady can pick up some—some unladylike attitudes."

"Sure," I said. "What's the attraction there? Bugsy?"

"It's a friendly place," she said slowly. "It's warm and plain and nobody tries to be anything they aren't." She opened the window on her side and threw her cigarette out.

I said, "You try to be something you aren't when you go there. Those aren't your kind of people."

"How do you know? What do you know about me?"

"I know you're rich and those people weren't. I can guess you're educated and I'm sure they aren't. Have any of them invited you to their homes?"

"Just the single ones," she said. "Are you lecturing me, Mr. Puma?"

"I'll quit it. It's only that I hate to see—oh, I'm sorry." I stopped for the light at Olympic, and looked over at her.

She was facing my way. "Go on. You hate to see what?"

"I hate to see quality degenerate."

The chuckle again. "How naive. Are you confusing quality with wealth, Mr. Puma?"

"Maybe." The light changed and I drove on toward Wilshire.

Two block this side of it, she asked, "Who recommended you to Dad?"

"Anthony Ellers, the attorney. I've done some work for him."

She was silent until I pulled the car into the lot behind Zuky's. Then she asked, "Don't you ever drink, Mr. Puma?"

"Frequently. But I don't *have* to."

She sighed. "Oh God, a moralist! Tony Ellers certainly picks them."

I smiled at her. "My credit rating's good, too. How about a sandwich with your coffee? It all goes on the expense account."

She studied me in the dimness of the car and then she smiled, too. "All right, all right. Get around here now and open the door for me like a gentleman."

•   •   •

Zuky's was filled with the wonderful smells of fine kosher food. From a booth on the mezzanine, Jean Hartley waved and made a circle with his thumb and forefinger. I ignored him.

We took a booth near the counter. Almost all the seats at the counter were taken, as were most of the booths. I said, "This is a warm and plain and friendly place and the food is good. Why not here instead of Bugsy's?"

Her gaze was candid. "You tell me."

I shook my head. "Unless you have some compulsion to degrade yourself. Cheap bars are for people who can't afford good bars. And all bars are for people who haven't any really interesting places to go. With your kind of money, there must be a million places more fun that Bugsy's."

Her smile was cool. "Like?"

"Oh, Switzerland or Sun Valley or Bermuda or the Los Angeles Country Club."

"I've been to all those places," she said. "They're no better."

The waitress came and we ordered corned beef sandwiches and coffee.

Jean Hartley materialized and said, "Joe, Joe old boy, gee it's great to see you."

"It's been nice seeing you, Jean," I said. "So long."

My welcome didn't dim his smile. "Joe boy, you're being difficult."

"Go, Jean," I said. "This isn't the *Palladium.*"

He looked from me to Miss Ladugo and back to me. He shook his head. "I don't blame you," he said, and went away.

"Handsome man," Angela said.

I shrugged.

"Tell me," she asked, "are you really as square as you sound?"

I shrugged again.

"That man wanted to meet me, didn't he? And he didn't know I'm rich, either, did he?"

"He probably does," I said. "He's worked his way into better fields since he milked the lonely hearts club racket dry."

"Oh? Is he what's called a confidence man?"

"No. They work on different principles. Jean trades on people's loneliness, on widows and spinsters, all the drab and gullible people who want to be told they're interesting."

Angela Ladugo smiled. "He seemed very charming. I suppose that's one of his weapons."

"I suppose. I never found him very charming."

"You're stuffy," she said. "You're—"

The waitress came with our orders and Angela stopped. The waitress went away, and I said, "I'm a private investigator. Decorum is part of what I sell."

She looked around and back at me. "Are you sexless, too?"

"I've never been accused of it before. I've never taken advantage of a drunken woman, if that's what you mean."

"I'm not drunk. I was, but I'm not now."

"Eat," I said. "Drink your coffee."

There was no further dialogue of any importance. She ate all of her sandwich and drank two cups of coffee. And then I drove her back to Beverly Hills and up the long, winding driveway that kept the Ladugo mansion out of view from the lower class drivers on Sunset Boulevard.

A day's work at my usual rates and it never occurred to me to be suspicious of the Buick four-door hardtop that seemed to have followed us from Santa Monica.

I billed Mr. Ladugo for mileage and the sandwiches and coffee and fifty dollars for my labor and got a check almost immediately. I had done what I was trained to do; the girl needed a psychiatrist more than a bodyguard.

I worked half a week on some hotel skips and a day on a character check on a rich girl's suitor. Friday afternoon, Mr. Ladugo called me.

What kind of man, he wanted to know, was Jean Hartley?

"He's never been convicted," I said. "Is it facts you want, sir, or my opinion of the man?"

"Your opinion might be interesting, considering that you introduced him to my daughter."

"I didn't introduce him to your daughter, Mr. Ladugo. Whoever told you that, lied."

"My daughter told me that. Could I have your version of how they happened to meet?"

I told him about Zuky's and the short conversation I'd had with Jean Hartley. And I asked, "Do you happen to know what kind of car Mr. Hartley drives?"

"It's red, I know that. Fairly big car. Why?"

I told him about the Buick that had followed us from Santa Monica. That had been a red car.

"I see," he said, and there was a long silence. Finally, "Are you busy now?"

"I'll be through with my present assignment at four o'clock. I'll be free after that." I was through right then, but I didn't want the carriage trade to think I might possibly be hungry.

"I'd like you to keep an eye on her," he said. "Have you enough help to do that around the clock?"

"I can arrange for it. Why don't I just go to this Jean Hartley and lean on him a little?"

"Are you—qualified to do that?"

"Not legally," I answered. "But physically, I am."

"No," he said, "nothing like that. I can't—afford anything like that. Angela's shopping now, but she should be home by five."

I phoned Barney Allison and he wasn't busy. I told him it would be the sleep watch for him; I could probably handle the rest of the day.

"It's your client," he said. "I figured to get the dirty end of the stick."

"If you don't need the business, Barny—"

"I do, I do." he said. "Command me."

Then I looked for Jean Hartley in the phone book, but he wasn't in it. He undoubtedly had an unlisted number. I phoned Sam Heller of the bunko squad, but Sam had no recent address of Jean's.

At four-thirty, I was parked on Sunset, about a block from the Ladugo driveway. At four-fifty, a Lincoln Continental turned in and it looked like Angela was behind the wheel.

I'd brought a couple sandwiches and a vacuum bottle of coffee; at six, I ate. At six-thirty, I was enjoying a cigarette and a disk jockey when a Beverly Hills prowl car pulled up behind my flivver.

The one who came around to my side of the car was young and healthy and looked pugnacious. He asked cheerfully if I was having car trouble.

I told him I wasn't.

"Noticed you first almost two hours ago," he went on. "You live in the neighborhood, do you?"

"About seven miles from here." I pulled out the photostat of my license to show him.

He frowned and looked at the other cop, who was standing on the curb. "Private man."

The other man said nothing nor did his expression change. It was a bored expression.

"Waiting for someone?" the younger one asked me.

I nodded. "If you're worried about me, boys, you could go up to the house and talk to Mr. Ladugo. But don't let his daughter see you. She's the one I'm waiting for and Mr. Ladugo is paying me to wait."

"Ladugo," the young man said. "Oh, yes. Ladugo. Well, good luck, Mr. Puma."

They went away.

Even in Beverly Hills, that name meant something. Puma, now, there was a name you had to look up, but not Ladugo. Why was that? I gave it some thought while I waited and decided it was because he was older, and therefore richer. But he wasn't as old as my dad, and my dad had just finished paying the mortgage on a seven thousand dollar home. He'd been paying on it for twenty years. I must learn to save my money, cut down on cigarettes, or something. Or get into another line of work, like Jean Hartley.

• • •

At seven-thirty, the Continental came gliding out of the Ladugo driveway, making all the Cadillacs on Sunset look like 1927 Flints. I gave her a couple of blocks and followed in the Continental's little sister.

There was a guilty knowledge gnawing at me. If we hadn't gone to Zuky's, she wouldn't have met Jean Hartley. And I wouldn't have been hired to follow her.

At a road leading off to the right, just beyond the UCLA campus, the Continental turned and began climbing into the hills. It was a private road, serving a quartette of estates, and I didn't follow immediately. If it dead-ended up above, Angela and I would eventually come nose to nose.

I waited on Sunset for five minutes and then turned in the road. The houses were above the road and four mailboxes were set into a field-stone pillar at the first driveway. Atop the pillar were four names cut out of wrought iron and one of the names was Ladugo. Her trip seemed innocent enough; I drove out again to wait on Sunset.

It was dark, now, and the headlights of the heavy traffic heading toward town came barreling around the curve in a steady stream of light. My radio gave me the day's news and some comments on the news and then a succession of platters.

A little before ten o'clock, the Continental came out on Sunset again and headed west. I gave it a three block lead.

It went through Santa Monica at a speed that invited arrest, but she was lucky, tonight. On Lincoln Avenue, she swung toward Venice.

Not back to Bugsy's, I thought. *Not back to that rendezvous of the literate and the witty, that charming salon of the sophisticated.* A block from Windward, she parked. I was parking a half block behind that when she went through the doorway.

I got out and walked across the street before going down that way. When I came abreast of the bar, I could see her sitting next to a man whose back was to me. I walked down another half block and saw the red Buick four-door Riviera. The registration slip on the steering column informed me that this was the car of Jean Hartley. His address was there, too, and I copied it.

Then I went back to wait.

I didn't have long. In about ten minutes, both of them came out of Bugsy's. For a few moments, they talked and then separated and headed for their cars.

I followed Angela's, though the Buick seemed to be going to the same place. Both of them turned right on Wilshire and headed back toward Westwood.

Westwood was the address on Jean Hartley's steering column. And that's where they finally stopped, in front of a sixteen unit apartment building of fieldstone and cerise stucco, built around a sixty foot swimming pool.

I waited until they had walked out of sight and then came back to the flood-lighted patio next to the pool. A list of the tenants was on a board here and one of the tenants was *Hartley Associates*.

Some associates he'd have. With numbers under their pictures. But who could guess that by looking at him? I went sniffing around until I found his door.

There was an el in the hallway at this point, undoubtedly formed by the fireplace in the apartment. It afforded me enough cover.

Hartley Associates. What could that mean? Phoney stock? I heard music and I heard laughter. The music was Chopin's and the laughter was Angela's. Even in the better California apartment houses, the walls are thin.

Some boys certainly do make out.

I heard a thud that sounded like a refrigerator door closing.

I wanted to smoke, but smoke would reveal me to others who might pass along the hall. Chopin changed to Debussy and I thought I heard the tinkle of ice in glasses. Light music, cool drinks and a dark night—while I stood in the hall, hating them both.

Time dragged along on its belly.

And then, right after eleven o'clock, I though I heard a whimper. There had been silence for minutes and this whimper was of the complaining type. I was moving toward the door, where I could hear better, when I heard the scream.

I tried the knob and the door was locked. I stepped back and put a foot into the panel next to the knob and the door came open on the second kick.

Light from the hall poured into the dark apartment and I could see Angela Ladugo, up against a wall, the palms of her hands pressed against the wall, her staring eyes frightened.

She was wearing nothing but that almost translucent skin and her fair hair. I took one step into the room and found a light switch next to the door.

When the lights went on, I could see Hartley sitting on a davenport near the fireplace and I headed his way. I never got there.

As unconsciousness poured into my reverberating skull, I remembered that the sign downstairs had warned me he had associates.

I came to on the floor. Hartley sat on the davenport, smoking. There was no sign of Angela Ladugo or anyone else.

I asked, "Where is she?"

"Miss Ladugo? She's gone home. Why?"

"Why? She screamed, didn't she? What the hell were you doing to her?"

He frowned. "I didn't hear any scream. Are you sure it was in this apartment?"

"You know it was. Who hit me?"

Hartley pointed at an ottoman. "Nobody hit you. You stumbled over that."

I put a hand on the floor and got slowly to my feet. The pain in my skull seemed to pulse with my heartbeat.

Hartley said, "I haven't called the police—yet. I thought perhaps you had a reason for breaking into my apartment."

"Call 'em," I said. "Or I will."

He pointed toward a hallway. "There's the phone. You're free to use it."

I came over to stand in front of him. "Maybe I ought to work you over first. They might be easier on you than I'd be."

He looked at me without fear. "Suit yourself. That would add assault to the rap."

I had nothing and he knew it. I wasn't about to throw the important name of Angela Ladugo to a scandal-hungry press. I was being paid to protect her, not publicize her. I studied him for seconds, while reason fought the rage in me.

Finally, I asked, "What's the racket this time, Jean?"

He smiled. "Don't be that way, Joe. So the girl likes me. That's a crime? She was a little high and noisy, but you can bet she's been that way before. Did she hang around? If she'd been in trouble, wouldn't she have stayed around to see that you were all right?"

"How do I know what happened to her?" I asked.

He looked at his watch. "She should be phoning any minute, from home. I'll let you talk to her if you want."

I sat down on the davenport. "I'll wait."

He leaned back and studied the end of his cigarette. "What were you doing out there, Joe? Are you working for her father?"

"No. I felt responsible for her meeting you. I'm working for myself."

He smiled. "I'll bet. I can just see Joe Puma making this big noble gesture. Don't kid me."

I said slowly, "This isn't the right town to buck anyone named Ladugo, Jean. He could really railroad you."

"Maybe. I can't help it if the girl likes me."

"That girl's sick," I said. "She has some compulsion to debase herself. Is that the soft spot you're working?"

"She likes me," he said for the third time. "Does there have to be a dollar in it? She's a beautiful girl."

"For you," I said, "there has to be a dollar in it. And I intend to see you don't ever latch onto it. I've got friends in the Department, Jean."

He sighed. "And all I've got is the love of this poor woman."

The phone rang, and he went over to it. I came right along.

He said, "Hello," and handed me the phone.

I heard Angela say, "Jean? Is everything all right? There won't be any trouble, will there?"

"None," I said. "Are you home?"

"I'm home. Jean—is that you—?"

I gave him the phone and went into the kitchen to get a drink of water. The lump on the back of my head was sore, but the rattles were diminishing in my brain.

If she was home, she was now under the eye of Barney Allison. I could use some rest.

I went out without saying any more to Jean, but I didn't go right home. I drove back to Venice.

•　　•　　•

The big man behind the bar greeted me with a frown when I came in. I said, "I'd like to talk to you."

"It's not mutual."

"I'd like to talk about Angela Ladugo. I'm being paid to see that she doesn't get into trouble."

He looked down at the bar to where a man was nursing a beer. He looked back at me. "Keep your voice low. I don't want any of these slobs to know her name."

I nodded. "The man who met her here tonight can do her more harm than any of your customers are likely to. His name is Jean Hartley. Have you ever heard of him?"

"I've heard of him." His eyes were bleak.

I said, "I'll have a beer if it's less than two dollars."

He drew one from the tap. "On the house. What's Hartley's pitch?"

"I don't know. What's *your* attraction, Bugsy?"

He looked at me suspiciously. "I knew her mother. Way, way back, when we were both punks. I was just a preliminary boy and her mother danced at the *Blue Garter*. I guess you're too young to remember the *Blue Garter*."

"Burlesque?"

"Something like that. A cafe. But Angela Walker was no tramp—don't get that idea. Her folks back in England were solid middle-class people."

"I see. And that's where Ladugo met her, at the *Blue Garter*?"

"I don't know. She was dancing there when she met him."

"And you kept up the acquaintanceship through the years?"

He colored slightly. "No. Not that she was a snob. But Venice is a hell of a long ways from Beverly Hills."

"She's dead now?"

"Almost three years."

"And Angela has renewed the friendship. Her mother must have talked about you."

"I guess she did. What's it to you, Mac?"

"Nothing, I guess. I'm just looking for a pattern."

"We don't sell 'em, here. I thought you were watching the girl."

"She's home," I said. "Another man will watch her until I go back to work in the morning. This is pretty good beer."

"For twenty cents, you can have another one."

I put two dimes on the counter, and said, "Hartley scares me. He's tricky and handsome and completely unscrupulous."

He put a fresh glass of beer in front of me. "I wouldn't call him handsome."

"Angela did. She went up to his apartment tonight. I broke in and somebody clobbered me. When I came to, she was gone. But she phoned him from home while I was still there."

Bugsy looked at me evenly. "Maybe the old man should have hired somebody who knew his business."

"You might have a point there. I'll go when I finish the beer."

He went down to serve the man at the other end of the bar. He came back to say, "I always mixed Angela's drinks real, real weak. She's got no tolerance for alcohol."

I said nothing, nursing the beer.

Bugsy said, "Can't you muscle this Hartley a little? He didn't look like much to me."

"He's a citizen," I said, "just like you. And the Department is full of boys who hate private operatives, just like you do."

"Maybe I resented the old man sending you down here to drag her home. Some of the joints she's been in, this could be a church."

"He didn't send me down *here*. I wound up here because she did. I don't think he knows where she goes."

Bugsy drew himself a small beer. He looked at it as he said,

"And maybe he doesn't care. Maybe he just hired you to keep the Ladugo name out of the papers."

"That could be," I said, and finished my beer. "Good night, Bugsy."

He nodded.

At home, I took a warm shower and set the alarm for seven o'clock. I wanted to write my reports of the two days before going over to relieve Barney.

I'd finished them by eight, and a little before nine, I drove up in front of the Ladugo driveway. There was no sign of Barney Allison.

He wouldn't desert a post; I figured Angela must have already left the house. I drove to the office. If Barney had a chance to leave a message, he would have left it with my phone-answering service .

Barney's Chev was parked about four doors from the entrance to my office. Angela wasn't in sight; I went over to the Chev.

Barney said, "She went through that doorway about fifteen minutes ago. Maybe she's waiting for you."

"Maybe. Okay, Barney, I'll take it from here."

He yawned and nodded and drove away.

Angela Ladugo was waiting in the first floor lobby, sitting on a rattan love seat. Her gaze didn't quite meet mine as I walked over.

When I was standing in front of her, she looked at the floor. Her voice was very low, "What—happened last night?"

"You tell me. Do you want to go up to the office?"

She shook her head. "It's quiet enough here." She looked up. "I—can't drink very well. You might think that's absurd, but it's—I mean, I really don't know what happened last night. I wasn't really—conscious."

"Didn't you drive home?"

She shook her head. "I'm almost sure I didn't. I think someone drove me home in my car. Was it Jean?"

"You don't need to lie to me, Miss Ladugo," I said gently. "I'm on your side."

"I'm not lying."

I said, "You phoned Hartley when you got home. You didn't sound drunk to me then. You just sounded scared." Her eyes were blank. "You were there?"

"That's right. You're not going to see Hartley again, are you?"

She shook her head. "Of course not. Are you—still going to follow me?"

"Shouldn't I?"

She took a deep breath that sounded like relief. "I don't know. Are you going to tell my dad about—last night?"

"Most of it is in the report I wrote. *Most* of it. I'm not sure where the line of ethics would be. It isn't my intention to shock your father or—hurt you."

She looked at the floor again. "Thank you."

The downcast eyes bit was right out of the Brontes; I hoped she didn't think I was falling for her delicate lady routine.

She looked up with a smile. "As long as you're going to be following me, why don't we go together?" Charm she had, even though I knew it was premeditated.

"Fine," I said. "It'll save gas."

We went to some shops I had never seen before—on the inside, that is. Like her poorer sisters, she shopped without buying. We went to *Roland's* for lunch.

There, under the impulse of a martini, I asked her, "Were you and your mother closer than you are with your father?"

She nodded, her eyes searching my face.

"You don't—resent your father?"

"I love him. Can't we talk about something else?"

We tried. We discussed some movies we'd both seen and one book we'd both read. Her thoughts were banal; her opinions adolescent. We ran out of words, with the arrival of the coffee.

Then, as we finished, she said, "Why don't we go home and talk to my father? I'm sure I don't need to be watched anymore."

"Might look bad for me," I said. So far as he knows, you're not aware I'm following you."

Some of her geniality was gone. "I'll phone him."

Which she did, right there at the table. And after a few moments of sweet talk, she handed the phone to me.

Her father said, "Pretend I'm taking you off the job. But keep an eye on her."

"All right, sir," I said, and handed the phone back to her.

When she'd finished talking, she smiled at me. "You can put

the check on the expense account, I'm sure. Good luck, Mr. Puma."

"Thank you," I said.

We both rose and then she paused, to suddenly stare at me. "I haven't annoyed you, have I? I mean, that report about last night—this doesn't mean you'll—make it more complete?"

I shook my head. "And I hope you won't betray your father's trust."

The smile came back. "Of course I won't."

I asked, "How do I get back to my car?"

"You can get a cab, I'm sure," she said. "I'd drop you, but I have so much more shopping to do."

She had me. I couldn't follow her in a cab and I couldn't admit I was going to follow her. I nodded good-bye to her and signaled for the check.

•   •   •

I got a cab in five minutes and was back to my car in ten more. And, on a hunch, I drove right over to Westwood.

I came up Hartley's street just as the Continental disappeared around the corner. A truck came backing out of a driveway, and, by the time I got started again, she must have made another turn. Because the big black car was nowhere in sight.

I drove back to Hartley's apartment building. There was an off chance he was home and she had arranged to meet him somewhere. I parked in front.

Ten minutes of waiting, and I went up to his door. I could hear a record player giving out with Brahms. I rang the bell. No answer. I knocked. No answer.

The music stopped and in a few seconds started over again. Hartly could be asleep or out, or maybe he liked the record. I tried the door; it was locked.

Was there another door? Not in the hallway, but perhaps there was one opening on the balconies overlooking the pool.

I found that there was a small sun-deck right off Hartley's door. The door was locked but I could see into his living room through a window opening onto the sun-deck. I could see Hartley.

He was on the floor, his face and forehead covered with dark blood. I didn't know if he was dead, but he wasn't moving.

I went along the balcony to the first neighbor's door and rang the bell. A Negro woman in a maid's uniform opened it and I told her, "The tenant in Apartment 22 has been seriously hurt. Would you phone the police and tell them to bring a doctor along? It's Mr. Hartley and he's on the floor in his living room. They'll have to break in, unless the manager's around."

"I'll phone the manager, too," she said.

I went to the nearest pay phone and called Mr. Ladugo. He wasn't home. I phoned Barney Allison and told him what had happened.

"And you didn't wait for the police to arrive? You're in trouble, Joe."

"Maybe. What I want you to do is keep phoning Mr. Ladugo. When you get him, tell him what happened. And tell him his daughter was just leaving the place as I drove up."

"Man, we could *both* lose our licenses."

"You couldn't. Do as I say now."

"All right. But I'm not identifying myself. And when the law nabs you, you'd better not tell them you told me about this."

"I won't. Get going, man!"

From there, I drove to Santa Monica, to one of the modest sections of that snug, smug suburb where one of my older lady friends lived. She was well past seventy, and retired. But for forty years, she had handled the society page for Los Angeles' biggest newspaper.

She was out in front, pruning her roses. She smiled at me. "Hello, stranger. If it's money you want, I'm broke. If it's a drink, you know where the liquor is."

"Just information, Frances," I said. "I want to know all you know about the Ladugos."

"A fascinating story," she said. "Come on in; I'll have a drink with you."

She told me what she knew plus the gossip.

Then I said, "Because Ladugo's wife was messing around with this other man, it doesn't necessarily follow that Ladugo wasn't the child's father. She and the other man could have been enjoying a perfectly platonic friendship."

"They might have been. But I don't think so. And neither did any of their friends at that time. I mean her good friends, not the catty ones. They were frankly scandalized by her behavior."

"All right," I said. "Your gossip has usually proven more accurate than some supposedly factual stories. May I use your phone?"

She nodded.

I phoned Barney Allison and he told me I could reach Mr. Ladugo at home. I phoned Mr. Ladugo.

He said, "My daughter's here now, Mr. Puma. She tells me that she never went into Mr. Hartley's apartment. She stayed there quite awhile, ringing his bell, because she could hear music inside and she thought he must be home."

"She told me this morning," I said, "that she was never going to see him again. She could be lying now, too."

A pause. "I—don't think she is. She's very frightened." Another pause. "How about Hartley? Is he dead?"

"I don't know. Did Hartley try to blackmail you, Mr. Ladugo?"

"Blackmail me? Why? How?"

"Let me talk to Miss Ladugo, please," I said.

His voice was harsh. "Is something going on I don't know about?"

"Could be. But I don't know about it either. Could I speak with Miss Ladugo?"

Another pause and then, "Just a moment."

The soft and humble voice of Angela Ladugo, "What is it you want, Mr. Puma?"

"The truth, if it's in you. Was Hartley blackmailing you? What was it, pictures?"

"I don't know what you're talking about, Mr. Puma."

"Okay," I said. "I'm supposed to be working for your father. But I'm not going to lose my license over a job. I'm going to the police now."

Silence for a few seconds, and then, "That would be stupid. That would be extremely poor business. Wait, here's Father."

After an interval Mr. Ladugo got on the wire. His voice was almost a whisper. "Will you come over here, first, Mr. Puma? And would you bring your reports along?"

"I'll be there in less than an hour," I said.

As I hung up, Frances said, "Scandal, eh? And do I get let in on it? No, no. I tell you all and you tell me nothing."

"Honey," I said, "you're a reporter. Telling all is your business. But *privacy* is what I sell."

"I'm not a reporter any more, Wop. I'm a lonely old woman looking for gossip to warm my heart over. Don't hurry back, you slob."

"I love you, Frances," I said. "I love you all the ways there are. And I'll be back with the gossip."

I didn't stop for the reports. I went over to the office for that purpose, but I saw the Department car in front and kept going. Sergeant Sam Heller would remember that I was asking about Jean Hartley the other day and that's why the law was waiting in front of my office. This would indicate that Hartley was either dead or unconscious, or the law would be parked somewhere else.

In the Ladugo home, Papa was waiting for me with Angela in his library. He sat in a leather chair behind his desk; Angela stood near the sliding glass doors that led to the pool and patio.

I said, "I couldn't get the reports. The police were waiting for me at my office, so I keep moving."

He nodded. "Somebody must have recognized you."

"I guess."

He looked at his daughter's back and again at me. "Why did you mention blackmail?"

"You tell me," I said. "Has it happened before?"

He colored. Angela turned. Her voice was ice. "What kind of remark was that, Mr. Puma?"

I looked at her coolly. "Blackmail could be a good way to milk your dad. Especially, if you worked with Hartley."

"And why should I cheat my own father? I'm his only child, Mr. Puma."

"Maybe," I suggested, "you get everything you want—except money. I don't know, of course, but that's one thought."

Ladugo said, "Aren't you being insolent, Mr. Puma?"

"I guess I am," I said. "Your daughter brings out the worst in me, sir." I took a deep breath and looked at him quietly.

He was rolling a pencil on this desk with the flat of his hand. "When you finally talk to the police, it wouldn't be necessary to tell them *why* you were at Hartley's apartment, would it."

"I'm afraid it would. If he's dead, I'm sure it would."

He continued to roll the pencil and now he was looking at it, absorbed in the wonder of his moving hand. "You'd have to tell them the truth? I mean, there could be other reasons why you were over there, couldn't there?"

I smiled. "For how much?"

He looked up hopefully. "For—a thousand dollars?"

I shook my head. "Not even for a million."

He was beet red and there was hate in his eyes. "Then why did you mention money?"

"Because I wanted you to come right out with a bribe offer. I don't like pussy-footing."

I looked over at his daughter and thought I saw a smile on that sly face. I looked back at Mr. Ladugo and was ashamed of myself. He was thoroughly humiliated. His hands were on top of the desk now and he was staring at them.

I said, "I'm sorry. Now that the damage is done, I'm sorry. But there has been such a mess of deception in this business, I was getting sick. Believe me, Mr. Ladugo, if I'm not forced to mention your name, I won't. Tell me honestly, though, have you been blackmailed before?"

He looked at his daughter and back at the desk. He nodded.

A MATTER OF ETHICS

A "Nick Delvecchio" Story
Robert J. Randisi

I got mugged on the way to meet a potential client.

Well, actually it wasn't really a "mugging," but more of an "asking."

My car was in the shop and I wasn't able to borrow one, so there I was taking the subway to meet with Mrs. Alex Randolph, who lived in the Canarsie section of Brooklyn. I hadn't been on the subway in years, having studiously avoided it.

I had switched to the double-L train—which I would ride to the last stop in Canarsie—when I was approached by a tall, young black lad who asked me for my wallet. When I refused he said he'd cut me. He asked me for my wallet again and I asked to see his knife. He showed it to me, and I gave him my wallet. It was a simple transaction. He got my wallet and I got to keep—well, whatever it was he would have cut off. The thirteen dollars in my wallet and one credit card that hadn't been taken away from me yet were not enough to get cut, or possibly killed, for.

So when I reached the last stop I was penniless, and the

Robert J. Randisi *is just now, with the publication of a St. Martin's private eye novel* NO EXIT FROM BROOKLYN, *beginning to get his critical due from the crime press. Previously, though he has been active as the founder of Private Eye Writers of America and as the creator of two very interesting private eye series, he was known in the main for writing more than fifty western novels in* The Gunsmith *series. His new St. Martin's novel will win him renewed critical acclaim and a wider audience.*

"asker" had gotten off the train ten or twelve stops back. There was no point in looking for a cop, so I simply walked to the address Mrs. Randolph had given me on 95th Street and rang the bell, determined to take the job whatever it was and get a retainer so I could take a cab back to my apartment/office on Sackett Street.

The woman who answered the door was handsomely approaching forty. She looked me up and down and asked, "Mr. Delvecchio?"

"That's right."

"Come in, please."

The house was huge and old and I had the feeling that she had lived there a long time. We went through a foyer into a livingroom, where she offered me a seat and nothing more. I could have used a drink after my experience on the train, but didn't mention it.

"Mr. Delvecchio, the job I want to hire you for is a very simple one, but it might sound strange to you."

"I've had a lot of strange jobs in my time, Mrs. Randolph."

"Well, rest assured that no matter how strange this sounds, I am very serious about hiring you."

"All right," I said, accepting her assurance. "What's the job?"

"I'd like you to follow my husband for the period of one week," she said, hesitating before adding, "to find out if he is cheating on his diet."

"Uh, cheating on his diet."

"Yes."

"Well," I said, "that certainly is, uh, strange."

"I'm serious."

"I'm sure you are, Mrs. Randolph," I said, "but could I ask why?"

"Is that necessary for you to know in order to do the job?"

"Uh, well no, not really, but—"

"I'd rather not say, then," she said, cutting me off. "I'll pay for standard rate . . ." she added, producing a checkbook and looking at me questioningly.

"Uh, that'd be two hundred dollars and day and expenses."

"Very well," she said, pressing what appeared to be a gold pen to the top check. "Will two days be enough of a retainer?"

"That'll be fine," I said, "but do you think I could get something in, uh, cash?"

"Cash?" she asked, looking at me with a puzzled expression. "I assure you, Mr. Delvecchio, my check is quite good. I usually conduct my business affairs with checks."

"Oh, I don't doubt that, Mrs. Randolph, it's just that, uh—"

She assumed what I'm sure she thought was an understanding expression and asked, "Did you forget your wallet, Mr. Delvecchio?"

"Not really," I said, and then wished I'd said yes. I sighed and went on to tell her what had happened on the train.

"One black boy with a knife took your wallet?" she asked, staring at me.

"He wasn't really a boy—"

"Mr. Delvecchio," she said, putting her pen down before she had signed the check, "perhaps I've hired the wrong man for this job."

"Why?" I asked. "Do you expect me to beat your husband up if I catch him cheating?"

Looking annoyed she said, "No, of course not . . . but I see your point." She signed the check, tore it out and handed it to me. "Of course, I'll want an itemized bill."

Taking it I said, "I assume your husband is not at home now?"

"No, he's at work."

"Does he drive or take the subway?"

"He drives a green Monte Carlo."

"Would you like me to pick him up there, or would it be all right to start tomorrow from here?"

"Tomorrow would be fine," she said. "That's when his diet starts."

"The diet goes on for only one week?"

"No, of course not," she said, "but if he lasts that long I'm sure he'll make it all the way. I only need you for the one week. As soon as he cheats—if he cheats—I want you to report to me immediately."

"All right," I said, standing up. When I didn't make for the door she reached into her purse and came out with some change.

"Would ninety cents for the subway be all right?"

"Uh, if you don't mind I've had my fill of the subway for the year. I'd much rather take a cab."

She studied me for a moment, then reached into her purse again and came out with a twenty.

"Would you like to use the phone to call a cab?"

"That won't be necessary," I said. "There's a car service right next to the subway stop."

"Oh, you noticed."

I gave her my best reproachful look and said, "I'm a detective, Mrs. Randolph. I'm trained to notice things."

I left before she could ask me why I didn't notice the black kid until he was right in front of me.

●   ●   ●

I picked Randolph up in front of his house and followed him for the week. I went to lunch with him and, when his business required him to go to dinner with clients, I was there, as well. The man never so much as cheated by stealing a french fry from someone else's plate. As far as his diet was concerned, he walked the straight and narrow.

As far as his marriage was concerned, however, it was a different story.

Randolph went home late five of the seven days I followed him. On two of those nights he had dinner with a client of his investment firm in downtown Manhattan—One Liberty Plaza, to be exact, in the shade of the twin towers. The other three nights, however, he drove back to Brooklyn to a small house in the Marine Park Section and enjoyed dinner and much more with a thirtyish blonde who lived there. She was no great catch as far as I could see, but then he was a few pounds towards portly himself. As fastidious as he had been about his diet I doubted that he cheated on it while inside this house, but I knew he was cheating on his wife. It was written all over the embrace he and the woman shared in the doorway just before he left each of those nights and went back to Canarsie.

Back in my office at the end of the week I had a decision to make. I could safely report to my client that after six days her hubby had not cheated on his diet even once, bill her, collect my fee and be satisfied that I had done what I was hired for. Beyond that, however, it was a matter of ethics. I knew her husband was cheating on her, but was I bound by ethics to tell her?

Was I ever bound by ethics before? I had always done what I thought was right for me. That's what had helped me to end up a P.I. instead of Police Commissioner. While on patrol one night I'd been attacked and beaten up pretty badly. In the hospital I made up my mind that I'd never take a beating like that again, from anyone. The next guy who tried it ended up dead and I ended up in hot water because he'd had a father who knew some people who knew some people. . . .

The deal had been a pension for me, and a P.I. ticket. Either that, or a prison sentence if I fought it. All it had cost me was my "career", and I'd been doing what was right for me ever since.

I'd had a case not long ago, however, where my client had ended up killing his wife because I'd found out what he hired me to find out and told him. His wife and her lover had stolen something from him with intentions of selling it back. I got it back, told him the story, and a week later his wife and her boyfriend were dead and I had a check for five thousand dollars for "services."

I tore the check up and turned him in. Had that been ethics? No, I just hadn't liked him thinking he could pay me off to keep my mouth shut about murder.

This wasn't murder, though. This was a cheating husband, and apparently his wife had no idea—or had she? Had she really hired me to see if he was cheating on his diet? Or had she been too proud to hire me to see if he was cheating on her, figuring that if I found out I'd tell her, anyway?

Now the question was, should I?

I took the question across the hall to my neighbor, Samantha Karson. Samantha was a pretty blonde who made her living— such as it was—as a writer. She wrote historical romance novels under the name "Kit Karson"—although you'd think it would be the other way around. Anyway, she had aspirations towards bigger things, which was why she had changed the name a bit. To date she'd published three novels and about a half a dozen short stories in the romance field, but she always felt that my occupation might be fodder for that something else, so we talked a lot. Sometimes we did more than talk when one or both of us got lonely, but we were good friends and not much more.

What more is there?

I knocked on her door and showed her the container of chinese food I'd bought down the block, and she invited me in to share it with her. Over beef with broccoli, pork lo mein, fried rice and ribs I told her my predicament and asked her for her opinion.

"That's a tough one, Nicky," she said. Aside from some friends from my childhood who still called me "Nicky D," she and my father were the only people who called me Nicky. Oh yeah, and nosy Mrs. Goldstein.

She licked some rib grease off her fingers and then picked up another one and bit into it.

"Thanks," I said, "I knew you'd help."

She shrugged her shoulders inside the knees length white sweatshirt she was wearing and said, "Tell her what she hired you to tell her. Why make her miserable?"

"Wouldn't you want to know if your husband was cheating on you?"

She smiled and said, "I would know."

"Well, maybe she knows, too," I said, "and that's why she hired me to check his diet."

"I don't think so."

"Why not?"

"Because if she was figuring you to find out anyway then what's there to hide? She might as well come out and hire you to find out without playing games."

"Then what the hell did she have me checking his diet for?"

"Maybe she really wants him to lose weight."

"Everybody wants to lose weight."

She was in the act of picking up a rib and seemed to take that remark personally.

"Except you, my love," I said quickly. "You're perfect the way you are."

She smiled, said, "Thanks," and picked up the rib.

•   •   •

As if to put off the decision of whether or not to tell Mrs. Randolph about her husband's indiscretion, I decided to follow Mr. Randolph one more day, to give it the full week.

His routine that day was similar to that of the previous days, and he ended up at that house in Marine Park. After he had let himself in with his key I parked down the block with a view of the house and settled down for the wait I had become used to when suddenly the front door opened again and he came out— running. He ran to his car, got in, gunned the engine to life and took off.

I sat still for a few moments. It wasn't really necessary to follow him. Where else could he be going but home? Whatever had happened in that house in the past few minutes had sent him running, and I was curious about what it was.

Curious, but not crazy.

I had seen enough "Rockford Files" and "Harry O" to know what I'd find if I went into that house now. Besides the fact that I'd have to break in illegally, I just knew that if I did go in there I was going to find a body, probably of the woman who lived there. If I didn't go in, then I wouldn't find it, and maybe she wouldn't be dead.

How's that for logic?

For her sake and mine I started my own engine and went home.

"You just left?" Sam asked in disbelief.

"That's right."

She had come over as soon as she heard me get home, to find out what I had decided to do.

"Weren't you curious?"

"Sure I was."

"Then how could you just leave?" she demanded. "He could have killed her, you know? She could be dead."

"First of all, he didn't have time to kill her," I said. "He was in and out in a couple of minutes, maybe less. Secondly, she doesn't have to be dead. They could have had a big fight—"

"In a couple of minutes?"

"Well, you just said he could have killed her in a couple of minutes. Why couldn't they have had a fight?"

"I don't understand why you didn't go into the house."

"Because I have a license to protect, Sam," I explained, "I can't go breaking into people's houses. This is not 'Riptide,' this is real."

"So, how will you find out what happened?"

"If they did have a fight he won't go back there this week," I reasoned.

"Especially if he killed her," she said in her best smart-aleck tone.

"If she's dead," I said, very distinctly, "It'll be in tomorrow's papers."

"You know what you're doing?"

"What?"

"You're waiting for your problem to resolve itself," she accused. "If they had a fight and broke up, you don't have to tell his wife he's been cheating, and if she's dead it comes out the same way. Either way, you can collect your fee with a clear conscience."

"Except for one thing."

"What's that?"

"If she is dead, it *is* possible that he killed her," I admitted, uncomfortably.

"Well, if that's the case, then you've got a whole new problem, my friend."

She turned to leave and I said, "Where are you going?"

"I left Lance and Desiree in a clinch," she said, referring to one of her romance novels.

As she left I thought, I wish I had left Mr. Randolph and his lady in one.

•   •   •

The next day it was in the papers, the Post and the Daily News. A woman was found murdered—strangled—in her house in Marine Park. Her name was being withheld until her family could be notified. The Police were seeking a mysterious male friend who had been visiting her regularly, and expected to make an arrest shortly.

I had the papers spread out on my desk and was wondering what I should do about it when there was a knock on the office door. At first I figured it was Sam coming to gloat, but she would have knocked on the apartment door.

The knocking became a banging and I circled my desk, calling out, "Coming!"

I opened the door expecting a potential client and instead looked down at Detective Vito Matucci. Behind him, was his partner, Detective Weinstock.

"Well, well," I said, looking down at him, "if it isn't Detective Tom Thumb."

Matucci, all five foot six or seven of him, shook with rage and said, "I don't take that from you, Scumbag!"

"Sure you do, Vito," I said. "All the time."

"We'd like to talk to you, Delvecchio," Weinstock said, trying to avoid a confrontation.

"Come on in, fellas," I said, walking away from the door to my desk. I closed the newspapers and folded my hands on top of them.

"I see you've been reading the papers," Matucci said, gesturing towards my desk.

"Actually, I was trying to housebreak my cat. Would you like me to read you the funnies, Vito?"

"Can the crap, Delvecchio," Weinstock said. "This is serious business."

"What can I do for *you*, Detective Weinstock?" I asked, making it plain that whatever it was I might do it for him, but not his partner. Matucci and I had managed to go through the academy together without speaking a civil word to each other, and things hadn't changed much since then.

"We got a request from the six-three precinct to check you out, Delvecchio."

"For what?"

"You read about that woman who was killed in her house in Marine Park?"

"Sure, it's all over the papers," I said, starting to sweat. I had a feeling I knew what he was going to say.

"Well, it seems that the detectives who caught the case in the six-three were told by some neighbors that a strange car had been parked on the block for the past week or so."

"Is that a fact?"

"Not every day, mind you," Weinstock said, "but enough to make it suspicious."

"And somebody took down the license plate number," Matucci added.

I knew it.

"Guess who the car checks out to?" Matucci asked with a shit-eating grin on his face.

"So?" I asked. "Is there a law against parking, now?"

"No law against it," Weinstock said, "it's just interesting that you should be parking on the same block where a woman was killed. Would you know anything about that, Delvecchio?"

"Not really."

"I say different," Matucci said.

"What you say, Vito, is a matter of no importance to me or anybody with half a brain."

Weinstock jumped in before Vito could come back at me. "You *were* there, weren't you?"

"Do these neighbors say I was parked in front of the dead woman's house?"

"No," Weinstock admitted, "down the block, but you could see the dead woman's house from there."

"Which one was it?" I asked. "The papers didn't give the address."

"If you don't know we ain't telling you," Matucci said.

"Fine."

"What were you doing there, Delvecchio?" Weinstock asked.

"I was tailing a wayward husband, Weinstock."

"What's his name?"

"I can't tell you that—"

"You have no right to withhold the name of your client, Delvecchio."

"No legal right, I know. I'd like to talk to my client, though, and clear it with them so I don't end up going to court to get my fee. Clients take a dim view when you get them involved with the cops, Weinstock. All of a sudden they don't want to pay you, you know?"

"All right, look," Weinstock said, "I'm gonna give you the name of the detective in the six-three. He wants to talk to you. I told him you'd cooperate."

"That was kind of you."

"Just don't make me out a liar, huh?" he asked. "Talk to your client, and then go and talk to Detective Walters in the six-three. I'll leave it to him to light a fire under your ass if you decide to clam up. Fair?"

"Fair."

"Wait a minute," Matucci said. "We can sweat this bum—"

"It's not our case, Vito," Weinstock said. "Let's go. We've got work to do."

"But—" Matucci said, but Weinstock was already out the door.

"Have a nice day," I said to Matucci. He took a few seconds to think up a good come back, then gave up and left in a huff, slamming the door behind him.

Technically speaking, I had no proof that the woman in the papers was the woman Randolph had been visiting. Once I satisfied myself that she was, I'd go and talk to Detective Walters.

I left my office and drove over the Brooklyn Bridge. I wanted to be at Randolph's office when he got there.

• • •

Of course, there was the chance that he wouldn't show up that morning, but that wouldn't look good if his wife or the cops looked closely at his movements.

He showed up at his regular time of eight forty-five, and I was waiting outside the building for him.

"Mr. Randolph?" I said, calling out to him as he approached the revolving door.

He stopped short and backed up a step, as if he thought I might be a street panhandler or worse.

"I'd like to talk to you, Mr. Randolph. My name is Nick Delvecchio."

"What do you want?"

"I'm the private investigator working for your wife."

"My wife?" he asked. "A p-private investigator?"

I nodded.

"I've been following you for a week."

The enormity of that statement struck him immediately.

"Can we talk in your office."

"No—" he said quickly.

"It would be more private."

"Oh—yes, of course. C-come upstairs."

I followed him up to his office, where he barrelled through the reception area without returning one of four different greetings. We entered his office which, unlike many of the others, was not just a glassed in cubicle, but an honest to goodness, four wall room. He wasn't the boss, but he must have been pretty close.

"Mr. Randolph," I said as he sank into the chair behind the desk with a stricken look, "I'm not here to make your life difficult."

"Why would my wife hire a detective?"

"The reason seemed pretty silly to me at the time, but apparently she was worried that you might be cheating on your diet."

"My diet?" he asked, staring at me incredulously. He started to laugh then, an ironic, almost hysterical laughter that I was afraid he would lose control of.

"My diet," he said, shaking his head as the laughter wound down. "I have a c-company physical coming up soon. A promotion could hang in the balance. That would mean more money. Myra would be worried about that."

"Needless to say, I followed you several times to Marine Park—including yesterday."

He stayed silent then, staring into space.

"You were only in the house a couple of minutes, Mr. Randolph. I don't think you killed her. I think she was dead when you got there, and you panicked and ran."

"Mary—" he began, shaking his head, then stopped short. "Do you intend to blackmail me?"

I shook my head irritably and said, "No, that's not why I'm here."

"Have you—told my wife anything?"

"Your wife hired me to check on your diet, Mr. Randolph, not to check on your fidelity. To be honest, I've been wrestling with myself as to whether or not I should tell her . . . but I honestly think that you should."

"I—can't—"

"And you'll have to talk to the police," I added. "I'll back your story that you were only in the house for a couple of minutes. That won't look too bad for you, believe me."

"I—"

"I'm giving you my expert advice, Mr. Randolph," I said, trying again. "Get yourself a lawyer, talk to the cops and your wife."

Randolph looked at me and asked, "How much time do I have?"

"Not much," I said. "The police have already talked to me. I didn't say anything, but I've got a license to protect." I stood up and added, "I'll have to talk to them today. I don't have much of a choice."

I didn't apologize to him because I was doing him a favor, and I didn't have to, but his wife was my client, and I didn't want to see him railroaded simply because he panicked.

•   •   •

Ethics are ethics, but a person has got to eat, too. After I left Randolph's office I drove to Canarsie. I wanted to give my report to Mrs. Randolph about her husband's diet and collect my fee before things got muddled.

"Mr. Delvecchio," Myra Randolph said as she opened the door. "I didn't expect you."

"May I come in, Mrs. Randolph?"

"Uh, yes, of course."

She seemed nervous as she backed up to allow me to enter. I closed the door behind me and followed her into her livingroom.

"Are you here to report on your progress?"

"Yes. I came to tell you that throughout the week that I followed your husband he never once cheated on his diet within my eyesight."

"That's wonderful," she said, reaching for her bag. It was then that I noticed that her purse was different from the one she'd had the first time I was there. She was wearing a chic two piece suit which matched the purse. A woman dresses with matching purse when she is going out.

"Have you prepared a bill?"

"As a matter of fact," I said, taking out the one I'd prepared that morning, "I have. My expenses are on it, as well."

"I'm sure it's in order," she said, glancing only at the bottom line and writing a check.

She handed me the check and dropped the checkbook on the chair between her purse and a copy of the Daily News. I folded the check and slid it into my pocket after noticing the number. She had written only one other check between this one, and the one she'd given me as a retainer.

"Thank you, Mrs. Randolph."

"On the contrary, Mr. Delvecchio," she said. "Thank you."

She saw me to the door rather hurriedly, bade me good-bye, and shut it quickly. I walked to my car, got in, and sat there a few moments. During that time she came out of her house carrying two suitcases, with her purse over her shoulder, got into a green Gran Prix parked in front of the next house, and drove away.

I waited a few more moments before getting out of the car and walking up to the front door.

I know what I told Sam about protecting my license by not breaking into the house in Marine Park, but I didn't think I'd be finding a body in this house. Besides, several things about Mrs. Randolph puzzled me enough to produce my lock picks, open the front door and illegally enter my client's house.

I went over it all again in my mind during the ride to La Guardia Airport.

For a woman who had been sure to advise me that she'd want an itemized bill, Mrs. Randolph had been very quick to look at the bottom line and write me a check for the amount without examining the bill further.

It was obvious that she'd been just about on the way out when I got there. She'd paid me off to get rid of me so she could leave for the airport. Of course, I didn't know that at the time, but I did wonder about her nervousness.

And then there was her checkbook, which had obviously been left behind by accident. It had slid down the cushion and between the pages of the newspaper, and she had simply picked up her purse and accidently left it behind. I knew she had written one check between the two she'd given me, and since it was the second week of the month, there were no monthly bills to be paid. (I hadn't thought of charge cards, where the bills come due at odd dates, but then if I had, I might not have gone into the house.)

Anyway, that other check had been made out to a Mary Burgess, and had then been voided. It had been dated the day before, the same day Alex Randolph's "Mary" had been murdered.

Of course, there was nothing concrete in all of that, but enough to make me suspicious enough to call the six-three and relay it to Detective Walters. I was hoping that just the fact that the wife of a murder suspect might be leaving town would be enough for him to send a car to the airport to stop her.

I was wrong.

"Look, Delvecchio," he said on the phone, "call me if you see *Mister* Randolph leaving. His wife is free to go."

"But Walters—"

"I've got to go. I've got cases up the ass to work on."

I'd shouted into the phone, but he'd hung up.

Now I was driving like a maniac to La Guardia Airport in Queens, hoping that I'd arrive before her plane left—whichever plane that was.

I parked in the longterm parking and took the elevator to the bridge between the indoor lot and the terminal.

La Guardia's different from New York's other major airport, Kennedy, in that all the terminals are connected in one big, semi-circular building, rather than each airline having their own building.

That would make it easier, if "easy" was a word to use. With as many major airlines as there were, how was I supposed to pick one out?

I began walking through the halls, stopping at each airline's ticket terminal to check the lines, and the monitors for the outgoing flights.

All I could figure was that since she was in such a hurry to leave, her plane had to be leaving soon. I also limited myself to major airlines, figuring that she would have been able to get a ticket on a flight at short notice.

There were three flights leaving within the half hour: Eastern to Florida, United to California, and American to Chicago. I made a mental note of the gates, and started with the Florida flight.

I had to stop at the metal detectors, and damned if I wasn't wearing my big western belt, the one that always makes the damned things go off. I had to take it off, hand it to a guard, walk through and reclaim the belt. I checked the gate for the Eastern flight to Florida, and she wasn't there. I checked with the ground attendants, and they checked their computer to see if she was confirmed on their flight. She wasn't.

I had to go through the same thing to get to the United gate, and had been dumb enough to loop the belt back on. Take it off, hand it to the guard, go through and run to the gate. I got there just as they were starting to board. This time I got smart. I had the ground attendant check her computer for her flight, then asked her if she could simply put the name in and check for all outgoing flights.

"I'm sorry, sir, but you would need a flight number in order for us to check it for you."

"Okay, thanks."

I thought I'd gotten smart, but now I had to run to catch the Chicago flight.

As I came within sight of the metal detector she was just about to go through it.

"Mrs. Randolph!" I called out.

She turned at the sound of my voice, frowning, and then recognized me. I had no proof of anything and she could have brazened it out, but instead she panicked. She pushed the woman in front of her aside and ran through the metal detector.

It started beeping like crazy and one of the guards called after her. It was still beeping when I ran through it with my belt.

"Hey!" the female guard yelled at me, too, but I kept running.

Actually, if I had stopped to think about it she wasn't going anywhere. They wouldn't have let the flight take off until she had been checked out, anyway, but neither one of us was doing any thinking at the moment. I didn't know at that moment what she had in her bag, and I still don't know how she expected to get it through the detector, unless she had simply forgotten all about it. After all, she did have a lot on her mind. . . .

As she reached the gate for her flight they were calling for first class passengers to board.

"Mrs. Randolph!" I shouted, trying to keep her from rushing into the boarding tunnel.

She turned and when she saw me she started reaching into her purse. I started for her like an idiot and couldn't believe it when she came out of her bag with a gun.

"Stay away!" she shouted.

"No, Mrs. Randolph, don't shoot!" The panic in my voice was apparent, even to me. Anyone who tells you they can look down the barrel of a gun *without* panicking is a fucking liar. I know, I've looked down the barrel at death before. The last time

I ended up taking a beating that almost killed me, and I swore that would never happen again. If I'd had a gun on me right then I would have gladly shot her. Since I didn't have a gun I was going to have to try and talk to her before I rushed her . . .

Suddenly people started shouting and screaming, and then they started to run for cover. Several of them passed between us and before I could say anything to her she suddenly turned and ran into the passageway.

"Jesus," I muttered, taking off after her. If she got onto the plane with passengers already on it, we'd have a situation here that I certainly wasn't equipped to handle—and one that I probably would have to take the blame for causing.

I ran through the doorway into the passageway, shouting to the attendant, "Call ahead and have them shut the door."

Please, I thought, make it a long passageway.

I saw her ahead of me, running unsteadily on high heels which slowed her progress. By the time she reached the door of the plane it was swinging shut in front of her. When she saw that I heard her scream, "No!" and then she whirled on me with the gun extended.

My heart began to pound. I had absolutely nowhere to go, and steeled myself to rush her. I had to hope she was nervous enough to miss her first shot.

"Put the gun down, Mrs. Randolph," a voice shouted from behind me.

I turned and saw Detective Walters, flanked by two airport security men who had their guns drawn and trained on my client.

"I didn't mean to kill her," she shouted as I turned back to her. I stood very still, afraid that if I moved she'd pull the trigger. Let the experts handle it.

"We know, Mrs. Randolph, but if you kill Delvecchio, or any of us, that will be deliberate murder. You don't want to do that."

She hesitated a moment, then the gun began to waver and she said through tears, "No, I don't want to do that . . ."

Walters moved roughly past me and I didn't move until he had her gun in his hand.

Mrs. Randolph, being an amateur murderer, had made several mistakes. She had used her own car, she had written that check so that the dead woman's name was in her checkbook, and she had finally panicked when the enormity of her deed struck her, and tried to leave town.

After hanging up on me Detective Walters had gotten a report from some men he had asking questions in the Marine Park neighborhood. One of them had come up with a description of Mrs. Randolph's car, and a partial plate. That had been enough to send him to La Guardia, where he heard someone talking about a crazy man running through the airport.

Walters said that Mrs. Randolph had obviously intended to buy the girl off, and when she wouldn't be bought, had strangled her in anger. (Why she didn't shoot her, no one knew. If she'd had the gun in the airport, why hadn't she taken it with her to see the girl? Mrs. Randolph wasn't talking, on advice from her attorney.)

Me, I think she planned it. I also think she planned for me to be a witness against her husband, which was why she'd put me on his tail in the first place—even though he really did have a company physical coming up. (Sam said if she'd planned it, why did she write the check? I still can't answer that one.)

Oh yeah, the cops got an anonymous phone call telling them to go to the house in Marine Park, where they might find a body—and would certainly have been able to find plenty of Alex Randolph's fingerprints, if not some belongings.

The call had come from a woman.

Of course, the matter of ethics still existed but after all, I *had* given my client what she had hired me for, and collected my fee.

Still, Sam might have been right. Maybe I stalled long enough for the situation to resolve itself, but then I think about what might have happened if I hadn't tailed Randolph that one last day.

TOUGH

John Lutz

*M*etzger watched through his old army binoculars as the car veered from the main highway that was barely visible as a distant, faint ribbon on the colored surface of the desert. A lazy plume of dust rose and hung in the air like a signal, telling Metzger that the car was on the old fork road, heading his way.

A lean, sun-browned man somewhere between fifty and seventy years of age, Metzger put down his binoculars, rubbed his gray and gritty beard and frowned. He lived alone, and he spent a lot of his time here at the window, watching the highway. His shack was one of fifteen deserted and dilapidated clapboard structures that were the remnants of a hippies' commune of the mid-Sixties. Metzger had lived nearby then, near a rise on the other side of the highway, and when the last of the commune people had left, he moved into the best of the shacks and the one with the clearest view of the faraway highway that was his one link with his fellow man.

John Lutz wrote the single best private eye novel of and about the 1970s, BUYER BE-
WARE. *Alo Nudger, his investigator, is his own man in all respects, not the least being
his point of view. Hemingway called it writing "truly," Wright Morris called it "angle
of vision." Whichever, Lutz's fiction is distinguished by a perception of the world that
manages to be both mordant and ennobling. One knows it's all a gag of sorts, Lutz seems
to say; one perseveres. His fiction is almost always troubling. His literary style is almost
always exemplary.*

He again raised his binoculars to his pale blue eyes. The car was only a few miles away now. Judging by the size and density of the dust cloud it raised, it was a big car.

The three men in the gray Lincoln sedan were cool despite the desert's ninety-eight-degree temperature. The car's powerful air-conditioner on high was more than a match for the late afternoon sun. All three men wore dark expensive suits and were neatly groomed. The two in the front seat were in their late thirties. The third man, Eddie Hastings, a dark-haired classically handsome man with white, even teeth and a curiously jaunty demeanor, was in his twenties. But Eddie considered himself tough enough for this company or for any company. He had held up his end of the job back in Vegas, which was one reason they were driving now with over half a million dollars of stolen casino money in the trunk. It was Vito Dellano, the car's driver, who had shot the man giving chase in the casino's parking lot. And Eddie knew that the man had posed no real threat. Big Vito had shot him because he felt mean at the moment. Plenty of reason for Vito.

The other man in the front seat provided a study in opposites. He was short while Vito Dellano was tall; fair while Vito was dark; blond and curly-haired while Vito was black-haired and approaching baldness. His name was Art Grogan. He had been an enforcer and bodyguard in the eastern mob for the last ten years. He had met Eddie Hastings during a brief stint in prison over a year ago, and the plan was born.

Vito provided the in they needed at the casino, and early this morning they had made the biggest score of their criminal careers, a dream score.

Now they needed to lie low for a while, divide the holdup proceeds, and then anonymously begin new lives. They had developed car trouble, a leaking oil line, a few miles back, and when they'd spotted the distant cluster of shacks from a rise in the highway they decided to conceal the car and themselves there and wait out the inevitable manhunt. Vito remembered the place from years ago. They were sharp, mean and Big City all the way. No one would expect them to hole up in a remote and crude desert ruin.

Metzger saw the three men and felt a sudden dread. They had spotted his run-down Jeep and parked near it. He could hear them talking.

"You think this pile of junk runs?" the hulking dark one said.

"The point is," a dapper, good-looking youngster answered, "it belongs to someone. It ain't been here forever like the rest of this wreckage. See how you can still make out its tire tracks in the sand?"

Then all three men gazed through shimmering desert air toward the nearest of the canted clapboard shacks, toward Metzger's home. The men glanced at one another, and then they spread out as if on a military maneuver and advanced on the shack.

Metzger quickly gathered up his boots, knife and a canteen of water and made for the back door.

But when he opened the door the blond man was standing outside smiling at him. The blond man was holding a revolver.

"It ain't hospitable to run out on your guests," he said, motioning with the gun for Metzger to go back inside. Metzger obeyed and the blond man followed.

"Were you goin' somewhere?" Eddie asked in an amused voice. "An important appointment, maybe?"

"So's we understand each other right off," Vito said, and stepped over and backhanded Metzger viciously across the face.

Metzger, backing away in a flurry of scrawny brown limbs, almost fell down. He raised a hand and felt blood on his lean cheekbone.

"Nice place you got here," Grogan said with a chuckle. He patted an errant lock of blond hair into place with his free hand and glanced around. "We're gonna be staying here for a while, old man. That is, if you invite us."

Metzger stood silently, staring at the bare wood floor. He had a radio in the shack. They would notice it soon, know that he might have heard about the casino robbery on the news. Three well-dressed men in a big car. Who else could they be? And they had killed a casino employee.

Vito stepped near enough to hit Metzger again if he so chose.

"Stay as long as you like," Metzger muttered, still staring at the floor.

"Very neighborly," Eddie remarked. He walked around, opened doors. "Hey, looka here, a freezer. Not big, but there's meat in it."

"No TV, though," Grogan said, "But look if it ain't a radio."

"You listen to the radio much, old man?" Vito asked.

Metzger shrugged bony shoulders.

"He knows," Grogan said. He absently twisted the large diamond ring he liked to flash. The ring was on the trigger finger of the hand holding the revolver. "Not that it makes any difference."

"How often you go into town for supplies?" Eddie asked Metzger.

"Every few months." The voice was a quaking whisper.

"How the hell do you live on just that?"

"I hunt."

Vito smiled. "Check around for a rifle, Eddie."

Eddie found the gun almost immediately, a modified old Enfield army rifle. "An antique," he said. "Like its owner."

"It looks to me like it'd fire," Grogan said. "That's what counts." He frowned and looked around at the bare walls, the glassless windows and the sink that supported a bucket of greenish well water. "How long do you figure we'll —"

Something suddenly rammed into Grogan. It was Vito. Grogan caught a glimpse of a fleeting shadow, tried to raise the gun in his hand. His wrist struck Vito's arm and the shot hammered harmlessly into the wood floor. Eddie, who was standing on the other side of the room, stared slack-mouthed at the window through which the old man had disappeared. It was almost as if the bearded desert creature had been an illusion. He'd been here; he was gone. Like that.

Vito cursed angrily. Then he smiled. He laughed. "He was laying back on us, the old bastard! He wasn't half so scared as he pretended. He was just waitin' his chance."

"He was quick when it come," Eddie said. "So quick I hardly seen him make it out the window."

"He's an old sand rabbit," Vito said, still grinning. "What do you expect? But there ain't no place he can go. Let's spread out and search all these shacks.

Guns at the ready, the three men from Las Vegas, sweating now and in shirt sleeves, began a systematic search of the ramshackle ruins.

Metzger was under the floor of the shack near the center of the old commune, in the dug-out space where once drugs had been hidden. He knew they would search for him, and before long they came. He lay perfectly still and listened to the cautious hollow footsteps overhead, saw the indistinguishable shape through the cracks in the floor boards. Then the searcher, satisfied that the shack was empty, moved on.

Metzger laughed soundlessly. He had caught them off guard, pretended that he was scared nearly numb. But he had sized up the three men almost immediately. Tough. City tough. But Metzger hadn't survived Korea, then all these years alone in the desert by being soft.

"I don't get it," Eddie said, forearming perspiration from his face. "He ain't in any of the shacks, so where did he go?"

Vito licked cracked lips and swiveled his head to take in the spread of weathered, leaning shacks. "Oh, he's still here somewhere."

"He ain't armed," Grogan said wearily. "He can't harm us none, and he ain't goin' to —" He suddenly raised a hand to his chin. "The Jeep!"

"Relax," Vito said through his wide grin. He held up a ring of keys. "I took these before we started lookin' for the old coot. And I took the distributor caps as well from both the Jeep and the Lincoln. He ain't goin' nowhere. Which gives me an idea."

The three men returned to Metzger's shack, and Vito explained that he would take Metzger's Jeep and drive to the crest of a distant rise. He had noticed a pair of binoculars in the shack, and on top of the rise he would be able to sit and use them to scan the array of run down structures until he saw some sign of the old man. He would note the location carefully, drive back to join the others, and then they would deal with their unexpectedly elusive quarry.

Vito took the binoculars, a canteen full of the brackish well water, and after making the ancient army surplus Jeep serviceable he set off in the midst of rattles, exhaust fumes and dust toward the distant rise of sand that shimmered in dancing heat waves. Eddie and Grogan hurried back into the dim comparative coolness of the shack's interior.

Less than an hour had passed when something came hurtling through the window and landed with a thump on the floor near Eddie. He yelled and jumped, unconsciously drawing his automatic from its shoulder holster. But the object on the floor was only something small and wrapped in a dirty gray rag.

Grogan came over to stand by Eddie, and both men stared down at the lump of cloth. Then Eddie felt a sudden anger at himself for letting the crazy old coot startle him. He knelt and carefully unwrapped the cloth.

"It's just a rock," Grogan said, watching studiously.

"Yeah," Eddie replied. Then he straightened violently. "Holy Mother!"

Grogan was staring wide-eyed at him, puzzled. "What is it?" And then he saw.

"*It's a finger . . .*" Eddie said. "*It's somebody's cut-off finger.*"

Both men knelt and stared at the small putty-colored member on the dirty cloth. It appeared to be a man's little finger. Grogan had seen something like it before when Larry Collissimo had been blown up in his car in St. Louis.

"A note," Eddie said, and he unfolded the slip of paper that had been in the cloth-wrapped package with the rock and blood-less finger.

"He's got Vito," he said in a flat voice after reading the scrawled note. "He says come now—just one of us—to the shack farthest west and trade him his freedom for Vito, or he'll give us the rest of Vito as dead as Vito's little finger."

Grogan was pale even for Grogan. His shirt was plastered to his short, muscular torso. He grinned a predator's grin. "He'll want all of our weapons and our car keys," he said. "And who knows what else? You know, you almost gotta admire the old bastard."

"Remember he's got Vito's gun now," Eddie said. "And the Jeep. Why do you figure he just didn't up and run?"

"How far would he get in that rattly old Jeep with us after him?" Grogan said. "Or maybe he ain't got enough gas to get anywhere. Anyway, we'll go see him."

"He said just one of us," Eddie cautioned.

"Just one of us will go to the front of the shack," Grogan said. "You'll be coming up from the other direction."

"What about Vito?"

"We'll save him if we can."

Both men stared at each other, both thinking about half a million dollars split two ways instead of three. They checked their weapons and left the shack.

As he doubled around to approach the rear of the shack where the old man waited, Eddied glanced at the ridge Vito had started out for. He could see nothing but blazing, lowering sun. All around him the desert was starkly shadowed and eerily desolate, wavering in the heat, with deep purples and reds cast over its undulating surface. Eddie spat, mustered his determination and cautiously moved forward.

"Old man!" Grogan called, when he was within fifty feet of the shack's half-hinged front door.

There was no answer. Grogan hefted his revolver and continued toward the shack.

A snap, a whir, a clod of sand at Grogan's feet.

At first he thought he'd been bitten by a rattlesnake. Then he stared with amazement at the knife protruding from his chest. The old man had rigged some kind of spring trap, concealed it beneath the sand. There was supple length of wire tied to the knife's handle and attached to something on the ground.

Breathing hoarsely, fighting the pain, Grogan fastened his fingers about the knife and slowly removed it. As it slid free, he screamed. He took three steps, whimpered and fell.

Eddied heard Grogan scream. Crouched low, he ran toward the front of the shack. In the distorting purple shadows, he almost fell over Grogan.

He glanced toward the shack. "Damn him!" he moaned. He did have enough sense to grab Grogan's revolver before running for cover.

Eddie had enough of the old man. The thing to do now was to get in the Lincoln, leaky oil line or not, and get as far away as possible.

As he reached the old man's shack, Eddie stopped and stood still, panting, feeling spasms of confusion and fear. The Jeep was parked alongside the Lincoln.

The shack's door opened and Vito stepped out onto the plank porch.

He glowered at Eddie. "Where the hell is Grogan?" he asked.

Eddie trudged forward, a gun in each hand, his shoulders slumped. "Grogan's dead," he said. He stared at Vito's hands.

Metzger sat leaning against the rough wall and expertly adjusted the bandage about the stump of the severed little finger of his left hand. He was grinning through his pain, his teeth crooked and yellow in his sun-darkened face. He had bagged one. If he could have grabbed the fallen one's gun, he'd have gotten two of the intruders. But the young one had been too quick for Metzger this time.

Metzger heard the Jeep drive away, watched it disappear in the direction of the ridge. He knew what their plan was, so he devised one of his own. Easy enough to stay out of sight. And a little finger was fair trade for his life. His idea had been worth a try and partially successful.

Sweat streamed down Metzger's lean face into his matted beard, but he didn't mind the heat. He had been frostbitten at the Chosin Reservoir in Korea. After living through that fiercest of battles and retreats, he had vowed never to be cold, hungry and afraid again. So after his discharge he had come to the desert and never once had he minded the heat or desolation. He knew how to get by in the inhospitable desert. He had learned how years ago from a uranium prospector who had befriended him.

"The old codger's tougher than we thought," Vito said, after Eddie explained what had happened. Vito had been driving back from the ridge when the confrontation took place.

"I say we climb in the car and get out," Eddie said.

"And leave the old bastard alive? There ain't that many turn-offs in this part of the country. No place to hide. If the cops come by here and talk to him, we'll be caught in a few hours. First we take care of the old man, then we leave."

"What'd you see from the ridge?" Eddie asked.

"Nothin'. He's stayin' holed up." Vito's dark brows lowered. "I did run into somethin' odd, though. A junkyard of old cars half buried in the sand. Must be dozens of 'em."

"Spare parts! Eddie said. "Maybe we can fix the oil line!"

"I got a better suggestion," Vito aid. "We siphon the gas outa the Lincoln, put it in the Jeep and take that. When we leave, the old man won't be in any condidtion to report it stolen."

Eddie silently chewed on the inside of his cheek. The old man. The rickety desert rat who couldn't weigh more than a hundred and forty pounds. He was proving to be a surprisingly difficult obstacle to overcome. And Eddie knew that Vito was right. In order for them to get away clean, the old man had to die. Eddie looked out the nearest window and saw that the desert was almost dark. Stars seemed to be staring down from the night sky like the eyes of animals. "Any ideas?" he asked Vito.

"One'll come," Vito assured him. "Here's the situation. We can't leave the old man, and he can't leave because he's got no transportation. That highway might be visible, but it's almost fifteen hard miles away—too far for an old heart-attack risk like that to walk to in the desert either by day or night."

"So it's a stand off," Eddie said.

Vito turned on a lamp fashioned from an old glass jug. "Not to my way of thinking," he said. "We've got food and water here. The old man might be able to find water, but not food."

Just then the light flickered and went out, and Vito and Eddie heard the freezer motor waver then gurgle to silence.

"Wait here!" Vito commanded. He went outside, got a flashlight from the glove compartment of the Lincoln and shone it about the exterior of the shack until he found the electrical hookup. Then he followed the lines away from the shack, playing the flashlight beam along the ground in front of him. He didn't want to die the way Eddie said Grogan had died.

Eddie waited nervously for almost fifteen minutes before hearing footsteps on the front porch. He was backed into a corner, his gun drawn, when the door opened and the faint moonlight revealed the unmistakable bulk of Vito.

"He's busted up the generator for keeps," Vito said.

"Then we're even up with the old man," Eddie said. "That meat in the freezer will spoil in no time. We gotta leave."

Vito stood scowling, occasionally wiping sweat from his thick brows. He knew Eddie was right, but he didn't like admitting that a whiskery old man had outsmarted them. And if they *were* going to leave, it might as well be as soon as possible and under the cover of darkness.

"You keep an eye out for the old coyote," Vito said. "I'll siphon the gas for the Jeep and transfer the money."

Eddie nodded, wondering if the old man had recovered his knife from Grogan's dead hand. He didn't like this a bit, not in the dark.

But Eddie had no reason to worry about nighttime sentry duty. Vito returned and told him that the tires on both the Jeep and the Lincoln had been slashed. Now hunter and prey were equally immobile. And there was something else about the slashed tires that sent a shiver of doubt and stifled terror through Eddie.

The old man didn't want them to leave. He had gone on the offensive.

Eddie cooked some partly spoiled ground beef that first night and again for breakfast. But by the second afternoon the rest of the meat in the now-hot freezer smelled strongly and was unfit to eat. At least Eddie and Vito were one day up on the old man. He hadn't eaten since yesterday morning.

The electric pump that drew water from the well was useless now, so they rationed the water in the bucket on the sink. There was plenty of it. But water proved a poor substitute for food. Eddie hadn't been hungry since his boyhood in Brooklyn, and he'd never been this hungry.

Through the fourth day Vito and Eddie did little but slump in opposite corners of the shack and endure the hunger and heat. They no longer tried even to talk. Eddie was sure that the old man must be dead by now, but he was too weak to care. They could only hope that someone would see the distant dots of the shacks from the highway, as Vito had, and make the mistake of driving over to investigate.

By late afternoon Eddie wondered if he might be hallucinating. He decided that he was only drifting in and out of sleep because of his weakened condition. But he dreamed, and the dreams were so real. Like this one. He could swear that the old man was standing before him, stacking all the weapons on a table. And Vito was sitting up in a chair, tied to it with thick rope. And Eddie was sitting up also. He suddenly knew that he wasn't dreaming at all. The old man was grinning down at him.

Eddie fought against the ropes that held him. Even at his strongest he wouldn't have been able to budge. He squinted at the old man and saw that he seemed to be none the worse for his ordeal. In fact, he appeared more well fed and healthy than when they had first seen him.

"The old bastard tricked us," Vito said weakly but with venom.

The gray-bearded man in front of Eddie smiled acknowledgement for the compliment. Grogan's diamond ring glinted on his scrawny middle finger. The stub of the little finger of the same hand was still neatly wrapped.

"What'd you eat," Eddie asked, "cactus?"

"That's where I got my water," the old man said. "I et meat."

"But where? . . ." A coldness suddenly spiraled through Eddie. He realized where the old man had gotten meat. He understood now, too, about the "junkyard" Vito had seen. He knew how the old man survived way out here alone in the vast, cruel desert.

"You get them from the highway, don't you?" Eddie asked.

"Ever once in a great while," the old man said. "Often as I need."

Vito squirmed helplessly in his chair. "What the hell are you two talkin' about?"

"Look at him," Eddie said, "and think about that junkyard of cars you saw. Think about Grogan."

"I still don't get it."

"He's a cannibal," Eddie said, hardly believing his own words, his own terrible but inevitable conclusion. "He killed Grogan and lived off his body while we were starving."

Vito stared at the old man with horror, then he began to laugh crazily, the whites of his eyes glittering.

When he was finished laughing, he looked at Eddie and actually winked. He was Big Vito again. "Don't let it get to you, kid. Our string's run out, that's all. When you're dead you're dead, and it don't matter what happens to the meat."

Eddie suddenly fixed wide eyes on the useless freezer and then on the old man. Something had occurred to him. "If Grogan was dead," he said, "how did you keep him from . . ."

"That was a problem I learned how to handle some years back," the old man said. He looked at Eddie and waited.

"Oh, dear God!" Eddie croaked.

"Your friend Grogan had passed out and lost a mite of blood, that's all," the old man said.

Eddie's face was contorted, his mouth open as if he were screaming, but the scream was soundless.

Vito stared at him, still not understanding. But he would understand.

"Now we'll see how tough you really are," the old man said. And he untied Vito's left arm.

THIS WORLD, THEN THE FIREWORKS

Jim Thompson

*M*ost of the city lay below the railway station. My taxi took me down through the business section, sparkling and scrubbed-looking at this early hour, and on down a wide palm bordered hill overlooking the ocean. Carol and Mom's house did not front on the water, as the best homes did, but it was still very nice, considering. After all, Mom had no income, and Carol's alimony was a mere two hundred and fifty a month.

My cab fare came to ninety-five cents. I had a total of two dollars. I would have had much more, but at the last moment I'd literally turned out my pockets to Ellen. It had to be done, I felt, her folks being the type they were. They wouldn't bar their doors to her, of course. But they doubtless would be very difficult—extraordinarily so—if she and the two kids could not pay a good share of their upkeep.

I can't understand people like that, can you? I mean, people

Jim Thompson took the crudest elements of paperback original fiction and transmuted them into literature. His "prayer" at the end of THE KILLER INSIDE ME *remains one of the saddest and most chilling utterances in the modern novel. Even in books which some critics consider minor such as* TEXAS BY THE TAIL, *Thompson brings to crime fiction a spiritual force that sweeps aside most ordinary literary considerations. Occasionally his narratives, like nightmares, fail to make sense; occasionally characters, again as in nightmares, seem to merge and become one. The story at hand is a good example. Max Allan Collins lent an editorial hand in clearing up a few points in this piece—yet even with certain flaws one sees here Thompson's power—part pathology, part poetry. This story appears here through the cooperation of Thompson's lovely and literate widow, Alberta.*

who extend adult conflict into the defenseless world of children. I don't condemn them mind you; everyone is as he is for sound reasons, because circumstance has so formed him. Still, I cannot understand such people, and they make me a little ill at my stomach.

I gave the cab driver my two dollars. I started up the walk to the house, broke but happier than I had been in years. It did not matter about being broke—Carol, dear child, had usually been very expert at obtaining money, and she was obviously in good form now. Anyway, broke or not, money or not, it didn't and wouldn't matter. We were together again. After three long years, the longest we had ever been separated, Carol and I were at last together. And nothing else seemed to matter.

Mom had heard the cab arrive, and was waiting at the door for me. She drew me inside, smiling with strained warmth, murmuring banal words of welcome.

I set down my suitcases, and returned the kiss she'd given me. She stepped back, and stared up into my face. Gazed at me with a kind of awed wonder, wonder that was at once worried and unwillingly proud.

"I just can't believe it, Marty." She shook her head. "You're even handsomer than you used to be."

"Oh, now," I laughed. "You'll make me blush, Mom."

"You and Carol. You get better-looking all the time. You never seem to grow a day older."

I said that she didn't look a bit older either, but of course she did. I had the impression, in fact, that she had aged about ten years since I stepped through the door of the house. There was a haunted, sickish look in her eyes. The only brightness in the sallow flesh of her face were the bluish pocks of that long-ago shotgun blast.

I remember how she got those pocks. I remember it well. It was our fourth birthday, Carol's and mine, and—"

"Where's Carol?" I asked. "Where's that red-headed sis of mine?"

"You eat your breakfast," Mom said. "I have it all ready."

"She's still in bed?" I said. "Which is her room?"

"Come eat your breakfast, Marty. I know you must be tired and hungry, and—"

"Mom. MOM!" I said.

Her eyes wavered nervously. She sighed, and turned away toward the kitchen. "At the head of the stairs, next to the bath. And Marty . . ."

"Yes?"—I was already at the stairs.

"You and Carol—you won't get into any trouble this time?"

"Get into trouble?" I said. "Why, that's pretty unfair, Mom. When were we ever in any trouble."

"Please, Marty. I j-just—I don't think I can take any more. Get yourself a job right away, son. You can do it. There's three newspapers here in town, and with your talent and experience and looks—"

"Now, Mom," I laughed. "You're making me blush again."

"Bring your family out right away. Set up your own household. I know how hard it must be on you to be around someone like Ellen, but you did marry her—"

"Better stop right there. Right there," I said.

"You'll do it, won't you? You won't stay here a bit longer than you have to?"

"Why, Mom," I said. "I know you don't mean it that way, but you almost sound as though I wasn't welcome."

I looked at her sorrowfully, with genuine sorrow. For it is rather sad, you know, when one's own mother fears and even dislikes him. It was almost unbearable, and I say this as one who has done a great deal of bearing.

"This saddens me, Mom," I said. "I quote you from section b., Commandment One-minus: If thy son be birthed with teeth in his tail, kick him not thereon. For this is but injury upon injury, and thou may loseth a foot."

A faint flush tinged her sallowness. She turned abruptly, and entered the kitchen.

I went on up the stairs.

I eased open the door of Carol's room, tiptoed across the floor and sat down on the edge of her bed.

•   •   •

We are only fraternal twins, fortunately; fortunately, since it would be a shame if she were as big as I. As it is, she is approximately a foot shorter—five feet to my six—and about eighty pounds lighter; and our physical similarities are largely a matter of coloring, skin texture, bone structure and contour.

I looked at her silently, thinking that I could look forever and never tire.

I am confident that she was awake. But knowing how much I like to see her awaken, she played 'possum for two or three minutes. Then, at last, she slowly opened her eyes— my eyes revealing their startling blueness to me.

And her lips curled softly, revealing the perfect white teeth.

"Mr. Martin Lakewood," she said.

"Mrs. Carol Lakewood Wharton," I said.

"Sister!"

—we said. "You wonderful, darling redhead!"

"Brother!"

And for the next few minutes we had no time nor breath for talk.

Finally, I got her robe for her, and accompanied her into the bathroom. I sat on the edge of the tub while she washed, and primped before the mirror.

"Darling—Marty." She touched a lipstick to her mouth. "How did that—uh—matter turn out in Chicago? I know you couldn't write me about it, and I was a little worried."

I didn't answer her immediately; I was only vaguely conscious of hearing the question. I was looking at her, you see, and now, so soon after our reunion, it was difficult to look at her and think of anything else.

"Mmm, darling?" she said. "You know the matter I mean. It was right afterwards that Mom went on her rampage, and dragged me out here."

I blinked and came out of my trance. I said that certainly I remembered. "Well, that worked out pretty well, darling. The cops had a guy on ice for a couple of other mur—matters. He was indubitably guilty of them, understand? So they braced him that one, and he obligingly confessed."

"Oh, how sweet of him! But of course, he had nothing to lose, did he?"

"Well, he was really a very nice guy," I said. "It's hard to repay a favor like that, but I did the little that I could. Always took him cigarettes or some little gift whenever I interviewed him for the paper."

She turned her head for a moment, gave me a fondly tender smile. "That's like you, Marty! You always were so thoughtful."

"It was nothing," I said. "I was only glad that I could make his last days a little happier."

Mom called up the stairway to us. Carol kicked the door shut, and picked up her eyebrow pencil.

"Goddamn her, anyway," she murmured. "I'll go down and slap the hell out of her in a minute. Well, I will, Marty! I'll—"

"I'm sorry," I laughed, "I'm not laughing at you, darling. It's just that it always seems so incongruous to me, the things you say and the way you look. Such words from such a tiny sweet-faced doll!"

I had reason to know that her words, her threats, were not idle ones. But still I was amused. She laughed with me, good sport that she was, but it was patently an effort.

"I guess I'm losing my sense of humor," she sighed. "I don't like to complain, but, honestly, I never saw such a town! Things have really been very difficult, Marty. I can't remember when I've seen a hundred-dollar bill."

"Oh? I thought it was supposed to be quite a lively place."

"Well, it may be. It may be just my luck."

"It'll change now," I said. "Things will be a lot better from now on."

"I'm sure they will be. I certainly hope so. I think if I go to bed with one more sailor I'll start saluting. Well"—she finished her primping and turned around facing me. "Now, what about you, darling? What was this little, uh, misunderstanding you were involved in?"

I said it was nothing at all, really. More a problem of semantics than ethics. The paper called it blackmail and extortion. I considered it a personally profitable public service.

"Uh-huh. But just what did you do, Marty?"

"Well, I was on the city hall beat, you know, and I had the good fortune to ferret out some smelly figurative bodies, and to identify the office-holders responsible for them . . ." I took out my cigarettes, and lighted two for us. I dragged the smoke in deeply, exhaled and went on. "Now, the paper's attitude was that I should have reported the story, but I couldn't see it that way. I couldn't and I still can't, Carol."

"Mmm-hmm. Yes, darling?"

"It would have simply meant the ousting of one bunch of crooks and the election of another. They'd either be crooked, the second bunch, or too stupid to be; incompetents, in other words. So . . . so I did the best possible thing, as I saw it. I made a deal with a friend of mine, an insurance salesman, and he had some confidential talks with the malefactors in question. They all bought nice policies. They seemed to feel pretty much as I did—that they were paying a just penalty for their malfeasance, and that I was no more than justly rewarded for a civic duty."

Carol laughed delightedly. "But how did you happen to get caught, Marty? You're always so clever about these things."

How? Why? I wasn't sure of the answer to that question. Or, perhaps, rather, I was more sure than I cared to be . . . I'd wanted to be caught? I'd subconsciously brought about my own downfall? I was tired, fed up, sick of the whole mess and life in general?

I wasn't conscious of feeling that way. I didn't want to believe that I did. For if I did, then I, and inevitably she, were lost. Time was already in the process of taking care of us. Of course, if we could accept the truth, see the danger, and completely alter our way of life—But how could we? We would have to, but how? Where the compromise between imperative and impossible? On either side, the possible truth showed the same hideous face. It could neither be accepted nor denied, and so I did neither. At any rate, I did my incoherent best to warn Carol, to put her on guard, without alarming her.

"That question," I said. "I'm a little wary of it, baby. I may have simply bungled or had some bad luck. Or it may have been another way. I could give you an explanation, and it would be completely believable. And it might even be true. But whether it actually was or not . . ." I shook my head, tossed my cigarette butt into the toilet. "As I say, I'm a little afraid of this one. It's too basic, the implications are too grave. At *some* point, you know—at *some* point—you'd better look squarely at the truth or look squarely away from it. You can't risk rationalizations. There is the danger that the rationalization may become truth to you, and when you have arrived at this certain point—"

I broke off abruptly. It had struck me with startling suddenness that this might be that certain point and this, the words I was speaking, a rationalization.

I sat stunned, unseeing, my eyes turned inward. For a terrifying moment, I raced myself about a swiftly narrowing circle. Faster and faster and—and never fast enough.

And then Carol was down on her knees in front of me. Hugging my knees. Her voice at once hate-filled and loving, her face an angel's and a fiend's.

"Shall I kill her, darling? Would you like sister to kill her?" The words were blurred together, smeared with tenderness and fury. "I don't mind. Brother would always do anything for sister, always, anything, so s-sister will j-just—"

"What?" I said. "What?"

"She was mean to you, wasn't she? She got you upset, and—a-and I'll kill her for you, Marty! She deserves to die, the old scarfaced hag! I ought to have killed her long ago, and now—"

"Don't!" I said. "DON'T CAROL!"

"B-but, darling, she—"

"It's too basic, understand? We can't think of such things. We can't use words like deserve and ought."

"Well . . ." The glaze went out of her eyes, and for a few seconds there was no expression in them at all. They were merely empty blue pools, blue and white pools. Blue emptiness and empty crystalline whiteness.

Then, I smiled, and instantly she smiled. We laughed, uncomfortably . . . And lightly.

"Now, didn't I sound silly!" she said. "I don't know what got into me."

"Forget it," I said. "Just put it out of your mind."

I boosted her to her feet, and she helped me to mine. We went down to breakfast.

·   ·   ·

I was prepared for Mom to be discomfiting, but she was not particularly so. Not nearly to the extent, at least, that she was capable of. I suspect that she was still a little cowed by Carol's outburst. Moreover, so soon after my arrival, she was unwilling—I might say, unable—to toss her weight around. To be annoying, a mild nuisance, was all the prosaic instincts would permit.

She was sure, she said, that Ellen and the kids would love this city. As for herself, an older person, she was beginning to feel that it might not be very healthy. It was too damp, you know. but for Ellen and the kids . . .

Did Ellen's folks still feel as they had? she said. Did they feel they had been unconscionably imposed upon, and were Ellen and the kids made to feel the brunt of their attitude?

She said—Well, that is about all she said. Her most annoying remarks.

I said virtually nothing, being busy with my breakfast.

Carol and I left the house soon after breakfast. We walked to-ward town a few blocks, then sat down on a bench in a small wayside park. Carol was very much concerned about the chil-dren. She was concerned for Ellen, too, of course—she and El-len have always been fond of each other. But Ellen was an adult. She was able to absorb things that children could not, and should not.

"Do you remember that time at Uncle Andrew's house, Marty? Uncle Frank had put us out because everyone in town was talking about us, and . . ."

I remembered. Uncle Andrew's three big boys had dragged Carol behind the barn, and when I took a club to them—I'd got-ten the life half-beaten out of me. By Uncle Andrew, with Mom helplessly looking on.

"I remember," I laughed. "But you know how we look on those things, Carol. They were normal, just what they should have been, broadly speaking. We weren't discriminated against, mistreated. What we endured was simply the norm; for us, for those particular times and situations."

"Yes, I know. But—but—"

But there could be no buts about this. You may be wrong, and exist comfortably in a world of righteousness. But you may not be right and live in a world of error, the kind of world we had once *seemed* to live in. It is impossible. Believe me, it is. The growing weight of injustice becomes impossible to bear.

"The norm is constantly changing," I said. "It is different with every person, every time, every situation. One person's ad-vantage may be the disadvantage of another, but the position of both is always normal."

"Uh-huh. Of course, Marty," said Carol. "But, anyway . . ."

She took a roll of bills from her purse, and thumbed through them rapidly. She pulled off a few of them for herself, probably a total of forty dollars, and pressed the others into my hand.

"You take this, Marty. I insist, now, darling! Keep what you need—I imagine you're broke, aren't you—and send the rest to Ellen. Wire it to her so she'll get it right away."

I counted the money. I looked up from it suddenly, with deliberate suddenness, and I saw something in her face I didn't like. I couldn't analyze the expression, say why it troubled me. And that in itself was alarming. We were so much alike, you know, we thought so much alike, that it was as though my brain and body had separated and I had lost contact with my own thoughts.

"You said things had been tough," I said. "But there's more than three hundred dollars here . . ."

"So?" She laughed nervously. "Three hundred dollars is money?"

"Your alimony would just about pay your rent," I went on slowly. "And you said Mom's doctor bills ran very high. So with your other living expenses, your clothes, groceries, household bills, personal expense—"

She laughed again, laying one of her beautifully delicate hands on my knee. "Marty! Stop making like an auditor, will you? I've never heard such a fuss over a little bit of money!"

"It's not a little bit, under the circumstances. It's around four hundred dollars with what you've kept. What's the answer, Carol?"

"Well . . ." She hesitated. "Well, you see, Marty, I was—I was saving this for something. I've saved it a few dollars at a time, and I knew that if you knew I needed—wanted—it for myself, you wouldn't want to—"

"Oh," I said, and I could feel my face clearing. "What was it you wanted, baby?"

"A—a mink. A cape stole. But I don't have to have it, darling. Anyway, now that you're here, we'll be rolling in money pretty soon."

I shoved the bills into my pocket. I hated to deprive her of anything, but since it was only temporary and not of vital importance . . .

She didn't have the clothes, the accessories, she'd used to have. I'd noticed that in glancing around her room that morning. She had sufficient to be very smartly turned out, mind you, but it was little by her standards. She had no jewelry at all. Even her wedding ring was gone—pawned, I supposed.

"Well, darling?" She smiled at me, her head cocked on one side. "Are you satisfied, now?"

I nodded. I had no reason to be anything else. Only a vague feeling of disquiet.

"Satisfied," I said.

We walked into town. It was a quiet walk, being largely up-hill. But we had had so little time together, and the walking gave us a chance to talk.

As I had imagined was the case, knowing her independent nature, she was carrying on on her own. The local vice syndicate was a laughable outfit. They had no real stand-in with the police, and their hoods were spineless oafs. Once, shortly after she had come here, they had tried to take Carol in tow, but they had left her strictly alone since then.

"Two of them came out to the house, Marty. I gave them some money, and then I fixed them both a nice big drink. And can you imagine, darling?—they gulped it down like lambs. I do believe they'd never heard of chloral hydrate! Well, fortunately, I had a car at the time, so . . ."

So when the stupes had awakened, they were out in the middle of the desert, sans clothes and everything else they owned. It was almost a week before the highway patrol found them. One of them died a few months later, and the other had to be committed to an insane asylum.

"That's my sister," I murmured. "That's my sweet little sis . . . Mom didn't know about the deal?"

"We-el, she didn't *know*. She was out somewhere that evening. But you know her. She always seems to sort of feel it when—when something's happened, and she was fussing around, nagging at me, for days. It was simply terrible, Marty! I almost went out and got a job just to shut her up."

"A *job*?" I said. "She wanted you to take a *job*!"

"Isn't it incredible?" Carol shook her head. "But what about you, Marty? You won't let her hound you into going to work, will you?"

I said that I wouldn't let anyone force me to do anything: my norm period for being forced had expired. Still, I probably would go to work. For a while, and when the notion struck me. A job could be amusing, and often very useful.

"I suppose," Carol nodded. "I guess it wouldn't hurt to work a little bit." She gave my hand a squeeze, smiled up at me sunnily. "I'll have to leave you here, darling. Have a nice day, and be sure to wire the money to Ellen."

She started toward the entrance of a swank cocktail lounge, her principal base of operations. Then, she paused and turned around again.

"Send a telegram with it too, will you, Marty? To the kids. Tell them Aunt Carol loves them more and more every day, and she wants them to be real good for their mother."

●　　●　　●

I went to work the following day on the first paper I applied to. I had no difficulty about it. Not since I was a child—and a very small child—have I had any difficulty in getting work. It would be very strange if I did. Personably and in intelligence, I am a generous cut above the average; I must admit to this, immodest as it seems. Also, and when I choose to, I can be exceedingly ingratiating. Then, there is my experience in job getting— my childhood training by earnest teachers. One gets work readily when the penalty for failure is a clubbing.

Carol did not get this valuable training. Being sorely undernourished and frequently raped, she had little energy and time for other endeavors.

However, as I was saying . . .

It was the best and biggest paper in town, which is not to say, of course, that it was either very good or very big. Most of the staffers were fair, about average, I suppose. They had been getting by nicely until I came along. Then, well, there I was, a *real* newspaper man, a towering beacon of ability, And by comparison, these average people looked like sub-moronic dolts.

The publisher no longer made his face to shine upon them. He griped at everyone—except me. No one—except me—could do anything to suit him.

Whenever I've cared to, when I've had an amusing objective in mind, I've always advanced in my work. But I set an all-time record on that paper. I was assistant city editor at the end of that week. Two weeks later, I was made city editor. And at the end of the month—Correction. It was the beginning of my fifth week . . .

By this time, the city room was in a mess. All the staffers were jumpy—almost to the point of total incompetence. The news editor had resigned. The copy-desk chief had reverted to alcoholism. The Newspaper Guild was raising hell. The—Well, as I say, it was a mess. Exactly the situation I had wanted. If it wasn't straightened out fast, the paper would be on the skids.

Now, the managing editor *was* a pretty good man. So much so that given a little time, and even with me around, he could have rerighted things. But the publisher was in no mood to give his time. The m.e. was a bum, he declared—in so many words. He was at the root of all the trouble, he would have to go. And his replacement should be you-know-who.

I held the job for two days, just long enough to make sure that the previous incumbent had left town. Then, I resigned. Needless to say, the publisher was shocked silly.

I couldn't do it! he sputtered. I simply couldn't do it! And when I pointed out that I just had done it, he virtually went down on his knees to me . . . Why was I doing it? he pleaded. What did I want from him?

I told him I already had what I wanted, and I was doing it because he was a wicked old man. He had violated Commandment One-minus, the commandment that had never been written since even a goddamned fool could be expected to know it.

"Yea, verily," I said. "It is the pointed moral of all happening from the beginning of creation; to wit: Take not advantage of thy neighbor with his pants down, for to each man there comes this season and in my house there are many mansions, and in the mansions are many bastards longer-donged than thyself."

He didn't argue with me any more. He was afraid to, I imagine, believing me insane and himself in actual physical danger.

I collected my pay from the cashier, and walked out.

It was now around three in the afternoon—my normal quitting time, since most of the work on afternoon papers is done in the morning. I had a couple drinks in a nearby bar. Then, feeling rather at loose ends, I wandered on down the street to the public square.

It was in the approximate center of the business section, a departure and arrival point for most of the city's bus lines. I found an unoccupied bench near the pseudo-Moorish fountain, and sat down. Letting my mind wander comfortably. Pleased with myself. A little amazed, as I sometimes am, that I could have risen so relatively high.

I had almost no formal education, no more than a few months of grammar school. I had learned to read from the newspapers—from the newspapers I hustled. And squeezing past this first barricade, leaping over it, rather, I had raced on up the casually tortuous trail of the newspapers. Street sales. Wholesale street. Circulation slugger. Copy boy. Cub reporter . . . The newspapers were grade school, high school and college. They were broad education, practically applied. And they never asked but one question, they were interested in only one thing: Could you do your job? I always could. I always had to.

Now, rather for some years past, I no longer had to. My norm for having-to had expired, I had expired it, if you forgive the verb. And for the future, the present—

I was quite pleased with myself. At the same time, the abrupt cessation of intense activity left me with a hanging-in-the-air feeling—restless and mildly ill at ease. And while what I had done was entirely logical and fitting, I was afraid I might have acted a trifle selfishly.

Carol wouldn't think so, of course. She would appreciate the joke as much as I. But still her luck was running very bad—there was still no prize chump in the offing, no one like that character in Chicago. And since she'd insisted on my sending most of my salary to Ellen—

Well, what the hell? I thought. We were bound to get a break before long. She'd latch onto some well-heeled boob, set him up where I could safely get at him; and that would be the end of him, and the end of our financial troubles.

I yawned and leaned back against the bench. Then, I sat up again; casually, oh so very casually, but very much alert. I got up, went down the flagstoned pathway, and stopped squarely in the middle of the sidewalk.

She smacked right into me. She'd been trying to look at me and not look at me for the past ten minutes, so we piled right together.

I had to catch her by the shoulders to keep her from going

over backwards. I continued to hold onto her, smiling down into her face.

It was what you might call a well-organized face, one that would have been pretty except for its primness and the severity of her brushed-back, skinned-back hairdo. Not that I place any emphasis on prettiness, understand. My wife Ellen is the ugliest woman I have ever seen.

She, this one, wore glasses, a white blouse, and a blue suit and hat. The blouse was nicely top-heavy, and the suit was curved in a way its maker had never intended.

"Well," I said, "if it isn't Alice Blueclothes! Boo, pretty Alice."

She was trying to look stern, grim, but she just wasn't up to it. Under my hands, I could feel her flesh trembling. I could feel it burn.

"L-Let—let go of me!" she gasped. "I'm warning you, mister, let go of me instantly—"

"Not 'instantly,' " I said. "Marty. You're thinking about my brother, Alice. He has pretty red hair, too."

"You l-let—I'll fix you! I'll—"

"But, Alice," I said. "We haven't had our waltz yet—or would you rather make it a square dance? I'm sure these smiling bystanders would be glad to join in."

She tore herself free. Red faced, acutely conscious of the aforesaid bystanders, she thrust a hand into her purse, came out with a leather-backed badge.

"P-Police officer," she said. "You're under arrest!"

•   •   •

I went along willingly, as the saying is. I had been sure from the beginning that she was a cop. She had a firm grip on my arm as we left the square, a grip strong with fury. But it rapidly grew weaker and weaker, and as we turned into a side street she let go entirely. She stopped. I stopped. I glanced at the plain black car at the curb, noted the absence of official insignia.

"All right, mister," she said, trying to look very stern, to sound very harsh. "I should take you in, but I'm off duty and—"

"Is this your car, Alice?" I said. "It matches your shoes, doesn't it?"

"Shut up! If you don't behave yourself, p-promise to behave, I'll—"

"Yes, it's an exact match," I said. "It matches your hair too. Are you brunette all over, Alice, or just where it shows?"

Her face went white. White then red again, about three shades redder than it had been. She turned away from me suddenly, jerked open the door of the car and literally stumbled inside. I slid into the seat with her.

"G-Go away," she whispered. "Please, go 'way . . ."

"I will," I said. "You say it like you mean it, and I will."

She hesitated. Then, she turned toward me, faced me, her chin thrust out. And her lips formed the words. But she did not speak them. I have played this same scene a hundred times, five hundred times, and never have I heard the words spoken.

Her eyes wavered helplessly. She looked down into her lap, shamefaced, her fingers twisting and untwisting the strap of her purse.

"W-We could . . ." She hesitated, went on in a barely audible whisper. "We c-could . . . go some place for a drink?"

"I wouldn't think of it!" I shook my head firmly. "I know something of your city, you see, and I know that cops in uniform may not drink."

"But—"

"I know something else, too. Local lady cops must be single; marriage is grounds for immediate dismissal. And one would also be dismissed, naturally—promptly—if her conduct were anything less than circumspect. She can't sleep around as other women might. A very small breath of scandal, and she'd be out. So—so what is our lady to do, anyway? What is she to do, say, if her womanly desires are somewhat stronger than the normal ones, if she is highly sexed, loaded with equipment which screams for action? What—yes, dear? You'll have to speak a little louder."

I had to bend forward to hear what she said.

"Well," I nodded, "that's fine. I'd like to go to your house. I always hate to take a woman to a hotel."

"No! I m-meant we could have dinner. We c-could talk. We— it's on the beach. We could swim, if you like and—"

I told her that of course, we could—and we would, if she still wanted to. We'd get right in bed first, and if she wasn't too tired afterwards . . .

I paused, looking at her inquiringly. I put a hand on the door latch.

"It's entirely up to you, dear. Don't consider me at all. I can walk a city block and pick up a half dozen women."

"I k-know . . ." she muttered humbly. "I know you could. But—"

"Well?"

"I—c-can't! You'd think I was awful! It would be bad enough, if we were acquainted and—"

"Don't apologize." I swung the door open. "It's quite all right."

"Wait! C-could I call you somewhere? If—if I t-thought about it and decided t-to—"

"But suppose I'd decided not to?" I pointed out. "No, I think we'd better forget it."

"B-But—" She was almost crying. "I c-couldn't respect my-self! You wouldn't respect me! You'd t-think I was terrible and— Wait! *Wait!*"

I smiled at her. I got out and slammed the door, and started up the street.

I really didn't care, you know. At least, I cared very little. She was a cop, of course, and it was a cop that Dad had killed. But I wasn't sure that I cared to do anything about that or her, to take care of that by taking care of her. I just didn't know. The situation had seemed to offer possibilities, but I just didn't know. Whether I wanted to do anything about it, and her. Whether there was anything suitable to do if I did want.

She called after me. She called louder, more desperately. I kept on going.

I heard the car door open. Slam. She called once more. Then, she was silent, she was running after me, a fiercely silent animal racing after an escaping prey.

She caught up with me. Her fingers sank into my arm, half yanked me around. And her face was dead white, now, even her lips were white. And her eyes were blazing.

"D-Don't you go 'way!" she panted. "Don't you dare go 'way! You come with me! Come right now, you hear? *N-now!* Now now now NOW or I'll—"

"But you won't respect me," I said. "You'll think I'm terrible."

"You better! You j-just better! You don't, I'll— *I'll do it here!*"

. . . It was the latter part of February, but it can be warm there in February and it was this night. Not hot-warm, but cool-warm. Balmy. The kind of night when bedclothes are unnecessary, and naked bodies warm each other comfortably.

I raised up on one elbow, reached across her to the ashtray. I held the cigarette over her a moment, letting its glow fall upon her body, moving the glow slowly downward from her breasts. Then, I crushed it out in the tray, and lay back down again.

"Very pretty," I said. "A very lovely bush. Not as extensive as my wife's, but then you don't have her area."

"Crazy!" She snuggled against me. "You and your four-hundred pound wife!"

"She probably weighs more than that now. She gets bigger all the time, you know. Elephantiasis. It's not fat, but growth. I imagine her head alone weighs as much as you do."

"I'll bet!" she snickered. "I can *see* you marrying a wife like *that*!"

"But who else would have married her?" And wasn't she entitled to marriage, to everything that could possibly be given her? It would have been better, of course, if she'd been put to sleep at birth as our first three children were—"

"Uh-huh. Oh, sure!"

"It's done. What kinder thing can you do for three hopeless Mongoloids? One you might take care of, but three of them—triplets—"

"Mmmm-hmm?" She yawned drowsily. "And what's wrong with the other two, the two you have now? They don't have all their parts, I suppose?"

"Well," I said, "they're my children. So, no, I don't suppose they do. Something is certain to be missing . . ."

A balmy gust of wind puffed through the partially opened window, swirling the curtains, sucking them back against the screen. They rustled there, scratchily, flattening themselves. Trying to push out into the moonlight. Then, they gave up limply, came creeping back over the sill. And slid down into the darkness.

I closed my eyes. I drew her into my arms, and pulled her tightly against me.

She shivered. Her lips moved hungrily over my face,

burning, pressing harder and harder. Whispering in ecstatic abandon. *"Marty . . . Oh, Marty, Marty, Marty! Y-You—you know what I'm going to d-do to you?"*

I had a pretty good idea, but I didn't say. She probably thought it was something original—her own invention—and there was no point in playing the kill-sport.

What I said was that that was beside the point! "It isn't what you're going to do to me, lady! It's what I'm going to do to you."

•   •   •

It was very late when I reached home. Mom was asleep—the doctor had come and given her a sedative. Carol let me in the door, and we swapped news briefly. Then, since both of us were tired and we didn't want Mom waking up on us, we turned in.

I had trouble getting to sleep—I don't think I'd slept more than an hour or so when my alarm clock sounded off. But I got up anyway, promptly at seven. Mom didn't know I'd quit my job. The longer she could be kept in ignorance the better.

I left the house, and had breakfast in a drugstore. Afterwards, I sauntered down to that little park I've mentioned and sat down to wait for Carol. We hadn't had a chance to talk much last night. She'd indicated that she had things to tell me, and I of course had things to tell her.

I yawned, blinking my eyes against the warm morning sunlight. I yawned again, and put on my sunglasses. Thinking about last night, about my lady cop. Putting together the bits of personal data I'd been able to get out of her.

Her name was Archer, Lois Archer. She was about twenty-eight years old. (My guess—she hadn't told me.) She'd been with the police department for five years. She'd worked as a secretary for three years, then there'd been an opening on the force so she'd shifted over to that. The pay was considerably higher. The work had promised to be much more interesting. She'd detested the job almost from the beginning; she simply wasn't the cop type. But she'd felt that she had to stick with it. Good jobs, even reasonably good jobs, were hard to get out there. So many people came here for the climate, and were willing to work for next-to-nothing to remain.

She had a brother overseas in the army. He and she owned the house jointly. She—well, that was about the size of things. The sum total of what I knew about her, and probably all it was important to know.

I saw Carol approaching. I stood up and waved to her. I'd been so busy that I'd hardly gotten a good look at her for weeks. And I noticed now that she seemed to have put on a little weight. It was hard to spot on anyone as small-boned as she; doubtless no one but I would have spotted it. I thought it made her even more attractive than she had been, and I told her so.

She laughed, making a face at me. "Now, that's a nice thing to say to a girl! You say that to your cop, and she'll probably pinch you."

"Well, turnabout," I shrugged. "Turnabout. I think she'll wish she could, incidentally, when she goes to sit down."

I filled her in on Lois, on the setup as a whole. I said that it looked quite promising.

"The house is on the outer outskirts of town; the nearest neighbor is blocks away. Of course, that's not all to the good. It would be worth a lot more if it was closer in."

"Uh-huh," Carol nodded. "But it's a nice place, you said, and it's on the waterfront."

"Yes. So, well, I'd say about fifteen thousand. That's at a forced sale—a fast sale—which naturally it would have to be. Now, this brother angle presents a bit of a problem. She'll have to get his okay, and I got the impression that he might be a pretty tough customer. She seemed rather uncomfortable whenever she mentioned him. But . . ."

I paused, remembering the way she'd acted. After a moment, I went on again . . . She'd been uncomfortable, conscience-stricken, about the whole situation, hadn't she? Afraid I wouldn't respect her, that I'd think she was awful and so on.

"Will it take very long, Marty?"

"I don't think so. She's already got the going-away notion—you know, just the two of us going off somewhere together. Possibly, probably I can swing it in a month."

"Oh," said Carol slowly. "Well, I suppose if"—she saw my expression, gave me a quick smile. "Now, don't you worry about me, darling. We'll get by all right. I'm a little behind on some of the bills, but my alimony is due next week and—well, something will turn up."

"I don't see how I can do it much faster," I said. "Not the main deal. But I might be able to promote a few hundred. Her brother is pretty certain to be half-owner of the car, and furniture, but there's quite a bit of pawnable stuff around, hunting and fishing gear that belongs to him, and—"

I broke off. It wasn't a good idea. In reaching for a few hundred, I might blow the main chance.

Carol said I shouldn't do it. She studied my face searchingly, so intently that I wanted to look away.

"Marty . . . You like her, don't you?"

"I like everyone," I said. "Except, possibly, for one William Wharton III—your ex-husband, in case you've been able to forget."

"You know how I feel about Ellen, Marty, and it's not out of pity. When a person thinks you're wonderful, knowing just about everything there is to know—well, I just about have to feel as I do. But . . . but I've thought a lot about it, Marty, and I think sometimes you really did it for me. You couldn't do anything about my marriage, but you could make yourself as miserable as I was."

"I didn't do it for you," I said. "I would have done it for you, of course—that, or anything else. But I didn't. Don't you remember, Carol? I did what I said I was going to do, back when we were kids. What we both said we were going to do."

"I know, darling, but—"

"Someone that no one else wanted. Someone scorned and shamed and cast-aside. Someone who had never known real love, or even simple kindness, and would never know unless we—"

Her hand closed over mine. She smiled at me mistily, winking back the tears in her sky-blue eyes.

I felt sick all over. I felt like my guts were being ripped out of me, and for a moment I wished they had been.

"Don't," I said. "For God's sake, don't cry, darling! I don't know how I could have been so stupid as to—"

"I—it's all right, Marty." She made the tears go away. "You didn't do it. I just happened to think of something, something that Mom said to me one night and—"

"What? What was it?"

"Nothing. I mean, she didn't actually say it. She started to, and then she—she just shut up. Let's forget it, hmmm?" She patted my hand, cocking her head on one side. "I'm probably wrong about it. She probably didn't intend to say anything at all like I thought she did."

"Well," I said, "I don't know what she could say that she hasn't said already."

"She didn't. She really didn't say anything, darling. Lend me your handkerchief, will you?"

I gave it to her, and she blew her nose. She opened her purse, took out her compact, and studied herself in the mirror.

"About afterwards, Marty. Will you have to dispose of her—Lois?"

"I don't know," I said. "I don't think I'd have to—I imagine she'd be too ashamed to squawk. But that still leaves the question of whether I should. It would seem kind of fitting, you know, something virtually required."

"Yes?" said Carol. "Well, perhaps. It seems that it would be, but on the other hand . . ." She shook her head thoughtfully, returning the compact to her purse. "Whatever you think, Marty, whatever you want. I just don't want you to feel you have to do it on my account."

"I won't," I promised. "For that matter . . . well, skip it. I have a feeling that it should be done, that it must, but—"

"Yes?"

"I don't know," I said. "I just don't know."

•   •   •

We walked into town together, and I left her at the cocktail lounge. I had a light second breakfast, and settled down in the public square. Except for a very vague sense of uneasiness, of something left undone, I felt quite happy. I had Carol; we were brought together again. I had Lois—at least, I would have her for a while. Life was back in balance, then, poised perfectly on the two essential kinds of love. And there was little more to be asked of it. There was much to be grateful for, to feel happy about.

I lolled back on my bench, basking in the sunlight. Warm inwardly and outwardly. Deciding that I should be able to send for the family in a few weeks. This would be a beautiful place for Ellen to die, I thought. And, of course, she was dying. I had been temporarily unable to go on watching the—process—and I had felt that her folks should be forced to do so. But in a few weeks, as soon as my emotional resources were replenished, and theirs, if they had any, depleted . . .

I would give her a beautiful death. It would make up for many things.

As for the present—

I got up quickly, and went out to the sidewalk.

The cocktail lounge was about a block away. Carol and a young navy officer had just emerged from it, and started up the street. And a man who had been loitering near the entrance had followed them.

I ran across the intersection. I ran part way up the block, then slowed to a walk as they, and subsequently he, rounded the corner. I reached the corner myself, and crossed to the other side of the street. I stood there, my back half-turned, ostensibly looking into a shop window.

They turned in at the entrance of one of those small, lobbyless hotels. He glanced up at its neon signs, consulted his watch and took out a notebook. He wrote in it briefly, looking again at his watch. Then, he returned it to his pocket, and walked on down the street.

I followed him at a discreet distance.

Some four blocks away, he entered a small office building. It was a shabby place, a diseases-of-men, rubber novelties, massage-parlor kind of building. At the foot of the steps, immediately inside the door, was a white-lettered office directory. It was divided into five sections, one for each story. Since the building was a walk-up, tenants became fewer and fewer after the second floor. And on the fifth there was only one.

He was all alone up there. J. Krutz, Private Investigations, "Divorce Cases a Speciality," was all alone.

I pulled my hat down low, readjusted my sunglasses and started up the steps.

There was a small lavatory, a chipped-enamel sink, in one corner of his office. He was bent over it, his back turned to the door when I arrived, and I stood back from the threshold for a moment, giving him time to dry his hands and face. Then, I strode in brusquely, curtly introduced myself, and sat down without waiting for an invitation.

He was a flabby-looking, owl-faced fellow. Obviously wounded by my manner—servilely hostile, if you know what I mean—he sat down across from me—at a scarred, untidy desk; memos to himself on a paper spike and an ash tray probably appropriated from a hotel overflowed with cigarette butts.

He was cert'n'ly glad, he said, to meet Mr. Wharton's West Coast representative. But wasn't we kind of rushing things? After all, he'd only been on the job four days; yessir, it was just four days since he'd got Mr. Wharton's wire from New York, and he'd already sent in two reports.

He paused, giving me a wounded look.

I ripped out a handsome curse.

"That Wharton"—I shook my head. "Always driving someone. Always trying to put on the squeeze. Why, he gave me the impression you'd been on the case for weeks!"

"Well," he hesitated cautiously. "I'm not criticizing, y' understand. But . . ."

"You should." I said firmly. "You have every right to, Mr. Krutz. Doubtless he can't help it, I bear him not the slightest ill-will, but the man is a bastard. This case itself is proof of the fact."

"Well . . ." He hesitated again. Then, he leaned forward eagerly, an oily grin on his owl's face. "Ain't it the truth?" he said. "Yessir, you really got something there, Mr. Allen. I know all about the case, even if there wasn't much of it got in the papers. Why, the guy was just as lowdown as they get—a washed-up, worn-out punk, pimping for a living. He was nothin', know what I mean, ten times lower than nothing. So somehow this swell little dish decides to marry him—I never will be able to figure that one out—and she starts getting him back on his feet. There's nothing he's any good at, so she supports 'em both. What time she ain't knocking herself out on a job, she's working to build him up. Nursing him, waiting on him hand and foot, actually making somethin' out of nothing, y'know, and she does so good at it that his family decides to take him back. Then . . ."

Then he'd given her a big fat dose of syphilis and divorced her for having it. She was very young, then. She was too dazed to fight. Probably she didn't care to fight.

"I see you know all the facts, Mr. Krutz," I said. "You're thoroughly grounded in the case.

"Sure. That's my business, know what I mean? . . . What's the matter with the guy, Mr. Allen? I'm tickled to have the job naturally, but why does he want it done? How can he do a thing like this just to save himself a few bucks?"

"I wonder," I said. "How can you do it to make yourself a few bucks?"

"Me? Well, uh"—he laughed uncertainly. "I mean, what the hell, anyway? That's my job. If I didn't do it, someone else would. I—Say, ain't I seen you somewhere be—"

"Would they do it?" I said. "How can you be sure they would, Mr. Krutz? Have you ever thought about the potentials in a crusade for not doing the things that someone else would do if you didn't?"

"Say, n-now," he stammered. "Now, l-looky here, mister—"

"I'm afraid you have sinned," I said. "You have violated Section A of Commandment One-minus. Yea, verily, Krutz—"

"Now, l-looky. Y-you—you—" He stood shakily. "You c-can't blame me f-for—"

"Yea, verily, sayeth the Lord Lakewood, better the blind man who pisses through a window than the knowing servant who raises it for him."

I smiled and thrust out my hand. He took it automatically.

I jerked him forward—and down. He came down hard on his desk, on its sharp steel paper-spike. It went through his open mouth and poked out the back of his head.

I left.

It just about had to be done that way, to look like an accident. But still I was not at all pleased with myself. It was too simple, a stingy complement to the complex process of birth, and there is already far too much of such studied and stupid simplicity in life. Catch-word simplicity—"wisdom." Idiot idealogy. Drop-a-bomb-on-Moscow, the-poor-are-terribly-happy thinking. Men are forced to live with this nonsense, this simplicity, and they should have something better in death.

That is and was my feeling, at least, and Carol shared it.

"The poor man," she said. "I wish I could have had him in bed with me. They're always so happy that way."

She did not, of course, receive her alimony check.

•   •   •

I went to work the following week, and quit at the end of it. Although I felt uncomfortable in doing so, I sent most of the money to Ellen at Carol's insistence. Mom was very cross that night, the eve of my resignation. She had learned, meanwhile, of my quitting the first job. And this seemed to be a little more than she could take.

"You just don't want to amount to anything!" she said furiously. "Neither of you do—you do your best not to! Well, all I have to say is . . ."

We were eating dinner at the time. Carol had been eating very little, and now she was beginning to look ill. I held up my hand, cutting off all that Mom had to say which was obviously interminable.

"Before you go any further," I said. "Before you say anything more, perhaps you should establish your qualifications for saying it."

"What—how do you mean?"

"I don't know how to make it any plainer. Not without being much more pointed than I care to."

She didn't understand for a moment; she was too absorbed in her tirade against us. Then, she understood, and her face sagged and her eyes went sick. Mouth working, she stared down dully at her plate.

"I . . . I couldn't help it," she mumbled. "I—I did the best I could."

I said I was sure of it. Carol and I didn't blame her at all. Now, why don't we finish our dinners and forget all about it?"

"I—I don't feel like eating." She pushed back her plate and stood up. "I think I'd better lie—" She staggered.

I jumped up and caught her by the arm, and Carol and I helped her up the stairs to bed. We fixed her some of the sleeping potion. She drank it down, looked up at us from her pillow; eyes dragging shut, face a crumpled, blue-dotted parchment.

"Just don't," she whispered. "Just don't do anything else."

And she fell asleep.

I was seeing Lois that night. Carol was also going out, having had poor luck that day; and she stood at the curb with me for a few minutes, while I waited for Lois to come by.

"Now, don't you worry about me, Marty," she smiled. "I feel

fine, and—and, well, after all, it's really the only way we can do anything very profitable."

"I know," I said. "But . . ." But it *was* the only way. If she was to pick up, or rather to be picked up by, a prize chump, there could be no witnesses to the act. It must be done unobserved, and night offered the least chance of observation.

"Well, don't wear yourself out," I said. "It's not necessary. I should be able to swing this other matter very soon."

"Don't you wear *yourself* out," she said. "Don't do anything at all, if you don't want to."

I promised I wouldn't. I added that I still hadn't decided what Lois' final disposition should be.

"It's an odd thing," I said, "but I have a feeling that it isn't necessary for me to decide. The fitting thing will be done, but I will have nothing to do with it."

Carol left as Lois drove up. We rode out to her house, and she was pouting and peevish throughout the trip. She just didn't see *why*, she kept exclaiming. My sister had money. She just had to have, the way she dressed and living in that big house and—and everything! So why—

"She'd die if she didn't live that way," I said. "She lived too long another way."

"Oh, stop talking nonsense! Tell me why, Marty. Just tell me why I should be expected to give up everything when you could just as well ask that fine sister of yours to—"

We had stopped in front of her house, in the driveway, rather. I turned suddenly and slapped her across the mouth.

Her eyes flashed. Her hand lashed out in instant, angry reaction—then stopped, just short of my jaw.

"Well?" I said. "Well, Lois, my peevish bluecoat?"

She bit her lip helplessly, trying to smile, to pass it off as a joke.

"Well, how about *this?*" I said, and I swung my hand again— I kept swinging it. "And this and this and—"

"P-please, Marty!" She tried to cover her face. "It'll s-show—I have to work, and—"

"All right," I said. "All right, my inky-haired incontinent, my sloe-eyed slut, my copulating cop. How about this?"

I caught my hand into the front of her blouse, her brassiere. I yanked, and her naked breasts bloomed out through the torn cloth. And . . . and she flung herself forward, crushing them against me.

"H-harder, dearest! Oh, Marty, I—I—"

"I'm trying to do you a favor," I said. "I love you, Lois, and I'm trying to—"

"D-don't talk darling. J-just—Marty! Where are you going?"

"Home," I said. "I'm walking up to the highway, and catching a cab."

"No! D-don't you dare! you just t-try to, and—"

I got as far as the highway, three blocks; then, I gave up and went back to her. Carried her in my arms. Carried her as I'd left her in the car. With every stitch of her clothes ripped off.

•   •   •

I stayed there that night. The next morning she phoned in to the department, reported herself sick and was given the day off. So I kept on staying.

It was a pretty wild day, a sweetly wild day, a perfect commingling of sweetness and wildness. We had breakfast. We took a bath together. We had a half-dozen drinks. Then, we stripped every damned picture in the house from the walls, dug up a couple of her brother's rifles and lugged the lot down to the beach.

They were the most hideous kind of crap, those pictures. Cute stuff—dime-store junk. Pictures of kewpie-doll babies with their pants falling off, and dogs smoking pipes, and cats rolling a ball of yarn. Her brother liked such junk, it seemed; he also liked to have his own way. So we carried it down to the beach, and we blasted it to pieces. Taking turns at it. One of us tossing an item into the air for the other to shoot at.

It was noon by that time. We went back to the house, ate and drank some more, and took another bath. We rested, dozed in each others arms. We got up, and went on another romp.

Her brother belonged to some half-assed lodge—one of the dress-up outfits. She got out his uniform hat, pulled the plumes off of it and made herself into a peacock.

She was a very lovely peacock. She crawled around on the floor, wiggling her bottom and making the plumes sway. I crawled around after her, snapping at them, barking and yipping like a dog. I caught up with her. We rolled around on the floor, locked together, working up static electricity from the carpet. We rolled into the living room—laughing, yelling and jerking with jolts of electricity. We knocked over the tables and chairs and lamps, making a mess of the place. And then I grabbed a bottle of whiskey, and we rolled back into the bedroom and under the bed.

We came out finally. We took our third bath, washing away the dirt and lint, and climbed into bed again. It was night. The balmy, cool-warm breeze of night, was drifting through the window. My back was to it, and she was afraid I might catch cold. She bent over me, shaking out her soft, black waist-length hair; she tucked it over and under my shoulders, her face pressed tightly to my chest, drawing herself against me with her hair. And we were wrapped together.

We had said nothing about money all day; we were afraid of spoiling that sweet wildness. We were afraid of spoiling this now, this gentle sweetness, so we still did not speak of money. We ignored that chasm and placed ourselves in the wonderland beyond, the green pastures of accomplished fact.

"Huh-uh, Marty . . ." she murmured. "I don't want you on any old newspapers. I want us to be all alone, away off somewhere by ourselves."

"Well, let's see, then," I said. "We might run a dairy. None of this mechanized stuff, mind you. I would operate it by hand, and you, my lamb, or I should say—"

"Now, Marty!" she snickered. "That's dirty."

"Well, I could write my book," I said. "My treatise on taxation. 'Cornucopia of Constipation or the Martin Lakewood Bowel-movement Single-tax.' "

"Crazy! You— *ha, ha*—you crazy sweet thing!"

"I would do away with all taxes on food and other necessities," I said, "and the only levy would be on bowel movements. It's really a very sensible plan, Lois. The most just, most equitable plan ever invented. The less money a man has, the less he eats, the less are his taxes."

"Uh-hmmm, and suppose he didn't have any money at all. What would he do then?"

"What does he do now?" I said.

"Oh, Marty! *Ha, ha, ha* . . ."

"What's so funny about it?" I said. "If it's right to let a man starve, then it's right to let him die of constipation. It's more right, goddammit! At least we give him a choice, a little control over his own destiny. We can deny him food, but we can't keep him from holding in his bowels. If he can hold in long enough— What's so funny? Goddammit, what are you laughing about?"

"Why, Marty!" She laughed nervously. "We're just talking, joking. There's nothing to be angry about."

"But"—I caught myself. "Yeah, sure," I said. "It's all a joke, and a pretty bad one; not even original. Just about the oldest joke there is."

We lay silent for a time. The curtains scratched restlessly against the screen, and far in the distance somewhere there was the faint howling of a dog.

"Marty . . ." She pressed in on me at the hips. "Love me, Marty? Love me very much?"

"Yes," I said. "I'm afraid I do."

"More than anyone else?"

We had been on this line before. I imagine almost every man has, and has been as frustrated by it as I.

"Do you, Marty? Love me more than you do your sister?"

"I've told you," I said. "It's two different things, entirely different kinds of love. The two aren't comparable."

"But you have to love one of us more than the other. You *have* to, Marty."

I said that, goddammit, I didn't have to, and no one out of his infancy would say that he did. It was a milk and high-ball proposition. Both were satisfying, but each in its own way. "Take your brother, now. As a brother, you love him more than—"

"I do not! I only love you, and I love you more than anyone else in the world!"

"Well," I said helplessly. "Well—"

The phone rang. She murmured to let it go, and I let it go. And after the second ring it stopped.

It was Carol's signal. I waited tensely for her to call back, and Lois waited for something else. She nudged me again, pressed forward with her thighs. The phone rang.

I turned suddenly, and grabbed for it. Lois let out with an angry *"Ouch!,"* sat up glaring at me, rubbing her scalp.

"What's the matter with you? You knew my hair was—"

"Please," I said. "Be quiet a minute!"

It was Carol. She spoke rapidly, her voice pitched just above a whisper.

". . . understand, Marty? A hunting lodge . . . take the left turn at the crossroad, and . . ."

"Of course, I understand," I said. "I'll start right away, Carol. As soon as mother gets to feeling better, I can come back."

We hung up. I gave Lois a kiss, and apologized for yanking her hair.

"I'll have to leave for a while now, baby. My mother's taken ill—nothing serious, but Carol thinks I ought to be there, and—"

"Oh, she does, huh?" She pushed me away from her. "Well, go on then, and call yourself a cab! You're not going to use my car to rush home to her!"

I started dressing. If I had to—and I was sure I wouldn't have to—I could get along without her car. It would take extra time; I'd have to go into town and rent one there. But I could do it.

"You and your darling Carol! I've seen the way you act around each other. You know what I think about you?"

"Something nasty, I'm sure," I said. "Something very naughty. Otherwise, you wouldn't be wearing that pretty blush."

She told me what she thought. Rather she yelled it. And I laughed, and kissed her again. Because she didn't actually think it, of course. She didn't mean it; it was meaningless. It was mere words, said not out of hate but love.

She was crying, apologizing, as soon as they were spoken.

"I'm s-sorry, darling. I just l-love you so much, and—"

"It's all right," I said. "I have to run now, baby."

I took the car, naturally. She insisted on it.

●　　●　　●

The lodge was about thirty miles up in the mountains, about a mile off the main mountain road. It was heavily wooded country up there. I shut off the car lights as soon as I left the road, and weaved my way through the trees by moonlight. I drove very slowly, holding the motor to a quiet purr. After a few minutes of this creeping, I stopped and got out.

I was on the edge of a clearing. The lodge was about fifty yards. It was a low, log-and-frame structure with a lean-to at one end. Inside the lean-to was a black sports coupe.

I glanced up at the sky, watched the moon drift behind a mass of clouds. In the brief darkness, as it vanished from view, I raced stooping across the clearing. I stopped in the sheltering alcove of the door, getting my wind back, reconstructing the interior of the place from the description Carol had given me.

This, immediately beyond the door, was the living room. The kitchen was straight on through. There was a bedroom on the right—of the living room, that is—and another at its left extreme. They were supposed to be in the one to the right.

I pressed gently down on the latch. I pushed against the door, ever so easily, and it moved silently open. I stepped inside.

A small lamp was burning on the fireplace mantle. I looked swiftly around the room, then crossed it and glanced into the kitchen. I couldn't see very well, but I could see enough. A wood stove with a row of implements above it. I lifted down one of them, a heavy meat cleaver, and reentered the living room.

It was an old place, and the floors were not what they had been. Several times, as I went toward the bedroom, there were dangerously loud squeaks. And just as I reached the door there was a *pop* like that of an exploding firecracker.

I stopped dead still in my tracks. Holding my breath. Listening.

There was no sound for a moment. Then, I heard the rattle of bedsprings, the rustle of bedclothes thrown back. The quiet but unmistakable sound of feet touching the floor. And crossing it.

I stepped to one side of the door. I raised the cleaver. I stood on tiptoe as the latch clicked softly, then clicked back into place. From the other side of the panels, there came a nervous whisper: "M-Marty . . . ?"

"Carol!" I laughed out loud with relief. "Are you all right, darling?"

"Fine"—she didn't sound exactly fine. "He let me fix him a drink, and—well, it's all over, Marty. I'll be out as soon as I dress."

I wiped the cleaver off and returned it to the kitchen. I sat down on a cowhide-covered lounge, and after a few minutes she came out. She sat down next to me, running a comb through her thick red hair, touching up the makeup on her innocent child's face.

There'd be no trouble, she said. There was no danger of future trouble. The guy had picked her up on a dark street, and they'd come directly to this place. Being unmarried and on a vacation, it might be days before inquiries were made about him.

"So it's all right—*that* part's all right." Carol smiled tiredly. "But look at this, Marty."

She opened her purse and handed it to me, a thick sheaf of bills with a rubber band around each end. I riffled it, and silently handed it back. It was a Kansas City roll, big bills, a couple of fifties on the outside; the inside, little stuff, ones and fives and a few tens.

Carol looked down at it, her blue eyes dull and empty.

I shook my head silently. It hardly seemed the time for words. I did a little wiping up with my handkerchief, and then we left.

She was sick once on the way back to town. I had to stop the car, and let her out by the roadside. We drove on again, she huddling against me, shivering with the cold mountain air. I talked to her—to myself. I talked to both of us, and for both of us. And if it was rationalization, so be it. Perhaps the power to rationalize is the power to remain the same. Perhaps the insane are so because they cannot escape the truth.

We were culpable, I said, only to the degree that all life, all society, was culpable. We were no more than the pointed instruments of that life, activated symbols in an allegory whose authors were untold billions. And only they, acting in concert, could alter a line of its text. And the alterations could best be impelled by remaining what we were. Innocence outraged, the sacred defiled, the useful made useless. For in universal horror there could be universal hope, in ultimate bestiality the ultimate in beauty and good. The blind should be made to see—so it was written. *They should be made to see!* And, lo, the Lord World was an agonized god, and he looked not kindly upon the bandaging of his belly whilst his innards writhed with cancer.

"Yea, verily," I said. "If thy neighbor's ass pains him, do thou not divert him with bullshit, but rather kick him soundly thereon. Yea, even though it maketh him thine enemy. For it is better that he should howl for a doctor than to drown in dung."

We had reached the house. Carol sat up, blinking her eyes sleepily.

"Don't worry about the money," she said, as she got out of the car. "It'll be a big help, more than I need, really."

I drove on out to Lois' house. I went inside just long enough to give her an ultimatum. She was to cable her brother immediately or at least the first thing in the morning. Otherwise, we were washed up.

She was too startled, too furious to speak for a moment. When she did it was to tell me to go to hell, that she would neither cable him in the morning nor any other time.

I got away fast—pleased, saddened. Glad that I had tried, but knowing that I had changed nothing. She was certain to relent. She had to. For she was a symbol also, one more character in the allegory of unalterable lines.

I don't know why I had been so long in identifying her, and seeing the part she had to play. Certainly, *I* should have seen it long before.

I got home and went quietly to bed. A few minutes later my bedroom door opened, and silently closed again. I sat up. I held out my hands in the darkness, and Carol found them, and I drew her down into the bed. I stroked her hair, whispered to her softly.

"Bad?" I said. "Is it bad, little sister?"

"B-bad . . ." She shuddered violently. "Oh, M-Marty, I keep—"

"Don't," I said. "Don't think, don't remember. It was the way it had to be. It was the best way, and you'll see that it was.

She shuddered again. And again. I drew her closer, whispering, and gradually the shaking subsided.

"Y-yes," she said. "Yes! Tell me a story, Marty."

I hesitated. I had told her so many stories, and I was not sure of the kind she wanted.

"Well . . ." I said. "Well, once upon a time there were three billion bastards who lived in a jungle. They ate dirt, these bastards, of which there was more than enough for all. A total of six sextillion, four hundred and fifty quintillion short tons, to be exact. But being bastards, they were not content with—"

"Marty."

"Another one? A different kind?"

"*The* other one, Marty. You know."

I knew. I remembered. How could I help but remember?

"Once upon a time," I said. "Once upon a time, there was a little boy and a little girl, and the little boy was her father and the little girl was his mother. They—"

The door banged open. The light went on.

Mom stood staring at us, her chest rising and falling. Her eyes gleaming with a kind of evil triumph.

I sat up. Carol and I both sat up. One of her breasts had slipped out of her nightgown, and I tucked it back inside.

"Yes, Mom?" I said. "I hope we didn't wake you up."

"I'll bet you do! I'll just bet you do!"

"But"—I frowned, puzzled. "Of course, I hope so. We tried to be as quiet as we could. Carol had a little trouble sleeping, so I was just—"

"I know what you were doing! The same thing you've been doing for years! Scum, filth—no wonder everyone hated you! They saw through you all right, you didn't fool them any. They should have beaten you to death, starved you to death, you r-rotten . . ."

She believed it. She had made herself believe it. It was justification; it excused everything, the moral cowardice, the silence in the face of wrong, the years of all-absorbing, blindly selfish self-pity. She had hoped for this—what she believed this was. Doubtless, she had hoped for it right from the beginning. That, abysmal degradation, had been her hope for her children. And who knew, who was to say, how much that hope had been expressed in our lives.

I wanted to say something, do something to comfort Carol. I could not.

I lay back down on the pillow, and covered my face with my hands. Carol laid one of her hands over mine.

She spoke very quietly, but somehow her voice rose above the tirade.

"You made Marty cry," she said. "You made my brother cry."

"I'll—I'll do worse than that!" Mom panted. "I'll—"

"There is nothing worse than that. Go to your room."

"Now-now, see here," Mom faltered. "Don't you tell me to—"

"Go to your room."

There was silence, complete suspension of movement, for a

moment. Then, Carol threw back the covers—I felt her throw them back. She climbed out of bed, and pointed—I could see her pointing.

"N-no!" It was Mom, but it was not her voice. "No, Carol! I'm sorry! I d-didn't mean it! I—"

"You meant it. I mean it. Go to your room."

"No! You can't! I'm your mother. Y-you—"

"Are you? Were you?"—she was moving away from the bed, and Mom was moving out of the door. Backing away as Carol advanced. "Go on. Go. You have to go to sleep."

"*No!*"

"Yes."

Their voices grew fainter and fainter. Then, right at the last, they rose again. Not strident but clear. A little tired but peaceful.

"That's right. Drink it all down. Now, you'll be a lot better."

"Thank you. Thank you, very much, Carol . . ."

•   •   •

Figuratively, at least, most people do die of oversedation; fumbling about fearfully, blindly, they grasp the sweet-smelling potions handed them with never a look at the label, and suddenly they are dead. They died "natural" deaths, then. As she died. At any rate, the doctor chose to call it natural—heart failure—and we could not, of course, dispute his word.

He, the doctor, left after a period of condoling with us. The undertaker came to supervise the removal of the body, and remained to discuss funeral arrangements. He thought something very nice could be done for about twelve hundred dollars, something that our loved one would have loved. The price fell gradually, his falling with it, until he was down to the rock bottom of "adequacy" which bore a price tag of four hundred and fifty.

Carol paid him. The funeral was set for the following afternoon. It was a little after he left us, with a barely pleasant good-morning, that Lois called.

"I've just got one thing to say to you," she began. "If you think for one minute that you can—Marty! Marty, darling! What's the matter?"

I couldn't answer her. How did I know what the matter was? Carol took the phone out of my hand and talked to her.

They talked for several minutes, and I could hear her weeping as Carol hung up. An hour or so later, as Carol was getting ready to go to town, she called back. I still couldn't talk, so Carol took a message for me.

Would I please, please call her as soon as I could? She didn't want to disturb me, feeling as I must, so—would I, please? It was important. It concerned something that I wanted.

I lay down. I hadn't felt at all sleepy, but I fell asleep instantly, and night had come when I awakened.

I called out to Carol. I got up and ran into her room, and there was a note pinned to her pillow:

Marty darling:
I storied to you about what I was going to do today. I knew you'd be worried, and there's really no need to because I'm going to be perfectly all right. I'll be with you as soon as I can, but I won't be able to be there for the funeral. Don't you go either, if it bothers you. And tell me a story tonight, darling. I'll be listening for it.

The signature was mixed up, jumbled. The initial letter was both *M* and *C* and the second letter was both *o* and *a*.

I fixed a bite of dinner. I shaved and started out to look for her, and then I remembered that this was tonight, so I came back. I went up to her room. I stretched out on her bed, and took her into my arms. And I told her a story, I told it all through the night. She was so frightened. She was trembling and shaking constantly. So I talked on and on, on and on through the night, holding her tightly against me.

Day came, at last.

At last, she slipped quietly out of my arms.

At last, she was asleep.

I lay watching her for a time, selfishly hoping that she would awaken. Because I had always loved to watch that awakening, the coming to life of purity and beauty, reborn by night and as yet untarnished by day. I waited and watched, but she did not awaken. She did not come to life. And finally I fell asleep at her side.

When I awoke, she was gone. I was anxious about her, naturally—I wondered where she had gone. I sat for a long time wondering, about her and the others who went. Then, it was almost time for the funeral, and I had to leave.

I went to the funeral, but I did not stay. I strolled away from the graveside and off toward the busline, meandering casually through the hummocked greensward, the marble and copper bordered streets of The City of Wonderful People. It was a crowded city; neighbor elbowed against neighbor. Yet no one felt the need for more room. They dwelt peacefully side by side, content with what they had. No one needing more than what he had, nor wanting more than he needed. Because they were so wonderful, you see. They were all so wonderful.

There was Annie, for example, devoted wife of Samuel. And there was William, faithful husband of Nora. There was Henry, dutiful son, and Mabel, loving daughter, and Father and Mother, who were not only devoted, faithful, dutiful and loving, but God-fearing to boot. One had to look closely to see that they were all these things, their gravestone being only slightly larger than a cigarette package. But one always does have to look closely to see virtue, and, as in this case, it is always worth the trouble.

Yes, hell. Yes, oh, God, yes, it was a wonderful place, The City of Wonderful People. Everyone in it was everything that everyone should be. Some had a little more on the ball, of course, than others; there was one guy, for instance, who was only humble. But think of that! Think of its possibilities! Think of what you could do with a guy like that on a world tour. Or if war prevented, as it indubitably would, you could put him on television. A nation-wide hookup. You could go to the network and say, look, I've got something different here. Something unique. I've got a guy that's—No, he doesn't do card tricks, he's not a singer or dancer. Well, he does have a sense of humor, but he doesn't tell—No, I'm afraid he doesn't have big tits, and his ass looks just like yours and mine. What he's got is something different. Something there's a hell of a need for. And if you'll just give him a chance.

They'd never go for it.

You'd have to nail him to a cross first.

Only here, only in The City of Wonderful People, was the wonderful wonderful.

• • •

The phone was ringing. Ringing again or still.

I let it go.

It would only be Lois weeping and apologizing and commis-
erating with me. Telling me she'd sent the cable. Begging to see
me. Telling me she quit her job, that she was giving up everything for me, so wouldn't I—couldn't I—come out for just a little while?

Yes, it would only be Lois. And, of course, I would go to see
her—I had to. But it was not time to yet. She had sent the cable
to Japan four days ago. Even in a suspicious world, where days
were hours and miles were feet, it was not yet time.

So I let the phone ring, even when it rang with that flat final-
ity which phones assume when ringing for the last time. I did
not want to talk. Carol would not want to talk. Carol was asleep
and must not be disturbed, and—

It wasn't Lois calling. Lois was answering it. The front door
was open, and she was speaking into the phone. Frowning,
stammering, her face slowly turning gray. She mumbled something that sounded like, "J-just a minute, doctor"—which made
no sense at all, naturally. She looked at me concernedly.

"Can you talk, Marty? It's some doctor down in Mexico. Just
across the border. He says—it's about Carol, darling—h-he,
says that . . . Oh, Marty, I'm so s-sorry—he says t-that—"

I took the phone away from her. It couldn't be about Carol,
but she was obviously in no condition to talk.

It was a poor connection and his English was poor. I had to
keep asking him to repeat things, and even then he was almost
impossible to understand. It was impossible to understand.

"You must be mistaken," I said. "Five months pregnant? What
the hell kind of doctor would abort a five-months pregnancy?"

"But I do not know, *senor*. She tell me is barely three months,
and it do not show mooch, you know. She is so small, an'—"

But he'd know, dammit. Any kind of doctor would. If he
wasn't completely stupid, willing to run any risk to pick up a few
dollars . . .

"I am so sorry *senor*. I do my ver' best. It is not much,
perhaps—but for twenty-five dollars, what would you? Soch as I
am, as leetle as I know, I—"

"Well, it doesn't matter," I said. "It's all a mistake. You've got the wrong party."

"No! Wait, *senor*!"

"Well?" I said.

"What should I do? What do you wish done? I am poor man, and you must know—"

"I'll tell you what I know," I said. "You're trying to work some kind of racket, and if you bother me again I'll sic the authorities on you."

"*Senor!* Please"—he was almost crying. "I mus'—you mus' do something! Almost four days it has been, an' the weather she is so hot, an'—What shall I do?"

I laughed. I imagined it must be a hell of a mess.

"What the hell do I care what you do?" I said. "Throw it in the ocean. Throw it on the garbage dump. Throw it out in the alley for the dogs to piss on."

"But she is—"

"Don't lie to me! I know where my sister is!"

I slammed up the phone.

Lois wet her lips. She came toward me hesitantly, wanting to protest, to take charge, to do what her essential primness and ingrained propriety demanded. She wanted to say, You'd better go, Marty. You must, or I'll do it. But she did not say that; she could not say it, I suppose. Her instincts had not changed during these past few weeks, but she was no longer sure of them. She no longer relished and took pride in them. They were something to be scorned, ignored, pushed out of the path of desire.

"Let's go out to my house, Marty. You need to get away from here."

"I think so, too," I said. "It's about time that I did."

•   •   •

I needed to be diverted. I needed to forget. I needed to make merry. I did. She said I did. So there was the sweet wildness again. Then, wildness without sweetness. Wilder and wilder wildness. Babel.

There was the lewd peacock, the weird, waggling, wiggling mutation of woman and bird. There was the breastless woman, the woman with three faces, with two bedaubed grinning faces for breasts. There was the serpent woman, the frog woman, the woman who was man. There was the man who looked like a dog, the man horse, the man who was woman, the man who was not man. There were the shrieks, the fierce grunts and growls, the howls and snarls, the cluckings, groanings, whinings, barkings, yippings, moanings. There was the rolling and crawling, the laughter and the prayers, the talk in unknown tongues. There was Babel.

And there was peace.

And there was night, and I was wrapped in Circe's hair.

". . . don't think I'm awful, do you, Marty? He's just, well, nothing. And he doesn't want to be anything. Just a big, stupid hateful boor. He's lucky I didn't do something like this long ago!"

"You should have," I said. "You should have split up with him, and gone your own way."

"Sweet"—she brushed her lips against my face. "You do think I'm right, then, don't you, Marty? He deserves to lose every last penny he's got! Every penny he put into this place."

"Why didn't you split with him?" I asked. "Why didn't you get married? Of course, there was your job, the department's single-woman policy. But couldn't you have kept it a secret?"

She hesitated. Her body moved in a small shrug. "I suppose, but you know how it is. I guess I just got in a rut, and, well, I guess there wasn't any one I cared about marrying."

I reached over her and lit a cigarette. We smoked it, taking turns, and I crushed it out in the ashtray. I turned a little on my side, looked out into the quiet night. It was early summer now. The air was sweet with the smell of budding trees, and the horizon still glowed with the golden pastels of the late-setting sun.

Lois laughed venomously; she could just see her brother, she said, when he received her cable. "He's always been so slow and stodgy, but I'll bet he moves fast for once. I told him I'd been offered thirty thousand dollars for the house."

I laughed with her. Thirty thousand dollars for *this* place! Yes, that would make him move all right.

"You don't think I'm awful, do you, Marty? About everything, I mean. You don't think I'm cheap and trashy and—and—"

"I want to tell you something," I said. "I want to tell you about my dad."

"But what's he—No, huh-uh, Marty. Don't tell me any of those crazy stories about—"

"Well, we'll say it's just a story," I said. "It isn't true, we'll say, but just a story."

"Well"—she squirmed uncomfortably. "Oh, all right! I suppose, if you simply *have* to."

"I've often wondered about him, Lois. He wasn't any genius, but he had at least average good sense. He must have known that fooling around with another man's wife—and a cop's wife, at that—was certain to cost him a lot more than it was worth. It was a continuing relationship, you see. Not just a one-night stand. She wasn't that kind of woman, and he wouldn't have been interested in her if she had been that kind. So I kept asking myself, why did he do it? Why did he carry on an affair that could only end in one way? And why did she, a woman of excellent reputation, ostensibly a model of womanly virtue—"

"Marty." She put her fingers over my mouth. "Please don't. Let's just talk about us, mmm?"

"We will." I pushed her hand away. "The woman killed herself that night, the same night Dad killed her husband. She didn't live long enough to explain, and Dad never chose to. It wouldn't have helped him any, and there was no point in looking like a bigger fool than he did already. So . . . so, Lois, I was left with a riddle. One that's nagged me for an answer for almost thirty years. And yet the answer's been before me all the time. In people. In hypocrisy and deception and self-deception. In walling ourselves up in our own little worlds.

"There was the husband, for example, a real cold fish. He minded his own business—was sufficient unto himself. We were his neighbors, but only geographically. So far as social contact went, we might just as well have been on another planet . . . It was a bad attitude. Inevitably, as it always does, it got him killed."

"*K-killed!* . . . Marty, please don't talk any—"

"It was a factor, certainly. If he'd been a little more sociable, friendly, talkative . . . But let's leave him there, and take up his wife. She was what you call a nice woman, as I say. Very proper. At the same time, she resented her husband. She might have gone to work on him, talked things out with him, reformed him into a reasonable facsimile of the man she'd loved and married.

But that would have been a lot of trouble, and she'd convinced herself that it wasn't worthwhile. It was easier to pick up another man—Dad. And there was a way she could do it and still cling to a few shreds of propriety. He was married, of course, and that was bad. But she could believe that it was his badness, rather than hers. If he thought, if he was willing to think that she—" I paused stroking her hair gently. "Don't cry, Lois. It can't be changed. There are not enough tears for this sorrow."

"M-Marty! Oh, Marty, Marty! H-how you must hate me!"

She wept uncontrollably. The tears were hot against my chest, and her flesh was icy.

"I've never hated anyone," I said. "Never anyone."

The lawn was bright in the moonlight. Soon a little girl would come trudging across the grass, it seemed that I could see her coming now, and she would be frightened because she was alone. And then she would not be alone . . .

"I love you, Lois," I said. "We're going to go away together. We'll all go away together."

A cab stopped in front of the house.

A man in uniform got out.

He was supposed to just cable her, give her permission to sell; he wasn't supposed to show up. Well, that was all right. We could all be together, now—brothers and sisters. But, of course, he wasn't her brother.

SOFT MONKEY

Harlan Ellison

*A*t twenty-five minutes past midnight on 51st Street, the wind-chill factor was so sharp it could carve you a new asshole.

Annie lay huddled in the tiny space formed by the wedge of locked revolving door that was open to the street when the document copying service had closed for the night. She had pulled the shopping cart from the Food Emporium at 1st Avenue near 57th into the mouth of the revolving door, had carefully tipped it onto its side, making certain her goods were jammed tightly in the cart, making certain nothing spilled into her sleeping space. She had pulled out half a dozen cardboard flats—broken-down sections of big Kotex cartons from the Food Emporium, the half dozen she had not sold to the junkman that afternoon—and she

*The late Dorothy Parker wrote: "It turns out that Mr. Ellison is a good, clean, honest writer, putting down what he has seen and known, and no sensationalism about it." During the twenty-five years since Parker set those words down, **Harlan Ellison** has become an even more singular and unique voice in American fiction. Woolrich, Collier, Bradbury, Ellison—these are the story writers our children and their children will read after we've passed on. And what a variety of dark delights Ellison will leave them—from the autumnal grief of* Paingod *to the Proustian solace of* Jeffty Is Five. *Here is a new Ellison story, a major one, a tale he would like introduced with the following:*

"Psychologists specializing in ethology know of the soft monkey experiment. A mother orangutan, whose baby has died, given a plush toy doll, will nurture it as if it were alive, as if it were her own. Nurture and protect and savage any creature that menaces the surrogate. Given a wire image, or a ceramic doll, the mother will ignore it. She must have the soft monkey. It sustains her."

had fronted the shopping cart with two of them, making it appear the doorway was blocked by the management. She had wedged the others around the edges of the space, cutting the wind, and placed the two rotting sofa pillows behind and under her.

She had settled down, bundled in her three topcoats, the thick woolen merchant marine stocking cap rolled down to cover her ears, almost to the bridge of her broken nose. It wasn't bad in the doorway, quite cozy, really. The wind shrieked past and occasionally touched her, but mostly was deflected. She lay huddled in the tiny space, pulled out the filthy remnants of a stuffed baby doll, cradled it under her chin, and closed her eyes.

She slipped into a wary sleep, half in reverie and yet alert to the sounds of the street. She tried to dream of the child again. Alan. In the waking dream she held him as she held the baby doll, close under her chin, her eyes closed, feeling the warmth of his body. That was important: his body was warm, his little brown hand against her cheek, his warm, warm breath drifting up with the dear smell of baby.

Was that just today or some other day? Annie swayed in reverie, kissing the broken face of the baby doll. It was nice in the doorway; it was warm.

The normal street sounds lulled her for another moment, and then were shattered as two cars careened around the corner off Park Avenue, racing toward Madison. Even asleep, Annie sensed when the street wasn't right. It was a sixth sense she had learned to trust after the first time she had been mugged for her shoes and the small change in her snap-purse. Now she came fully awake as the sounds of trouble rushed toward her doorway. She hid the baby doll inside her coat.

The stretch limo sideswiped the Caddy as they came abreast of the closed repro center. The Brougham ran up over the curb and hit the light stanchion full in the grille. The door on the passenger side fell open and a man scrabbled across the front seat, dropped to all four on the sidewalk, and tried to crawl away. The stretch limo, angled in toward the curb, slammed to a stop in front of the Brougham, and three doors opened before the tires stopped rolling.

They grabbed him as he tried to stand, and forced him back to his knees. One of the limo's occupants wore a fine navy blue cashmere overcoat; he pulled it open and reached to his hip. His hand came out holding a revolver. With a smooth stroke he laid it across the kneeling man's forehead, opening him to the bone.

Annie saw it all. With poisonous clarity, back in the V of the revolving door, cuddled in darkness, she saw it all. Saw a second man kick out and break the kneeling victim's nose. The sound of it cut against the night's sudden silence. Saw the third man look toward the stretch limo as a black glass window slid down and a hand emerged from the back seat. The electric hum of opening. Saw the third man go to the stretch and take from the extended hand a metal can. A siren screamed down Park Avenue, and kept going. Saw him return to the group and heard him say, "Hold the motherfucker. Pull his head back!" Saw the other two wrench the victim's head back, gleaming white and pumping red from the broken nose, clear in the sulfurous light from the stanchion overhead. The man's shoes scraped and scraped the sidewalk. Saw the third man reach into an outer coat pocket and pull out a pint of scotch. Saw him unscrew the cap and begin to pour booze into the face of the victim. "Hold his mouth open!" Saw the man in the cashmere topcoat spike his thumb and index fingers into the hinges of the victim's jaws, forcing his mouth open. The sound of gagging, the glow of spittle. Saw the scotch spilling down the man's front. Saw the third man toss the pint bottle into the gutter where it shattered; and saw him thumb press the center of the plastic cap of the metal can; and saw him make the cringing, crying, wailing victim drink the Drano. Annie saw and heard it all.

The cashmere topcoat forced the victim's mouth closed, massaged his throat, made him swallow the Drano. The dying took a lot longer than expected. And it was a lot noisier.

The victim's mouth was glowing a strange blue in the calcium light from overhead. He tried spitting, and a gobbet hit the navy blue cashmere sleeve. Had the natty dresser from the stretch limo been a dunky slob uncaring of what *GQ* commanded, what happened next would not have gone down.

Cashmere cursed, swiped at the slimed sleeve, let go of the victim; the man with the glowing blue mouth and the gut being boiled away wrenched free of the other two, and threw himself forward. Straight toward the locked revolving door blocked by Annie's shopping cart and cardboard flats.

He came at her in fumbling, hurtling steps, arms wide and eyes rolling, throwing spittle like a racehorse; Annie realized he'd fall across the cart and smash her flat in another two steps.

She stood up, backing to the side of the V. She stood up: into the tunnel of light from the Caddy's headlights.

"The nigger saw it all!" yelled the cashmere.

"Fuckin' bag lady!" yelled the one with the can of Drano.

"He's still moving!" yelled the third man, reaching inside his topcoat and coming out of his armpit with a blued steel thing that seemed to extrude to a length more aptly suited to Paul Bunyan's armpit.

Foaming at the mouth, hands clawing at his throat, the driver of the Brougham came at Annie as if he were spring-loaded.

He hit the shopping cart with his thighs just as the man with the long armpit squeezed off his first shot. The sound of the .45 magnum tore a chunk out of 51st Street, blew through the running man like a crowd roar, took off his face and spattered bone and blood across the panes of the revolving door. It sparkled in the tunnel of light from the Caddy's headlights.

And somehow he kept coming. He hit the cart, rose as if trying to get a first down against a solid defense line, and came apart as the shooter hit him with a second round.

There wasn't enough solid matter to stop the bullet and it exploded through the revolving door, shattering it open as the body crashed through and hit Annie.

She was thrown backward, through the broken glass, and onto the floor of the document copying center. And through it all, Annie heard a fourth voice, clearly a fourth voice, screaming from the stretch limo, "Get the old lady! Get her, she saw everything!"

Men in topcoats rushed through the tunnel of light.

Annie rolled over, and her hand touched something soft. It was the ruined baby doll. It had been knocked loose from her bundled clothing. *Are you cold, Alan?*

She scooped up the doll and crawled away, into the shadows of the reproduction center. Behind her, crashing through the frame of the revolving door, she heard men coming. And the sound of a burglar alarm. Soon police would be here.

All she could think about was that they would throw away her goods. They would waste her good cardboard, they would take back her shopping cart, they would toss her pillows and the hankies and the green cardigan into some trashcan; and she would be empty on the street again. As she had been when they made her move out of the room at 101st and First Avenue. After they took Alan from her . . .

A blast of sound, as the shot shattered a glass-framed citation on the wall near her. They had fanned out inside the office space, letting the headlight illumination shine through. Clutching the baby doll, she hustled down a hallway toward the rear of the copy center. Doors on both sides, all of them closed and locked. Annie could hear them coming.

A pair of metal doors stood open on the right. It was dark in there. She slipped inside, and in an instant her eyes had grown acclimated. There were computers here, big crackle-gray-finish machines that lined three walls. Nowhere to hide.

She rushed around the room, looking for a closet, a cubbyhole, anything. Then she stumbled over something and sprawled across the cold floor. Her face hung over into emptiness, and the very faintest of cool breezes struck her cheeks. The floor was composed of large removable squares. One of them had been lifted and replaced, but not flush. It had not been locked down; an edge had been left ajar; she had kicked it open.

She reached down. There was a crawlspace under the floor.

Pulling the metal-rimmed vinyl plate, she slid into the empty square. Lying face-up, she pulled the square over the aperture, and nudged it gently till it dropped onto its tracks. It sat flush. She could see nothing where, a moment before, there had been the faintest scintilla of filtered light from the hallway. Annie lay very quietly, emptying her mind as she did when she slept in the doorways; making herself invisible. A mound of rags. A pile of refuse. Gone. Only the warmth of the baby doll in that empty place with her.

She heard the men crashing down the corridor, trying doors. *I wrapped you in blankets, Alan. You must be warm.* They came into the computer room. The room was empty, they could see that.

"She *has* to be here, dammit!"

"There's gotta be a way out we didn't see."

"Maybe she locked herself in one of those rooms. Should we try? Break 'em open?"

"Don't be a bigger asshole than usual. Can't you hear that alarm? We gotta get out of here!"

"He'll break our balls."

"Like hell. Would he do anything else than we've done? He's sittin' on the street in front of what's left of Beaddie. You think he's happy about it?"

There was a new sound to match the alarm. The honking of a horn from the street. It went on and on, hysterically.

"We'll find her."

Then the sound of footsteps. Then running.

Annie lay empty and silent, holding the doll.

It was warm, as warm as she had been all November. She slept there through the night.

The next day, in the last Automat in New York with the wonderful little windows through which one could get food by insertion of a token, Annie learned of the two deaths.

Not the death of the man in the revolving door; the deaths of two black women. Beaddie, who had vomited up most of his internal organs, boiled like Chesapeake Bay lobsters, was all over the front of the *Post* that Annie now wore as insulation against the biting November wind. The two women had been found in midtown alleys, their faces blown off by heavy caliber ordnance. Annie had known one of them; her name had been Sooky and Annie got the word from a good Thunderbird worshipper who stopped by her table and gave her the skinny as she carefully ate her fish cakes and tea.

She knew who they had been seeking. And she knew why they had killed Sooky and the other street person: to white men who ride in stretch limos, all old nigger bag ladies look the same. She took a slow bite of fish cake and stared out at 42nd Street, watching the world swirl past; what was she going to do about this?

They would kill and kill till there was no safe place left to sleep in midtown. She knew it. This was mob business, the *Post* inside her coats said so. And it wouldn't make any difference trying to warn the women. Where would they go? Where would they *want* to go? Not even she, knowing what it was all about . . . not even she would leave the area: this was where she roamed, this was her territorial imperative. And they would find her soon enough.

She nodded to the croaker who had given her the word, and after he'd hobbled away to get a cup of coffee from the spigot on the wall, she hurriedly finished her fish cake and slipped out of the Automat as easily as she had the document copying center this morning.

Being careful to keep out of sight, she returned to 51st Street. The area had been roped off, with sawhorses and green tape that said *Police Investigation—Keep Off*. But there were crowds. The streets were jammed, not only with office workers coming and going, but with loiterers who were fascinated by the scene. It took very little to gather a crowd in New York. The falling of a cornice could produce a *minyan*.

Annie could not believe her luck. She realized the police were unaware of a witness: when the men had charged the doorway, they had thrown aside her cart and goods, had spilled them back onto the sidewalk to gain entrance; and the cops had thought it was all refuse, as one with the huge brown plastic bags of trash at the curb. Her cart and the good sofa pillows, the cardboard flats and her sweaters . . . all of it was in the area. Some in trash cans, some amid the piles of bagged rubbish, some just lying in the gutter.

That meant she didn't need to worry about being sought from two directions. One way was bad enough.

And all the aluminum cans she had salvaged to sell, they were still in the big Bloomingdale's bag right against the wall of the building. There would be money for dinner.

She was edging out of the doorway to collect her goods when she saw the one in navy blue cashmere who had held Beaddie while they fed him Drano. He was standing three stores away, on Annie's side, watching the police lines, watching the copy center, watching the crowd. Watching for her. Picking at an in-grown hair on his chin.

She stepped back into the doorway. Behind her a voice said, "C'mon, lady, get the hell outta here, this's a place uhbizness." Then she felt a sharp poke in her spine.

She looked behind her, terrified. The owner of the haberdashery, a man wearing a bizarrely-cut gray pinstripe worsted with lapels that matched his ears, and a passion flame silk hankie spilling out of his breast pocket like a crimson afflatus, was jabbing her in the back with a wooden coat hanger. "Move it on, get moving," he said, in a tone that would have gotten his face slapped had he used it on a customer.

Annie said nothing. She *never* spoke to anyone on the street. Silence on the street. *We'll go, Alan; we're okay by ourselves. Don't cry, my baby.*

She stepped out of the doorway, trying to edge away. She heard a sharp, piercing whistle. The man in the cashmere topcoat had seen her; he was whistling and signalling up 51st Street to someone. As Annie hurried away, looking over her shoulder, she saw a dark blue Oldsmobile that had been double-parked pull forward. The cashmere topcoat was shoving through the pedestrians, coming for her like the number 5 uptown Lexington express.

Annie moved quickly, without thinking about it. Being poked in the back, and someone speaking directly to her . . . that was frightening: it meant coming out to respond to another human being. But moving down her streets, moving quickly, and being part of the flow, that was comfortable. She knew how to do that. It was just the way she was.

Instinctively, Annie made herself larger, more expansive, her raggedy arms away from her body, the dirty overcoats billowing, her gait more erratic: opening the way for her flight. Fastidious shoppers and suited businessmen shied away, gave a start as the dirty old black bag lady bore down on them, turned sidewise praying she would not brush a recently Martinized shoulder. The Red Sea parted miraculously permitting flight, then closed over instantly to impede navy blue cashmere. But the Olds came on quickly.

Annie turned left onto Madison, heading downtown. There was construction around 48th. There were good alleys on 46th. She knew a basement entrance just three doors off Madison on 47th. But the Olds came on quickly.

Behind her, the light changed. The Olds tried to rush the intersection, but this was Madison. Crowds were already crossing. The Olds stopped, the driver's window rolled down and a face peered out. Eyes tracked Annie's progress.

Then it began to rain.

Like black mushrooms sprouting instantly from concrete, Totes blossomed on the sidewalk. The speed of the flowing river of pedestrians increased; and in an instant Annie was gone. Cashmere rounded the corner, looked at the Olds, a frantic arm motioned to the left, and the man pulled up his collar and elbowed his way through the crowd, rushing down Madison.

Low places in the sidewalk had already filled with water. His wing-tip cordovans were quickly soaked.

He saw her turn into the alley behind the novelty sales shop (*Nothing over $1.10!!!*); he *saw* her; turned right and ducked in fast; *saw* her, even through the rain and the crowd and half a block between them; *saw* it!

So where was she?

The alley was empty.

It was a short space, all brick, only deep enough for a big Dempsey Dumpster and a couple of dozen trash cans; the usual mounds of rubbish in the corners; no fire escape ladders low enough for an old bag lady to grab; no loading docks, no doorways that looked even remotely accessible, everything cemented over or faced with sheet steel; no basement entrances with concrete steps leading down; no manholes in the middle of the passage; no open windows or even broken windows at jumping height; no stacks of crates to hide behind.

The alley was empty.

Saw her come in here. *Knew* she had come in here, and couldn't get out. He'd been watching closely as he ran to the mouth of the alley. She was in here somewhere. Not too hard figuring out where. He took out the .38 Police Positive he liked to carry because he lived with the delusion that if he had to dump it, if it were used in the commission of a sort of kind of felony he couldn't get snowed on, and if it were traced, it would trace back to the cop in Teaneck, New Jersey from whom it had been lifted as he lay drunk in the back room of a Polish social club three years earlier.

He swore he would take his time with her, this filthy old porch monkey. His navy blue cashmere already smelled like soaked dog. And the rain was not about to let up; it now came sheeting down, traveling in a curtain through the alley.

He moved deeper into the darkness, kicking the piles of trash, making sure the refuse bins were full. She was in here somewhere. Not too hard figuring out where.

Warm. Annie felt warm. With the ruined baby doll under her chin, and her eyes closed, it was almost like the apartment at

101st and First Avenue, when the Human Resources lady came
and tried to tell her strange things about Alan. Annie had not
understood what the woman meant when she kept repeating *soft
monkey, soft monkey*, a thing some scientist knew. It had made no
sense to Annie, and she had continued rocking the baby.

Annie remained very still where she had hidden. Basking in
the warmth. *Is it nice, Alan? Are we toasty; yes, we are. Will we be very
still and the lady from the City will go away? Yes, we will.* She heard
the crash of a garbage can being kicked over. *No one will find us.
Shh, my baby.*

There was a pile of wooden slats that had been leaned against
a wall. As he approached, the gun leveled, he realized they ob-
scured a doorway. She was back in there, he knew it. Had to be.
Not too hard figuring that out. It was the only place she could
have hidden.

He moved in quickly, slammed the boards aside, and threw
down on the dark opening. It was empty. Steel-plate door, locked.

Rain ran down his face, plastering his hair to his forehead. He
could smell his coat, and his shoes, oh god, don't ask. He turned
and looked. All that remained was the huge dumpster.

He approached it carefully, and noticed: the lid was still dry
near the back side closest to the wall. The lid had been open just
a short time ago. Someone had just lowered it.

He pocketed the gun, dragged two crates from the heap thrown
down beside the Dempsey, and crawled up onto them. Now he
stood above the dumpster, balancing on the crates with his knees
at the level of the lid. With both hands bracing him, he leaned
over to get his fingertips under the heavy lid. He flung the lid
open, yanked out the gun, and leaned over. The dumpster was
nearly full. Rain had turned the muck and garbage into a swimming porridge. He leaned over precariously to see what floated
there in the murk. He leaned in to see. *Fuckin' porch monk—*

As a pair of redolent, dripping arms came up out of the muck,
grasped his navy blue cashmere lapels, and dragged him head-
first into the metal bin. He went down, into the slime, the gun
going off, the shot spanging off the raised metal lid. The coat
filled with garbage and water.

●   ●   ●

Annie felt him struggling beneath her. She held him down, her feet on his neck and back, pressing him face-first deeper into the goo that filled the bin. She could hear him breathing garbage and fetid water. He thrashed, a big man, struggling to get out from under. She slipped, and braced herself against the side of the dumpster, regained her footing, and drove him deeper. A hand clawed out of the refuse, dripping lettuce and black slime. The hand was empty. The gun lay at the bottom of the bin. The thrashing intensified, his feet hitting the metal side of the container. Annie rose up and dropped her feet heavily on the back of his neck. He went flat beneath her, trying to swim up, unable to find purchase.

He grabbed her foot as an explosion of breath from down below forced a bubble of air to break on the surface. Annie stomped as hard as she could. Something snapped beneath her shoe, but she heard nothing.

It went on for a long time, for a time longer than Annie could think about. The rain filled the bin to overflowing. Movement under her feet lessened, then there was hysterical movement for an instant, then it was calm. She stood there for an even longer time, trembling and trying to remember other, warmer times.

Finally, she closed herself off, buttoned up tightly, climbed out dripping and went away from there, thinking of Alan, thinking of a time after this was done. After that long time standing there, no movement, no movement at all in the bog beneath her waist. She did not close the lid.

When she emerged from the alley, after hiding in the shadows and watching, the Oldsmobile was nowhere in sight. The foot traffic parted for her. The smell, the dripping filth, the frightened face, the ruined thing she held close to her.

She stumbled out onto the sidewalk, lost for a moment, then turned the right way and shuffled off.

The rain continued its march across the city.

No one tried to stop her as she gathered together her goods on 51st Street. The police thought she was a scavenger, the gawkers tried to avoid being brushed by her, the owner of the document copying center was relieved to see the filth cleaned up. Annie rescued everything she could, and hobbled away, hoping to be able to sell her aluminum for a place to dry out. It was not true that she was dirty; she had always been fastidious, even in the streets. A certain level of dishevelment was acceptable, but this was unclean.

And the blasted baby doll needed to be dried and brushed clean. There was a woman on East 60th, near Second Avenue; a vegetarian who spoke with an accent; a white lady who sometimes let Annie sleep in the basement. She would ask her for a favor.

It was not a very big favor, but the white woman was not home; and that night Annie slept in the construction of the new Zeckendorf Towers, where S. Klein-On-The-Square used to be, down on 14th and Broadway.

The men from the stretch limo didn't find her again for almost a week.

She was salvaging newspapers from a wire basket on Madison near 44th when he grabbed her from behind. It was the one who had poured the liquor into Beaddie, and then made him drink the Drano. He threw an arm around her, pulled her around to face him, and she reacted instantly, the way she did when the kids tried to take her snap-purse.

She butted him full in the face with the top of her head, and drove him backward with both filthy hands. He stumbled into the street, and a cab swerved at the last instant to avoid running him down. He stood in the street, shaking his head, as Annie careened down 44th, looking for a place to hide. She was sorry she had left her cart again. This time, she knew, her goods weren't going to be there.

It was the day before Thanksgiving.

Four more black women had been found dead in midtown doorways.

Annie ran, the only way she knew how, into stores that had exits on other streets. Somewhere behind her, though she could not figure it out properly, there was trouble coming for her and the baby. It was so cold in the apartment. It was always so cold. The landlord cut off the heat, he always did it in early November, till the snow came. And she sat with the child, rocking him, trying to comfort him, trying to keep him warm. And when they came from Human Resources, from the City, to evict her, they found her still holding the child. When they took it away from

her, so still and blue, Annie ran from them, into the streets; and
she ran, she knew how to run, to keep running so she could live
out here where they couldn't reach her and Alan. But she knew
there was trouble behind her.

Now she came to an open place. She knew this. It was a new
building they had put up, a new skyscraper, where there used to
be shops that had good throwaway things in the cans and sometimes on the loading docks. It said Citicorp Mall and she ran inside. It was the day before Thanksgiving and there were many
decorations. Annie rushed through into the central atrium,
and looked around. There were escalators, and she dashed for
one, climbing to a second storey, and then a third. She kept
moving. They would arrest her or throw her out if she slowed
down.

At the railing, looking over, she saw the man in the court below. He didn't see her. He was standing, looking around.

Stories of mothers who lift wrecked cars off their children are
legion.

When the police arrived, eyewitnesses swore it had been a
stout, old black woman who had lifted the heavy potted tree in
its terracotta urn, who had manhandled it up onto the railing
and slid it along till she was standing above the poor dead man,
and who had dropped it three storeys to crush his skull. They
swore it was true, but beyond a vague description of old, and
black, and dissolute looking, they could not be of assistance.
Annie was gone.

On the front page of the *Post* she wore as lining in her right
shoe, was a photo of four men who had been arraigned for the
senseless murders of more than a dozen bag ladies over a period
of several months. Annie did not read the article.

It was close to Christmas, and the weather had turned bitter,
too bitter to believe. She lay propped in the doorway alcove of
the Post Office on 43rd and Lexington. Her rug was drawn
around her, the stocking cap pulled down to the bridge of her
nose, the goods in the string bags around and under her. Snow
was just beginning to come down.

A man in a Burberry and an elegant woman in a mink
approached from 42nd Street, on their way to dinner. They
were staying at the New York Helmsley. They were from

Connecticut, in for three days to catch the shows and to celebrate their eleventh wedding anniversary.

As they came abreast of her, the man stopped and stared down into the doorway. "Oh, Christ, that's awful," he said to his wife. "On a night like this, Christ, that's just awful."

"Dennis, *please!*" the woman said.

"I can't just pass her by," he said. He pulled off a kid glove and reached into his pocket for his money clip.

"Dennis, they don't like to be bothered," the woman said, trying to pull him away. "They're very self-sufficient. Don't you remember that piece in the *Times*?"

"It's damned near Christmas, Lori," he said, taking a twenty dollar bill from the folded sheaf held by its clip. "It'll get her a bed for the night, at least. They can't make it out here by themselves. God knows, it's little enough to do." He pulled free of his wife's grasp and walked to the alcove.

He looked down at the woman swathed in the rug, and he could not see her face. Small puffs of breath were all that told him she was alive. "Ma'am," he said, leaning forward. "Ma'am, please take this." He held out the twenty.

Annie did not move. She never spoke on the street.

"Ma'am, please, let me do this. Go somewhere warm for the night, won't you . . . please?"

He stood for another minute, seeking to rouse her, at least for a *go away* that would free him, but the old woman did not move. Finally, he placed the twenty on what he presumed to be her lap, there in that shapeless mass, and allowed himself to be dragged away by his wife.

Three hours later, having completed a lovely dinner, and having decided it would be romantic to walk back to the Helmsley through the six inches of snow that had fallen, they passed the Post Office and saw the old woman had not moved. Nor had she taken the twenty dollars. He could not bring himself to look beneath the wrappings to see if she had frozen to death, and he had no intention of taking back the money. They walked on.

In her warm place, Annie held Alan close up under her chin, stroking him and feeling his tiny black fingers warm at her throat and cheeks. *It's all right, baby, it's all right. We're safe. Shhh, my baby. No one can hurt you.*

YELLOW GAL

Dennis Lynds

*T*hat night a warm rain fell on the city. Charlie Johnson limped slowly toward the cafe. It blinked red and yellow through a wet haze like the distant lights of signals on the tracks guiding to a town with a bar where you could sing for supper and a bed. Forty years is a long time, but the cafe was the same. A little brighter maybe, with its neon signs, but the same cafe. The girl would be waiting inside. He walked slowly from the concert hall to make sure she would be there first, telling himself all the way that he was crazy.

Charlie, you're crazy! The moment he stepped from the train that morning, the moment his feet touched the platform, he told himself he was crazy. Charlie, he said, Charlie you're a damned old fool. But maybe it was just the feel of the platform under his feet, hard, respectable, not shifting like the loose gravel of the roadbed the first time he came to this city, sliding down the embankment and holding his guitar over his head. Maybe it was the people meeting him—the polite, respectful people carrying his bag and guitar to the long, black automobile.

Dennis Lynds/Michael Collins writes the Dan Fortune private eye novels which, by the time this anthology appears, may well have begun to receive the recognition long due them. Like Bill Pronzini, Lynds writes histories of our time in the guise of detective stories. To be sure, Lynds' books are thrillers (in the sense that they thrill) but they are also in a real sense novels. His book THE SILENT SCREAM is especially notable, along with many short stories published in leading literary magazines.

He limped down the dark, wet street toward the cafe. The people passed on the street, bent against the rain, some of them smiling at him, but he did not recognize anyone. That was what being old meant when you were famous. They knew him as he passed, but he didn't know them. He wondered if it was better to be old and famous, or old and unknown. You did not know anyone either way.

In the old days it was different. Into a bar, unsling the guitar, and sing as long as anyone would buy a drink and listen. He didn't know anyone then either, started to play alone, but always ended with harmonicas, banjos, and squeeze-boxes all around just like it was his home town. It didn't matter in the old days, but now, in New York, they came and sat where he could not touch them and listened to his music that was just music to them.

"Charlie Johnson," he said aloud, "you are plumb damn swampwater crazy."

Hundreds of letters like hers. Kids who wanted to see what a real-live-jailbird-singing-legend was like. Goddamned kids who never had no idea what he was singing about. But her letter was different. He told himself her letter was different. This one he had to go and answer. This one he had to tell to meet him in the old cafe where he met Jenny forty years ago.

"You ain't crazy, Charlie, you is soft in the head."

Maybe he done it because she wrote she liked "Yellow Gal" the best of all his songs. That song came with him out of the swamp the first time, right across Mississippi, through Tennessee, and way up North. Up North and right into the penitentiary. The husband had come with his knife low the way he should, low and fast, too fast, creasing his side and past when he brought the bottle down on the husband's skull. The knife was under the body when they took it away. That was all that saved him that time. Five years for manslaughter and he sang his way in and out with "Yellow Gal." It was his song. The others, the ones they shouted for from the big money seats in the big halls, they were other men's songs. "Jenny" was his song, too. He always ended with "Jenny."

He stood on the stage, tall and white-haired with a thin body in a black suit, and sang for anyone who knew what he was singing about. He sang the deep hopelessness of thin black men meeting in unpainted temples under the thin rain of scrub pine forests.

> *We shall walk through the valley in the shadows of death,*
> *We shall walk through the valley in peace;*
> *If Jesus himself shall be our leader—oh,*
> *We shall walk through the valley in peace.*

He sang the songs of lean, dusty men in pits and quarries and turpentine forests; the songs of sweat in the sun of railroad road-beds; the songs of men chained together and swinging hammers to make ballast for roads they would never use.

> *Take this hammer—Whah!*
> *Carry it to the Captain—Whah!*
> *Take this hammer—Whah!*
> *And carry it to the Captain—Whah!*
> *If he asks you—Whah!*
> *Was I laughin'—Whah!*
> *Tell him I was cryin'—Whah!*
> *Tell him I was cryin'—Whah!*

He sang the sun on his back, the rain in his eyes, the heat of raw whisky running inside. He sang the smell of sweat, the smell of the swamp where he was born, the smell of a hard woman on a hard mattress late at night; and he sang the wail of a freight train slowing for a curve.

He liked to sing, and tonight had been a good concert, but he was tired and should be home in bed in the hotel, not walking through the rain in the narrow streets of a city of his youth. A lot of years and a lot of distance. Forty years. Jenny had been a field woman with big hands, and a long razor scar on her face. That was all he remembered except the long nights and the bed and Jenny laughing, smelling of sweat like a woman should at night. After work when he sat in the big chair her grandmother left her and listened to her sing as she cooked his supper. She taught him the song "Jenny." That was why he called her Jenny. He did not remember her right name. He sat in the big chair and watched her feed the kid he hadn't seen since they sent him up again after she died.

Limping on his bad leg, he crossed the sour smelling street, smelling sour from the odor of wet garbage in the back alleys, crossed through the falling rain to the red-and-yellow cafe. Rain made his leg ache but he never minded too much because it was the rain that saved him the time he got the bullet in that leg. He never did know if the man he left on the ground was dead or not. Just ran through the wet woods on the hillside. In West Virginia it was, like old John Hardy. Only he wasn't caught like poor John. The rain had hidden him and covered his scent and a day later he was three states away.

She was the only white person in the cafe. After twenty years or so in New York he was used to white girls, and yellow girls, and brown girls, and he couldn't say why he jumped inside when he saw her. Maybe it was just that he had not expected her to be small and round, with black hair that hung below her shoulders and was shiny even in the dim light of the cafe, and a small, straight nose, and soft red lips that said every night was Saturday night with her. Small breasts moved high under the tight silk of her white blouse. Her straight gray skirt clung close over her belly showing its curve when she breathed. There was a time, he thought now, when she would not have left the section alive.

"Hello," she smiled, "I'm June, June Padgett, Mr. Johnson."

"Like you wrote," he said. "Glad to meet you."

"It was a wonderful concert, Mr. Johnson."

"Call me Yellow," he said, "they always called me Yellow in here. They knowed it didn't mean nothing like it sounds. Yellow Johnson, on account of I'm so black," he laughed, shaking his big, thin frame.

"I thought it might be because of the song," she said.

"Guess maybe that, too," he laughed. "Always wore a yellow shirt in them days, too."

His trademark, that yellow shirt. It was Pete's shirt. Jenny gave it to him when he came to her after they killed Pete. He carried that shirt through prison the second time and put it on the first day he came out. Wore it all the time, even on the roads where the railroad bulls could spot him a mile off in it. Wore it all the way to Frisco where he got "discovered" like he'd just been born or something.

"Always liked yellow," he said. "What you drinkin', honey?"

"Gin and ginger ale," she said.

"You can bring me a little rye, son," he said to the waiter. The hell with the doctors. When you're sixty-nine you ain't got time for worrying about dying young. Like Pete when he asked him if he was scared. *"Sure I'm scared, kid, but I wasn't fixin' I should live forever."* Old Pete.

"Tell me about yourself, honey," he said. "You sing?"

"Oh, yes, Mr. Johnson, I sing ballads mostly . . ."

He could not decide where he and Jenny had been sitting that first night, or any other night. He thought it was in the corner near the bar where the juke box was now. But he wasn't sure. Forty years makes a lot of changes.

". . . I can't sing like you—more like Susan Reed. Do you like Susan Reed, Mr. Johnson, she's not as . . ."

Somehow, the girl looked a lot like Jenny. The only trouble was that he did not remember what Jenny looked like. Forty years he'd been singing about a girl named Jenny, who wasn't named Jenny, and who he could not really remember. He tried to remember Jenny, but he was tired and the whisky was hot in him, and his head ached when he tried. He remembered a lot of faces, but which one was Jenny? Maybe all of them were Jenny.

"This is my friend Eddie," the girl said, holding the sleeve of a small man who stood beside her. The man was really only a boy. "He plays guitar. I asked him to come down and meet you."

"That's okay," he said, shaking the boy's hand. "That's fine."

"Can I get you a drink?" the boy asked. He had a guitar case and leaned it against the wall behind. Charlie wondered if it was a good guitar.

"Never turned down a drink in my life," he said. "Make it rye."

"Eddie plays good guitar," the girl said, "like Sam Madison a little."

"Sam's great," the boy said, returning with the drinks. "I heard him last year and . . ."

The whisky by now was very hot inside him, and smooth, easing the pain in his leg, loosening the old muscles until he felt ready to run over a mountain again. Sam Madison was old Red Madison's boy, at least Red figured he was but had to admit that Sam's mother was mighty popular and Red wasn't sure where she was while he was blowing his trumpet nights. Sam was a good singer, except maybe he sang a little too much like the cover-charge customers wanted. They were talking about Josh and about Sonny who was one of the best maybe because he was blind and didn't have much cause to play except like he wanted to play. They talked about Bessie who just sang the way things are and who was dead now.

". . . yeh, Sam's great, but he can't sing things like 'Jenny' the way you can, Mr. Johnson," the boy was saying. "I can tell . . ."

Jenny was Pete's woman. Pete killed Jenny's old man to get her and they got Pete for that. Pete liked him. He was only a kid then, in for that first killing over the yellow gal.

You was lucky this time, kid, but they'll get you just like they got me, Pete said.

Not me, Pete. I aim to live a while, he said.

Pete laughed at that, an easy laugh that made deputies look around for help when they had to take Pete in.

Hell, boy, a good man ain't gonna live no long time, specially if he's poor and black and got the gals in his eye. You got the good liquor and the no-damn-backtalk look in your eye. If them don't get you, the gals will sooner'r later. You just like me, kid. You better live while you got time.

What you wanta live for if you gotta slack up to make it, Pete said. If he got the feel to get livin' ain't much man if he worry about livin' old.

He laughed out loud, thinking of what Pete would say if he could see him now. Yellow Johnson, old, white-haired, with money in the bank and talking to a white girl in the same town where Pete killed his man to get Jenny. Pete would have one hell of a laugh on himself.

"Did I say something funny?" the girl said, smiling at him.

He waved his hand to the waiter. "Hell no, honey, just thinkin' of something. What's yours, son?" he said to the boy.

"Just beer, Mr. Johnson."

"Play somethin' for me, son," he said.

The waiter came and he ordered gin and ginger ale, beer, and more rye for himself. The boy got his guitar out. It was a shiny new guitar but the boy handled it well.

"What'll I play?" the boy asked.

"Anythin' son. How 'bout 'Rock Island Line'?" he said. The boy began to play and he swung back to the table and listened. As he listened he knew that Pete would not be laughing. Pete would not know him.

You ain't Yaller Johnson, mister. Shuffle off. Yaller Johnson's dead.
Killed a long time ago like I said he would. I know Yaller Johnson.

He could hear Pete real plain, standing right there behind the white girl, sneering at him.

I am too Johnson, Pete. Listen, I'll play you a little tune like I done before they come for you. That'll show you. Listen, Pete. It's Yellow Johnson, Pete.

I don't hear you, mister.

Listen, Pete, I'm singing for you like I always done. Please Pete, I'm singing.

"What did you say, Mr. Johnson?" the girl asked.

The whisky made her seem to float very near, very close, smelling of perfume and sweat.

"I thought you said you'd sing," she said. "I'd like that."

"Me, too," the boy said, laying his guitar down.

He blinked. He opened his guitar case and took out his old guitar. It wasn't the same one as forty years ago, but it was old enough. The bartender turned off the juke box to listen.

" 'Yellow Gal,' " the girl said, touching his arm.

He ripped into the fast, happy drive of the old song he had brought from the swamps where there wasn't much to do but work and sing and drink your own liquor and find a woman, and where it was worth staying alive just to spit at the swamp sitting like a giant cottonmouth waiting for you to crack.

I went home with a yellow gal,
I went home with a yellow gal,
Didn't say a thing to the yellow gal,
Didn't say a thing to the yellow gal.

He took the song through the dry hills of Texas and up into that Memphis factory where he got a steady job because he had to go and marry Susy Washington who had four kids of his in three years and hated his guts until he made money in New York and the whole passel tracked him down with their cotton-picking hands itching in his pockets.

She was pretty and fine, oh me yellow gal,
She was pretty and fine, oh me yellow gal,
She wasn't none of mine, oh the yellow gal,
She wasn't none of mine, oh the yellow gal.

Singing the song for pennies on the streets of the old South Side, and in all-night speakeasies when Louis and the King were riding high and stood a touch when his luck got real low. The King was dead now, dead and gone, leaving the blues in the royal garden, the blues in the alleys where he sat watching the yellow gals pass by.

She was long and tall, the yellow gal,
She was long and tall, the yellow gal.
She was my downfall, it's the yellow gal,
She was my downfall, it's the yellow gal.

Singing on a slow freight stretching from coast to coast and twice back. Singing behind the bars of big jails and little jails. The jails he knew and the jails he didn't know. The other men's jails.

Got thirty years for the yellow gal,
Got thirty years for the yellow gal.
Yellow, oh me yellow, oh me yellow gal.
Yellow, oh me yellow, oh me yellow gal.

Ending on the long descending note like a faint foghorn out in the delta.

"Beautiful," the girl said. "Now 'Jenny.' "

Jenny was Pete's woman. They killed Pete because of Jenny. Pete didn't think about that. The only thing worried Pete was what was going to happen to Jenny.

I killed her old man and they gonna kill me. Ain't left that gal no man 'tall, Pete said.

Yaller, you go get Jenny when you gets out. Tell her I said for you and her to stick together. I'm givin' her to you. You tell her, Pete said.

I ain't wanting your woman, he said.

I ain't about to need no woman, Pete said. You do like I say.

Jenny taught him the song. She sang it like no one ever sang it. He always figured he never would have run out on Jenny. He wasn't ever tired with Jenny. Heaving sacks all day at the mill, but he wasn't ever tired. Never too tired for bed, never too tired to play and sing at night. Not with Jenny. He nearly killed the cop who shot her in the mill riot. They sent him up the second time for that. Only what did Jenny look like?

"That's wonderful, Mr. Johnson," the girl said.

"I like it," he said. "Call me Yellow, honey."

"Who was Jenny, Yellow?" she asked, smiling at him.

"She was a gal kinda like you," he said.

She smiled again and picked up his scarred right hand. Her hand was so small she could hold only three of his thick, bent fingers. He felt her thigh against his under the table. His hands were wet on the guitar strings.

"We all ready for another round?" the boy asked.

He nodded and the boy got up and walked to the bar. He slid into the hard sadness of "Empty Bed Blues." Full beds and empty beds. The girl sat listening with her chin propped on one hand, eyes closed, lips parted. There ain't nothing so empty as an empty bed. The girl sang along with him under her breath, her lips moving with the music. So many empty beds, the ones he was in and the ones he had left the women in, and all of them fading into the empty bed the night Jenny was killed. Jenny had a scar. But what did Jenny look like? He leaned across the table and kissed the girl's mouth.

Her eyes opened wide—leaping open. With a soft gasp she jerked back. He held her arm, the muscles strained on his back. He dropped his guitar, pulling her to him, pulling her closer as she fought.

She screamed.

The boy at the bar whirled around, a glass in each hand. The glasses fell and smashed on the floor. The girl tore loose, stumbling across the room to the boy at the bar.

"You goddamn old bastard!" the boy cried, stepping closer, trying to shake the clinging girl away.

"Don't, Eddie, please, he's drunk," the girl said.

"I'll kill him," the boy said, pulling free.

"Please, Eddie, let's go."

Roaring with laughter, he leaped. His fist caught the boy full on his red, angry face. The boy went down dragging the girl with him, blood running over his chin onto his white shirt. The girl struggled to get up, her skirt up to her waist. He watched the boy but his eyes saw the girl's long white thighs. He saw her blue silk pants, blue silk, tight to her smooth body and dark at the crotch. The boy stumbled to his feet. The girl wore bright blue pants. It was worth fighting for a girl who wore bright blue pants.

As the boy swung the bottle he felt his knife spring open in his hand. Sidestepping, he swung the knife low and close across the boy's arm. Just a little cut. Just a small one. The bottle fell to the floor, rolling across the room into a corner. The bottle was bloody. The boy held his arm. Outside in the street the girl was screaming.

"Get him out of here," someone shouted.

Hands pushed him toward the rear of the cafe. Hands gripped his arm, pushing. The girl out in the street, screaming, and the boy leaning on the bar holding his arm.

Then he was outside and running. The rain splashed on his face. His guitar bounced against his back as he ran. No shiny black case now. Over a fence he was in an alley. The rain was cool on his face. His leg did not ache any more. Turning, twisting, he limped through the alleys until the noise from the cafe was gone. As he ran he laughed. He laughed until he could no longer run from the pain in his sides.

Leaning against a wall, he laughed so much the tears washed down his face, rippling across the deep wrinkles like shallow water over rocks, faster and wetter than the rain. He slid down the wall into a sitting position, his back against the wall, his legs stretched before him in the inch-deep alley water. He unslung his guitar. Man, he could use that girl in the blue pants. Oh man, but he could use a woman. A low-down yellow woman who raped him with her eyes, who wore blue pants and squeezed with her long, brown, field-muscled legs. In the falling rain of the alley he began to sing.

> *Oh, big fat woman with the meat shakin' on her bones.*
> *I love my woman and I tell the world I do,*
> *I love my woman and I tell the world I do,*
> *Oh Lord, I love my woman, tell the world I do,*
> *She was good to me, just like I to you.*

His fingers were wet and slippery on the strings; the music would not come right. He dropped the guitar, lay flat on the ground and stared up into the low, dark sky. Mouth open, he let the rain wash through him. He started to laugh again.

"Pete," she shouted, "Pete man! What do you think of this one?"

The noise of the car hummed into his mind. It grew louder slowly, very slowly, as if the car were creeping along the street and stopping at each corner. The car was looking for something.

"Charlie," he said, "that means cops."

Struggling to his feet, he picked up his guitar and ran away down the alley. At the first corner he turned into a street. Running fast, he was in the middle of the street before he could stop. A police car sat parked under the nearest street lamp. Two policemen stood beside it.

"There he is!" one policeman shouted, and then ran toward him calling out, "Hold it now, hold it!"

He shook his head and looked wildly up and down the street. The policeman reached to hold him. Laughing, he swung his guitar, felt it smash against the policeman's face. The other policeman ran from the car. He dropped his broken guitar into the gutter. One of them shouted to him again. He ran on, limping over the broken concrete. He whooped aloud as he ran. He felt good, good. He ran and laughed.

When he heard the shots behind him he began to weave and dodge, running more slowly, running in irregular spurts to confuse the shooters. At the corner he turned to see where they were.

It felt as if he had run full into a brick wall. He was still running but his legs would not move. The wall lay on top of him, pressing him down into the wet street. He heard voices. Jenny was looking down at him, the long scar standing out white on her black face. She grinned at him. He wondered if her pants were blue. The voices kept talking, talking. Talking so loud he could not hear Jenny. She raised her skirt so he could see the color of her pants. They were blue. He laughed happily when he saw them.

"He's trying to talk," a voice said.

"I didn't mean to hit him," a voice said. "Jesus! He just turned and stopped. Jesus!"

"Shut your fat yap, he's trying to talk!"

"I just wanted to scare . . ."

"Always the gun! You gotta go for the gun."

"The poor bastard's laughing."

"Wait till the papers get this."

"Shut up! All of you! Where's the friggin' ambulance?"

Jenny was trying to say something. He wished they would stop shouting. If he kept running maybe he could get away from the voices. Pete was way ahead, running fast with that easy run that could drive a hound into the ground. He ran fast to catch up. Like a turkey through the corn, boy, like a turkey through the corn.

We're long gone, Pete man, we're long gone, he laughed.

Pete laughed, too, running alongside. *Come on, Pete, run, man, run!*

The rain washed all over him. He could feel it wet inside. Wet and warm, like Jenny in the dark on the old iron bed. Wet and warm and dark. He ran faster. The more he ran the more he laughed. He could hardly hear the voices at all now.

"All he does is laugh!"

"Goddamn that ambulance!"

Then he did not hear the voices any more. Jenny and Pete stopped running. They were grinning at him now.

SCRAP

A "Nathan Heller" Story
Max Allan Collins

*F*riday afternoon, December 8, 1939, I had a
call from Jake Rubinstein to meet him at 3159 Roosevelt, which
was in Lawndale, my old neighborhood. Jake was an all right
guy, kind of talkative and something of a roughneck, but then on
Maxwell Street, when I was growing up, developing a mouth and
muscles was necessary for survival. I knew Jake had been existing
out on the fringes of the rackets since then, but that was true of a
lot of guys. I didn't hold it against him. I went into one of the
rackets myself, after all—known in Chicago as the police department—and I figured Jake wouldn't hold that against me, either.
Especially since I was private, now, and he wanted to hire me.

The afternoon was bitterly cold, snow on the ground but not
snowing, as I sat parked in my sporty '32 Auburn across the
street from the drug store, over which was the union hall where
Jake said to meet him. The Scrap Iron and Junk Handlers Union, he said. I didn't know there was one. They had unions for
everything these days. My pop, an old union man, would've
been pleased. I didn't much care.

Max Allan Collins *is most famous for his Nathan Heller historical mystery novels. But
for all of Heller's following, Collins' other series also have their admirers—Quarry, the
professional killer; Nolan the professional thief; Mallory, the professional mystery writer.
To this list Collins has now added a series about Eliot Ness, the bane of Capone-era hood-
lums. Whatever the form he chooses, he's always an exciting and powerful writer to read.
In the story here, Nathan Heller faces a new nemesis.*

I went up the flight of stairs and into the outer office; the meeting room was adjacent, at my left. The place was modest, like most union halls - if you're running a union you don't want the rank and file to think you're living it up—but the secretary behind the desk looked like a million. She was a brunette in a trim brown suit with big brown eyes and bright red lipstick. She'd soften the blow of paying dues any day.

She smiled at me and I forgot it was winter. "Would you be Mr. Heller?"

"I would. Would you be free for dinner?"

Her smile settled in one corner of her bright red mouth. "I wouldn't. Mr. Rubinstein is waiting for you in Mr. Martin's office."

And she pointed to the only door in the wall behind her, and I gave her a can't-blame-a-guy-for-trying look and went on in.

The inner office wasn't big but it seemed bigger than it was because it was under-furnished: just a clutter-free desk and a couple of chairs and two wooden file cabinets. Jake was sitting behind the desk, feet up on it, socks with clocks showing, as he read the Racing News.

"How are you, Jake," I said, and held out my hand.

He put the paper down, stood and grinned and shook my hand; he was a little guy, short I mean, but he had shoulders on him and his grip was a killer. He wore a natty dark blue suit and a red hand-painted tie with a sunset on it and a hat that was a little big for him. He kept the hat on indoors—self-conscious about his thinning hair, I guess.

"You look good, Nate. Thanks for coming. Thanks for coming yourself and not sending one of your ops."

"Any excuse to get back to the old neighborhood, Jake," I said, pulling up a chair and sitting. "We're about four blocks from where my pop's bookshop was, you know."

"I know, I know," he said, sitting again. "What do you hear from Barney these days?"

"Not much. When you'd get in the union racket, anyway? Last I heard you were a door-to-door salesman."

Jake shrugged. He had dark eyes and a weak chin and five o'clock shadow; make that six o'clock shadow. "A while ago," he allowed. "But it ain't really a racket. We're trying to give our guys a break."

I smirked at him. "In this town? Silly Skidmore isn't going to put up with a legit junk handler's union."

Skidmore was a portly, dapperly dressed junk dealer and politician who controlled most of the major non-Capone gambling in town. Frank Nitti, Capone's heir, put up with that because Skidmore was also a bailbondsman, which made him a necessary evil.

"Skidmore's got troubles these days," Jake said. "He can't afford to push us around no more."

"You're talking about the income tax thing."

"Yeah. Just like Capone. He didn't pay his taxes and they got 'im for it."

"They indicted him, but that doesn't mean they got him. Anyway, where do I come in?"

Jake leaned forward, brow beetling. "You know a guy named Leon Cooke?"

"Can't say I do."

"He's a little younger than us, but he's from around here. He's a lawyer. He put this union together, two, three years ago. Well, about a year back he became head of an association of junkyard dealers, and the rank and file voted him out."

I shrugged. "Seems reasonable. In Chicago it wouldn't be *unusual* to represent both the employees *and* the employers, but kosher it ain't."

Jake was nodding. "Right. The new president is Johnny Martin. Know him?"

"Can't say I do."

"He's been with the Sanitary District for, oh, twenty or more years."

The Sanitary District controlled the sewage in the city's rivers and canals.

"He needed a hobby," I said, "so he ran for president of the junk handler's union, huh?"

"He's a good man, Nate, he really is."

"What's your job?"

"I'm treasurer of the union."

"You're the collector, then."

"Well . . . yeah. Does it show?"

"I just didn't figure you for the accountant type."

He smiled sheepishly. "Every union needs a little muscle.

Anyways, Cooke. He's trying to stir things up, we think. He isn't even legal counsel for the union anymore, but he's been coming to meetings, hanging around. We think he's been going around talking to the members."

"Got an election coming up?"

"Yeah. We want to know who he's talking to. We want to know if anybody's backing him."

"You think Nitti's people might be using him for a front?"

"Could be. Maybe even Skidmore. Playing both ends against the middle is Cooke's style. Anyways, can you shadow him and find out?"

"For fifteen a day and expenses, I can."

"Isn't that a little steep, Nate?"

"What's the monthly take on union dues around this joint?"

"Fifteen a day's fine," Jake said, shaking his head side to side, smiling.

"And expenses."

The door opened and the secretary came in, quickly, her silk stockings flashing.

"Mr. Rubinstein," she said, visibly upset, "Mr. Cooke is in the outer office. Demanding to see Mr. Martin."

"Shit," Jake said through his teeth. He glanced at me. "Let's get you out of here."

We followed the secretary into the outer office, where Cooke, a man of medium size in an off-the-rack brown suit, was pacing. A heavy top coat was slung over his arm. In his late twenties, with thinning brown hair, Cooke was rather mild looking, with wire-rim glasses and cupid lips. Nonetheless, he was well and truly pissed off.

"Where's that bastard Martin?" he demanded of Jake. Not at all intimidated by the little strongarm man.

"He stepped out," Jake said.

"Then I'll wait. Till hell freezes over, if necessary."

Judging by the weather, that wouldn't be long.

"If you'll excuse us," Jake said, brushing by him. I followed.

"Who's this?" Cooke said, meaning me. "A new member of your goon squad? Isn't Fontana enough for you?"

Jake ignored that and I followed him down the steps to the street.

"He didn't mean Carlos Fontana, did he?" I asked.

Jake nodded. His breath was smoking, teeth chattering. He wasn't wearing a topcoat; we'd left too quick for such niceties.

"Fontana's a pretty rough boy," I said.

"A lot of people who was in bootlegging," Jake said, shrugging, "had to go straight. What are you gonna do now?"

"I'll use the phone booth in the drug store to get one of my ops out here to shadow Cooke. I'll keep watch till then. He got enough of a look at me that I don't dare shadow him myself."

Jake nodded. "I'm gonna go call Martin."

"And tell him to stay away?"

"That's up to him."

I shook my head. "Cooke seemed pretty mad."

"He's an asshole."

And Jake walked quickly down to a parked black Ford coupe, got in, and smoked off.

I called the office and told my secretary to send either Lou or Frankie out as soon as possible, whoever was available first; then I sat in the Auburn and waited.

Not five minutes later a heavy-set, dark-haired man in a camel's hair topcoat went in and up the union-hall stairs. I had a hunch it was Martin. More than a hunch: he looked well and truly pissed off, too.

I could smell trouble.

I probably should have sat it out, but I got out of the Auburn and crossed Roosevelt and went up those stairs myself. The secretary was standing behind the desk. She was scared shitless. She looked about an inch away from crying.

Neither man was in the anteroom, but from behind the closed door came the sounds of loud voices.

"What's going on?" I said.

"That awful Mr. Cooke was in using Johnny . . . Mr. Martin's telephone, in his office, when Mr. Martin arrived."

They were scuffling in there, now.

"Any objection if I go in there and break that up?" I asked her.

"None at all," she said.

That was when we heard the shots.

Three of them, in rapid succession.

The secretary sucked in breath, covered her mouth, said, "My God . . . my God."

And I didn't have a gun, goddamnit.

I was still trying to figure out whether to go in there or not when the burly, dark-haired guy who I assumed (rightly) to be Martin, still in the camel's hair topcoat, came out with a blue-steel revolver in his hand. Smoke was curling out the barrel.

"Johnny, Johnny," the secretary said, going to him, clinging to him. "Are you all right?"

"Never better," he said, but his voice was shaking. He scowled over at me; he had bushy black eyebrows that made the scowl frightening. And the gun helped. "Who the hell are you?"

"Nate Heller. I'm a dick Jake Rubinstein hired to shadow Leon Cooke."

Martin nodded his head back toward the office. "Well, if you want to get started, he's on the floor in there."

I went into the office and Cooke was on his stomach; he wasn't dead yet. He had a bullet in the side; the other two slugs went through the heavy coat that had been slung over his arm.

"I had to do it," Martin said. "He jumped me. He attacked me."

"We better call an ambulance," I said.

"So, then, we can't just dump his body somewhere," Martin said, thoughtfully.

"I was hired to shadow this guy," I said. "It starts and ends there. You want something covered up, call a cop."

"How much money you got on you?" Martin said. He wasn't talking to me.

The secretary said, "Maybe a hundred."

"That'll hold us. Come on."

He led her through the office and opened a window behind his desk. In a very gentlemanly manner, he helped her out onto the fire escape.

And they were gone.

I helped Cooke onto his feet.

"You awake, pal?"

"Y-yes," he said. "Christ, it hurts."

"Mount Sinai hospital's just a few blocks away," I said. "We're gonna get you there."

I wrapped the coat around him, to keep from getting blood on my car seat, and drove him to the hospital.

Half an hour later, I was waiting outside Cooke's room in the hospital hall when Captain Stege caught up with me.

Stege, a white-haired fireplug of a man with black-rimmed glasses and a pasty complexion—and that Chicago rarity, an honest cop—was not thrilled to see me.

"I'm getting sick of you turning up at shootings," he said.

"I do it just to irritate you. It makes your eyes twinkle."

"You left a crime scene."

"I hauled the victim to the hospital. I told the guy at the drugstore to call it in. Let's not get technical."

"Yeah," Stege grunted. "Let's not. What's your story?"

"The union secretary hired me to keep an eye on this guy Cooke. But Cooke walked in, while I was there, angry, and then Martin showed up, equally steamed."

I gave him the details.

As I was finishing up, a doctor came out of Cooke's room and Stege cornered him, flashing his badge.

"Can he talk, Doc?"

"Briefly. He's in critical condition."

"Is he gonna make it?"

"He should pull through. Stay only a few minutes, gentlemen."

Stege went in and I followed; I thought he might object, but he didn't.

Cooke looked pale, but alert. He was flat on his back. Stege introduced himself and asked for Cooke's story.

Cooke gave it, with lawyer-like formality: "I went to see Martin to protest his conduct of the union. I told Martin he ought to've obtained a pay raise for the men in one junkyard. I told him our members were promised a pay increase, by a certain paper company, and instead got a wage cut—and that I understood he'd sided with the employer in the matter! He got very angry, at that, and in a little while we were scuffling. When he grabbed a gun out of his desk, I told him he was crazy, and started to leave. Then . . . then he shot me in the back."

Stege jotted that down, thanked Cooke and we stepped out into the hall.

"Think that was the truth?" Stege asked me.

"Maybe. But you really ought to hear Martin's side, too."

"Good idea, Heller. I didn't think of that. Of course, the fact that Martin lammed does complicate things, some."

"With all the heat on unions, lately, I can see why he lammed.

There doesn't seem to be any doubt Martin pulled the trigger. But who attacked who remains in question."

Stege sighed. "You do have a point. I can understand Martin taking it on the lam, myself. He's already under indictment for another matter. He probably just panicked."

"Another matter?"

Stege nodded. "He and Terry Druggan and two others were indicted last August for conspiracy. Trying to conceal from revenue officers that Druggan was part owner of a brewery."

Druggan was a former bootlegger, a West Side hood who'd been loosely aligned with such non-Capone forces as the Bugs Moran gang. I was starting to think maybe my old man wouldn't have been so pleased by all this union activity.

"We'll stake out Martin's place," Stege said, "for all the good it'll do. He's got a bungalow over on Wolcott Avenue."

"Nice little neighborhood," I said.

"We're in the wrong racket," Stege admitted.

It was too late in the afternoon to bother going back to the office, now, so I stopped and had supper at Pete's Steaks and then headed back to my apartment at the Morrison Hotel. I was reading a Westbrook Pegler column about what a bad boy Willie Bioff was when the phone rang.

"Nate? It's Jake."

"Jake, I'm sorry I didn't call you or anything. I didn't have any number for you but the union hall. You know about what went down?"

"Do I. I'm calling from the Marquette station. They're holding me for questioning."

"Hell, you weren't even there!"

"That's okay. I'm stalling 'em a little."

"Why, for Christ's sake?"

"Listen, Nate—we gotta hold this thing together. You gotta talk to Martin."

"Why? How?"

"I'm gonna talk to Cooke. Cooke's the guy who hired me to work for the union in the first place, and . . ."

"What? Cooke hired you?"

"Yeah, yeah. Look, I'll go see Cooke first thing in the morning—that is, if you've seen Martin tonight, and worked a story out. Something that'll make this all sound like an accident . . ."

"I don't like being part of cover-ups."

"This ain't no fuckin' cover-up! It's business! Look, they got the state's attorney's office in on this already. You know who's taken over for Stege, already?"

"Tubbo Gilbert?"

"Himself," Jake said.

Captain Dan "Tubbo" Gilbert was the richest cop in Chicago. In the world. He was tied in with every mob, every fixer in town.

"The local will be finished," Jake said. "He'll find something in the books and use that and the shooting as an excuse to close the union down."

"Which'll freeze wages at current levels," I said. "Exactly what the likes of Billy Skidmore would want."

"Right. And then somebody else'll open the union back up, in six months or so. Somebody tied into the Nitti and Guzik crowd."

"As opposed to Druggan and Moran."

"Don't compare them to Nitti and Guzik. Those guys went straight, Nate."

"Please. I just ate. Moran got busted on a counterfeit railroad-bond scam just last week."

"Nobody's perfect. Nate, it's for the best. Think of your old man."

"Don't do that to me, Jake. I don't exactly think your union is what my pop had in mind when he was handing out pamphlets on Maxwell Street."

"Well, it's all that stands between the working stiffs and the Billy Skidmores."

"I take it you know where Martin is hiding out."

"Yeah. That secretary of his, her mother has a house in Hinsdale. Lemme give you the address . . ."

"Okay, Jake. It's against my better judgment, but okay . . ."

It took an hour to get there by car. Well after dark. Hinsdale was a quiet, well-fed little suburb, and the house at 409 Walnut Street was a two-story number in the midst of a healthy lawn. The kind of place the suburbs are full of, but which always seem shockingly sprawling to city boys like yours truly.

There were a few lights on, downstairs. I walked up onto the porch and knocked. I was unarmed. Probably not wise, but I was.

The secretary answered the door. Cracked it open.

She didn't recognize me at first.

"I'm here about our dinner date," I said.

Then, in relief, she smiled, opened the door wider.

"You're Mr. Heller."

"That's right. I never did get your name."

"Then how did you find me?"

"I had your address. I just didn't get your name."

"Well, it's Nancy. But what do you want, Mr. Heller?"

"Make it Nate. It's cold. Could I step in?"

She swallowed. "Sure."

I stepped inside; it was a nicely furnished home, but obviously the home of an older person: the doilies and ancient photo portraits were a dead giveaway.

"This is my mother's home," she said. "She's visiting relatives. I live here."

I doubted that; the commute would be impossible. If she didn't live with Martin, in his nifty little bungalow on South Wolcott, I'd eat every doilie in the joint.

"I know that John Martin is here," I said. "Jake Rubinstein told me. He asked me to stop by."

She didn't know what to say to that.

Martin stepped out from a darkened doorway into the living room. He was in rolled-up shirt sleeves and no tie. He looked frazzled. He had the gun in his hand.

"What do you want?" he said. His tone was not at all friendly.

"You're making too big a deal out of this," I said. "There's no reason to go on the lam. This is just another union shooting—the papers're full of 'em."

"I don't shoot a man every day," Martin said.

"I'm relieved to hear that. How about putting the heater away, then?"

Martin sneered and tossed the piece on a nearby floral couch. He was a nasty man to have a nice girl like this. But then, so often nice girls do like nasty men.

I took it upon myself to sit down. Not on the couch: on a chair, with a soft seat and curved wooden arms.

Speaking of curves, Nancy, who was wearing a blue print dress, was standing wringing her hands, looking about to cry.

"I could use something to drink," I said, wanting to give her something to do.

"Me too," Martin said. "Beer. For him, too."

"Beer would be fine," I said, magnanimously.

She went into the kitchen.

"What's Jake's idea?" Martin asked.

I explained that Jake was afraid the union would be steam-rolled by crooked cops and political fixers, should this shooting blow into something major, first in the papers, then in the courts.

"Jake wants you to mend fences with Cooke. Put together some story you can both live with. Then find some way you can run the union together, or pay him off or something."

"Fuck that shit!" Martin said. He stood up. "What's wrong with that little kike, has he lost his marbles?"

"A guy who works on the west side," I said, "really ought to watch his goddamn mouth where the Jew-baiting's concerned."

"What's it to you? You're Irish."

"Does Heller sound Irish to you? Don't let the red hair fool you."

"Well fuck you, too, then. Cooke's a lying little kike, and Jake's still in bed with him. Damn! I thought I could trust that little bastard . . ."

"I think you can. I think he's trying to hold your union to-gether, with spit and rubber bands. I don't know if it's worth holding together. I don't know what you're in it for—maybe you really care about your members, a little. Maybe it's the money. But if I were you, I'd do some fast thinking, put together a story you can live with and let Jake try to sell it to Cooke. Then when the dust settles you'll still have a piece of the action."

Martin walked over and pointed a thick finger at me. "I don't believe you, you slick son of a bitch. I think this is a set-up. Put together to get me to come in, give myself up and go straight to the lock-up, while Jake and Cooke tuck the union in their fuckin' belt!"

I stood. "That's up to you. I was hired to deliver a message. I delivered it. Now if you'll excuse me."

He thumped his finger in my chest. "You tell that little kike Rubinstein for me that . . ."

I smacked him.

He didn't go down, but it backed him up. He stood there

looking like a confused bear and then growled and lumbered at me with massive fists out in front, ready to do damage.

So I smacked the bastard again, and again. He went down that time. I helped him up. He swung clumsily at me, so I hit him in the side of the face and he went down again. Stayed down.

Nancy came in, a glass of beer in either hand, and said, "What . . . ?" Her brown eyes wide.

"Thanks," I said, taking one glass, chugging it. I wiped the foam off my face with the back of a hand and said, "I needed that."

And I left them there.

The next morning, early, while I was still at the Morrison, shaving in fact, the phone rang.

It was Jake.

"How did it go last night?" he asked.

I told him.

"Shit," he said. "I'll still talk to Cooke, though. See if I can't cool this down some."

"I think it's too late for that."

"Me too," Jake said glumly.

Martin came in on Saturday; gave himself up to Tubbo Gilbert. Stege was off the case. The story Martin told was considerably different from Cooke's: he said Cooke was in the office using the phone ("Which he had no right to do!") and Martin told him to leave; Cooke started pushing Martin around, and when Martin fought back, Cooke drew a gun. Cooke (according to Martin) hit him over the head with it and knocked him down. Then Cooke supposedly hit him with the gun again and Martin got up and they struggled and the gun went off. Three times.

The gun was never recovered. If it was really Cooke's gun, of course, it would have been to Martin's advantage to produce it; but he didn't.

Martin's claim that Cooke attacked and beat him was backed up by the fact that his face was badly bruised and battered. So I guess I did him a favor, beating the shit out of him.

Martin was placed under bond on a charge of intent to kill. Captain Dan "Tubbo" Gilbert, representing the state's attorney's office, confiscated the charter of the union, announcing that it had been run "purely as a racket." Shutting it down until such time that "the actual working members of the union care to continue it, and elect their own officers."

That sounded good in the papers, but in reality it meant Skidmore and company had been served.

I talked to Stege about it, later, over coffee and bagels in the Dill Pickle deli below my office on Van Buren.

"Tubbo was telling the truth about the union being strictly a racket," Stege said. "They had a thousand members paying two bucks a head a month. Legitimate uses counted for only seven hundred bucks' worth a month. Martin's salary, for example, was only a hundred-twenty bucks."

"Well he's shit out of luck, now," I said.

"He's still got his position at the Sanitary District," Stege said. "Of course, he's got to beat the rap for the assault to kill charge, first . . ." Stege smiled at the thought. "And Mr. Cooke tells a more convincing story than Martin does."

The trouble was, Cooke never got to tell it, not in court. He took a sudden turn for the worse, as so many people in those days did in Chicago hospitals, when they were about to testify in a major trial. Cooke died on the first Friday of January, 1940. There was no autopsy. His last visitor I was told, was Jake Rubinstein.

When the union was finally re-opened, however, Jake was no longer treasurer. He was still involved in the rackets, though, selling punchboards, working for Ben "Zuckie the Bookie" Zuckerman, with a short time out for a wartime stint in the air force. He went to Dallas, I've heard, as representative of Chicago mob interests there, winding up running some strip joints. Rumor has it he was involved in other cover-ups, over the years.

By that time, of course, Jake was better known as Jack.

And he'd shortened his last name to Ruby.

AUTHOR'S NOTE: I wish to acknowledge my debt to two books, *Maxwell Street* by Ira Berkow, and *The Plot to Kill the President* by G. Robert Blakey and Richard N. Billings; however, the bulk of the research (conducted by myself and George Hagenauer) for this work of historical fiction came from newspapers of the day.

M.A.C

SET 'EM UP, JOE

Barbara Beman

*T*he pay-off was only $10,000, and God knows
people die every day. But something about this one smelled like
ten day old hamburger trying to pass for fresh. I couldn't quite
put my finger on it, but something didn't compute.

For one thing, the life insurance policy was only six months
old, which meant an automatic review. And although the
deceased, William Crocker, had passed his physical with flying
colors, the death certificate read cirrhosis of the liver. Crocker
had just turned 23.

The beneficiary of the policy was Crocker's employer, Joseph
Callahan. I guess I could buy that. The policy was strictly small
potatoes. Maybe this Callahan had been a father figure, a friend
as well as a boss. But Crocker had only applied for a social security card directly before taking out the life insurance with
Consolidated.

As I said, something down in Florida was in the state of rotten. I could smell it all the way from the main office. And I had
to go to Miami anyway, on another case. Some broad holding a
million dollar policy had tried to poison her husband.

Turned out the old man was running around with a young

Barbara Beman has written under pen-names in two or three genres and is only now
attaching her real name to her droll, stylish and occasionally violent tales of modern urban
warfare. By the time this book has appeared, two new novels by her will have appeared
and Beman the brand-name will be launched.

nurse, who foiled the plot. Now the old lady was screaming for her premiums back.

I made a note to check on the Crocker-Callahan mess while I was down there. At least I figured it was a mess. Something about a 23-year-old kid dying of liver failure stuck in my craw. I've been a scotch drinker all my life and never had more than an occasional twinge the morning after a bad night. Or maybe it's the mornings that are bad, after a good night.

Anyway, I decided to do a little investigating. Ask a few questions. Sometimes my hunches paid off. And I was pretty damned curious.

By the time I reached the southwest section of town, I was parched for a cold beer. But I pulled over to a U-Tote-Em and bought a Dr Pepper instead. August in Miami is enough to make a man kill for a cold beer, and the air conditioning in my Chevy rental was on the blink. But something about my talk with the doctor—the one who signed Crocker's death certificate—had me spooked. Thus the pepper upper.

"Ah, yes, William Crocker. Some case," Dr. Ortega had told me. He was a compact man, slate gray eyes, rimless spectacles, a nervous giggle. He wrinkled his nose at me. "The young man clearly drank himself to death. Jaundiced skin, yellow eyeballs, distended abdomen."

"Any sign of drug use?" As an insurance investigator, I knew that heavy drug use led to liver damage. And we had a clause that covered us on that one.

The good doctor proceeded to lecture me on alcohol as a potent drug, but I didn't want to hear it. The upshot of our conversation was that it was possible for Crocker to heap that much abuse on his poor liver since the date of his physical. Extreme, but possible.

It appeared, from the evidence of his malnourished body, that our man Crocker had been a rummy. That explained why only recently, in the last year of his life, had he applied for a Social Security card. Consolidated required it. Chances were, Crocker had no previous work record, before he tied up with Callahan. He had been unemployable.

I checked back with the other doctor, the one who had given Crocker his physical. No surprises there. Crocker had been wearing brand new jeans and smelled like he'd hoisted a few beers, but his heart, lungs and liver checked out okay. The reason this doctor remembered so clearly, Crocker had been taken into his office by his boss, a big, blustery man who kept hovering over them and asking questions. A laugh a minute, this other fellow was.

I could just bet. My soda was turning warm and syrupy. Up ahead on my right, just off franchise row, was Callahan's place of business. The Body Beautiful—auto bodies, get it? I got it but I didn't like it.

A big, cinderblock garage with an attached office. Out front, the freshly painted carapaces of old gas hogs gleamed in the sun. Mostly pre-oil crisis Caddies and a few Lincoln Continentals.

There was a high-assed, heavily chromed, twin exhaust fuschia pick-up in the yard. Above the fancy price tag scrawled on the windshield, some joker had written, Shit-Kicker Special. It went with the new gun club bumper sticker.

I wasn't ready to approach Callahan yet. I'd dug up plenty to think on for now, and I'd had my daily dose of cute. I pulled into a joint about a block up the street, the Coral Rock Lounge. I needed a cold one. The hell with Dr. Ortega.

It was dark as a tomb in there, but the artic blast from the air conditioner felt good. As my eyes adjusted to the dim light, I saw I wasn't the only one with the same idea. Looked like a goodly mix of local yokels, the kind of regulars who warm up the same barstools every day.

I must have sat in one that was reserved. The dumpy phony redhead behind the horseshoe-shaped bar asked if I would move over one, because I was sitting in Al's place. Al had been gone long enough to let his seat get cold, but I didn't argue. I moved over and ordered a beer.

It was the best beer I'd had in a long time, ice cold with flecks of foam that tickled my upper lip. I downed it and ordered another. I saw looks of approval from the regulars, though I was still regarded with suspicion. Good drinking bars rarely take kindly to strangers, straight off. I might have to put a few kinks in my own liver, to get any information here.

You can always tell a good drinking bar from the complexion of its patrons. These were a clannish lot with identical barroom tans. Their faces had a darkened almost purplish cast to them under the neon. Artificial health. In the sun, you'd need a calculator to count the broken capillaries that gave them that ruddy look.

Real sunlight was a shocker. I winced when the front door opened and an old man ambled over to the barstool next to me. His reserved seat. He flipped a quarter to the barmaid and told her to play E-5 after she brought him a shot and a beer. His fingers were doing a St. Vitus dance over the shotglass by the time the jukebox started blaring out a song about rainbow stew.

"You must be Al," I said. "Buy you a drink?"

He nodded sourly and sipped his brew. Still, a free drink was a free drink. He grimaced at me. "You new around here?"

"Yeah," I grunted. "A friend of mine said I could get a good deal on a new paint job for my car down the street here, but I don't know. . . ."

He grunted back at me and downed his second shot. Old Al wasn't much of a talker.

"You know anything about Callahan's shop, the Body Beautiful?" I figured I'd have to work fast to get anything out of this guy before he slid off his reserved seat.

"Know something about Callahan," Al said. "Him and me used to be drinking buddies."

The redhead behind the bar listened in on our conversation. The novelty got her, I guess. She wasn't used to Al saying more than three words: shot, beer and E-5. "Joe Callahan don't drink no more," she offered.

"You mean no more than he used to?" I asked, picking up on an old joke she probably heard about ten times a day around here.

"No. I mean he don't drink at all."

Al, the redhead and I pondered this shocker. I shook my head sadly as Al volunteered, "Callahan's been off the sauce three years now."

Red nodded as if contemplating a three century drought. "And he used to be one of my regulars, a real fun guy. I hear he's done real good for himself, though . . . got that double trailer paid for and the shop going good. Still. . . ."

"Hard to trust a man who don't drink," I said. For a man from Yankeeland, I was picking up on the venacular real quick. I even got some right friendly nods when I bought the house a round. "I hear that Billy Crocker who worked for Joe was a real drinker, though. Did you know him?"

"Him," Red snorted. "He was a bum, one of them true alkeeholics."

"Sad case, huh?" I prompted.

"So bad I wouldn't serve him," she stated. That told me a lot, but she elaborated. In fact, she got downright righteous on the topic, because Crocker used to come in four sheets to the wind—after getting his load on at the liquor store up the street.

"Geez," I commiserated, "that must have put you in a tough spot . . . it's a wonder a guy like that could hold a job."

I kept the conversation well oiled. Callahan had taken the kid in, put him to work, and sobered him up for a few months. I was getting the picture. I realized why Crocker had passed the physical. The liver is a strange thing. It's one of the few organs that will heal up and rejuvenate, given half a chance. Enough to pass an insurance physical, anyway.

"What I couldn't figure," the barmaid told me, leaning over and breathing sen-sens in my face, "is why Calahan paid all the kid's liquor bills after Crocker fell off the wagon."

"Yeah," Al broke in. "The damndest thing . . . for a guy who don't drink no more. He let Crocker sleep in the back of the garage and opened up an unlimited account for him up the street . . . beer, tequila, Wild Turkey. . . ." Al grew glassy eyed and a little green, like a kid who knows the boy up the street can get anything he wants at the candy store. Or could. Until the cirrhosis did him in.

Back at the motel, I reviewed the situation. Callahan had worked a scam on Consolidated all right, but there wasn't a damn thing I could do about it. Not legally. Crocker drank himself to death, and there was nothing on the books that Callahan could be charged with—even though he had provided the ways and means. And there wasn't anything I could do to fight the life insurance payoff. Technically, Crocker's death was not murder or suicide. It was just rotten and ugly.

And it left me feeling rotten and ugly. I called the main office to ask if I could present Callahan's life insurance check in person while I was down here. Strictly speaking, this is not the way we operate, but I had my reasons, and I got Accounting to go along with me.

Then I called Callahan at the Body Beautiful and told him I

was on my way out there with a check. His voice was bluff and hearty. He hadn't been expecting the company to act so quickly. Poor Billy was barely cold in his grave. And me delivering in person . . . well, that was one swell company I represented. And I must be one swell guy, to go out of my way for him. Yes sir, he would be expecting me.

And he was. Fresh coffee was brewing in his office and the grin on his face threatened to split it in two. Besides the Mr. Coffee machine, there was an old Philco t.v. and a worn desk. We shook hands. His were smooth and steady.

"Guess you don't do too much work with your hands," I commented.

"No sir," Callahan tee-heed. I hate a man who tee-hees. "Me and Manual don't get along too good, and I can always hire some . . . slob . . . to do the work." He had stopped himself from saying some drunk. Maybe my Yankee accent, or the look in my eye, made him wary.

He overexplained, "Well, you see, I get along much better sitting back here making the deals, and there's always someone needing a job. . . ."

"Like poor Billy," I said.

"Yeah . . . it was a shame about poor Billy. But I guess some good comes out of the worst of things, heh, heh."

"Yeah." I waved the check before his eyes, so he could see $10,000 printed across the face of it. "This money ain't exactly chopped liver."

At the mention of liver, his eyes took on a narrow, calculating look, but he smiled. "No siree, not exactly chopped liver is right . . ."

I had him sign a few papers. He was so eager his hands shook. I played him along. "Too bad the kid had no friends or relatives, but I guess he had you."

"He was like a son to me," Callahan said, too quick. "I gave him a real nice funeral."

"I bet." I had checked it out. They practically had to fold Crocker over to fit him in the least expensive casket, and a cut-rate preacher had said a few words over his grave—as part of the package.

"Say," I beamed, slapping my thigh, "how about we hoist a few to poor Billy when I turn this check over to you? That place up the street looks real inviting, and my mouth's about as dry as a popcorn fart."

Callahan looked real uneasy, but the last line reassured him. Unless it was the way I held the check just out of his reach that led him on. At any rate, he followed me up the street like a dog after a bone, and we hit the entrance of the Coral Rock at a dead run.

Old Al was in his seat, and the redhead was waiting behind the bar. If they were surprised to see Callahan, they didn't say a word. They probably knew what it had taken me one sleepless night to figure out: drunks can be reconstituted just like orange juice, lemonade, instant coffee. All you have to do is mix them with booze and they look, smell and taste like drunks again.

Joe Callahan had known that, when he had taken Billy Crocker on, dried him out, then handed him a drink. And maybe Callahan was one of the smart ones, who knew that same vulnerability applied to him. Maybe.

Like a homing pigeon, the ex-drunk sidled up beside me and I slapped the check in his palm. "Set 'em up, Joe," I said.

And he did, with a double for himself.

It almost made me want to take out a policy on him.

Shut the Final Door

Joe L. Hensley

*T*he night was gentle and so Willie sat out on the combination fire escape and screened play area that hung in zigzags from the north side of the government-built, low-rent apartment building. He stayed out there in his wheelchair for a long time watching the world of lights from the other buildings around him. He liked the night. It softened the savage world, so that he could forget things he saw and did in the day. Those things still existed, but darkness fogged them.

He reached around, fumbling under his shirt, and let his hand touch the long scar where it started. He couldn't reach all of it for it ran the width of his back, a slanting line, raised from the skin. Sometimes it ached and there was a little of that tonight, but it wasn't really bad anymore. It was only that he was dead below the scar line, that the upper half of him still lived and felt, but the lower felt nothing, did nothing.

Once they'd called him Willie the Runner, and he had been very fast: the running a defense from the cruel world of the apartments, a way out, a thing of which he'd been quite proud. That had been when he was thirteen. Now he was fifteen. The

*Publicists love to note that **Joe L. Hensley** is a Judge. Which is true. But long before he donned the black mantle of the court, he had written some singularly haunting novels about injustice, not least being* THE COLOR OF HATE, *which Walker Books will reissue this year in hardcover. Hensley covers turf most modern crime writers forego, small-town America, which he writes about in a troubled and poetic way entirely his own.*

running was gone forever and there was only a scar to remind him of what had been once. But the new gift had come, the one the doctors had hinted about. And those two who'd been responsible for the scar had died.

A cloud passed across the moon and a tiny, soft rain began to fall. He wheeled off the fire escape and into the dirty hall. It was very dark inside. Someone had again removed the light bulbs from their receptacles. Piles of refuse crowded the corners and hungry insects scurried at the vibration of Willie's wheelchair. In the apartment his mom sat in front of the television. Her eyes were open, but she wasn't seeing the picture. She was on something new, exotic. He'd found one of the bottles where she'd carefully hidden it. Dilaudin, or something like that. It treated her well. He worked the wheelchair over to the television and turned off the late-night comic, but she still sat there, eyes open and lost, looking intently at the darkened tube. He went on into his own bedroom, got the wheelchair close to the bed, and clumsily levered himself between the dirty sheets.

He slept and sleeping brought the usual dreams of the days of fear and running. In the dream they laughed coldly and caught him in the dark place and he felt the searing pain of the knife. He remembered the kind doctor in the hospital, the one who kept coming back to talk to him, the one who talked about compensation and factors of recovery. The doctor had told him his arms might grow very strong and agile. He'd told him about blind men who'd developed special senses. He'd smiled and been very nice, and Willie had liked him. The gift he'd promised had come. Time passed in the dream and it became better and Willie smiled.

In the morning, before his mother left for the weekly ordeal with the people at the welfare office, Willie again had her wheel him down to the screened play area and fire escape. In the hall, with the arrival of day, the smell was stifling, a combination of dirt and urine and cooking odors and garbage. The apartments in the building were almost new, but the people who inhabited the apartments had lived in tenement squalor for so long that they soon wore all newness away. The tenants stole the light bulbs from the hallways, used dark corners as toilets of convenience, discarded the leftovers of living in the quickest easiest places. And they fought and stole and raped and, sometimes, killed.

Sometimes, Willie had seen a police car pass in the streets outside, but the policemen usually rode with eyes straight ahead and windows rolled up tight. On the few times that police came into the apartment area they came in squads for their own protection.

Outside the air was better, Willie could see the other government apartments that made up the complex, and if he leaned forward he could, by straining, see the early morning traffic weaving along the expressway by the faraway river.

His mother frowned languidly at the sky, her chocolate-brown face severe. "It'll maybe rain," she said, slurring the words together. "If it rains you get back in, hear?"

"Okay," he said, and then again, because he was never sure she heard him, "Okay!" He looked at her swollen, sullen face, wanting to say more, but no words came. She was so very young. He'd been born almost in her childhood and there was within him the feeling that she resented him, hated caring for him, abominated being tied to him, but did the dreary duty only because there was no one else and because the mother-feeling within warred with all the other wants and drives and sometimes won an occasional victory. Willie remembered no father, and his mother had never spoken of one.

"None of them bad kids bother you up here, do they?" she asked, always suspicious.

He smiled, really amused. "No," he said.

She shook her head tiredly and he noticed the twitch in the side of her dark face. She said, "Some of them's bad enough to bother around a fifteen-year-old boy in a wheelchair. Bad enough to do 'most anything I guess. When we moved in here I thought it would be better." She looked up at the sky. "It's worse," she ended softly.

Willie patiently waited out her automatic ministrations, the poking at the blanket around his wasting legs, the peck on the forehead. Finally, she left.

For a while then he was alone and he could crane and watch the expressway and the river and the downtown to the north. He could hear the complex around him come to angry life, the voices raised in argument and strife. Down below four boys came out of a neighboring building. They were dressed alike, tight jeans, brown jackets, hair long. He saw them gather in front of the building and one of them looked up and saw him watching. That one nudged the others and they all looked up, startled, and they went away like deer, around the far corner of their building at a quick lope. Willie only nodded.

A block away, just within his vision, a tall boy came out of the shadows and engaged another boy in a shouting argument. A small crowd gathered and watched indolently, some yelling advice. Willie watched with interest. When the fight began they rolled out of sight and Willie could only see the edges of the milling crowd and soon lost interest in watching.

The sun came out and the sky lightened and Willie felt more like facing the day. He looked down at his legs without real sorrow. Regret was an old acquaintance, the feeling between them no longer strong. Willie leaned back in the wheelchair. With trained ears alert to any sudden sound of danger, he dozed lightly.

Memory again became a dream. When he had become sure of the gift he had followed them to their clubhouse. It was in a ruined building that the city was tearing down to build more of the interminable housing units. He rolled right up to the door and beat on it boldly and they came and he saw the surprise on their faces and their quick looks to see if he'd brought police along.

"Hello, Running Willie, you crippled bastard," the one who'd wielded the knife said. The one who'd held him and watched smiled insolently.

He sat there alone in the chair and looked back at them, hating them with that peculiar, complete intensity, wanting them dead. The sickness came in his stomach and the whirling in his head and he saw them move at him before the sunlit world went dark brown.

Now they were dead.

A door opened below and Willie came warily awake. He looked down and saw Twig Roberts observing the day.

"Okay to come on up, Willie?" Twig asked carefully.

"Sure," Willie said negligently.

Twig came up the stairs slowly and sat down on the top one,

looking away into the distance, refusing to meet Willie's eyes. He was a large, dark boy, muscled like a wrestler, with a quick, foxy face. He lived in the apartment below Willie's.

"What we goin' to do today, Willie boy?" Twig asked it softly, his voice a whine. "Where we headin'?" He continued to look out at the empty sky and Willie knew again that Twig feared him. A small part of Willie relished the fear and fed on it, and Willie knew that the fear diminished both of them.

Willie thought about the day. Once the trips, the forays, into that wild, jackdaw land below had been an exciting thing, a thing of danger. That had been when the power was unsure and slow, but the trips were as nothing now. Instead of finding fear below he brought it.

He said softly, "We'll do something, Twig." Then he nodded, feeling small malice. "Maybe down at Building Nineteen. You been complaining about Building Nineteen, ain't you?" He smiled, hiding the malice. "You got someone down there for me?"

Twig looked at him for the first time. "You got it wrong, Willie. I got relatives in that building. I never even taken you around there for fear . . ." He stopped and then went on. "There's nothing wrong with Nineteen." He watched earnestly until Willie let his smile widen. "You were puttin' me on, Willie," Twig said, in careful half-reproach.

"Sure, Twig," Willie said, closing his eyes and leaning back in the wheelchair. "We'll go down and just sort of look around."

The fan in the elevator didn't work and hadn't worked for a long time, but at least today the elevator itself worked. The odor in the shaft was almost overpowering and Willie was glad when they were outside in the bright sun that had eaten away the morning fog.

Twig maneuvered him out the back entrance of the building. Outside the ground was covered with litter, despite the fact that there were numerous trash receptacles. A rat wheeled and flashed between garbage cans and Willie shivered. The running rat reminded Willie of the days of fear.

They moved on along the sidewalks, Willie in the chair, Twig dutifully behind. Ahead of them Willie could almost feel the word spread. The cool boys vanished. The gangs hid in trembling fear, their zip guns and knives forgotten. Arguments quieted. In the graveled play yards the rough games suspended. Small children watched in wonder from behind convenient bushes, eyes wide. Willie smiled and waved at them, but no one came out. Once a rock came toward them, but when Willie turned there was no one to be seen. There was a dead zone where they walked. It was always like that these days.

A queer thought came to Willie as he rode along in solitary patrol. It was an odd thought, shiny and unreal. He wondered if someplace there was a someone with the gift of life, a someone who could set stopped breath to moving again, bring color back to a bloodless face, restart a failed heart, bring thought back to a dead mind. He rather hoped that such a gift existed, but he knew that on these streets such a gift wouldn't last. In this filth, in this world of murderous intent the life-giver would have been torn apart. If the life-giver was Willie—if that had been the gift—they would have jerked him from the moving casket he rode, stomped him, mutilated him. And laughed.

There were other worlds. Willie knew that dimly, without remembrance, without real awareness. There was only a kind of dim longing. He knew that the legs were the things that had saved him from a thousand dangers. He remembered the leering man who'd followed him one day when he was twelve, the one who wanted something, who touched and took. He remembered the angry ones with their knives and bicycle chains, the gangs that banded together to spread, rather than absorb, terror. He looked at his world: the ones who'd roll you for the price of a drink and the ones who'd kill you for a fix. It was the only world he knew. Downtown was a thing of minutes spent. It wasn't life. Life was here.

The legs had been survival. A knife had taken them. The doctor had promised something and Willie had believed. Survival was still necessary and the world savage.

So was the compensating gift.

Twig pushed on into a narrow alley between trash cans. The sound of their coming disturbed an old white man who was dirtily burrowing in one of the cans. He looked up at them, filthy hands still rooting in the can. His thin, knobby-armed body seemed lost in indecision between whether to dig deeper in the muck or take flight. Hunger won.

"What you doin' there, man?" Twig demanded, instantly pugnacious at the sight of the dirty, white face.

The old man stood his ground stubbornly and Willie felt an almost empathy with him, remembering hungry days. The man's old eyes were cunning, the head a turtle's head, scrawnily protruding up from its shell of filthy clothing. Those eyes had run a thousand times from imagined terror, but they could still calculate chances. Those eyes saw only a boy in a wheelchair, a larger boy behind.

The old man reached in his pocket. "Ge' away, you li'l black bassurds. Ge' away fum me." The hand came out and there was a flash of dull metal. A knife.

Willie saw Twig smile triumphantly. Those who stood their ground were hard to find in these days of increasing fear.

"Hate him, Willie," Twig said softly. "Hate him now!"

Willie smiled at the old man and hated him without dislike. He had to concentrate very hard, but finally the wrenching tearing feeling came in his head and the brownout and the sickness became all. He faded himself into the hate and became one with it, and time stopped until there was nothing. When it was done and he was again aware he opened his eyes.

The old man was gone. There was nothing left to show he'd ever existed, no clothes, no knife.

"Did he run?" Willie asked.

Twig shook his head. "He smoked," he said, smiling hugely. "That was the best one yet. He smoked a kind of brown smoke and there was a big puff of flame, and suddenly he ain't there anymore." He cocked his head and clapped his hands in false exuberance. "That one was good, Willie. It was sure good." He smiled a good smile that failed to reach his eyes.

The sun was warm and Willie sat there and knew he'd been alone for all fifteen of his years and now, with the gift, that he could remain alone and that he was quite sanely mad.

He looked again at the children playing their rough games in the measured gravel and he knew he could explode them all like toy balloons, but the insanity he owned, he realized, should be worse than that.

The sun remained warm and he contemplated it and thought

about it and wondered how far the gift extended. *If I should hate the sun . . .*

There was another thought. He worked it over in his head for a long time, while his fingers absently reached and stroked the long scar on his back.

There was a way out, a possible escape.

Tomorrow he might try hating himself.

DEATH
AND THE DANCING SHADOWS

James M. Reasoner

*I*mages flickered in the darkness.

I hesitated before going into the little screening room. The picture up on the screen was in black-and-white, circa 1940, born about the same time I was. Right at the moment, it was a long shot of an old-fashioned train barrelling through a mesquite-dotted plain. Two figures were struggling on top of a boxcar.

As I watched, the camera cut to a medium close shot of the two fighters. Both wore western outfits, one of them in lighter shades, the other in dark. They were trading vicious punches that should have knocked them off the train but didn't. A sky filled with fluffy white clouds rolled along behind them in a process-shot.

The man in dark clothes had a broad, ugly face with a thin black moustache. His hat was black, too, low and flatcrowned. His expression seemed to be frozen in a permanent leer. It was funny how his hat never came off, even when the other man punched him hard in the face.

That other man wore a white hat, and underneath it his face

James Reasoner was one of the stars of the old Mike Shayne Mystery Magazine. *For it he wrote a number of memorable novelettes and short stories, a sample of which you can find here. His first novel* TEXAS WIND *is a cult classic, one of those small masterpieces that is more talked about than read—in this case because of its unavailability. Presumably an intelligent publisher will help it find the readership it deserves.*

was strong, open, and handsome. You could tell just by looking at him that here was a good, honest man. I recognized him instantly as Eliot "Lucky" Tremaine, the man who had called me earlier in the day at my West Hollywood office and told me he wanted to hire me.

The fight was reaching a crucial point on the movie screen. The black-hatted villain, whom I had recognized as veteran B-movie heavy Paul McBain, had knocked Lucky Tremaine off his feet with a sneak punch. Lucky sprawled at the edge of the speeding boxcar, only a desperate grip saving him from going over. His leer growing wider McBain stepped closer and swung a booted foot at Lucky's head in a kick that would surely finish him off.

But Lucky ducked, grabbed that boot, and twisted. With a scream and a crescendo of background music, McBain staggered backwards and went off the other side of the train, just as it obligingly crossed a deep gorge.

The rest of the movie was the usual stuff, Lucky being reunited with the female lead of the picture and the promise of living happily ever after. I had been standing at the rear of the room for less than ten minutes when the studio's insignia flashed on the screen and then blank white leader flapped out of the projector.

There was a light switch just inside the door. I flipped it up, and when the fluorescent strips in the ceiling flashed on, I said, "*Six-Gun Raiders*, right?"

Eliot Tremaine was sitting in the middle of the third row of seats. He turned to look at me and said, "Right. We filmed it in nine days, with only half a script. The writer was too drunk to finish it, so the director and I made up the second half as we went along. How do you think it plays?"

"It plays good. Of course, it bears a certain resemblance to other films in the series."

Tremaine laughed. "Hell, all them pictures were alike. The fans didn't seem to care. You want some lunch, Markham? You *are* Markham, aren't you?"

"I'm Markham."

Eliot Tremaine stood up and went into the cubicle at the back of the room to shut off the projector. I couldn't help but think that he looked smaller in real life than he did on screen. I would have recognized him anywhere, though. There were more lines on his face and more gray in the black hair, and his waist was quite a bit thicker, but he was still unmistakably Lucky Tremaine, hero of countless B westerns and Saturday afternoon serials.

I stepped aside to let him lead the way out of the screening room. It was a fairly new addition to the sprawling old ranch house. The rest of the house looked almost like a set from one of Lucky's old movies.

He was wearing boots, jeans, and a blue work shirt, and he looked more like a working rancher than he did the retired star of cowboy movies. He looked back over his shoulder at me and asked, "You don't mind eatin' in the kitchen, do you?"

"Not at all."

I was hungry. It was quite a drive out here into the valley to Tremaine's ranch, and the clock had gone around to a little after noon. If he wanted to postpone telling me why he wanted to hire a private detective, that was his business and all right with me.

We went out into the kitchen, his boots clopping on the tile floor. The white-haired lady who had let me into the house and directed me to the screening room was taking a roast out of the oven. Tremaine pulled out a chair at the table, waved me to another one, and said, "Could you whip us up a couple of sandwiches out of that roast beef, Mrs. Rankin?"

"Of course, Mr. Tremaine," she replied in her soft voice, and I wondered idly if there was more between them than an employer-housekeeper relationship.

The hot roast beef sandwiches were good. We washed them down with a can of cold beer apiece, then Tremaine clasped his big rough hands on the table in front of him and said, "I guess you wonder why I want to hire you, Markham."

"I figured you would tell me whenever you were ready."

He fixed his direct gaze on me. Those clear blue eyes were more powerful in real life than they had ever been staring into a camera. "You're supposed to be a good man for handlin' delicate matters. At least that's what the county sheriff told me, and he got the word from a friend of yours on the L.A. force."

"I do my best."

"Come back to the movie room with me. There's something I want you to see."

He kept talking as we went back through the house. "I made

my last movie in 1953. One hundred and forty-two pictures in a little over fifteen years. You seen many of 'em?''

"Quite a few. Old movies are all they show on TV in the middle of the night."

"Ain't it the truth. Anyway, when I saw the way things were going in the industry, I told myself it was time to quit. I had saved my money. I never was one to live high and fancy. So my wife and I bought this ranch."

We went into the screening room. Tremaine paused at the projection booth, taking a film carton off a shelf. He removed the reel from it and began threading the film into the projector with practiced ease. He went on, "I watch my pictures a lot. I suppose that seems vain. But it ain't, really. I just like to see something that reminds me of the way things used to be in Hollywood. Good, clean, excitin' stories with a hero and without all this trashy stuff they put in today. You go to the movies much, Markham?''

"Tickets cost too much. I can't afford it." I didn't really want to get into a discussion of morality in the movies with him.

He had the projector ready to go, but he didn't turn it on. Instead, he said, "My wife died not long after we bought this place. I raised our boy pretty much by myself. I worried about him not having a mother around, but he turned out all right. Married a fine girl and had a daughter of his own. He and his wife were killed in a car wreck five years ago. The little girl was thirteen then. Get the lights, will you, Markham?''

I snapped them off, and he turned the projector on. There were no credits on this film and no dialogue. The soundtrack was raucous, driving music. The actors were three young men and a beautiful brown-haired girl in her late teens. They were all naked.

"That's my granddaughter Stacy," Eliot Tremaine said in a voice that trembled just slightly.

"You don't have to show me all of it, Mr. Tremaine."

He cut the projector off and I turned the lights back on. With motions that were automatic and detached, he began to rewind the film. His face was set in a tight mask.

"That came in the mail yesterday," he said. "There was an unsigned note with it saying that the film hadn't been released yet, but that it would be, with plenty of publicity about who

Stacy really is, unless I show up at five o'clock today in the bus
depot in Los Angeles with ten thousand dollars in a brief case—
in exchange for the only other copy of the film."

I told him bluntly, "There're probably a dozen copies of it,
Mr. Tremaine."

The mask on his face sagged, and suddenly he looked his age.
"I know that, Markham. But I don't know what else to do. Stacy's all the family I've got left."

It was a messy situation, with no good solutions that I could
see. I said, "The best thing for you to do would be to turn the
film and the note over to the police. It would be rough, but it
would probably do the least damage in the long run."

"I though of that—" He smacked a fist into an open palm.
"—but I just can't bring myself to do it. I have to protect her if I
can."

"Do you have the money?"

"Yeah. Enough for this time. It'll run out sooner or later,
tough, and then where will Stacy be?"

I hated to see the man going through this. He wasn't really
what I would call one of the heroes of my youth, but he seemed
to be a good man, and I had seen a lot of his movies and enjoyed
them. I decided I wanted to help him if I could.

"Have you talked to Stacy about this?" I asked.

"I tried to call her last night. That's another thing that's got
me real worried. She's a freshman at USC, and her roommate
in the dorm told me that Stacy hasn't been around for the last
three days."

I felt a little cold prickle on the back of my neck. That didn't
sound good. I thought for a moment and then said, "All right.
Here's what we'll do. You be at the bus terminal at five just like
you're supposed to be, but don't take the money. I'll be there
covering you. Tell whoever contacts you that you've decided not
to pay."

Tremaine started to protest, but I held up a hand and stopped
him. "I'll trail the blackmailer and do what I can to get him off
your back, short of killing him, that is."

"What about Stacy?"

"I'm heading back to L.A. right now. I'll have a couple of
hours to check around before that five o'clock meeting. I'll need
to know where she lives and the name of her roommate."

Tremaine gave me the information and I wrote it down in my notebook. We discussed my fee briefly, settling on a figure that satisfied both of us. Then I shook hands with him, admiring his firm grip, and headed back toward the city of the angels.

The drive along the freeways didn't take much concentration, traffic being fairly light on a weekday afternoon. My mind was free to occupy itself with Lucky Tremaine and his problem.

Stacy Tremaine had been at USC for a semester-and-a-half, staying in reasonably close contact with her grandfather, with whom she had made her home after her parent's death. She had visited the ranch often, at least until recently. Tremaine also thought that she was doing well in her studies.

It seemed like a very good possibility that the film had been produced somewhere in the Los Angeles area. It was also a good bet that whoever had produced the film was the would-be blackmailer as well. The stuff had probably been shot with that in mind, rather than as the commercial pornography it resembled.

Right now, my best course of action would be to isolate the blackmailer and throw a scare into him, try to get him to abandon the scheme. If that failed, Tremaine would have little choice but to either go to the police or pay off and keep paying off as long as he could. Whatever happened, I wanted to find Stacy and set his mind to rest about her safety.

I got back to the city a little before three and stopped at my office long enough to call a sergeant I knew on the Vice Squad and ask him about porno movie-making in the area.

"You got all day?" he asked, and I could almost see his shrug. "It goes on all the time, and we do our best to stop it, but there's just too much. Anybody with a camera and some willing bodies can make the stuff."

Naturally, he wanted to know why I was asking, but I stalled him off and headed for the university. I wanted to have a talk with Stacy Tremaine's roommate before five o'clock.

The dormitory Stacy lived in was set in the middle of a big lawn dotted with trees. It was a very nice setting. I parked my Ford not too far away and strolled back to it among well-dressed students. Out of place is a mild description of the way I felt.

It had been a hell of a long time since I had called for a girl in a college dorm, but it looked like it still worked the same way. I gave my name to a coed behind a desk in the lobby and asked to see Beverly Graham. I was surprised when she gave me the room number and told me to go on up.

The room was on the second floor. I could hear quite a few female voices as I walked down the hall, and I discovered that I felt vaguely uncomfortable. It *had* been a long time.

Beverly Graham turned out to be a tall, angular blonde with glasses and a very nice smile. When she answered my knock on the door, I told her who I was and that I was working for Eliot Tremaine. "I was wondering if you could give me some information about Stacy," I finished.

"Sure," she said and gave me that nice smile. "Come on in."

She was wearing jeans and a USC sweatshirt. She sat on one of the neatly made twin beds and I took a straight-backed chair next to a desk. "When was the last time you saw Stacy?" I asked.

"It was Sunday afternoon. I'd been home for the weekend, but I got back here about four in the afternoon. Stacy was here then, but she went out a few minutes after I got here. She didn't say where she was going, and she never came back."

"Did she seem to be upset about anything?"

"No. But then we're not what you would call close friends."

"Meaning you didn't confide in each other?"

"No, not very often."

Beverly seemed to be a nice girl, but it looked like she was going to be no help at all in locating Stacy. I said, "Has Stacy ever disappeared like this before?"

"Not since we've been roommates."

"Do you know if the police have been notified?"

Beverly shrugged. "I haven't called them. The dorm director knows that Stacy is gone, of course. She may have called the police. I just don't know."

"Do you know who Stacy's friends are, someone she might go to stay with?"

"Not really. To tell the truth, I never saw much of Stacy. She didn't hang around here much."

This was getting me nowhere fast. I looked around the tidy little room with its bright curtains and well-filled bookcases. There was a picture of Lucky Tremaine as he had appeared in his movies on the desk. I stood up and said, "Thanks for your time, Miss Graham. I'm sure Stacy will turn up."

"I didn't help you very much, did I?"

Something prompted me to be honest. "No, I'm afraid not."

I saw a shadow of concern flicker over her face. "I really would hate for anything bad to happen to Stacy."

"So would I."

I still had some time before the five o'clock meeting at the bus terminal, so I asked around in the lobby downstairs and located several girls who knew Stacy Tremaine. None of them were able to give me any useful information, though. Evidently Stacy was a girl who had kept pretty much to herself, a legacy, perhaps, of spending the last few years with her grandfather.

I went back to my car and drove toward downtown L.A., parking two blocks aways from the terminal. The place was busy, as usual, and I didn't think I would have any trouble blending into the crowd. It was a little after four-thirty.

At five o'clock, Eliot Tremaine walked through the big front doors. He was wearing a dark blue business suit now but still had his boots on. There was a black briefcase in his hand. I hoped that he had followed my suggestions and that it was empty.

I was sitting on a bench with a newspaper, between an elderly man and a girl with a small baby. I watched as unobtrusively as I could as Tremaine walked slowly through the big room. He kept his eyes straight ahead.

He had come about halfway across the room toward my position when another man approached him from the side. The man put out a hand and spoke to him, too softly for me to hear. Tremaine stopped.

The exchange was interesting. I couldn't overhear any of what was said, but I could see their faces. Tremaine's was flushed and set in angry lines. I could tell that he was barely able to contain his emotions. The other man was calm at first, but he too began to look angry, undoubtedly right after Tremaine told him that he didn't have the money.

I had never seen the man before. He was around thirty, dressed casually, with dark curly hair and a moustache. He spoke sharply to Tremaine as I watched, then turned quickly on his heel and stalked away.

I thought for a second that Tremaine was going to go after him. I got to my feet quickly and hurried toward the former cowboy actor, hoping to forestall any hasty action on his part. By the time I got there, though, he had visibly regained control of himself.

"That filth," he said when he saw me. "That utter filth."

There was the same deadly intensity in his voice as there had been when he faced down a score of movie bad guys. Only this time it was for real.

"Settle down, I said. "Was that him?"

"It was. He wanted to know if I had the money. I told him I didn't."

"What did he say then?"

"That he was sorry, it was too bad the world would have to know Lucky Tremaine's granddaughter was a porno star."

I didn't have time to talk anymore. I said quickly, "I'll handle it now. You go back to the ranch. I'll be in touch."

"Did you find Stacy yet?"

I shook my head and hurried away. I didn't want to look at the pain and worry that were etching themselves on his rugged face.

When I hit the sidewalk, the blackmailer was just getting into a ten-year-old Cadillac. I made a mental note of the license number, then hurried around the block to my own car. I caught up with him at a red light four blocks later.

Trailing him wasn't hard. He wasn't expecting to be followed. From the looks of him in the terminal, he wasn't a professional at this sort of thing. That made my hopes of scaring him off go up.

I followed him to an apartment complex not far from the university. He parked the Caddy and got out as I cruised by. He still looked mad. I parked in the next block and walked back.

With my hands in my pockets, I sauntered past his car and glanced in through the open window. There was a film can lying on the front seat.

There didn't seem to be anyone around. I reached in and plucked the can off the seat almost without pausing. As I strolled on into the courtyard of the complex, I turned it over in my hands and examined it. A piece of tape with the name *Stewart* on it was stuck to one side.

That was a stroke of luck. The row of mailboxes next to the manager's apartment told me that an H. Stewart lived in

Apartment 106. That was on the first floor, at the far end of the courtyard.

I opened the can as I walked toward H. Stewart's apartment. There was a reel of film inside. I pulled one end of it loose and held it up, seeing the cloudy darkness of bland, exposed film. Tremaine's ten thousand would have bought him exactly nothing.

I snapped the can shut and knocked on the door of Apartment 106. It took H. Stewart almost a minute to answer it.

He had shed his sports coat, but it was the same man, the same moustache and bushy hair. He looked at me blankly, traces of anger and tension still visible on his face, and said curtly, "Yeah?"

I held up the film can and said, "Tremaine wouldn't have gotten his money's worth, would he?"

His eyes widened and he said, "Where'd you get—"

I interrupted him by putting my free hand on his chest and pushing. He took an involuntary step back into the apartment, with me following closely. I shut the door behind me with my foot.

"You can't just barge in here," he began to bluster.

"Blackmail is against the law, too."

That shut him up for a second. He was confused and a little bit scared, and he didn't know what to make of me.

Music was coming from another room, music I had heard before, and with it was the sound of a movie projector. A girl's voice called out, "Who was it, Hal?"

Somehow, I knew. I felt my heart sinking right down into my stomach. I pointed a finger at Stewart and said, "Tell her to come out here."

He looked like he wanted to argue, but I guess my expression was pretty bleak right then. He swallowed and said over the music, "Come out here a minute, Stacy."

She appeared in the doorway to other other room, wearing a halter top and cutoff jeans. Beyond question, she was a lovely girl. That didn't stop me from disliking her on sight.

Her smooth brow furrowed in a frown when she saw me. She asked Stewart, "Who's this?"

I answered her. "I'm the guy your grandfather hired to help you, Miss Tremaine. Only it looks like you don't need any help."

"Listen, you'd better get out of here," Stewart said, "or I'll call the cops."

"Fine. I'm sure they'd love to nail you for blackmail and making porno movies."

Stacy came closer to me, her gaze cool and appraising. She said, "I'll bet you're a private detective. Good old Lucky. Something goes wrong with his little world and who does he call on for help? Another hack movie cliche."

My dislike for her was growing rapidly. I said wearily, "Why would you want to hurt him, Miss Tremaine? He loves you very much."

There was bitterness in her voice as she said, "Do you know what it's like to have to watch old movies day after day and listen to an old man lecture on the evils of today's morality? Hell, I figure he deserves whatever he gets, and we might as well make some money out of it, hadn't we?"

There was no way I could answer her. If she and her grandfather lived in two different worlds, at least I was a lot closer to his than hers. I could see now that Stewart wasn't the driving force in this business. Trying to scare Stacy Tremaine off would be futile. She was beyond being scared by me.

"Go ahead and call the cops, Hal," she suddenly said. "We'll admit it all, and let the old man's heart break. Might as well get it over if he's not going to pay."

She was probaby bluffing, but I didn't feel like calling it. "Don't bother," I said. "I'm leaving."

"What are you going to tell Lucky?"

"Not to waste his money or his love on you. He won't believe me, but it's all I can do."

She laughed, and there was a slight cutting edge of hysteria to it. "It doesn't matter. I never expected to get too much out of the old man. There's other ways to go. We can always get money."

I turned my back on her and walked out of the apartment, anger and disgust making me feel sick. I was halfway back to my car before I realized that I was sill holding the film can tightly in my hand.

I paused on the sidewalk and looked at it, thinking that it was as worthless as whatever was in Stacy Tremaine's heart, when a car door opened and closed behind me and a hard voice said, "Give me the film."

I started to turn my head to look at the speaker. He snapped, "Don't turn around. Just reach around behind you with the film."

I was in no mood for this. I said, "What the hell?" and started to turn around anyway. I wasn't expecting what happened next. Something hit me on the head.

It sounds simple, but it wasn't. Lights flashed and sirens went off and the film can slipped from my fingers.

After that, I don't remember a thing, at least not for a while.

I was in another screening room when I woke up. The overhead lights were out, but the screen was lit with a brilliant white light. It stabbed into my eyes and right into my brain. I had a headache to start with from being hit, and the light didn't help it any.

Somebody was fumbling with something in the back of the room and cursing as he had trouble with it. I started to turn my head and look in that direction when something round and hard poked into the back on my neck and a quiet voice said, "Eyes front, please."

I kept my eyes front. The soft voice went on, "We're going to take a look at that film you had, Mr. Markham. I want to see what I'm buying this time."

I wished that my head didn't hurt so bad, because whoever this was, he had just given me several things to think about. He had obviously gone through my wallet and found out my name, and just as obviously, he thought I was part of the blackmail scheme. His words implied that he had made at least one payoff already. It looked as if Stacy Tremaine and Hal Stewart had more than one pigeon. If the man sitting behind me had already bought a blank film from them, he was probably in no mood now to haggle with someone he thought was one of the blackmailers, namely me. I had to convince him otherwise.

"Look," I ventured, "you've got this all wrong—"

"Shut up. I want to see this film first." The sound of his voice changed, and I could tell that he had turned his head. "Haven't you got that projector going yet?"

Another voice, harder and slower, answered, "Not yet. This crazy thing always gives me trouble."

The man right behind me spoke to someone else. "Go give him a hand."

A few minutes went by, and still the film didn't roll. Every time I tried to say something, the guy behind me told me to shut up. Finally I decided to keep quiet for the time being.

One of the men in the back of the room called out, "You'll have to help us with this, boss. We can't make this projector work."

The man behind me cursed under his breath and then said, "All right. Just a minute." To me, he said, "Don't try anything. I'm a good shot, and I'd just as soon kill you and get it over with, now that I know where the other two are."

I didn't like the sound of that at all. I had the feeling that he would be even less happy when he saw that the film was blank.

I didn't move while he went back to the projection booth. There were three of them and only one of me. Besides, I didn't even know where I was.

They got the projector running after a few minutes. My estimation of the head man's reaction when he saw the blank screen was right.

The gun in his hand bounced off the side of my head as the lights came on. I yelped, "Dammit!" and started to my feet. Strong hands grabbed me and pushed me back down.

"You must be pretty damn stupid, Markham, to think you could sell me a blank film twice. Did you honestly think I wouldn't have your boy Stewart followed after the first payoff? I want the real films and I want them now!"

Slowly, I put my finger to my head and felt blood oozing from the gash his gun had opened up. "You've got it all wrong," I grated. "You've been though my stuff. You know I'm a private cop. I've seen the films you're talking about, but I didn't have anything to do with blackmailing you!"

"No? Then why were you at Stewart's place? There was another payoff set for six o'clock. Are you trying to tell me you weren't on your way there when we grabbed you?"

My head throbbed. "That's exactly what I'm trying to tell you. I didn't know anything about a six o'clock meeting. I was hired to stop the blackmailers."

"Hired by who?"

"Someone who wants to protect the girl in the film. That's all I can tell you."

"It's not nearly enough. I don't believe you. Now you're going to tell us where the real films are."

He wasn't going to believe anything I said as long as I was denying any involvement with blackmail scheme. I sighed wearily and said, "All right. They're in Stewart's apartment. I'll show you. Let's get over there and get it over with."

"What's to stop me from getting rid of you now?"

"I could be lying. Hadn't you better keep me alive until you've checked it out?"

He was silent for a moment as he thought it over. Then he said, "Come on. We'll all go. And you'd better be telling the truth, Markham."

All I wanted was to get out of this little screening room so that I would have some room to maneuver. I stood up and turned around, this time meeting no opposition. For the first time, I saw the man who had been holding the gun on me.

He was a little shorter than me and about the same age. His hair had gone prematurely silver. The revolver in his hand didn't go too well with the expensive suit he wore. I could have sworn I had seen him somewhere before.

Flanking him were two bigger men who had the look of not-too-bright hired help. They closed in on me and the man with the gun said, "Don't give us any trouble, Markham."

I wasn't planning to—yet.

With the two big men on either side of me and the man with the gun behind, we walked out of the screening room and into a hall. From the looks of things, we were in a fairly expensive home.

It only took a few seconds to walk down the hall and out the front door. My guess was right. Even though darkness had fallen, I could tell we were in a fashionable neighborhood. A Lincoln Continental was parked in the driveway, and that's where we were headed.

The man with the gun opened the rear door and said, "You and I will ride back here." He got in first, keeping the gun trained on me.

It looked like the best chance I was going to get. My foot lashed out against the car door, slamming it shut and trapping the man's arm. He let out a howl and dropped the gun.

I rammed a shoulder into one of the other men, knocking him backwards. There was welcoming darkness in an adjacent yard only a few feet away, and I sprinted for it. I heard the man shout, "Get him!"

I plunged through a hedge and ducked into the shadows alongside a garage. The two big men were blundering after me. It was easy to keep track of where they were and manage to be somewhere else. I kept working my way slowly away from them.

Thirty minutes later I was walking along a boulevard and looking for a phone. I found one outside of a convenience store and called a cab. My aching head was ready for this night to be over, but there were still things to do.

My abductors had left me my wallet, so I was able to pay the cab driver when he dropped me off at my two room office. I wanted to give Eliot Tremaine a call, since he was probably waiting on pins and needles to hear from me.

It was worse than that. He was waiting on my doorstep.

He stood up when he saw me, looking as haggard as I felt. I said, "I thought I told you to go back to the ranch."

"I started to," he said. "I got halfway there before I decided to come back. I wanted to be able to see Stacy tonight if you found her."

I put my key in the lock and twisted it. "I found her."

"Well, my God, Markham," he said, gripping my arm, "is she all right?"

"She's not hurt. At least not physically." I couldn't find the words to tell him. He was staring at me imploringly. I shrugged and said, "Hell, come on in."

He followed me in and stood there as I sat down wearily behind the grey metal desk. I said, "You won't like it."

"Tell me anyway."

I told him. Every bit of it. I told him that Stacy had been a willing participant in the film and that she might have even planned the whole thing. I told him that she and Stewart were blackmailing other people besides him. He stood there and took it, his face slowly turning to granite.

"So that's where it stands," I finished.

He stood there silently for a moment, then said, "I'll write you a check for your time, and then you're fired. I don't want you workin' for me no more."

"I was afraid you'd feel like that. You don't believe a word of what I said, do you?"

"Not one damn word. I'll find somebody else to help me and Stacy."

"Whatever you want."

He scribbled out a check and dropped it on my desk, then turned and walked out of the office without another word. I felt like hell. The job had been a complete bust from the first, and I had wound up having to hurt a man that I liked and admired. Lucky Tremaine deserved better.

I didn't feel like going back to my apartment. I stretched out on the cot in the back room, thinking that my head hurt way too much for me to sleep.

I was wrong.

It was a little after seven when I woke up the next morning. I was groggy and stiff from spending the night on the cot, but my head felt a little better. I ran a hand over my raspy jaw and decided that the first thing I had better do was pick up my car so that I could go home and clean up.

Another taxi took me back to the street near Stewart's apartment where I had left my Ford the afternoon before. It was still there.

The neighborhood was beginning to wake up. It was nearly time to go to work for most of these people. I had just unlocked the front door of the Ford when the neighborhood woke up even more.

Someone started screaming.

It was coming from the direction of the apartment house where Hal Stewart lived. Frowning, I told myself not to worry about it. It was none of my business anymore.

I told myself that for about two seconds. Then I started running in the direction of the screams.

I could tell before I got there that the screams were coming from Apartment 106. Some of the people from the other apartment were sticking their heads out, but no one was making a move toward 106. I pounded up to it and grabbed the knob. The door was unlocked.

Hal Stewart was lying on the floor near the little makeshift projection room. From the size of the bloodstain growing on his chest, I knew he was either dead or soon would be. I sniffed the air. It hadn't been long since he was shot.

And Stacy Tremaine was standing over him, screaming and holding a gun.

I walked across the room toward her, moving slowly so as not to alarm her. She put up no resistance as I plucked the gun from her hand. In fact, she didn't seem to be taking any notice of me at all. I let her scream while I looked for the phone.

It wouldn't take the police long to get there. As soon as I had hung up, I began to look around the apartment. There was an empty film can on the floor of the projection room. The projector wasn't running, but when I touched a finger to the big bulb, it was hot. It looked like they had been watching movies, and I thought I knew which one.

A couple of uniformed officers were the first to arrive, and they summoned a homicide lieutenant, a technical crew, and the Medical Examiner. The apartment got pretty crowded in the next hour.

The homicide lieutenant's name was Hoskins. I knew him slightly. I gave him all the facts I had, all the details of the blackmail scheme. He was younger than me and wanted to know who the hell Lucky Tremaine was.

By mid-morning, Stacy Tremaine had been booked for Hal Stewart's murder. A search of the apartment had turned up three copies of the film. I went downtown with Hoskins, sat in an uncomfortable chair in his office and said to him, "You know, it's very likely that the girl didn't kill Stewart."

He looked at me with his face a mixture of skepticism and weariness. "What are you talking about, Markham? I've been on duty for fourteen hours now. You're not trying to make more work for me, are you?"

"What would Stacy's motive be?"

"Lover's quarrel, maybe? It doesn't make any difference, Markham. Their neighbors there in the apartment house place the shot at approximately twenty until eight. You get there at fifteen till and find the girl standing over the body with a gun. What more do you want?"

"What about the blackmail scheme? What about the guys who grabbed me yesterday?" It seemed to me that Hoskins was being unnecessarily stubborn in looking for the easy way out.

"We're trying to identify the three boys in that film. When we do, maybe we'll have a lead to whoever roughed you up. You can press kidnapping and assault charges then."

I fingered my still-sore head. "You're damn right I will."

Hoskins let me hang around until he got a report on the three young men in the film. While we were waiting, he told me what Stacy Tremaine had said in her statement.

"She claims she had passed out from too much wine and marijuana. She and Stewart were going at it pretty good, and she says she doesn't remember anything after about midnight. According to her, the gunshot woke her up this morning, but by the time she came out of her fog enough to know what was going on, there was nobody there but Stewart, and he was already dead with the gun laying beside him. She claims she picked it up without thinking. Except for a few of yours, her prints are the only ones on it."

"Whose gun was it?" I asked.

"It's registered in Stewart's name. By the way, if you're interested, until today he ran a little camera shop. Making porno films was just a sideline."

An officer came in then with a folder, which he handed to Hoskins. Inside there were some photos and typed sheets.

He scanned them quickly and then said, "This looks like what you wanted to see, Markham." He handed it across the desk to me. "I thought that the three guys in the film might be students at USC, since the girl was."

They all went to USC, all right, all sons of wealthy, respectable families. Ideal targets for a blackmail scheme. Their fathers were a banker, a judge, and an electronics tycoon.

That last one jogged something in my memory. I looked at the boy's picture more closely and read his name on the back: Jeffrey Wayne Olney. Son of industrialist Raymond Olney. Now I knew why the man with the gun had looked vaguely familiar. I had seen his picture in the business section of the paper not long before.

Hoskins still wasn't too sure he believed my story, and he advised me not to push the charges against someone who could afford high-priced lawyers. I could see the logic in that but it didn't make my head any less sore.

I convinced Hoskins to check on Olney's alibi, if any, for the time of Stewart's death, and also on the alibis of everyone else involved in the film. He grumbled about it but agreed to do it.

"Now it's time you got out of here, Markham, and let me get back to work. We do have some physical facts to base this case on, you know."

"I know," I agreed grudgingly.

Despite what I had said earlier, I knew the odds were good that Stacy had indeed killed Stewart. I wanted to believe she was innocent, for Lucky's sake, but it was hard to deny the things I had seen with my own eyes. It was possible that someone else had pulled the trigger and then ducked out, leaving Stacy to take the blame, but it wasn't very likely.

I told Hoskins I'd be checking with him later and went out into the corridor outside his office. Lucky Tremaine was sitting in a chair, waiting for the Lieutenant to interview him.

I stopped and said, "Mr. Tremaine . . . I'm sorry." He looked up at me, eyes as hard as chips of agate, and said, "Some detective you are."

"Yeah," I agreed softly. "Some detective I am."

I went back to my apartment for the first time in over twenty-four hours, shaved, showered and took a two hour nap. When I woke up, I felt quite a bit better, at least physically. I made myself a sandwich and then got Hoskins on the phone.

The first thing he said was, "Maybe you were right, Markham. I've talked to Raymond Olney, and he acts like a man who's got something to hide. He's got an alibi for this morning though; he was home under sedation. Seems he picked up a broken arm somewhere last night."

"What about his men?"

"They alibi each other. You know how much that's worth."

I felt some hope at his words. If someone could prove that Stacy Tremaine was innocent of murder, then at least Lucky wouldn't have to live out the rest of his life with the knowledge that his granddaughter was a killer.

"It goes against the evidence," Hoskins was saying, "but I suppose it's just possible that one of Olney's men could have gone in there, shot Stewart, grabbed the film, and slipped away just before you got there. Still, we have to go with the evidence as it is and that means the Tremaine girl."

"You still think I shouldn't press charges against Olney?"

"It would be your word against his, Markham. Who do you think most people would believe?"

We both knew the answer to that one. Olney wouldn't be getting away completely unscathed, though. His son's part in the film would be common knowledge soon enough. That's the kind of thing that gets around. I was still a little disgruntled. It hadn't been the kid who had hit me in the head.

Something else Hoskins had mentioned was catching in my brain. I said, "What was that about grabbing the film? I thought you found three copies of it."

"That's the one thing that doesn't really jibe," he answered. "The girl has admitted freely to the blackmail plan, and she says there were four copies of the film. We found three of them, but that leaves one copy missing."

He was right. I remembered the empty film can on the floor now. I said "Doesn't that do something to your case?"

"The District Attorney doesn't think so. He thinks we can go with the physical evidence that *was* there and get a conviction. You'll be glad to know that he's decided to drop the charge to manslaughter, though."

The D.A. was probably right, I thought glumly. He was likely to get a conviction, unless something else turned up. I thanked Hoskins for the information, urged him to keep checking on Olney, and hung up.

I didn't feel like going into the office. One of the virtues of being self-employed is the ability to give in to such feelings. So I fixed myself another sandwich, heavy on the peanut butter this time, snapped on the television set, and stretched out on the sofa.

The audio came on before the picture. A very familiar voice was saying, "Drop those guns and reach for the sky, hombre."

It was a Lucky Tremaine movie.

I had seen it before, and my mind started to wander.

It wandered a long way.

The screening room was dark again, just as it had been the morning before. The projector was humming along, throwing its images on the screen. The film was *Riders on the Wind*, possibly the best of the Lucky Tremaine series.

The star was sitting in the darkness watching himself. Something kept me from interrupting right then. I stood in the back of the room and let the scene play itself out.

Up on the screen, a much younger Lucky was riding along slowly, talking to a young boy who rode beside him. I didn't remember the child actor's name, but I remembered seeing the scene before.

"But you're the bravest man I know!" the boy was enthusing.

"Bein' brave ain't all that makes a man," Lucky responded. "Bein' a man is a mixture of a whole bunch of things, Joey. Bravery's only part of it. There's carin' about other people, and bein' a good citizen, and takin' responsibility for whatever you do. Bein' scared ever so often don't make a fella any less of a man. Not if he goes ahead and does what he knows to be right."

I snapped the lights on. "Those are good words, Lucky. Who wrote them?"

Tremaine jerked his head around to look at me. When he had gotten over his initial surprise at seeing me there, he said, "I put that dialogue in myself."

"I thought maybe you did. Do you still believe what it said?"

"Yes, sir, I do."

"Even the part about taking responsibility for your actions?"

He frowned. "Just what are you gettin' at, Markham?"

I looked up at the images on the screen. They weren't people anymore. The bright fluorescent lights had washed them out so that were only shadows now, dancing aimlessly in a world that no longer existed. I said, "Were you really going to let Stacy take the blame for a murder you committed?"

He stood up, his body breaking into the beam thrown by the projector. "You're crazy. You'd better get outta here."

"Not just yet, Lucky." I took the reel of film from under my coat. "You should have gotten rid of this while you had the chance, instead of leaving it in your bedroom."

He had aged a lot since the first time I had seen him. Now I would have had trouble recognizing him. He replied heavily, "I reckoned somebody would figure it out. I should've known it would be you."

"It was only luck that put me one to you," I said. "Stewart was watching the film just before he was killed. Afterwards, that copy of the film was gone. The killer had only a couple of minutes to rewind the film and get it out of the projector. I happened to know that the only other good suspects in the case were very clumsy with projectors. There was no way they could have taken the film in that amount of time. And then I remembered watching you work the projector here at the ranch."

"I thought maybe that was the only copy of the film. I didn't have time to look for any more." He sat down and rubbed his eyes, looking very tired. "It was kind of an accident, Markham. After I talked to you at your office, I drove around the town all night. I sure didn't want to believe what you'd told me, but I couldn't figure out why you'd lie about it. So when it got to be mornin', I looked up this Stewart's address in the phone book and went to see him."

A shudder ran through Lucky's body, but he continued, "Stacy was there, all right, passed out on the floor. Stewart was drinkin' and lookin' at that filthy movie. He just laughed at me when I told him I was takin' Stacy home with me. I told him I wanted the film too."

He paused and drew a deep breath. "He started talkin' dirty then, sayin' dirty things about Stacy. I . . . I got mad and threw a punch at him." Lucky grimaced. "I missed. He got that gun out of a desk and started wavin' it at me. I went to take it away from him and . . . it went off. Stacy started to stirrin' around, so I wiped my prints off the gun, got the film, and got out of there."

"And I came in a couple minutes later to find Stacy standing over a dead man with a gun in in her hand. Didn't you think about how it would look?"

"Hell, Markham, I wasn't thinkin'! I never meant to kill nobody." He pulled a piece of paper out of his pocket. "But I never meant for Stacy to get in trouble, neither. That's why I wrote it all down, just the way it happened, and signed it. That's why I didn't burn the film. I wanted to be able to prove what I did. If it looks like Stacy's goin' to be convicted, I'll come forward and tell what I did.

There was a bitter taste in the back of my throat. I suppose it was disillusionment. I said, "You'll come forward sooner than that, Lucky."

He was still holding the confession in one hand. With the other, he reached down into the seat beside him. It come up holding a big Colt revolver the likes of which I hadn't seen in years. It looked just like the gun he used to carry in his films.

"What's to stop me from pluggin' you right now?"

I swallowed the fear that had replaced disillusionment in my throat and answered truthfully, "Because I called the county

Sheriff and asked him to meet me here at seven o'clock. It's nearly that now."

Lucky considered for a long moment, then lowered the gun and said, "You know somethin', Markham? I believe you. And I don't think I could shoot you anyway." He stared down at the gun in his lap. "Well, hell, I guess it's all over."

"Yeah," I said, reaching into the little booth and turning the forgotten projector off, "I guess so."

He looked up at me again with pleading in his eyes. "Could you maybe go away and leave me alone for a minute or two, Markham? I'll give you this paper I wrote up. You already got the film. You can clear Stacy." His expression became wistful. "Back in the old days, a man knew what he had to do. A man knew how to go out when his time came."

It would have been easy, so easy, to go along with him but I shook my head. It was one of the hardest things I had ever done.

"Only in the movies," I said.

A KILLER
IN THE DARK

Robert Edmond Alter

*I*t had been a long hot dry summer and the little mice had come down from the foothills and into the residential district to look for water. And that was why the diamondback had left the hills; not to look for water—to look for mice.

Daylight was on the ebb. The hot, splintery sun was on its way down the far side of the western hills and the diamondback hadn't had any luck. He was in a garden, in the soft loam of a rose bed, and the back of a house was right in front of him. There were weeds there, banked along the sill, and he was going to have a look in them.

The reason he didn't know about the little boy on the wall was because he was deaf and his eyes were only accurate up to about fifteen feet. The boy watched him slither along for a moment with a sort of spellbound fascination. Then he pulled his slingshot from his jeans and loaded it, drew back, aiming, and let the elastic fly.

The stone would have missed by six inches at any rate, but

Robert Edmond Alter died brave and young. Before his time passed, he wrote several hard-boiled novels that resonate with nightmares peculiar to their author. Alter, a man who prided himself on his professionalism, was never better than when he looked at the brutal side of the mundane. In an interview shortly before he died, he wrote: "This is the dark moment . . . for a quarter of a century now I have been fascinated by the fearful realization that eventually I would have to face the moment of truth . . . I wrote so many characters in and out of their dark moments . . . it gives me an obligation to pay back in spirit some part of the courage that I created in print." Two days later cancer claimed him.

even before it struck the dirt the diamondback knew about it and he S-shaped his glistening body and took off in zigzag alarm.

"Mom!" the boy yelled. "Mom! Come quick! I hit a rattler!"

About ten minutes earlier Peter Douglas had made the last cut on his lawn and, leaving the mower standing idle at one corner of his yard, he had strolled down to George Hudson's house, three doors away. George had been out weeding; now both men were standing in George's driveway chatting and smoking. They were half-seriously thinking of going in together on a power mower.

Then Mrs. Ferris, Peter's neighbor on the west, came down Peter's driveway in a state of agitation and called to him very excitedly.

"Pete! Pete! Jimmy found a rattlesnake in your backyard!"

Peter turned, narrowing his eyes at the distant woman.

"What did she say?"

George's mouth formed a down-cornered smile. "Something about a snake in your yard. Leave it up to that busybody and her kid to know more about what's going on in *your* yard than in her own."

Pete! Pete, you better hurry!"

Peter grinned, lowering his head, and flipped his cigarette away.

"Better go see what has her bugged, I suppose," he murmured.

Both men started across the Thompson's lawn, both still smiling, the way men do whenever they encounter the exaggerated fears of a female. But Peter's smile felt a little forced in his cheeks. A snake, he wondered. Had she said a *rattle*snake?

Mrs. Pedroni came out on her front porch as the two men cut across Ed Pedroni's lawn. "What is it, Pete? Something wrong?"

George answered, casually. "Little Jimmy thinks he saw a snake in Pete's backyard."

Mrs. Ferris was acting like a child holding up her hand in the classroom when no question had been asked. Her large eyes were shifting about in her face in a very distracted manner. She was actually wringing her hands anxiously.

"Hurry, Pete," she said. "Jimmy was sitting on our wall and

he saw it come through your rose bed and he hit it with his slingshot."

Which probably accounts for the broken pane in my basement window two weeks ago, Peter thought. He was still wearing the inquiring halfsmile on his face, and it still didn't feel quite right. Mrs. Ferris was already trotting back up his drive, calling, "Jimmy! Where *are* you? I told you to stay out in the *drive*way!"

Mrs. Pedroni was coming along behind George and Peter. And now the ten-year-old Jimmy appeared at the head of the drive. He had his slingshot in his hands, loaded too.

"F'goshsake, Mom. He can't hurt me. He's gone already."

Somehow, those words made Peter feel a lot better. He was a little surprised, now, to realize just how apprehensive Mrs. Ferris' news and agitated manner had made him. He didn't suppose everyone reacted the same way to snakes, but . . .

"He went down that hole in your basement window, Mr. Douglas. I seen him. I was sittin' up there on the wall and he came right along through those roses—and *boy* was he big! And I took my slingshot—"

"All right, all right, Jimmy!" Peter snapped without meaning to. The apprehension was back again. It wasn't overpowering or anything like that, but it was there. He felt it in his stomach.

"Are you sure it went through the window?"

"Sure!" The boy scampered across the lawn toward the small fourpane window which sat on the sill. One of the lower panes was smashed.

"He scooted into these weeds and went right in through here."

"Jimmy! Get away from those weeds!"

Peter sucked in his breath. He wished that Mrs. Ferris would put a soft-pedal on her voice. She was getting on his nerves.

Jimmy turned to his mother with a pained expression. "I tol' you, Mom, he ain't here any more. He's down in Mr. Douglas' cellar."

George was grinning at Peter. "That's a nice little visitor to come calling. Maybe you can charge him room and board."

Peter smiled mechanically, saying, "Yeah." He looked at the boy.

"You sure it was a rattler, Jimmy? Not just a garden snake?"

"Aw naw. I seen him. He was a great big ol' rattler."

That's swell, Peter thought. That's really a swell thing to have in your basement. "Well," he said brightly. "I think a telephone call to the sheriff's office is in order right about—"

The backdoor opened and Madge Douglas in her apron looked out at the five people with friendly curiosity.

"Well, what on earth is all this?"

Peter started toward here with a smile.

"It's all right, hon. Jimmy thinks he saw a snake" (and even before he finished he saw the apprehension come into her eyes and he knew his intuition had been right all along—that it was going to be bad; because fear, he supposed, was atavistic in women. All the way back to the dim females of the caves it had been kids and accidents, kids and sickness, or husbands and wars, husbands and heart attacks) "go down in our basement."

There was a pause as she stared at his eyes, as she took a breath to say it with a rush. And in that brief moment they were the only two people there—man and wife, parents.

"Peggy's down there."

Already she was turning away, moving toward the closed basement door in the back-porch. Peter went after her with a start, clumping up the steps and through the open door, and caught her by the shoulders, turning her back.

"All right, he said quietly. "Now wait a minute, take it easy."

Her eyes didn't jump about like swallows trapped in a barn, the way Mrs. Ferris' did. They were fixed, frozen, staring up at him.

"She and little Glady went down to play Monster."

He nodded jerkily, saying, "All right. Phone the sheriff. I'll go down now. It's all right, honey."

He reached for the light switch by the side of the closed door . . . but he was hearing in memory what Madge had said to him a week ago: *Pete, you'll have to put a new bulb in the basement. The light's burned out.* And himself answering absently, his mind half on the evening papers: *Yeah, I'll get it. Tomorrow. . . .*

Tomorrow, tomorrow . . . . Peggy in the dark basement. Seven years old. Happy blue eyes in a pale tender face, standing in a blonde mist of hair, at his elbow, as he watched TV. *'Night, Daddy. . . .*

"Pete, you didn't—"

"It's all right, he insisted, reaching for the doorknob instead. "Give me the flashlight from the drawer there." And again he saw it in her eyes and he knew that that wasn't going to work either.

"Oh, Pete, the batteries . . . I forgot to buy the batteries!"

"Okay. Okay. A candle—give me one of the candles."

They had followed him up to the door, Mrs. Pedroni, Mrs. Ferris, Jimmy and George. George had a peculiar look on his face. He was saying, "I've got a gun, Pete. A thirty-two. I'll—"

Peter swung on him. "I can't take a pistol down there! Not with two little girls!"

"Well," George murmured. "Well . . ."

Then he knew that George wasn't going with him, and there wasn't any sense in embarrassing him by asking him to. *Can I blame him? Would I, if Peggy wasn't down there? For someone else's kid?* At that moment he didn't honestly know.

"Phone the sheriff, George," he said. He took the candle from Madge and he jerked his head at her. In movies—at this moment—there always seemed to be ample time for the man to reassure the girl; oceans of time for him to tell the woman he loved just how much she meant to him. But it wasn't true. He didn't have a spare second. Just a quick reluctant nod. That's all the time there was.

He opened the door and started down the breakneck steps into a waiting black pit, fishing for a match in his pocket.

The stairs were in a well. You stepped straight down until you reached the concrete floor. Then you turned left around the corner of the plastered wall and you were in the basement.

The basement was large and dark and very cluttered. It had been the Douglas catch-all for nearly ten years. Peter couldn't see anything—except, here and there, the far-away little windows, like small, square, opaque eyes. They didn't help him at all. Dusk was settling outside, quietly bringing along the threat of night.

He hesitated at the corner of the stairwell, peering into the dark, listening. But there wasn't anything to hear.

"Peggy?" He hadn't whispered consciously, and it startled him to hear the tremulous, wispy sound come out of his throat.

"Peggy?" he said clearly.

Monster was their favorite game. Peggy and her little friend Gladys would rather play Monster than eat. It had to be played in the dark, of course, otherwise they couldn't scare themselves into delicious hysterics. So they would hide in a dark place and one would be Monster and the other would be Victim. Monster had to remain stationary; Victim had to move about. When Victim sneaked close to Monster, Monster would let out an awful mouth noise—which not only shocked poor Victim into delighted shrieks of horror, but also managed to scare Monster half to death as well. Then Monster would chase Victim in the dark. It was a very merry little game.

"Peggy!" His voice turned insistent. He scraped the matchhead along the plaster wall, dragging a flare of orange fire after it, and held the quivering little bulb of light to the candlewick.

Then he heard a noise. *Ggggggheehee.* Low and throaty and restrained. He let out his breath, raised the little island of candlelight against the black set of the basement. Inky shadows lurched away from him, turning into a multitude of orange and brown objects.

"Peggy. Glady. I hear you. Don't move . . . don't move at all, girls. Just tell Daddy where you are. I'm going to play Monster with you."

There was a pause; then the faint ghostly little gurgle of giggling again, from the far end of the basement. *Ggggggheehee.*

"Peggy, are you by the furnace, honey? Don't move. Just tell me."

And suddenly, shockingly, the little outraged voice of his seven-year-old, coming at him from nowhere like an unexpected blow.

"That's not fair, Daddy! You can't use a light! My goodness!"

By the water heater—wasn't it? He thought so.

"All right, honey. I'll blow it out in a minute. I'll be the Monster and come find you and Glady."

"No! *You're* supposed to hide and jump out on us when we—"

"Yes, I know. But let's play it this other way. It'll be more fun. Just stay where you are, now. Gladys—where are you, honey?"

"Over here." Behind the furnace. Good. That put both of them at the same end of the cellar. He started forward, slowly, holding the candle high, peering everywhere, sharply.

Stacks of old newspapers and magazines . . . the fat, smiling, dust covered face of Khruschev on the cover of a *Life* . . . old inner tubes, tools, a fallen rake . . . cardboard boxes packed with all the nameless, seemingly purposeless articles that wives never really discard . . . a steamer trunk that had belonged to Peter's father . . . an old backless bookshelf filled with paint cans and brushes and old jars . . .

Maybe the damned thing wasn't down here at all . . . except in Jimmy's imagination. But what if he had seen a snake? *Calling* it a rattler was just the kind of thing a ten-year-old would think of, even if it was only an old garden snake. Still, that rake would make a good weapon, just in . . .

CH-CH-CH-CH-CH-HHH!

It went off like a telephone right behind him, and its immensity of sound seemed to fill the entire basement. It jerked him to full stop and the short hairs on the back of his neck felt just like pins and needles in his flesh.

It didn't sound the same as it did in movies or TV. It didn't really sound like a baby's rattle. It was too overpoweringly loud, and it went on and on. At that moment, all he could think of was a freight train rattling and bouncing and lurching along, endlessly coming.

He jumped, spun about, seeing it there on the dusty cement floor, coiled neatly near a stack of old encyclopedias with the flat triangular head cocked down in the center, the forked tongue flicking through the closed traplike mouth as if tasting the cool air, the beady-bright, vertical eyes watching him dispassionately, and the caudal rattle vibrating the horny epidermal rings warningly.

Panicky, he wondered how long the rattler would wait before it decided to strike; or would it wait indefinitely, as long as he didn't move? *It's cold*, he thought, *sluggish, but it's awake enough to know that it doesn't like me.*

"*Ooooh*, Daddy! What's the funny noise, Daddy?"

He couldn't help himself. He was triggered as tightly as a bear trap. He stepped backward in a rush, his right foot coming down on the iron prongs of the rake. The handle swished up and slammed him just behind the right shoulder, snapping the candle from his hand.

In the vivid instant before the falling light winked out he saw the rattler uncoil all at once, shooting its flat head at the candle as it hinged mouth jerked open and those two hypodermic needle-like fangs snapped forward.

Then, for a gut-grabbing moment, there was nothing. No

sound, no sight. Peter was on his left knee, both hands touching the floor. He wasn't exactly sure how he had come to this crouching position. The right side of his back was stabbing him with pain and his entire right arm was tingling. He was afraid to move.

He didn't know much about rattlesnakes, only a few vaguely remembered facts he'd read somewhere, or been told. The snake's eyesight wasn't good, and it was utterly useless in the dark. And he was stone deaf. But those things didn't matter, because the snake had a built-in gimmick in his head which made him as deadly as a highpowered rifle in the hands of an insane expert marksman.

Some said it had to do with the facial pit between the snake's eye and nostril; others said it had to do with the tongue or an inner organ of the throat—Jacob's Organ. Whatever it was, it acted as a specialized sense organ which reacted to warm and cold objects. It could strike unerringly at a temperature aura.

"Daddy! Daddy!" Peggy's voice came imperiously. "No fair starting yet. You know where we are. Wait till we hide again. Okay, Daddy?"

"*NO!*' Then he caught himself, his nerve, and lowered his tone.

"No, wait, honey. Don't move yet. Gladys, don't you move either. Daddy wants to do something first. Just a minute, honey."

He leaned back on his haunches to put his left hand into his pants pocket. But the pocket was empty. No matches.

Peter wet his lips and put his right knee down and his left hand, to try in his right pocket. His left hand descended on something round and cold and slightly yielding.

A surging cry gagged in his throat and he threw himself backwards with a slam against the metal face of the furnace, creating a hollow *tooomm* of sound.

Wait! Wait! he told himself. *It wasn't him. Not the snake. Garden hose! A piece of plastic garden hose.* For a crazy moment he thought he was going to giggle. He checked himself, and remembered the matches. He dug into his right pants pocket.

It was like reaching his hand into blank despair. He wouldn't believe it—that in his frantic anxiety he hadn't even had the sense to check for matches before he came down into the cellar.

He felt his shirt pockets. His pack of cigarettes was still there, but not—of course—the half-empty book of matches he had started the day with.

"*Keep 'em,* he heard himself saying to George again, as they stood and talked in George's driveway. *I've got some kitchen matches.*

He started to edge around the furnace, groping with his left hand.

"Glady—Glady, are you there, honey?"

He heard her leather soles crunch on the grit of the cement floor. She giggled quietly in the dark in front of him.

"No, don't move, Gladys. Come here, dear. I want to explain about the game before we start."

Then his trembling fingers found the fabric of her play clothes and he almost grabbed he violently. Bu he restrained himself, taking her gently under the armpits and lifting her.

"We're going to play it differently," he whispered. "Now sit here and wait while I go for Peggy."

He fumbled with the little girl's soft body, setting her up on the top of the furnace, telling her, "Now take ahold of one of the ducts—the pipes. Got it?"

"It's all dusty dirty," she told him.

"That's all right. Just hold on to it, so you won't fall. Okay? Now I'll be right back."

He let go of her and turned in the dark, hating the thought of making his blind way from the furnace clear over to the water heater. Why didn't that fool sheriff hurry?

"Pete?" The shock of the sudden voice in the dark almost unmanned him. His heart lurched. Then he steadied himself. It was Madge calling from the stairwell.

"Pete, are you all right?"

"Yes. Yes, Madge. We're all right. Madge—don't come down here!"

"Is Peggy—"

"Yes, they're both all right."

"Pete, is the—is it down there?"

She was thinking of the kids; they would know what the word Snake meant, and it would probably scare them. Peter didn't want to scare her. He lied. "I don't think so. I haven't seen it."

"Mrs. Ferris is bringing a flashlight."

"All right. All right, Madge. We'll be up in a minute."

Why did I say that? he wondered. *We won't be. We don't dare try to move out of here. We'll have to sit tight until the sheriff's men get here.*

"When're we gonna start the game, Daddy? You said we were gonna play Monster!"

We're playing it, honey. Oh, yes, we're really playing it.

"In just a minute, Peg. Just as soon as I get everything ready."

There was just the faintest flicker of dull light on the floor before him. The covered pilot light in the water heater. He reached out, feeling for his daugher. "Now—here Daddy is."

Ch-CH-CH-CH-CH-HHH!

He couldn't believe it. But he had to because it was there, rattling—it seemed—right beside him. Frantically, he sprang away from the heater and heard almost instantly the sharp *sssip* of the snake's momentum as it snapped blindly forward. Then he sprang again, to divert the thing's attention away from the vicinity of the heater and his daughter.

"*Ooooh,* Daddy! You're making that funny noise again!"

"*Don't move, Peggy!* Don't move. Peggy, you mind Daddy— don't move an inch."

"Pete! Pete, what's that noise? Is it the—"

"Shut *up*, Madge! Stay there."

He was gasping now, standing in the dense dark in a half crouch, trying to listen. He thought he could hear the soft slither of the snake's belly sliding across the gritty floor.

Coming this way? he asked. God—is he coming this way?

It was inconceivable to him that this soulless, vicious little length of muscle, bone and venom might cost him his life. It was senseless and mad. He was the product of innumerable generations, the result of a complicated process of evolution since the creation of the earth. It was outrageous to think that that filthy little pitviper could kill him.

Because death was something that happened to other people in other cities, other lands. It didn't happen to your friends or family. It never really happened to you.

Not Peggy, he prayed. *Not Gladys—because she's as much my responsibility as my own child is.*

"Pete! I've got Mrs. Ferris' flashlight. Shall I—"

"Don't come down here, Madge!" He half turned in the direction of the stairwell.

CH-CH-CH-CH-HHH!

It went off again, surrounding him in the horror of its clamor, and he sprang to the left . . . right into the shelves of old paint cans and jars. He went down, his equilibrium lost in the black crash of falling objects, tin cans clattering and glass shattering.

He rolled in the mess, trying to get the leverage to get up and get out of there, and his right hand caught something and he grabbed, and then—too late—he couldn't let go.

It quivered, jerked, seemed to kick in his hand. He felt his whole arm jolt. It was like grabbing a live wire, only it was cold and slick and it rippled with writhing muscle and it wrapped around his wrist and forearm. The caudal rattle went off in his ear.

Throw it away! My God, throw it away! But he wouldn't, couldn't. He was wild with fear and revulsion, and he was all turned around. He might unwittingly throw it into his daughter's face.

The sinuous length of body coiled and tightened and whipped around his arm, the rattle going going going.

He couldn't think. He started staggering into the dark aimlessly, holding his jerking arm out. Far far away he heard the sad wail of the siren coming. But it didn't have meaning to him. It belonged to the normal outside world. He was here in blackness with this damned thing wrapped around his arm and he didn't know what to do with it.

"It hasn't struck me," he muttered dazedly. "I must have it right behind the head, and it can't get the swing. But dear God, what am I to *do* with the filthy thing?"

His feet blundered into something and he almost went down. Tools . . . tools under my feet. He dropped to his knees, his left hand groping among the clutter of metal and wood and plastic, and found a hammer.

Ch-CH-CH-CH-HHH!

"Shut up!" he hissed. "*Shut up!*"

He put his right hand down on the cement floor and held the thrashing, rattling thing there and swung the hammer at it.

The first blow caught the knuckle of his forefinger and he gasped against the white jolt of pain, and he swung again and again and . . .

He wasn't himself when he came up the stairs; he knew it, but couldn't seem to do anything about it. He felt like a sonmambulist.

The two deputies had already pushed by him with their flash-lights to go down into the basement and Madge was on her knees on the back-porch with one arm around Peggy and the other around Gladys, and Peggy was explaining to her how he, Daddy, hadn't played the game correctly, how he had tried to scare them merely by making a "funny old noise."

And Madge was saying, "Yes, dear, yes dear," over and over, and doing her best not to cry.

The deputies had brought an ambulance with them, and now the intern was leading Peter down the backsteps, plucking at the sleeve of his shirt trying to see the mangled hand.

It seemed as though half the neighborhood was in his back-yard. George was there with his .32 and with a sheepish look on his face.

"I brought the gun anyhow, Pete," he said apologetically.

Peter nodded. "Thanks, George."

"Come on," the intern insisted. "Let's go out to the wagon and have a look at that hand."

Peter let himself be led down the drive. People were stepping aside all along the way, staring at him. He blinked and looked around dully when he heard Jimmy call to him.

"Gosh, Mr. Douglas, why'd you have to kill it? Couldn't you just hold it till the cops got here? I'd like to keep that ol' rattler."

Some of the spectators chuckled, watching Peter askance.

"Sorry, Jimmy," Peter murmured.

"C'mon," the intern ordered.

He closed the doors in the rear of the ambulance and had Pe-ter sit on the cot. He gave Peter a penetrating glance, and then he gave him a shot of something. After that he offered him a cigarette.

"All right now?" he asked.

Peter nodded. "Yeah, sure."

Then he grinned spastically at the intern.

"I got him, huh? I couldn't see in the dark, you know? Couldn't see my hand before my face. I think he must have launched himself when I blundered into the paint cans. Then, before he could collect himself again, I caught him by accident. I just kept pounding him and pounding him until he was pulp— or my hand was. Couldn't tell. Then all at once I found myself standing and I was feeling my right hand with my left and the snake was gone. I—I couldn't stop pounding him, you know? I just kept . . . "

Abruptly the emotional discharge of words ran out. He fumbled for something to say, as a rapt look of horrified revulsion came into his eyes.

The intern nodded, watching him.

All at once Peter was sobbing, his entire body trembling violently. He dropped his cigarette and his head went down, as the intern reached for him, wrapping one arm around his bowed shoulders, and holding him like a frightened child.

PERCHANCE TO DREAM

Michael Seidman

*J*unior was tired, bone-tired, which was good. He was also having the dream again, which wasn't. It was because of the dream that he had taken the walk. Starting at Lincoln Center and heading down Broadway all the way to Battery Park. And back, but this time not going straight. Instead, he followed the traffic lights, crossing at each corner according to the green—going east, going west—but always going north until he got back to the brownstone tenement on Columbus Avenue, across the street from the Harp & Lager.

Now he leaned against the mailbox on the corner, tired and thirsty. A couple of brews to start, then into the Black Jack straight up with the beers back. He'd be able to sleep tonight; he thought, and so deeply that the dream wouldn't reach him. He patted himself down, searching for a cigarette.

From his pants he got the old Zippo with his initials scratched onto its side, a parting gift from his father. He put his thumb on the bottom and first two fingers on top and snapped it open, smelling the lighter fluid and feeling the slick film it had left on the worn, dented metal. He spun the wheel and brought his

Michael Seidman is a New York writer and editor whose short fiction shares certain qualities with the late Frederic Brown's. His prose, and formal prose it is, manages to convey a certain haunted quality while still remaining somewhat ironic. Amusing and bleak. Presently, Seidman's fiction and articles appear in a variety of magazines, and one assumes that he will someday give us a novel.

head down to the cupped flame, sucking it up toward the dangling Lucky. The rich smoke filled his lungs and he held it there for a moment, waiting to see if the coughing would begin again. No, Just a scratching. He blew a smoke ring toward the street lamp and smiled as he tossed the lighter up and caught it.

He told everyone that the Zippo was an heirloom, that his father had carried it through World War II, that his brother had used it in Korea, that he had taken it to 'Nam.

"In fact," he'd say, "this little beauty saved my life, got me a Purple Heart instead of a body bag. We was outsida Da Nang when some sniper took it into mind to blow me away an' I had the lighter in my pocket, right here," tapping his left breast, "and the bullet deflected offa it and just scraped 'tween my arm and chest."

It was a good story, one that was usually worth a beer or two. But that's all it was, a story.

He watched the door of the tavern; it didn't look too crowded so maybe Smitty would let him in again. Junior loved the Harp & Lager, a neighborhood bar with a pool table in the back, nuts and pickled eggs on the bar. It was just like the beer halls back home in the mining towns along Rum Creek. Except for the fights: At home, twelve, thirteen years ago, when he was eighteen, you could count on someone taking a beer bottle upside someone's head at least once a week. Here in New York things were more civilized. Except for that time six months ago.

Junior'd been having the dream then, too, and was drinking too much. It was really bad going to sleep—or trying to. He'd toss and turn, twisting the sheets between his legs and around his waist, cutting off the circulation. The bedding would be soaked with sweat and if he did manage to doze off, he'd only wind up screaming himself awake. All he could do then was lie there, smoking one cigarette after another, nipping at whatever bottle he'd brought home, and watch the reflection of the neon signs and traffic lights smear across his ceiling. Then it was that Wednesday, after an impossible Tuesday night.

He'd gone to work at the garage red-eyed and reeking and dropped a wrench on the hood of the sleek Porsche he was supposed to tune up and he watched the wrench bounce off the now-marred finish and crack the windshield. The boss had screamed at him, and sent him packing.

He'd walked the streets that night, too, then headed for the Harp. It was good there, right somehow, and he started drinking and talking with his friends, guys who understood about dreams and nightmares and would stand him to rounds and ask him to sing. And it was good shooting some pool, a little eight ball. With the cue stick in his hand he calmed down, stroking shots, "just showin' off" like that guy on television said. He wasn't a hustler, exactly; just good at the game like he was good with an engine. Breeding shows, he'd been told, and that's what he'd been bred to do.

When the guy with the big nose came in—Herb something—and looked for some action at the table, they all told him to play Junior. The Nose wasn't a regular here, and nobody felt they owed him anything. Junior lost a game or two, to keep it interesting, but he could afford to buy The Nose an occasional beer, what with all the free ones he was getting.

Then The Nose decided he could out-hustle the bar's main man.

"Hey, Junior, isn't it, how about making it interesting?" The Nose stroked his cue, then reached for the chalk. "Say a dollar a ball, and fifty for the game?"

Junior laughed. "No way. I ain't got that kinda dough. But I'll tell you what, how about fifty cents a ball and ten bucks for the game?"

It began. Three hours later, about eleven o'clock, he had won a lot, lost a little, and was about seventy-five dollars ahead. Side bets were going down and the Harp & Lager was filled with regulars and smoke and the good noise of men at play.

"Tell you what, Herb. I got enough of a stake now, let's play like you wanted, a dollar and fifty."

The Nose looked around. Seemed safe enough. He had the turkey where he wanted him. "Sure, fellow."

It took only fifteen minutes. The Nose was down six hundred and sweating. Junior smiled at him and took a long pull at his Rheingold. Smitty, the Harp's owner, and the bartender, Kevin, exchanged looks. Trouble coming.

Smitty walked over to the table and hefted the cue ball. "Okay, guys, I think that's about enough now. Game's gettin' a little too rich, don't you think?"

Junior shrugged. It was okay with him; he'd made enough to

keep himself going until he got another job. Herb, though, felt differently.

"No way, man. He's just about got me at tap city. You gotta give me a chance to make something back." The Nose looked around, feeling belligerent, realizing that the blond guy with the dirty fingers and shitkicker's drawl had taken him. The guy was good, no arguing with that, but he was better when something heavy was on the line. "Look," he went on, "let me try double or nothing. Ya gotta gimme a shot."

Junior leaned against the table, staring at the wall. He didn't care; it was up to Smitty.

The owner put the cue ball back on the table and racked the balls. Turning to The Nose, he said, "Okay. But two things. First, show me you got enough to cover if you lose. And second, this is the last rack, no matter what.

"Now, my friend behind the bar may look big, but he's even tougher than he looks. He's gonna come around and stand at the table, here. When the eight ball sinks, he's taking the stick from your hand. You can sit and drink then, or you can leave. Got it?"

The Nose watched Kevin walk to the table, all six-three, two-forty of him. He took out his wallet and passed seven hundred dollar bills to Smitty.

Kevin pulled a Kennedy half out of his pocket. "Herb, you call it in the air for the break." The silver disk jumped into the air.

"Tails."

JFK's face looked up at them from the felt. Junior winked at him, set the cue ball, took a deep breath, and stroked.

The three ball broke out of the pack, fell lazily into the corner pocket. He chalked, walking around the table. Stroke. The one ball fell into the side pocket; the eight popped toward the far corner, coming to rest against the rail, its roll stopping just short of ending the game.

Stroke. Click. Thunk.

Stroke. Click. Thunk.

The Nose felt the sweat running down his spine as he watched Junior set up for his last shot. *Stroke.* The shooter turned away from the table, walked toward the bar where another bottle waited for him. *Click.* The cue ball kissed the eight ball. *Thunk.*

"*Goddamnit!*" The Nose screamed, starting to swing his stick at Junior's back.

Kevin moved, stopping the arc cold. "We warned you, boy-o." He tossed the cue to Smitty and stepped in front of the shaking loser. "You were leaving now, right?"

"I ain't leavin' nowhere. You guys hustled me, you and that moth. . . ."

Junior spun, face red, drool edging out of his mouth. "Don't call me that, cocksucker. Don't ever. . . ."

"Motherfu—"

Junior's cue cut the air, the thick handle connecting with The Nose's face just above the right eye. There were two cracks, as stick and skull broke. *"Never sound on my mother. Never. Never!"*

A couple of guys pulled him back, while Kevin supported the sagging weight with the bleeding face. Smitty ran over and the two of them dragged The Nose out between them and brought him to the little alley around the corner, where the dumped him. All the while they could hear the screams from inside, incoherent noises being shouted into the night.

Kevin came back first and watched Junior's struggles to break free slow down. He walked up to him, a man almost as big as he, and waved everyone off. "It's okay now, he's gone."

Junior fell back onto a stool, shaking his head, watching the floor. "I'm sorry Kevin. But he shouldn'ta started calling me that, though. You know."

"I know, Junior. Look, it's okay now, it's all right."

They were joined by Smitty, looking glum. He put his hand on Junior's shoulder, shook him just a little. Like he says, Junior, it's okay. But I think you should stay away from here for a while, at least until this cools down. That guy might want to get back some of what he lost tonight—pride more than money. Whattaya say?"

So Junior stayed away. The first couple of nights he'd watched from his window to see if The Nose was around, but there was no sign of him. Still, Smitty'd said stay away. He'd gotten another job and he was feeling good . . . except that the dream was starting again. And he missed the Harp & Lager.

He looked at his watch. Seven-thirty. There was nothing on the tube he wanted to see, but the Yankees were playing tonight and he knew Smitty had gotten one of those seven foot screen jobs. He tossed the butt toward the drain on the corner and crossed to the tavern.

He paused, then pushed the door open and smelled home. The voices from inside greeted him and Kevin, seeing him stand in the entrance, waved him in, shouting something about where the hell you been and let me buy you a beer.

Junior laughed, certain now that tonight, at least, he wouldn't dream.

•　　•　　•

The Checker pulled into traffic, joined the flow down Broadway at Ninety-ninth Street. The driver shifted his forty-seven year old bones and pulled the .45 out from behind him, dropping it into the dark green nylon flight bag on the seat next to him. Coming to a stop at the corner of Ninety-third, he pushed his shoulders back into the seat, zipped the bag shut and turned it so that he could see the silver parachute and wings, the Airborne jump insignia, printed on its side, with the big, white MP beneath it.

He moved out with the light, jockeying the heavy cab through the moderate traffic with the agility and unconcern of a seasoned New York cabbie. He'd been hacking for two years, ever since that trouble down at Bragg.

When Lilah insisted that they move north, ex-Master Sergeant Paul Reegan agreed. They had some money stashed away and he did have a pension, and he knew he'd land a job in security somewhere. What he hadn't taken into account was that the city was filled with ex-cops taking security jobs and that the cost of living was more than the living was worth. Finally, he'd gotten a job as a guard in a small, exclusive bank on Fifth Avenue and began pushing the cab nights. Between the two jobs, and what the bitch was bringing in from waitressing at the Greek's place, they had a life as good as he could hope for.

As he got to Seventy-second Street, he caught someone waving him down from the far corner, near a fruit store. Hell, the whole neighborhood up here was filled with fruits, not that he could object too much. He didn't have to worry about sharing a foxhole with one of 'em. Anyway, the building he lived in on Fifty-seventh, near Ninth, was filled with them. He turned his head a bit to get a good look at who was hailing him, then stared intently in the other direction. Now that he'd put the gun away, he wasn't about to stop for some half-assed pimp.

He drove on another few blocks. A good looking couple was standing near Juilliard and he pulled over.

"Evenin' folks. Where to?"

"Third and Eighty-sixth, please."

Oh damn, across town and back up. And the traffic on the East Side at this hour's a bitch and a half. "Okay." He leaned forward and pressed the button starting the meter. He pulled over into the left lane, turned onto Sixty-fifth and headed for the transverse. He knew he could get through the park without too much trouble. Up ahead he saw the lights strung in the trees around The Tavern on the Green.

"Looks pretty, doesn't it? It's nice, being able to see things like that once in a while."

He didn't get a response from the back and looked into the little mirror he'd placed up near the roof of the cab, aimed so that he could get an eyeful of whatever might be going on in the back seat. The things people would do, as if he didn't exist. He hadn't figured these two for action, though.

He hadn't been wrong. The two of them just sat in the back staring angrily straight ahead. Reegan let his thoughts roam.

"Go to school, boy, get on a team, get outta here." That's what his Daddy used to tell him. But school was a drag, and even if Daddy was management and didn't have to dig in the mines every day, even if he did run the company store, you were still hungry, or cold, or tired and didn't want to put up with the drag. You may have been rich compared to some of the other people along the Creek, but you didn't have anything, really. Your credit was better, because your father issued the credit, but he still had to pay it off. And you'd be awake at night, listening to your parents fight about who was cheating on who and hearing your father's fist lose itself in your mother's body while you lay in the dark smelling the coal dust; or you were out drinking beer, or whoring, or both.

And because your father was important, you found you had your own importance, that girls and women were nice to you, very nice to you, and most of the time their husbands and fathers knew just how nice they were and insisted that they stay nice, because cold beer was better than warm water. So why bother about school, it would all work out, and in the meantime old man Waltham was on the night shift and his red-haired wife looked good and the brat would be asleep by now and NO!

Reegan pulled to a sudden stop. The couple in back was

thrown forward and back again and the man was shouting and *Jesus!*

"Sorry, folks. It looked like that dog over there was gonna run out in front of us. Oughta keep those things on a leash."

He stepped on the gas, gently, and rolled more than drove the last block. As he made change, and thanked the guy for the tip, Paul realized he was shaking. He had promised himself not to think about Gina Waltham ever again, but he kept going back to that night just before he turned eighteen over and over. God, *she was beautiful, about thirty-two, long, thick red hair, natural red hair, tall. She'd kept her shape, even with the high-starch diet, and the baby and.* . . .

Paul's head jerked up at the sound of the horns blaring behind him. *Shit.* He saw a parking spot up ahead, near a coffee shop, and decided it was time to take a break. He looked at his watch. Nine-fifteen. *Sure, take a half hour. Call Lilah. Yeah.*

He felt better after the coffee. It was ten, and he headed downtown and west, hoping to catch a fare at Penn Station when the Metroliner got in from D.C. The only thing bothering him was the unanswered phone at home.

•   •   •

"Hi, the boss around?"

Kevin looked at the blonde hoisting herself onto the stool at the door end of the bar. A good-looking woman in her early thirties, definitely not a working girl or junkie. And that honeyed voice. . . . "He's in back, should be up in a few minutes. Anything I can do for you?"

She smiled, liking the fact that the question wasn't a proposition. She tossed her head a little, so that her hair swung. "I'd just like to wait and talk with him, if that's okay?" Her blue eyes took in the scene with a practiced glance. The place was busy, and it looked like they just had the bartender working it. Maybe she'd get lucky. Her feet were tired and there was a dull ache in the small of her back. Everything was going wrong. Almost everything—at least she wasn't pregnant. The thoughts were stopped, cold, by the sound of a voice at the back of the room. Rising in song, it sounded just like her husband. She looked back, saw the man standing next to the pool table, swaying a bit, beer bottle in hand, singing "Behind Closed Doors." Damned if that didn't sound like her old man.

"Miss? Miss?"

"Oh, I'm sorry." She turned to Smitty, standing next to her. "Are you . . . ? She let the question hang, feeling foolish.

"The boss? Yeah. Kevin said you wanted to speak to me."

"Yes. I'm, well, I was wondering if you could use any table help, a waitress or something? I'm looking for a job, I got laid off today and things being what they are. . . ." Again, she didn't finish.

Smitty looked her up and down, frankly appraising. She seemed decent enough and when he'd watched her from the small kitchen she hadn't been playing games with anyone, just sitting and waiting, watching.

"Kevin—Miss, would you like a drink of anything? Kevin would you get—"

"Joyce, well actually, it's Lilah Joyce. Lilah Joyce Reegan, but only my husband calls me Lilah. Anyway, yes, a Coke would be nice."

"—Joyce a Coke? Thanks. What happened to your other job?"

"I was tablehopping over at a coffee shop . . . well, business has been off, and the boss had his family working there? And, well, you know. They'll give me references. And I've worked bars before and I'm reliable. And," she continued breathlessly, rushing to a finish, "I can short order and mix drinks if you need it."

She looked away from Smitty, down at her hands clutched in her lap, watching the light glint off the plain gold wedding band. In the background, the singing man shifted into another song— the third? Fourth?—and she listened to the voice, so much prettier, really, than Paul's, but definitely similar.

Smitty and Kevin exchanged little shrugs. Kevin didn't care; he could handle the rush himself or use help, whatever. Business had been good, though, and as the neighborhood gentrified, as they were calling it, young people and couples were coming in, mixing well with the older regulars. He looked at Smitty and nodded.

The older man looked at her again, sitting quietly, almost like a child about to be bawled out. He liked the way she could shift from wide-eyed innocence to hands-off sultry without seeming to be aware of it. Maybe it was the night, maybe hearing Junior's tenor again, maybe just a wish to be young, but what the hell.

"Okay, Joyce, you got it. We'll start you on Monday, I guess. For now, let's make it from six 'til eleven, that'll be thirty hours a week with Saturdays, two-fifty an hour . . . that's seventy-five plus tips, a meal if you want it, how's that?"

They couldn't tell if she was laughing or crying. "Oh, that's fine, Mr.—Oh, I don't even know your name!"

"I'm Smitty. Kevin's the hulk behind the bar. Now, let's have a drink to celebrate. What'll you have?"

"If you could just put a little bourbon in with this Coke?"

Smitty faked a shiver, then laughed. "What in the hell do you call that?"

Before she could answer, Junior's voice boomed. "Smitty, my friend, you call that down home."

Joyce looked up at him. *Here we go, Lilah girl. It had to happen, didn't it?*

He took her hand in his, lifted it to his lips. "Sure is a pleasure to meet someone from down around home, ma'am, and welcome to the Harp & Lager."

"Why, thank you, *suh.*" She gave a mock bow with her head. "And it is shore a pleasure to make your acquaintance." She barely got through the sentence before the giggles overwhelmed her. They both broke down in laughter, leaving Kevin and Smitty to stare, dumbfounded.

"Sure, and this must be culture shock," was Kevin's reaction. It brought new gales of laughter from the couple.

"Joyce, if you can stop laughing for a minute, I'd like you to meet Junior. Junior, this is Joyce, known to her husband as Lilah. She's coming to work here on Monday."

The pretty blonde smiled. "Well, I guess I'd better get going. Paul'll be home soon and if'n I'm not there, there'll sure enough be hell to pay."

"Ain't that the truth, though." Junior smiled and offered his hand as Joyce got off the stool. "May I help you get a cab?"

"Thanks, but no. Actually, I've got one but my husband's driving it now." She made a low sound, somewhere between a sigh and a chuckle. "I'll just get a bus on Broadway; I don't have that far to go. See y'all Monday. And thanks." And with a wave to them all she was gone into the night.

Junior watched her walk to the corner and stand waiting for the light to change. As it did, and before she stepped into the street, she made a half turn and looked back, catching a hint of Junior's profile in the window. She smiled, trusting that he wouldn't see it in the dark, and began moving more quickly toward Broadway. It was only eleven blocks home, but she was hot and tired. And a little scared. But she was used to that, now.

•   •   •

It had started when she was fifteen, and took the job at the drive-in outside of Fort Bragg, North Carolina. That's all there was for her to do, really, serve food to soldiers with some time on their hands. They hadn't wanted her around the U.S.O.—she wasn't good enough—she wasn't well born, she was nothing, not even an Army brat. She'd tried at school, but her mother wanted her to work, bring some money in instead of wasting her time. As far as anyone was concerned, her future was set, she would be Mrs. Corporal Someoneorother and that was that.

She was a very pretty girl and the customers tipped her well and songs would be played for her, dedications on the local station, but most of the guys got grabby before they even said hello. She'd go out with them, get rides home, maybe neck a little. But she heard the cries and whimpers of too many bastards, including her older sister's twins, to go much further. The re-tread condoms they sold in the men's rooms weren't anything to put faith in, any more than the guys were. It was funny how they all shipped out the day after you put out for them.

What wasn't funny was sitting in the car in front of the small, white frame house with the J.P.'s sign on the lawn, waiting for your mother's fifth wedding ceremony to end. It wasn't funny, either, to be twenty-five and to have lost the guy you finally gave it up to. He was a townie, not a soldier, and now, four years later, he's marrying your own goddamned mother who's twenty-three years older than he is.

That night, after dropping her *parents* off at the bus station—they were moving to Elkton, Maryland, for some reason she neither understood nor questioned—she took a ride home from the drive-in with a good looking sergeant. He'd been sniffing around for a while, and she didn't much give a damn what happened.

Six months later, when he proposed, she didn't have to give it much thought. It was security, he had only a few years to go before retirement.

Within weeks she recognized her mistake. The walls of the trailer they had rented as their first home began to close in around her. Paul, her *husband*, the man who had sworn eternal love to her as they lay naked on the grass, was making it with the wife of a private three trailers down the row.

When she threw it up to him after work one night, dead tired and really not in the mood to go belly-to-belly with him, when she said, "Why don't you just trot down to Cindy if you want to get your rocks off," he beat her for the first time, punching blindly and telling her to mind her place, and as she fell bleeding to the floor he stopped and ran from the trailer. He came back two days later and Lilah knew she had won. She didn't know what she had won, but he was back; he probably did love her. That's just what love was like around the Army. Pretty stories were for the books and the rich.

With that confidence, and knowing that she was trapped, she took a lover. The satisfaction wasn't in the sex, but in the fact of doing it, in giving back to Paul even if he could only suspect. She knew enough to be careful. If the beating was any indication at all, he was capable of killing her.

So she'd wait for those nights when he had duty in town, or the unit was on maneuvers. There was a slim possibility of his slipping away to check up on her—they all seemed to do that regularly, all those loving husbands—but he had a pride in doing his job right. He owed the Army, he said. She'd never drive away with anyone, but would slip them notes, telling them where to meet her. She wasn't worried about being caught flirting: That was part of the job, you had to do it. That's where the tips came from.

It became easier to take lovers. At times—sweating and frustrated in the back of someone's car, or stretched naked on a blanket in some dark corner of Bragg—she couldn't believe that she was the same girl who had waited until she was twenty-one before losing her virginity in a town where the joke was that a virgin was a seven-year-old who ran faster than her father. Her father was gone long before she was seven. The one thing she could thank her mother for was that she had kept the stepfathers away. Some of her friends hadn't been that lucky. Lilah could laugh about that now, and about how she should have kept the boyfriend away from her mother.

Then Paul had gotten caught up in that brutality thing and managed to work a deal because there were a lot of people who owed him favors (including his commanding officer, though Paul would never know about that, that Lilah had taken care of that long before it was necessary) and she pushed him to move to New York, to get away from this town, and the Army. Hell, she was only thirty, maybe she could still make something of herself.

•   •   •

Since coming to New York she'd been straight. She'd wanted to go back to school, learn something, typing, anything. But the pressures here were different and money was a problem and here she was, still serving and flirting and waiting.

She got on the bus and sat up front near the driver, staring out of the windshield as they moved downtown. She brushed her hair back, ran her fingers though it. Smiled. *Junior.*

•   •   •

It was dark in the room, and quiet. The window over the bed was open in an attempt to catch some breeze. The thin curtains waved, brushing the face of the man turning restlessly beneath them.

"Ya gotta pay the piper, Gina."

You hear the curtain being drawn and soft sounds and then a woman crying saying yes saying no not that and the sound of a slap and you reach under your pillow for your new knife and hold it while the woman cries and says hush Paulieboy you'll wake the child and the man says so what he can join the party and did he used to suck on these this way and oh Gina and you want the food don't you and you take the knife and creep silently from the bed in the darkness and walk to the curtain you can't see but feel and crawl under it and the light is reflecting on the woman's body and the skinny kid from the store is pulling her beautiful hair that smells so good when she lets you play with it and he's pushing her down in front of him like in church and it isn't the same as when you saw mommy and daddy playing and the crying is wrong and with all the strength of your five-year-old body you leap at the man crying out your hunger and fear and you strike at the man but the knife doesn't penetrate you're too weak the man is too strong and he pushes you away knocking you into a wall with such force that the whole house shakes and you are crying and your mother is screaming and the knife is on the floor and the man is holding the knife and mommy is pushing him while people run from all over and the man turns to push your mother away so he can get you you know he wants to get you and the knife probes deep into your mother's breast and you can't see but know that her body is sticky with red blood and you see him jump naked through the open window while people chase him screaming and it is getting darker and someone giggles because they think it's funny that the little naked boy is lying on the naked body of his mother her hair still smells so sweet *and you're being held and you cry while an old woman holds you to her and you cry some more as she croons and soon you are asleep.*

And when you wake again it is because of the screams and they're your own and it is still night always night but twenty-five years later and you think you see mommy but now she's blonde and your age and walking across the room to you and you reach out and she's gone but you can smell her and someone pulls you off the bed and is smothering you with a pillow and you scream and scream until there is a knock at the door and you are awake in New York and sweating and shaking and the dream came back but almost ended differently.

Junior Waltham spent the rest of the night pacing. And thinking of Joyce.

•   •   •

Joyce was quickly comfortable at the Harp & Lager. The regulars, the older, almost-beaten-but-definitely-not-out, men took to her warmth and patter. Sometimes Paul would come in with her, at about five, before she had to start, and they accepted him, laughing along with him and promising to keep an eye on his girl.

The young crowd also liked her, especially when she and Junior would go into a duet off the country charts. Paul was always gone by the time Junior would show up, for which Smitty was eternally grateful. Reegan was a dangerous man, you could see it in the way he moved, the way he was always watching what was going on, who was coming in. No, the last thing Smitty needed was those two bulls challenging each other. Reegan might win the horn-locking, but if Smitty was any judge, and he was, he'd lost the woman. It was better than *Dallas*, and more dangerous.

Then, one rainy Tuesday night in August, after she'd been there for three months, and after walking her to the bus stop, Junior called her Lilah for the first time.

They stood in a doorway, waiting for the bus, holding hands and looking at each other.

"Lilah," he said, "Lilah, I can't remember ever being this happy."

"Me, too, hon." She pulled him to her in a tight hug, stood on tiptoe to kiss him lightly on the lips, then more searchingly, longingly. A first kiss.

"Lilah, do you think maybe, if I took a day off . . . ?"

"Yes."

"Thursday? If I give the boss some notice, I'm sure he'll say okay."

"Yes."

"Where?"

Where? Oh it would have been so easy back at Bragg. The woods, places to get lost. Where? Where?

"Look, sugar, why don't you come over about eleven. Paul'll be at the bank, right, and he don't get home until about four."

"I don't know. I'm scared of coming to your house, Lilah." Junior stepped away from her and moved out into the rain, looking up Broadway. He could see the lights of her bus. "You're sure it'll be okay?"

"Oh yes, love, yes. It'll be fine."

He started back to the Harp, whistling in the rain, waving to people on the way. A cab drove slowly past him, sending up a small spray from the puddles in the street.

It was still raining on Wednesday, and the Harp was steamy with heat and humidity. Junior got there early, bouncing. As he came in he saw Lilah standing next to some big guy sitting at one of the tables, his arm around her waist, hers around his neck. He moved moved quietly to a stool at the bar and watched her in the mirror. Kevin came down to him quickly, putting a beer up and warning him with his eyes.

Lilah turned her head to listen to something being called out by one of the regulars and froze as she saw Junior's face in the backbar mirror. Paul felt her stiffen and looked up at her. "Somethin' wrong honey?"

"No, no. Just a chill, someone walking over my grave." She ran her fingers through his hair. "I'm okay, really." Moving free, she looked at her watch. "I'd better get ready, it's almost six."

"Sure, I'll just have another brew, then hit the road."

Lilah leaned over, passed a kiss at his face, her eyes locked on the mirror. *He suspects something.* She felt it, heard it in his voice. *That's why he's started coming to the tavern, like when he used to pick me up at the drive-in.*

She went into the kitchen to get her apron, feeling Paul's eyes on her back and Junior's watching from the bar. She didn't come out again until her husband had gone.

Junior moved to the pool table, setting up some trick shots. He smiled at her, winked, and went back to the game. As she walked by behind him, brushing him with her hand, she heard him kiss the air. *Everything was going to be fine. Everything.*

When she left that night, she waved him off. Across the street, at the corner, she saw the yellow Checker parked, its off-duty sign lit. *He knew.*

"I'll call you in the morning, okay? Just another twelve hours, honey, that's all. Just don't walk out with me now, stay away from the door. Please."

"Sure, but—"

"Don't argue with Momma, sugar. Listen," she said, seeing the hurt on his face, "I think Paul's parked across the street, so just stay put and I'll see you tomorrow."

"I love you, Lilah."

"And I, you." She looked at him and he thought he saw tears beginning to pool in her eyes. But that must have been a trick of the light.

She walked into the night, feeling the drizzle coat her face. It hid her tears. The cab door opened and Paul waved to her. "Cab, lady?"

She managed a smile and hoped her fear stayed inside, hoped she'd be alive to love Junior in the morning.

The ride was quiet, uneventful; lethal. When she asked, Paul just said that he was nearby and knew she was getting off, so why not give the old lady a lift, right? He dropped her off in front of their apartment building. "See you later, sugar."

She opened the door at his first, tentative knock, kissing him and leading him into the apartment. He opened his mouth to speak, and she put a finger on his lips, shaking her head.

Across the street, Paulieboy Reegan sat in the coffee shop, as he had every morning this week, and watched the two figures move across the room. He reached into the flight bag and felt the heavy weight of the gun as his fingers closed around the butt, and he clicked the safety off and on. There was time; he called for a refill.

Light flickered through the room as the drapes moved, but it was dark. The couple in the bed were freckled with sweat. Junior's eyes were closed and he was feeling comfortable listening to Lilah's dream. There was a scraping sound at the door and comfort hid under the bed, flew out the window.

Junior was up as the front door slammed. Lilah lay stiffly, hands on her ears, as if not hearing the sounds would erase what they meant. Junior moved to a corner so anyone entering would not see him. The light from the hallway shone on yesterday's nightmare.

Junior stiffened, became a shadow. Reegan filled the door, his screams building from a whisper.

"Bitch! Christ, you fuckin' bitch. In my bed!"

Then he was slapping the crying woman in the bed, beating at her head, his voice a deluge of sounds as he beat at Lilah who screamed and covered her head with her arms and Paulieboy pulled his pistol while Junior went silently to the drapes which he felt but could not see and heard Reegan scream: *"Where is he? Let him join the party,"* and Junior whispered, *Paulieboy!* Then there was a gunshot and Junior screamed now: *MOMMA!"*

There was sudden quiet punctuated by labored breathing. Reegan moved from the bedside, going toward the window while Lilah rose behind him and Junior couldn't see but knew her body was sticky with red blood and as Paulieboy lunged for the son of the woman he murdered, the woman he married pushed him and the drapes tore as he grabbed for them and Reegan went through the window, crushing himself five stories down.

Junior felt the drapes pulled from his hands, felt a naked woman with sweet-smelling hair press against him, but there were no other sounds until the shouts from the street began and Junior knew that he would sleep now, always.

HORN MAN

Clark Howard

*W*hen Dix stepped off the Greyhound bus in New Orleans, old Rainey was waiting for him near the terminal entrance. He looked just the same as Dix remembered him. Old Rainey had always looked old, since Dix had known him, ever since Dix had been a little boy. He had skin like black saddle leather and patches of cotton-white hair, and his shoulders were round and stooped. When he was contemplating something, he chewed on the inside of his cheeks, pushing his pursed lips in and out as if he were revving up for speech. He was doing that when Dix walked up to him.

"Hey, Rainey."

Rainey blinked surprise and then his face split into a wide smile of perfect, gleaming teeth. "Well, now. Well, well, well, now." He looked Dix up and down. "They give you that there suit of clothes?"

Dix nodded. "Everyone gets a suit of clothes if they done more than a year." Dix's eyes, the lightest blue possible without

---

Clark Howard's Animals *may just be one of the best stories ever published in the crime field. I tried to get it for this anthology but another anthologist got there first.* Horn Man *is, in a very different way, its equal. Howard, who has written everything from westerns to category action novels to major bestsellers, is a man nobody mentions when discussing the best writers in the field. It may be that he is punished for limiting his outlet to short stories. The fact that many of them are brilliant seems not to matter. Yet long after some of the more amiable but less serious practitioners of the craft are gone, Howard's stories will remain.*

being gray, hardened just enough for Rainey to notice. "And I sure done more than a year," he added.

"That's the truth," Rainey said. He kept the smile on his face and changed the subject as quickly as possible. "I got you a room in the Quarter. Figured that's where you'd want to stay."

Dix shrugged. "It don't matter no more."

"It will," Rainey said with the confidence of years. "It will when you hear the music again."

Dix did not argue the point. He was confident that none of it mattered. Not the music, not the French Quarter, none of it. Only one thing mattered to Dix.

"Where is she, Rainey?" he asked. "Where's Madge?"

"I don't rightly know," Rainey said.

Dix studied him for a moment. He was sure Rainey was lying. But it didn't matter. There were others who would tell him.

They walked out of the terminal, the stooped old black man and the tall, prison-hard white man with a set to his mouth and a canvas zip-bag containing all his worldly possessions. It was late afternoon: the sun was almost gone and the evening coolness was coming in. They walked toward the Quarter, Dix keeping his long-legged pace slow to accommodate old Rainey.

Rainey glanced at Dix several times as they walked, chewing inside his mouth and working up to something. Finally he said, "You been playing at all while you was in?"

Dix shook his head. "Not for a long time. I did a little the first year. Used to dry play, just with my mouthpiece. After a while, though, I gave it up. They got a different kind of music over there in Texas. Stompin' music. Not my style." Dix forced a grin at old Rainey. "I ever kill a man again, I'll be sure I'm on *this* side of the Louisiana line."

Rainey scowled. "You know you ain't never killed nobody, boy," he said harshly. "You know it wudn't you that done it. It was *her*."

Dix stopped walking and locked eyes with old Rainey. "How long have you knowed me?" he asked.

"Since you was eight months old," Rainey said. "You know that. Me and my sistuh, we worked for your grandmamma, Miz Jessie DuChatelier. She had the finest gentlemen's house in the Quarter. Me and my sistuh, we cleaned and cooked for Miz

Jessie. And took care of you after your own poor mamma took sick with the consumption and died—"

"Anyway, you've knowed me since I was less than one, and now I'm *forty*-one."

Rainey's eyes widened. "Naw," he said, grinning again, "you ain't that old. Naw."

"Forty-one, Rainey. I been gone sixteen years. I got twenty-five, remember? And I done sixteen."

Sudden worry erased Rainey's grin. "Well, if you forty-one how old that make *me*?"

"About two hundred. I don't know. You must be seventy or eighty. Anyway, listen to me now. In all the time you've knowed me, have I ever let anybody make a fool out of me?"

Rainey shook his head. "Never. No way."

"That's right. And I'm not about to start now. But if word got around that I done sixteen years for a killing that was somebody else's, I'd look like the biggest fool that ever walked the levee, wouldn't I?"

"I reckon so," Rainey allowed.

"Then don't ever say again that I didn't do it. Only one person alive knows for certain positive that I didn't do it. And I'll attend to her myself. Understand?"

Rainey chewed the inside of his cheeks for a moment, then asked, "What you fixin' to do about her?"

Dix's light-blue eyes hardened again. "Whatever I have to do, Rainey," he replied.

Rainey shook his head in slow motion. "Lord, Lord, Lord," he whispered.

Old Rainey went to see Gaston that evening at Tradition Hall, the jazz emporium and restaurant that Gaston owned in the Quarter. Gaston was slick and dapper. For him, time had stopped in 1938. He still wore spats.

"How does he look?" Gaston asked old Rainey.

"He *look* good," Rainey said. "He *talk* bad." Rainey leaned close to the white club-owner. "He fixin' to kill that woman. Sure as God made sundown."

Gaston stuck a sterling-silver toothpick in this mouth. "He know where she is?"

"I don't think so," said Rainey. "Not yet."

"*You* know where she is?"

"Lastest I heard, she was living over on Burgundy Street with some doper."

Gaston nodded his immaculately shaved and lotioned chin. "Correct. The doper's name is LeBeau. He's young. I think he keeps her around to take care of him when he's sick." Gaston examined his beautifully manicured nails. "Does Dix have a lip?"

Rainey shook his head. "He said he ain't played in a while. But a natural like him, he can get his lip back in no time a'tall."

"Maybe," said Gaston.

"He can," Rainey insisted.

"Has he got a horn?"

"Naw. I watched him unpack his bag and I didn't see no horn. So I axed him about it. He said after a few years of not playing, he just give it away. To some cowboy he was in the Texas pen with."

Gaston sighed. "He should have killed that fellow on this side of the state line. If he'd done the killing in Louisiana, he would have went to the pen at Angola. They play good jazz at Angola. Eddie Lumm is up there. You remember Eddie Lumm? Clarinetist. Learned to play from Frank Teschemacher and Jimmie Noone. Eddie killed his old lady. So now he blows at Angola. They play good jazz at Angola."

Rainey didn't say anything. He wasn't sure if Gaston thought Dix had really done the killing or not. Sometimes Gaston *played* like he didn't know a thing, just to see if somebody *else* knew it. Gaston was smart. Smart enough to help keep Dix out of trouble if he was a mind. Which was what old Rainey was hoping for.

Gaston drummed his fingertips silently on the table where they sat. "So. You think Dix can get his lip back with no problem, is that right?"

"Tha's right. He can."

"He planning to come around and see me?"

"I don't know. He probably set on finding that woman first. Then he might not be *able* to come see you."

"Well, see if you can get him to come see me first. Tell him I've got something for him. Something I've been saving for him. Will you do that?"

"You bet." Rainey got up from the table. "I'll go do it right now."

George Tennell was big and beefy and mean. Rumor had it that he had once killed two men by smashing their heads together with such force that he literally knocked their brains out. He had been a policeman for thirty years, first in the colored section, which was the only place he could work in the old days, and now in the *Vieux Carré*, the Quarter, where he was detailed to keep the peace to whatever extent it was possible. He had no family, claimed no friends. The Quarter was his home as well as his job. The only thing in the world he admitted to loving was jazz.

That was why, every night at seven, he sat at a small corner table in Tradition Hall and ate dinner while he listened to the band tune their instruments and warm up. Most nights, Gaston joined him later for a liqueur. Tonight he joined him before dinner.

"Dix got back today," he told the policeman. "Remember Dix?"

Tennell nodded. "Horn man. Killed a fellow in a motel room just across the Texas line. Over a woman named Madge Noble."

"That's the one. Only there's some around don't think he did it. There's some around think *she* did it."

"Too bad he couldn't have found twelve of those people for his jury."

"He didn't have no jury, George. Quit laying back on me. You remember it as well as I do. One thing you'd *never* forget is a good horn man."

Tennell's jaw shifted to the right a quarter of an inch, making his mouth go crooked. The band members were coming out of the back now and moving around on the bandstand, unsnapping instrument cases, inserting mouthpieces, straightening chairs. They were a mixed lot—black, white, and combinations; clean-shaven and goateed; balding and not; clear-eyed and strung out. None of them was under fifty—the oldest was the trumpet player, Luther Dodd, who was eighty-six. Like Louis Armstrong, he had learned to blow at the elbow of Joe "King" Oliver, the great cornetist. His Creole-style trumpet playing was unmatched in New Orleans. Watching him near the age when he would surely die was agony for the jazz purists who frequented Tradition Hall.

Gaston studied George Tennell as the policeman watched Luther Dodd blow out the spit plug of his gleaming Balfour trumpet and loosen up his stick-brittle fingers on the valves. Gaston saw in Tennell's eyes that odd look of a man who truly worshipped traditional jazz music, who felt it down in the pit of himself just like the old men who played it, but who had never learned to play himself. It was a look that had the mix of love and sadness and years gone by. It was the only look that ever turned Tennell's eyes soft.

"You know how long I been looking for a horn man to take Luther's place?" Gaston asked. "A straight year. I've listened to a couple dozen guys from all over. Not a one of them could play traditional. Not a one." He bobbed his chin at Luther Dodd. "His fingers are like old wood, and so's his heart. He could go on me any night. And if he does, I'll have to shut down. Without a horn man, there's no Creole sound, no tradition at all. Without a horn, this place of mine, which is the last of the great jazz emporiums, will just give way to" —Gaston shrugged helplessly, "—whatever. Disco music, I suppose."

A shudder circuited George Tennell's spine, but he gave no outward sign of it. His body was absolutely still, his hands resting motionlessly on the snow-white tablecloth, eyes steadily fixed on Luther Dodd. Momentarily the band went into its first number, *Lafayette,* played Kansas City style after the way of Bennie Moten. The music pulsed out like spurts of water, each burst overlapping the one before it to create an even wave of sound that flooded the big room. Because Kansas City style was so rhythmic and highly danceable, some of the early diners immediately moved onto the dance floor and fell in with the music.

Ordinarily, Tennell liked to watch people dance while he ate; the moving bodies lent emphasis to the music he loved so much, music he had first heard from the window of the St. Pierre Colored Orphanage on Decatur Street when he had been a boy; music he had grown up with and would have made his life a part of if he had not been so completely talentless, so inept that he could not even read sharps and flats. But tonight he paid no attention to the couples out in front of the bandstand. He concentrated only on Luther Dodd and the old horn man's breath intake as he played. It was clear to Tennell that Luther was struggling for breath, fighting for every note he blew, utilizing every cubic inch of lung power that his old body could marshal.

After watching Luther all the way through *Lafayette*, and half-way through *Davenport Blues*, Tennell looked across the table at Gaston and nodded.

"All right," he said simply. "All right."

For the first time ever Tennell left the club without eating dinner.

As Dix walked along with old Rainey toward Gaston's club, Rainey kept pointing out places to him that he had not exactly forgotten, but had not remembered in a long time.

"That house there," Rainey said, "was where Paul Mares was born back in nineteen-and-oh-one. He's the one formed the original New Orleans Rhythm Kings. He only lived to be forty-eight but he was one of the best horn men of all time."

Dix would remember, not necessarily the person himself but the house and the story of the person and how good he was. He had grown up on those stories, gone to sleep by them as a boy, lived the lives of the men in them many times over as he himself was being taught to blow trumpet by Rozell "The Lip" Page when Page was already past sixty and he, Dix was only eight. Later, when Page died, Dix's education was taken over by Shepherd Norden and Blue Johnny Meadows, the two alternating as his teacher between their respective road tours. With Page, Norden, and Meadows in his background, it was no wonder that Dix could blow traditional.

"Right up the street there," Rainey said as they walked, "is where Wingy Manone was born in nineteen-and-oh-four. His given name was Joseph, but after his accident ever'body taken to calling him 'Wingy.' The accident was, he fell under a street car and lost his right arm. But that boy didn't let a little thing like that worry him none, no sir. He learned to play trumpet *left-handed*, and *one-handed*. And he was *good*. Lord he was good."

They walked along Dauphin and Chartes and Royal. All around them were the French architecture and grillework and statuary and vines and moss that made the *Vieux Carré* a world unto itself, a place of subtle sights, sounds, and smells—black and white and fish and age—that no New Orleans tourist, no Superdome visitor, no casual observer, could ever experience, because to experience was to understand, and understanding of the Quarter could not be acquired, it had to be lived.

"Tommy Ladnier, he used to live right over there," Rainey said, "right up on the second floor. He lived there when he came here from his hometown of Mandeville, Loozey-ana. Poor Tommy, he had a short life too, only thirty-nine years. But it was a good life. He played with King Oliver and Fletcher Henderson and Sidney Bechet. Yessir, he got in some good licks."

When they got close enough to Tradition Hall to hear the music, at first faintly, then louder, clearer, Rainey stopped talking. He wanted Dix to hear the music, to *feel* the sound of it as it wafted out over Pirate's Alley and the Café du Monde and Congo Square (they called it Beauregard Square now, but Rainey refused to recognize the new name). Instinctively, Rainey knew that it was important for the music to get back into Dix, to saturate his mind and catch in his chest and tickle his stomach. There were some things in Dix that needed to be washed out, some bad things, and Rainey was certain that the music would help. A good purge was always healthy.

Rainey was grateful, as they got near enough to define melody, that *Sweet Georgia Brown* was being played. It was a good melody to come home to.

They walked on, listening, and after a while Dix asked, "Who's on horn?"

"Luther Dodd."

"Don't sound like Luther. What's the matter with him?"

Rainey waved one hand resignedly. "Old. Dying. I 'spect."

They arrived at the Hall and went inside. Gaston met them with a smile. "Dix," he said, genuinely pleased, "it's good to see you." His eyes flickered over Dix. "The years have been good to you. Trim. Lean. No gray hair. How's your lip?"

"I don't have a lip no more, Mr. Gaston," said Dix. "Haven't had for years."

"But he can get it back quick enough," Rainey put in. "He gots a natural lip."

"I don't play no more, Mr. Gaston," Dix told the club owner.

"That's too bad," Gaston said. He bobbed his head toward the stairs. "Come with me. I want to show you something."

Dix and Rainey followed Gaston upstairs to his private office. The office was furnished the way Gaston dressed—old-style, roaring Twenties. There was even a wind-up Victrola in the corner.

Gaston worked the combination of a large, ornate floor vault and pulled its big-tiered door open. From somewhere in its dark recess he withdrew a battered trumpet case, one of the very old kind with heavy brass fittings on the corners and, one knew, real velvet, not felt, for lining. Placing it gently in the center of his desk, Gaston carefully opened the snaplocks and lifted the top. Inside, indeed on real velvet, deep-purple real velvet, was a gleaming, silver, hand-etched trumpet. Dix and Rainey stared at it in unabashed awe.

"Know who it once belonged to?" Gaston asked.

Neither Dix nor Rainey replied. They were mesmerized by the instrument. Rainey had not seen one like it in fifty years. Dix had *never* seen one like it; he had only heard stories about the magnificent silver horns that the quadroons made of contraband silver carefully hidden away after the War Between the States. Because the silver cache had not, as it was supposed to, been given over to the Federal army as part of the reparations levied against the city, the quadroons, during the Union occupation, had to be very careful what they did with it. Selling it for value was out of the question. Using it for silver service, candlesticks, walking canes, or any other of the more obvious uses would have attracted the notice of a Union informer. But letting it lie dormant, even though it was safer as such, was intolerable to the quads, who refused to let a day go by without circumventing one law or another.

So they used the silver to plate trumpets and cornets and slide trombones that belonged to the tabernacle musicians who were just then beginning to experiment with the old *Sammsamounn* tribal music that would eventually mate with work songs and prison songs and gospels, and evolve into traditional blues, which would evolve into traditional, or Dixie-style, jazz.

"Look at the initials," Gaston said, pointing to the top of the bell. Dix and Rainey peered down at three initials etched in the silver: BRB.

"Lord have mercy," Rainey whispered. Dix's lips parted as if he too intended to speak, but no words sounded.

"That's right," Gaston said. "Blind Ray Blount. The first, the best, the *only*. Nobody has ever touched the sounds he created. That man hit notes nobody ever heard before—or since. He was the master."

"Amen," Rainey said. He nodded his head toward Dix. "Can he touch it?"

"Go ahead," Gaston said to Dix.

Like a pilgrim to Mecca touching the holy shroud, Dix ever so lightly placed the tips of three fingers on the silver horn. As he did, he imagined he could feel the touch left there by the hands of the amazing blind horn man who had started the great blues evolution in a patch of town that later became Storyville. He imagined that—

"It's yours if you want it," Gaston said. "All you have to do is pick it up and go downstairs and start blowing."

Dix wet his suddenly dry lips. "Tomorrow I—"

"Not tomorrow," Gaston said. "Tonight. Now."

"Take it, boy," Rainey said urgently.

Dix frowned deeply, his eyes narrowing as if he felt physical pain. He swallowed, trying to push an image out of his mind; an image he had clung to for sixteen years. "I can't tonight—"

"Tonight or never," Gaston said firmly.

"For God's sake, boy, take it!" said old Rainey.

But Dix could not. The image of Madge would not let him.

Dix shook his head violently, as if to rid himself of devils, and hurried from the room.

Rainey ran after him and caught up with him a block from the Hall. "Don't do it," he pleaded. "Hear me now. I'm an old man and I know I ain't worth nothin' to nobody, but I'm begging you, boy, please, please, please don't do it. I ain't never axed you for nothing in my whole life, but I'm axing you for this: *please* don't do it."

"I got to," Dix said quietly. "It ain't that I want to; I *got* to."

"But why, boy? *Why?*"

"Because we made a promise to each other," Dix said. "That night in that Texas motel room, the man Madge was with had told her he was going to marry her. He'd been telling her that for a long time. But he was already married and kept putting off leaving his wife. Finally Madge had enough of it. She asked me to come to her room between sets. I knew she was doing it to make him jealous, but it didn't matter none to me. I'd been crazy about her for so long that I'd do anything she asked me to, and she knew it.

"So between sets I slipped across the highway to where she had her room. But he was already there. I could hear through the transom that he was roughing her up some, but the door was locked and I couldn't get in. Then I heard a shot and everything got quiet. A minute later Madge opened the door and let me in. The man was laying across the bed dying. Madge started bawling and saying how they would put her in the pen and how she wouldn't be able to stand it, she'd go crazy and kill herself.

"It was then I asked her if she'd wait for me if I took the blame for her. She promised me she would. And I promised her I'd come back to her." Dix sighed quietly. "That's what I'm doing, Rainey—keeping my promise."

"And what going to happen if she ain't kept *hers*?" Rainey asked.

"Mamma Rulat asked me the same thing this afternoon when I asked her where Madge was at." Mamma Rulat was an octaroon fortuneteller who always knew where everyone in the Quarter lived.

"What did you tell her?"

"I told her I'd do what I had to do. That's all a man *can* do, Rainey."

Dix walked away, up a dark side street. Rainey, watching him go, shook his head in the anguish of the aged and helpless.

"Lord, Lord, Lord—"

The house on Burgundy Street had once been a grand mansion with thirty rooms and a tiled French courtyard with a marble fountain in its center. It had seen nobility and aristocracy and great generals come and go with elegant, genteel ladies on their arms. Now the thirty rooms were rented individually with hotplate burners for light cooking, and the only ladies who crossed the courtyard were those of the New Orleans night.

A red light was flashing atop a police car when Dix got there, and uniformed policemen were blocking the gate into the courtyard. There was a small curious crowd talking about what happened.

"A doper named LeBeau," someone said. "He's been shot."

"I heared it," an old man announced. "I heared the shot."

"That's where it happened, that window right up there—"

Dix looked up, but as he did another voice said, "They're bringing him out now!"

Two morgue attendants wheeled a sheet-covered gurney

across the courtyard and lifted it into the back of a black panel truck. Several policemen, led by big beefy George Tennell, brought a woman out and escorted her to the car with the flashing red light. Dix squinted, focusing on her in the inadequate courtyard light. He frowned. Madge's mother, he thought, his mind going back two decades. What's Madge's mother got to do with this?

Then he remembered. Madge's mother was dead. She had died five years after he had gone to the pen.

Then who—?

Madge?

Yes, it *was* her. It was Madge. Older, as he was. Not a girl any more, as he was not a boy any more. For a moment he found it difficult to equate the woman in the courtyard with the memory in his mind. But it was Madge, all right.

Dix tried to push forward, to get past the gate into the courtyard, but two policemen held him back. George Tennell saw the altercation and came over.

"She's under arrest, mister," Tennell told Dix. Can't nobody talk to her but a lawyer right now."

"What's she done anyhow?" Dix asked.

"Killed her boyfriend," said Tennell. "Shot him with this."

He showed Dix a pearl-handled over-and-under Derringer two-shot.

"Her boyfriend?"

Tennell nodded. "Young feller. 'Bout twenty-five. Neighbors say she was partial to young fellers. Some women are like that."

"Who says she shot him?"

"I do. I was in the building at the time, on another matter. I heard the shot. Matter of fact, I was the first one to reach the body. Few minutes later she come waltzing in. Oh, she put on a good act, all right, like she didn't even know what happened. But I found the gun in her purse myself."

By now the other officers had Madge Noble in the police car and were waiting for Tennell. He slipped the Derringer into his coat pocket and hitched up his trousers. Jutting his big jaw out an inch, he fixed Dix in a steady gaze.

"If she's a friend of yours, don't count on her being around for a spell. She'll do a long time for this."

Tennell walked away, leaving Dix still outside the gate. Dix waited there, watching, as the police car came through to the street. He tried to catch a glimpse of Madge as it passed, but there was not enough light in the back seat where they had her. As soon as the car left, the people who had gathered around began to leave too.

Soon Dix was the only one standing there.

At midnight George Tennell was back at his usual table in Tradition Hall for the dinner he had missed earlier. Gaston came over and joined him. For a few minutes they sat in silence, watching Dix up on the bandstand. He was blowing the silver trumpet that had once belonged to Blind Ray Blount; sitting next to the aging Luther Dodd; jumping in whenever he could as they played *Tailspin Blues,* then *Tank Town Bump,* then *Everybody Loves My Baby*.

"Sounds like he'll be able to get his lip back pretty quick," Tennell observed.

"Sure," said Gaston. "He's a natural. Rozell Page was his first teacher, you know."

"No, I didn't know that."

"Sure." Gaston adjusted the celluloid collar he wore, and turned the diamond stickpin in his tie. "What about the woman?" he asked.

Tennell shrugged. "She'll get twenty years. Probably do ten or eleven."

Gaston thought for a moment, then said, "That should be time enough. After ten or eleven years nothing will matter to him except the music. Don't you think?"

"It won't even take that long," Tennell guessed. "Not for him."

Up on the bandstand the men who played traditional went into *Just a Closer Walk with Thee*.

And sitting on the sawdust floor behind the bandstand, old Rainey listened with happy tears in his eyes.

SHOOTING MATCH

A "Joe Hannibal" Story
Wayne D. Dundee

"*L*et me tell you how it is in pro wrestling,"
The Bomber was saying. "Ninety percent of what you see on
TV is hokum, just like everybody figures. That's the buildup,
the ballyhoo, the advertising that sells the tickets to the live
matches all across the country. In the arenas, though, it's a little
different story. Oh, there's plenty of hokum there, too, because
the boys know they have to give the folks a good show in order to
keep them coming back. But most of the time, especially in your
top contender matches, it truly is the better man who gets his
hand raised in victory."

I nodded tolerantly. "Thanks for the sports lesson, professor.
Now what about this 'shooting match' you mentioned?"

"A shooting match," The Bomber explained, "is an insider's
term for the one kind of match where there is absolutely no hokum. No gimmicks, no showboating, and usually no holds
barred. Just two guys flat out trying to beat each other."

"You mean a grudge match?"

He made a face. "So-called grudge matches are as common as
jock itch. You get a couple hundred of them every year, each

Wayne Dundee *is just starting out. He publishes a magazine of hard-boiled fiction called,
appropriately enough,* Hard-Boiled. *He also writes. To date he has sold several short stories and he is working on a novel whose first hundred pages seem certain to win him nomina-
tion for a* "Shamus" *and* "Edgar." *He writes about the working class with tough but
wary respect and not a teardrop of sentimentality (Rocky Balboa please note).*

one carefully planned by some promoter and milked for all it's worth on a dozen different cards in a dozen different towns. A shooting match is a grudge match, yeah, because the guys involved have some kind of beef to settle—but it's the real thing."

I turned to the third person in the room and said, "And your husband is going to be involved in an upcoming shooting match, is that it, Mrs. McGurk?"

Lori McGurk was a delicately pretty woman, thirtyish, with straw-colored hair, a cupid's bow mouth, and wide, trusting eyes. The three of us—Lori, The Bomber, and myself—were seated in the basement office of The Bomb Shelter, the State Street bar Bomber had purchased upon his retirement from the grunt-and-groan circuit and turned into one of Rockford's most popular watering holes. It was half past ten in the morning and overhead we could hear muffled footfalls and the occasional scrape of a barstool as Liz Grimaldi, Bomber's Gal Friday, took care of the light mid-morning drinking crowd. The Bomber, by the way, is Bomber Brannigan; former pro boxer and wrestler and nowadays frequent friend in need to a certain hard-drinking private eye whose bar tab regularly exceeds his accounts received.

"That's right," Lori said in response to my question. "My Tommy steps into the ring this coming Friday night against El Bandido. Like Bomber says, there won't be any choreographed moves or crowd-pumping antics. Their sole intent is to try and destroy each other."

"This is all very interesting, it really is," I said. "But where do I fit in?"

The Bomber and Lori exchanged glances and some unseen signal passed between them that delegated the task of explanation to her. She took a deep breath, cleared her throat, and said, "I think someone is trying to force Tommy to throw the match."

I laughed out loud. I couldn't help it. I cut it short, however, when I saw that I was the only one who found any humor in what had been said. The Bomber scowled at me and Lori looked indignant. I weighed the idea of the whole thing being a put-on and decided it wasn't.

"Sorry," I said, somewhat lamely. "I guess the thought of a pro wrestler taking a dive just doesn't sound too serious to me. With all due respect to your husband's profession, Mrs. McGurk, and in spite of what my friend The Bomber says about the best man getting his hand raised and all . . . Well, let's face it, we all know there are a heck of a lot of prearranged matches in the wrestling game. I don't see where one more is anything to get very concerned over."

"You have no right to say that," Lori McGurk said with her chin thrust out defiantly. "You don't know my Tommy. You don't know how important all of this is to him."

I sighed, starting to wither under Bomber's glare as well as from Lori's rebuttal. "I guess you're right," I said. "I don't know any of those things. I shouldn't have laughed."

"Damn right you shouldn't have," The Bomber growled.

I shot him a look that said, "thanks, pal," then turned to Lori again. "Let's start over. When you say someone is trying to 'force' your husband to throw the match, that implies a threat of some kind has been made."

"There have been phone calls. They started a couple weeks ago, just after the match with El Bandido had been signed. I never tried to listen in or anything, so I don't know exactly what was said. But Tommy was always very upset afterward, I could tell even though he tried to hide it from me. Those calls left him moody, even surly at times. If you knew Tommy, you'd know how out of character that is for him. And then he came up with the suggestion that Tommy Jr. and I spend some time with my folks down in Missouri. He made up some silly excuse about feeling guilty because I hadn't seen them often enough in the past few years, but by then I'd already started to put two and two together. Whoever was making those calls—those threats—must have tried to apply extra pressure by threatening Tommy Jr. and I."

"So you never went to Missouri?"

"Oh, I went all right. But I could only stand it for one day. I kept imagining all sorts of terrible things that might be happening up here. I decided a wife's place was at her husband's side, no matter what. So I left Little Tommy with Mom and Pop and hightailed it back. I drove all night. On the way, I thought of The Bomber and came straight to him for help. I haven't been home yet. I'm . . . not quite ready to face Tommy."

"That's why I called you, Joe," The Bomber said. "I know the wrestling game inside and out, but you're the experienced detective. I figure it's going to take both of us to get to the bottom of this."

"What's your connection with McGurk?" I wanted to know. "Why did Lori come to you?"

"A few years back, when I was still wrestling and Tommy was just starting out, I took him under my wing for awhile and sort of showed him the ropes."

"Kept him from getting his block knocked off during those first couple years, the way Tommy tells it," Lori put in.

The Bomber shrugged. "A lot of the veteran wrestlers get a big kick out of intimidating rookies. They don't mean any harm, it's just one of their roughhouse ways of having fun. But they leave some of those boys so battered and discouraged in the early going that they drop out of the business without really giving it a fair shot. Tommy was too nice a kid and too talented for me to stand by and risk letting that happen to him."

Lori beamed. "Isn't he just a big teddy bear?"

I chuckled. "Oh, yeah, I've often heard him described just that way."

The Bomber blushed furiously. "Knock it off, you two. How about it, Joe? You willing to help with this thing?"

"I'll be happy to pay your regular fee, Mr. Hannibal," Lori said, bringing those damn trusting eyes into play.

I waved a hand. "Don't worry about that," I said. I looked from one of them to the other, then heaved another sigh. "All right, count me in. It still sounds like a crazy deal, but I'm in because this big jerk—" I jabbed a thumb to indicate The Bomber— "is going to poke around with or without me. And without me, he just might get his teddy bear ass chopped off."

•　•　•

Alex Mekapolis was a dapper little guy in his early sixties. He looked more like a distinguished old stage actor than how I would have imagined a wrestling promoter. No chewed cigar stub or baggy-in-the-seat trousers, instead razor cut snow white hair, a sunlamp tan, and a five hundred dollar pinstripe suit.

"Bomber Brannigan, as I live and breathe!" he exclaimed when The Bomber and I were ushered into his small, neat office. He got to his feet and came around the end of the desk with outstretched right hand. "Damned if you don't look fit enough to climb back into the ring this very minute."

The Bomber grinned. "You making me an offer, Al?"

"You know me. I'm ready to make the whole wide world an offer if it would just stop and listen."

They laughed and pumped hands vigorously.

Mekapolis' gaze fell on me. "What've you got here? A protege maybe? A new baby-face for me?"

"Al, this is Joe Hannibal, a good friend of mine. The only guy ever knocked me down in a fair fight."

Mekapolis grabbed my hand in a surprisingly strong grip. "Hey, that's some recommendation, kid. Where you been wrestling before this?"

It was my turn to grin. Being called a kid at my age was cause enough for that, even without the bad guess as to how I made my living.

"Afraid you don't understand," I said. "I'm a private detective, not a wrestler. That knockdown took place in a barroom brawl, by the way. And whenever The Bomber makes that introduction he fails to mention how he got back up and proceeded to throw me through a wall."

"A regular pier sixer, eh? Hot damn, I'd've loved to seen that." The little promoter paused to frown deeply. "But you say you're a private detective. Is this business? Is there some problem that brings you to see me?"

"Afraid so, Al," The Bomber said. "Can you spare us a few minutes of your time?"

Mekapolis gestured us into chairs and resumed his position behind the desk. After he had buzzed his secretary and told her no interruptions, The Bomber laid it out for him. Told him of the mysterious phone calls, of Tommy McGurk's moody behavior, and of Lori's subsequent suspicions.

"You know Lori McGurk as well as I do," Bomber summed up. "She's not the type to get hare-brained ideas or jump to conclusions. I believe there *is* something rotten going on and I figure she's probably right about what it is."

Mekapolis frowned some more over steepled fingers. "I appreciate your sharing this information, old friend. But what is it you want from me?"

The Bomber shifted his three hundred-plus pounds in the too small chair. "Dammit, Al, you promote matches all over northern Illinois and southern Wisconsin. You give the boys a fairer shake than most promoters do, but you still rule your territory with an iron fist. You don't maintain the kind of control you've got without keeping your ear to the ground, without knowing every time somebody dribbles in their jock strap. So what's going on? What makes this upcoming match between Tommy McGurk and El Bandido important enough for somebody to try and rig it by threatening a man's family?"

Scowling now, Mekapolis gave a firm shake of his head. "I don't know. I swear to you I don't. I also swear to you that I intend to do everything in my power to find out. But at this point you have caught me completely by surprise."

"What happened between McGurk and El Bandido?" I asked. "Why is their match Friday night going to be a shooting match?"

Mekapolis moved his eyebrows around. "Ah, that was a bad one. I was there. It happened up in Milwaukee about a month ago. El Bandido was going against a popular babyface from that area by the name of Irish O'Cady. It was a long, tough match but finally El Bandido got the Irishman in his patented submission hold, The South Of The Border Legbreaker. Only after O'Cady submitted, El Bandido wouldn't release the hold. He just kept cranking away. When the referee tried to make him stop, he knocked the ref from the ring and cranked away on the hold some more. By the time some of the other wrestlers came out of the dressing room and put El Bandido on the run, both of O'Cady's legs were severely damaged. I'm talking a couple bad fractures, some torn cartilage, the whole nine yards. He won't wrestle for months, maybe never again if everything doesn't heal properly."

"But what does that have to do with McGurk?"

"Tommy and Irish were good friends," The Bomber answered. "I remember they both turned pro about the same time."

Mekapolis nodded. "That's exactly right. Tommy was on the card that night, too. He was one of the boys who finally got El Bandido out of the ring. When he saw how badly his friend was hurt, I never saw a guy so crazy mad in my whole life. This wasn't the first time El Bandido had gone overboard like that and he likely would have been suspended if Tommy and some of the other wrestlers hadn't demanded to have a shot at him.

Tommy grabbed me right there at ringside that night and made me promise to get him a match with El Bandido as soon as possible. He was so wild I was actually a little frightened by him. I knew right then and there I was going to have a shooting match on my hands."

"This El Bandido sounds like a real sweetheart," I commented. "What's the story on him?"

"A Mexican kid, as the name implies," Mekapolis said. "Wrestles in a mask like so many from down there do. Comes into the ring wearing a sombrero and bandoleers crossed over his chest. Big and strong, average talent, but real hungry. Mean hungry, you know? Like a dog that hasn't been fed regularly. That's what gives him the edge in most of his matches, that hunger. I guess it's also what gives him that rage he can't always control."

"In your opinion, can Tommy take him?"

"Whew, that's a tough call to make. Ordinarily, I guess I'd have to say no. Even with size and talent on his side, Tommy is basically too nice a kid while El Bandido obviously doesn't care what he has to do to keep winning and get to the top. But right now Tommy's got this anger, see, this self-righteous fury. And he'll be in front of a hometown crowd. I'd say this one time he could maybe pull it off."

"Unless his head is all screwed up from threatening phone calls and worry over the safety of his wife and kid," I said pointedly.

Mekapolis leaned forward in his chair. "You mean you think El Bandido could be the one behind it?"

I shrugged. "Sure seems like a possibility. You say he's hungry for success, doesn't care what he has to do to get to the top. This match is getting a lot of attention, right? It would be a big step backward for him if he loses. What's more, if I were El Bandido I think I'd be at least a little worried that McGurk might take this revenge business literally. You know, an eye for an eye? That could mean even more than just the loss of the match, it could mean serious injury for the Mexican."

Mekapolis banged the desktop with his fist. "By God, if he's the one I'll have him barred from the sport!"

"Calm down, Al," The Bomber said easily. "Joe was just conjecturing. Detectives do that all the time."

"Yeah, well it sounded like damned sensible con . . .

cong . . . what*ever* it was." Mekapolis pointed a finger at me. "I'll make you a deal, Hannibal. You get to the bottom of this, find out who's behind the threats. Do it before the match Friday night and I'll pay you a bonus on top of whatever else you got going."

Since I had zilch else going, it was a deal I promptly accepted. I'd been feeling a little desperate ever since turning down Lori McGurk's offer of payment earlier. Noble gestures may enrich the soul, but they do damn little for your bank account.

We killed another fifteen minutes talking with the little promoter. Among other things, he told us that both Tommy McGurk and El Bandido had matches that night, but on different cards in different towns.

"No way I'm putting those two in the same arena, not even in separate matches," he explained. "It's too much of an explosive situation. They might go after each other in the dressing room or something. No, when they meet I want it be be in the middle of the ring on Friday night in front of a sellout crowd."

When Bomber and I stood to leave, Mekapolis came around the desk once more. He reached up to clap me on the back and, in a subtly different tone of voice, said, "Tell me, Joe, you sure you never did any wrestling?"

I shrugged. "Fooled around some as a kid, you know how that goes."

"Uh-huh. Pretty big guy, though, aren't you? Not as big as The Bomber here, but then who is, right? What do you go, about two thirty, two forty maybe?"

"Somewhere in there, yeah."

"How does the private eye racket treat you moneywise?"

The Bomber rolled his eyes. "Oh-oh. Here it comes."

Mekapolis made a point of ignoring him and continued to bend my ear. "Hey, everybody could use a little extra income these days, right? While we were sitting here talking, I got this dynamite idea. Let me get your reaction—The Masked Investigator! How does it grab you?" But he was on a roll and didn't wait for an answer. "I'd have you spend a couple weeks in the gym, see, learn some of the routines, trim that gut a little, maybe bulk up some around the neck. Then, when you were ready, we'd have to come up with the right costume to wear into the ring. I'm picturing a trench-coat and turned-down fedora, maybe even a shoulder holster and a gun. Of course the gun would have to be fake, a water pistol or something. Yeah, that's it, we could make you a heel and you'd have some kind of solution in the gun that you'd squirt in your opponents' eyes when the referee wasn't looking, something that'd supposedly blind them long enough for you to make your pin. The crowd would love it. They'd hate your guts, but they'd lap up the bit like chocolate ice cream. Whatya think?"

I must have looked like I might be considering it, because The Bomber suddenly grabbed me by the arm and hustled me out the door ahead of him. "He'll give it some serious thought, Al," he called back over his shoulder. "We'll let you know. Don't call us, we'll call you."

● ● ●

That night, up in Janesville, Wisconsin, in the main event of a card held in the high school gymnasium, Tommy McGurk pinned his opponent in less than three minutes. Lori, The Bomber, and I were watching from back row bleacher seats and both of them were quick to comment on the uncharacteristic savagery of Tommy's style.

After leaving Alex Mekapolis' office, The Bomber and I had returned to his apartment where we'd left off Lori to rest up from her all night drive. The three of us had then put our heads together over the kitchen table and, at my suggestion, had agreed that before going any further with this thing we ought to confront Tommy with Lori's suspicions and give him the opportunity to level with us about exactly what was going on and, hopefully, welcome our help.

Hence our evening trip across the state line. The remote seats once we got there were at Lori's insistence. She wanted to be sure we weren't spotted, stressing we do nothing to upset her husband before his match.

When the lights came up and the crowd started boiling out, we cut across the flow and made our way back toward the locker rooms. Lori flashed a plastic-coated ID card that got us past the security guards and we found ourselves in a narrow, empty hallway with our heels clacking hollowly off the tile floor. We pulled up in front of a thick wooden door on which someone had stuck strips of masking tape with the neatly printed message: PRIVATE—WRESTLERS ONLY.

As we leaned back to wait, Lori said, "Why do I suddenly feel so guilty? Tommy's going to come through that door in a few minutes and see me standing here and I'm going to have to explain that not only didn't I stay in Missouri like he wanted but that I brought you two in on something he obviously considers a very personal and private problem. I feel as if I've betrayed him somehow."

"You did the right things for the right reasons," Bomber told her reassuringly. "He'll be able to see that."

I lit a cigarette and said nothing. I wasn't so sure. Tommy McGurk was a big, physically powerful man; the kind of guy who'd take pride in being able to solve his own problems. If he accepted our help at all, it would mean having to swallow a big chunk of that pride. But what might be harder yet for him to swallow, I thought, was the realization that his wife hadn't had faith in his ability to handle the situation and had sought outside help in the first place. I sucked some smoke deep into my lungs and wished I wasn't any part of it.

Some of the wrestlers began filing out. Most of them knew The Bomber, of course, so there was plenty of shoulder punching and good-natured ribbing before they moved on.

Lori McGurk lit a cigarette also and smoked it in long, hard drags. She was growing visibly more nervous by the minute. Every time the door opened, her head would snap around to see who it was.

Finally, it was Tommy. Up close, he as a moon-faced young giant with a bull neck thrusting up out of a checkered sports shirt and huge, wedge-fingered hands dangling from corded forearms. He stood nearly as tall as The Bomber's six-and-a-half feet, but was trimmer, harder, weighing somewhere in my range. His gaze scanned the three of us, came to rest on Lori, and he frowned.

"Lori? What on earth are you doing . . . And Bomber! Hey, what gives?" Sudden balls of muscle appeared at the hinges of his jaw. "Something hasn't happened to Tommy Jr. has it?"

Lori hurried forward and slid her arms around his waist. "Oh no, honey. Nothing like that."

Tommy's frown deepened as he let his duffel bag drop to the floor and hesitantly put his arms around his wife.

"It's Tommy Sr. we're worried about," The Bomber said.

"What do you mean?"

"I think you know what I mean. We're here to help, Tom. You need to talk to somebody. Tell us about it."

The young giant grinned foolishly and looked down at Lori. "What's going on, babe? This some kind of joke?"

Without meeting her husband's eyes, Lori said, "I know all about it, Tommy. I've known for days. That's why I couldn't stay in Missouri. I came back and I told Bomber about the phone calls and I asked him to help you."

Tommy glared at The Bomber with anger and sudden suspicion in his eyes. "Who's this guy?" he said, jerking his chin to indicate me.

"His name is Joe Hannibal. He's a friend of mine. He also happens to be a private detective."

Tommy pulled away from his wife and threw his hands in the air. "Good God, woman, what have you gone and done!?"

"I'm just trying to help you, you bullheaded fool," Lori shot back, stiffening now with her own anger.

"The only help I needed from you was to stay the hell down in Missouri like I told you."

I didn't feel like standing by while this turned into a domestic squabble, so I said, "How about it, McGurk? Is someone trying to make you throw the fight Friday night?"

He spun on me. "I ain't *about* to answer no questions from you, you window-peeping freak. So you'd just better shut up. Better yet, get the hell out of here before I throw you all the way back down that hall."

"You might have some trouble doing that," The Bomber said easily. "First off, you'd have to get by me."

"What are you, his babysitter?" Tommy fumed. "I don't want him around me, you hear? Come to think of it, I don't want you around either!"

Tension filled the narrow hallway, crowding all four of us.

And then, very softly, Lori said, "How about me, Tommy? Do you want me around?"

The words—and whatever implications they carried—impacted visibly on McGurk. He seemed to deflate as some of the anger left him. He turned to his wife with a brow furrowed by uncertainty.

"What kind of question is that?" he said hoarsely.

"If you don't want me around, Tommy, then just say so and I'll leave. But if you do want me around, then I expect you to be honest with me. I've watched this thing tearing you up from the inside out. No matter how big and strong and wonderful you are, you can't fight every battle alone. I'm your wife, I love you and I want to fight this battle with you."

Tommy pulled a hand slowly down over his face. Then, with both hands, he made a frustrated gesture. "There's no way of knowing how nasty this thing could get. I'm afraid for you to be near it."

"I already *am* near it," Lori said stubbornly. "I'm married to you."

Ever so slowly, you could see an expression of grudging acceptance—maybe even relief—settle over Tommy McGurk's face. He pulled Lori back into his arms and buried his face in her hair. They stood like that for a long time and somewhere in there I started to feel glad I was on hand after all, glad to be a part of helping them.

•   •   •

The bedside alarm coaxed me awake around seven the next morning. I got up, plugged in the coffee pot, and while it was brewing stood under a hard shower spray until the slamming water had done a passable job of clearing the sleep cobwebs from my eyes and brain.

Once I had some coffee in me, I sat down over a bowl of corn flakes and mentally reviewed the events of the previous day and night. After leaving the Janesville high school gym, the four of us had gone to a nearby diner where Tommy proteined up on steak and eggs while relating his side of the story. It turned out Lori's suspicions were right on the money. The phone calls had started two weeks ago. Always the same voice on the other end of the line, a middle-aged-sounding male with no distinguishing accent or dialect. At first he'd tried to buy Tommy off. When he was told to go climb his thumb, the threats started. In the beginning they were directed against Tommy himself, but it wasn't long before they became aimed at Lori and Tommy Jr.

"I didn't—and still don't—know what the hell to do,"

McGurk had said dejectedly. "If I throw this match, I won't be able to face myself in the mirror. If I don't throw it, and something happens to my family . . . well, I can't even think about that."

"With a little luck," I had told him, "you won't have to make that choice. We intend to find out who's behind those phone calls and take them out of the picture."

Big talk. Now, in the harsh light of morning, I didn't feel so cocky. The whole thing seemed so ludicrous it was almost impossible to figure. Professional wrestling matches were rigged every day of the week. Why go to so much trouble over this one? In my mind, it kept coming back to El Bandido. He was the one who would benefit most obviously from a fixed outcome. Not only would he walk away victorious, but the risk of a revenge injury would be eliminated.

"I don't know," Tommy McGurk had said when I ran that train of thought by him. "El Bandido may be a creep, but I just can't picture him being behind this. For one thing, he's such an egotistical bastard the wouldn't feel it was necessary. He's confident he can beat me straight up."

"How about somebody close to him?" I'd suggested. "A manager? A friend?"

Tommy snorted derisively. "He doesn't have a manager that I know of, and he damn sure doesn't have any close friends."

So call me stubborn. But with no other leads at hand, the foremost item on my agenda for the new day was to have a chat with Mr. Bandido and see what kind of vibes I picked up.

Before leaving my southside apartment, I made two phone calls. The first was to a St. Louis-based P.I. I'd dealt with in the past, a guy named Finch. I got him out of bed and briefed him on the McGurk situation. He agreed to send a man out to the rural area where Lori's folks lived, to keep a discreet eye on Tommy Jr. in case the tentacles of this thing reached down that far. I offered to wire him a retainer but he said to hang on to it and he'd bill me when the whole business was wrapped up.

My second call was to The Bomber. We'd decided last night that our best plan of action was for him to stick close to Tommy and Lori while I remained mobile and put my investigative skills to work. In keeping with that, he had spent the night in the McGurks' guest bedroom. He sounded well rested and chipper this morning but his closing words carried an ominous warning:

"You watch out for that crazy Mexican, Joe. I've seen his kind before. They plain like to hurt people."

I was on the road shortly past eight. I put Rockford behind me and drove east on Route 20. The home address Alex Meka-polis had provided for El Bandido—real name Horace Garcia— was in Crystal Lake, a smallish bedroom community on the northwestern fringes of Chicago. I skirted Belvedere, northern Illinois' mini-Detroit with its sprawling Chrysler plant, then left 20 and jogged north through the farm village of Marengo before catching Highway 176 and heading east again. After a while, to the south of me, I began to sense the pulsing mass of The Windy City, its unseen presence oozing out over the green fields like the fetid breath of some ancient dragon threatening to lay waste the land.

It was ten on the nose when I hit the Crystal Lake city limits. I stopped at a Dunkin' Donuts for coffee and directions and a dozen minutes later I pulled up in front of the appropriately numbered house on the appropriately named street.

The day was warming rapidly. Overhead, the climbing sun seemed to have forgotten that the calendar had turned to Sep-tember and was striving mightily to produce one more dog day. I left my jacket in the car and walked to the front door in my shirtsleeves.

Repeated jabs at the doorbell produced no response. I cursed my luck and was about to turn away when I heard noises from the rear of the house. Voices and the irregular clank of metal. I walked around one end of the split level and back to where a chest-high wooded fence enclosed the back yard.

The yard was treeless and ablaze with sunshine. In its center a muscular, glistening brown man was doing bench presses with a heavily weighted bar bell. A woman with rich cinnamon skin and thick blue-black hair that reached to the small of her back stood watching him. Both wore the barest minimum in match-ing crimson swim attire.

The woman was counting the man's reps out loud and seemed every bit as intent on the task as he was.

". . . eighteen . . . nineteen . . . twenty!"

The man locked out on the latter, exhaled a huge gust of air, let the bar settle gently into its support hooks. He sat up and reached for a towel to mop the rivulets of sweat that ran from his face.

"How much weight?" I said from my side of the fence.

Two faces snapped in my direction, their expressions guarded, on the verge of being hostile.

After several beats, the man said, "Three hundred."

I nodded. "Pretty impressive."

"What is it you want?"

"Are you Horace Garcia? The wrestler they call El Bandido?"

"Who wants to know?"

"My name's Hannibal. I'm a reporter for The Rockford Bulletin." I dangled a phony press card over the fence to back up the lie.

Neither the man nor the woman moved to examine the card. "So?" he said.

"So I'm doing a story on the big match tomorrow night. I'd like to talk with you, ask you some questions."

"Since when do the pompous newspapers of this country bother to cover my husband's sport?" the woman said sneeringly.

I shrugged. "I just go where my editors tell me, lady. I guess this match is generating so much interest they can't afford to ignore it. And then, of course, there's also the threats Tommy McGurk has been receiving."

El Bandido pounced on that. "What threats?" he demanded.

I had him hooked now, it was time to introduce a few of my rules to the game.

"Look," I said, "can we do this without a fence between us?"

They exchanged glances. I thought I saw the woman give a quick, almost imperceptible shake of her head. But if she did, El Bandido chose to ignore it. He marched over, unlatched the gate, motioned me in.

Once I was through the gate, the woman held out her hand for the press card and this time gave it a scowlingly close examination. It was a good counterfeit, having served me well for a number of years, so I wasn't concerned she'd find any fault with it. Besides, if she was like most people she had no idea what a press card was supposed to look like in the first place.

"Now what of these threats you mentioned?" El Bandido wanted to know. "Who is making them?"

"That's a good question. At this point nobody knows."

"What is their content?"

"They've been warning McGurk to lose the match tomorrow night or harm will come to his wife and child."

"That is loco! Of course McGurk will lose. I, El Bandido, will be victorious. It is already a certainty in the minds of all but the very foolish. There is no need for threats!"

I spread my hands. "Apparently somebody doesn't see it that way."

"I say it is nothing but a trick of the crybaby gringo McGurk. He knows I will punish and humiliate him when I get him in the ring. He just wants to have an excuse."

"Look, I'm a reporter, not an announcer on one of your phony TV spots. Spare me the bluster and the bullcrap, okay?"

He regarded me with narrowed eyes. "So you are one of the many who think my sport is nothing by a phony game, is that it?"

I saw a wild gleam start to dance in those slits and I knew instinctively that he was going to try and push me into a confrontation. My instincts also told me something else: The man standing before me had nothing to do with the threats against Tommy McGurk and his family. The idea that someone apparently felt it was necessary to "help" him by threatening McGurk had insulted and angered him. And it was that anger he now intended to vent on me.

"Does it really matter what I think of your sport?" I said.

"You come onto my property, you interrupt my training, you insult my profession. You think that does not matter?"

"Okay. If I offended you in some way, I apologize."

"And now you back down from your words as quickly as shifting sand. It is disappointing that such a big man—so muy macho in appearance—is so sadly lacking in cojones."

It was a childish taunt and I shouldn't have let it get to me. But I did. I felt the heat crawling up my neck and the hands dangling at my sides were suddenly bundled into fists.

We stood like that for a while. Nose to nose, him grinning like a shark, me fighting inwardly to keep my cool.

The woman moved up beside us and said, "Do not do anything foolish. Either of you."

I broke eye contact with El Bandido, glanced at his woman, then swung my gaze back. "She's right," I said. "I think it's time I was going."

His taunting smile broadened. "Yes, why don't you?"

And then the sonofabitch shoved me.

Still smiling, he reached out almost casually, placed both palms on my chest, and shoved like a fourth grade schoolyard bully. There wasn't a lot of force behind it, but there was more than enough to make me lose whatever cool I had left. I won't be pushed around. Not by anybody. I leaned back into him, feinted with my left, then threw a right uppercut that should have wrapped his bottom lip up around his eyebrows.

Only his chin wasn't where it was supposed to be. The punch missed by a full six inches. Damn, he was quick!

My fist shot high into the air, dragging me off balance. El Bandido grabbed my arm, pivoted a half turn, levered my elbow across his shoulder, and flipped me as neatly as you or I might tip a drinking straw from a paper cup. I sailed through the air and landed like a sack of firewood.

Somewhere between the time my feet left the ground and my ass returned to it, it occurred to me that taking a poke at him might not have been a real good idea. But the jarring humiliation of impact made me too damn mad to care. I scrambled to my feet and charged, throwing a roundhouse right.

He ducked the blow and hammered a forearm across my stomach. When I stopped short and started to fold, he hooked my right arm with his, then leaned away and at the same time pulled. Again I went sailing through the air. I landed even harder than the first time—if that was possible—and wasn't so quick to get back up. It looked like it could turn out to be a very long morning.

"What the hell did you expect?" a voice demanded from somewhere inside my rattled noggin. "The guy's a pro, for crying out loud. You may be a pretty good street scuffler and barroom brawler, but you're not ready to go head to head against a pro."

Maybe not. But it didn't look like I had a choice any longer. El Bandido was moving toward me in a wrestler's crouch, still smiling that damned smile.

I considered the derringer in my boot. It's a two-shot .22 Magnum, strictly an emergency piece. I'm never without it and it's saved my bacon more than once. But I decided this wouldn't be another one of those times. Guns are for when your life is on the line. With his professional reputation to think of, I doubted El Bandido was out to seriously injure me. Beside, even if it meant taking a beating I didn't want to give the cocky fucker the satisfaction of knowing he'd made me feel threatened enough to reach for a gun.

I got to my feet. Instead of another foolhardy charge, I shrugged into a boxer's stance that seemed to confuse my opponent momentarily. I moved to my right and flicked out with a couple left jabs that found their mark, stinging him, irritating him, but doing no real damage. When I tried to push a good thing too far and threw a third jab, he had it timed and was waiting. He grabbed my arm, pivoted, pulled, and once again I went flying ass over tea spout.

When I landed this time, I rolled into the weight bench and various other pieces of training hardware that were clustered in the center of the yard. For a couple seconds I couldn't be sure if all the clanging I heard was from the equipment being scattered of if some of it was inside my head.

My jabs had finally wiped the smile from El Bandido's face. It stayed gone as he advanced now, looking intent on finishing me.

I put my hands down and started to push myself up to meet him. My right palm came to rest on a weight belt, about a five pounder, one of those vinyl-covered, weighted straps that athletes wear around their wrists or ankles during a workout to increase endurance.

When El Bandido leaned and reached for me, I brought the weight belt up and clapped it against the side of his head. He rocked back on his heels, teetered there for a moment, then fell onto his rump. I steam-rollered forward and threw a shoulder block high into his neck and the edge of his jaw that flattened him like a fifty cent throw rug.

I dropped to the grass beside him, sucking air, still shaken from the series of flips as well as from the impact of my own block.

I became aware of the woman standing over me.

"If you are still here when he comes to," she said, "I cannot be responsible for his actions. He was toying with you before. He took you too lightly. He will not make that mistake a second time. If he puts his hands on you again, he will break you in half."

I got to my feet. Slowly. The anger and adrenaline had started to subside and I suddenly felt a couple hundred years old.

The woman positioned herself between El Bandido and I. There was nothing menacing in her stance but I sensed a panther-like readiness about her. If I meant her man any further harm, I would have to go through her to do it. She stood close enough that I could smell her mixed scent of perfume, suntan oil, and perspiration. She had the bold features of a full-blooded Latina, the kind of beauty that is indeed enhanced by anger and other strong emotions. Behind her, El Bandido stirred and lifted one hand to the side of his head. He was a durable bastard, you had to give him that. But I wondered if he'd ever be aware that his greatest strength lay not in his bulging biceps but in the fierce loyalty of his woman.

I showed her a weary smile. "Like I said before, I think it's time I was going."

I plucked the bogus press card from between her fingers, turned and walked across the yard.

At the gate, I paused. "Someone told me earlier that your husband has no friends," I said. "I'll make it a point to let them know how wrong they were."

I could feel her eyes on my back until I rounded the corner of the house.

•   •   •

It was past noon by the time I got back to Rockford. I decided a drink was in order, something to soothe my aches and to relax the knot of frustration that was tightening in my gut. Time was running out and the case was going nowhere. I hadn't realized it, but I'd had my hopes pinned too strongly on El Bandido as the culprit in this thing. With that a washed out solution, I was feeling discouraged and aimless and temporarily unmotivated.

I climbed into my usual stool at The Bomb Shelter. Liz Grimaldi was behind the bar, dispensing drinks and thick sandwiches to the tail end of the lunch hour crowd. She put a shot and a beer in front of me without my having to say a word and in a little while, when she got a break in the action, returned to lean on the bar opposite me. Liz is a buxom, dark-haired beauty in her middle thirties, given to frequently wearing tight

V-necked sweaters. She had one on today and the sight of her leaning in my direction was a fine way to start the afternoon.

"How goes the battle, shamus?" she said.

I shook my head. "Don't ask."

"That bad, huh?"

"I've had better mornings."

"The Bomber told me what you two are up to. Is he with the McGurks now?"

"Uh-huh. He's supplying the extra brawn to keep them while I'm supposed to be supplying the brains to find the source of their trouble. Half of us aren't doing too hot."

Liz chewed her bottom lip. "I'm a little worried about that whole business, Joe. Especially Bomber's part in it."

That shoved my eyebrows up. "Since when does anyone need to worry about The Bomber?"

"Oh sure, he's physically huge and all that. But you've got him mixed up in something that could be pretty damned dangerous."

I held up a hand, palm out. "Wait a minute. Haven't you got that a little backwards? He's the one who dragged me into this mess."

"The bottom line is still the same. Anyone ruthless enough to threaten a man's wife and child could certainly be ruthless enough to try and carry out that threat. And since their target is the family of a professional wrestler, they obviously aren't intimidated by physical size or strength. A gun can be a great equalizer. What chance would The Bomber have against a bullet?"

"About the same as anybody else."

"I don't mean to sound as if I'm not concerned for you, too, Joe, but this is the kind of thing you do for a living. You pack your own gun and you know the rules of the game."

"There are no rules in this kind of game, kid."

"That's just it. I'm not sure The Bomber realizes that."

I lit a cigarette and blew some smoke. "Look, you know damn well I don't want anything to happen to the big ox any more than you do. But he dealt himself into this long before I ever entered the picture and I know him well enough to know that nothing or nobody is going to convince him to back out now. All I can do is promise to stick close and try to get everybody out with their asses intact."

"Including yours?"

"That's priority one."

"Like hell it is. You're as bad as The Bomber when it comes to sticking your neck out for somebody else. Worse. Jesus, here it is the nineteen eighties, the era of Alan Alda and Phil Donahue, and the two men in *my* life run around acting like John Wayne and Victor McLaglen!"

It gave me a funny feeling to hear Liz say that. I knew her relationship with The Bomber, close as it was, was purely platonic. And while my own relationship with her was equally platonic, there was something more there; a spark that we both chose to leave unfanned because of past bad experiences. Neither of us wanted to risk ruining a good friendship with a lousy romance. But the spark continued to smolder, and so did the possibility of it one day bursting into flame. It sounded good being called one of the men in her life, but at the same time it scared the hell out of me.

Liz got busy with other customers again and I decided I couldn't afford to hang around any longer. I gave her a wink and a wave on the way out and she responded with a smile, albeit a troubled one.

I drove out to the McGurk home on Spring Creek Road and reported on my morning, glossing over the fight and stressing my conviction that El Bandido wasn't our man. I then spelled The Bomber for a couple hours while he left to get a change of clothes and to take care of some personal matters. Tommy and Lori both seemed introspectively quiet, which suited my own mood, so very little of my time with them was spent in conversation.

When The Bomber returned, I headed out again and did what I should have done in the first place. I started working the streets, contacting snitches, dropping into dives of both high and low class, spreading the word that I wanted—and was willing to pay for—information on whoever was pressuring Tommy McGurk.

When I ran out of dives, I went to my Broadway office and hung out there for a while, hoping somewhat naively that the phone would ring and it would be a quick response to my seeding. Evening had turned into night and my rumbling stomach reminded me that I hadn't eaten since morning. I ordered up a pizza and spent some time munching on that, washing it down with hits from the office bottle.

Around nine, I decided to call it a night. After checking in with The Bomber, I switched the phone answering machine back on and drove home to my apartment. A hot shower felt good on the various bumps and bruises my skirmish with El Bandido had left me with. I hit the sack and fell asleep quickly, but my slumber wasn't without some rough spots.

I dreamed I was out on a date with Liz and we went to the movies. The picture was a DeMille-like Biblical epic based on the story of David and Goliath. But when the climax came, David—who remained a shadowy, faceless figure throughout—pulled from his tunic not a slingshot but a .357 Magnum revolver and blew a hole the size of a chariot wheel in Goliath's chest. As the giant toppled down—in obligatory slow motion—the camera zoomed in for a closeup and his face was the face of Bomber Brannigan!

•   •   •

Nine o'clock the next morning found me back at the McGurk house, seated over coffee at the kitchen table with Lori, Tommy, and The Bomber.

I'd dialed into the office answering machine before leaving my apartment but there were no messages. A phone message *had* been received during the night, however—by Tommy McGurk.

"The same voice spouting the same crap," he was saying now. "Lose tonight's match or else."

"So what did you tell him?" I wanted to know.

He made a face. "I told him to, uh, go and do something with himself that from all reports is physically impossible."

"That's your stance then? You're definitely going for the win?"

Tommy's head hung under the weight of uncertainty. "I wish it was that easy," he said. "But I really don't know." He glanced briefly at Lori, then hung his head even lower and stared down at his hands, bunched into huge but futile fists that rested on either side of his coffee cup. "Damn it, I just don't know."

Lori watched him silently for a long moment, then leaned forward and took one of his hands in hers. "There's only one thing you *can* do, and we all know what it is. You'll go into that ring tonight and you'll do your level best to beat El Bandido."

McGurk lifted his head. "But what about you and Little Tommy? If anything—"

"Don't even think about it. Bomber and Joe are looking after us, aren't they? Trust them. I do."

"Hey, we could still get a break in this thing." Bomber said. "Joe's got feelers out all over town and it's almost a dozen hours till fight time."

"Besides," I pointed out, "after what you told them on the phone last night I'd say you're already locked into it. They aren't likely to call again so even if you did decide to throw the match the'd have no way of knowing. Whatever steps—if any—they figure on taking to back up their threats are already planned and possibly already in motion. All we can do now is keep on our guard and be ready for them if and when they make their move."

We kicked it around a while longer but it kept coming back to pretty much the same place. When Tommy mentioned that his usual routine on the morning of a match was to go to the gym for a light workout, I said I saw no problem with that as long as Bomber or I accompanied him. Bomber told me to go ahead, he'd stay with Lori.

The gym where Tommy worked out turned out to be a drafty old brickpile just off South Main. Not wanting to stand around like a suspicious-eyed slug, I borrowed some sweats and did a little hanging and banging of my own. All the puffing I'd done after my prelim with El Bandido the previous day had served to remind me that I wasn't getting any younger and I really ought to be doing something on a regular basis to keep in better shape. I warmed up with some calisthenics and rowing, then did a series of lifts at one of the Universal machines and finished up on the heavy bag. Tommy's "light" workout, in the meantime, made my efforts look about as strenuous as a yawn and a stretch before climbing out of bed in the morning.

You had to hand it to the guy. In the past couple days, I'd gained a good deal of respect for him and his profession. At the core of the whole thing, masked by all the ballyhoo and cheap carnival theatrics, were some truly fine athletes. Athletes like Tommy McGurk—and, yeah, even El Bandido—as dedicated and sincere as any you'd find anywhere. Maybe even more so, considering the way they were snubbed by the media and the rest of the pro sports brotherhood.

Lori had lunch ready when we got back. The four of us sat down over broiled steaks and tossed salad. Afterwards, still following his usual match day routine, Tommy lay down for a nap.

Lori cleared the table, Bomber washed, I dried. When that was out of the way, Lori asked Bomber to take her shopping for some things she hadn't stocked because she'd figured on her and Tommy Jr. being away for several days.

I got on the phone after they'd left and tried my answering machine again. There were a couple messages from prospective clients, but nothing I wanted to hear right then. I cradled the receiver with an impatient curse.

I roamed through the silent house, feeling restless. I found a stack of magazines and tried to get interested in three or four different articles, but couldn't. I lit a fresh cigarette from the end of one I was getting ready to put out, then prowled some more.

Waiting isn't my strong suit. I usually get results—sometimes in ways that haven't been particularly healthy for me—by kicking around in the middle of a situation, shaking the walls now and then, until I jar something loose, something I can sink my teeth into. But this time I was damned if I could figure out what walls to shake and until I did all I had to sink my teeth in was the bitter taste of frustration.

Bomber and Liz returned a little past three. The rumble of the automatic garage doors rolling back announced their arrival. I'd flipped on the TV out of boredom and, so help me, had gotten interested in some game show I can no longer remember the name of. A chinless Georgia housewife and a ramrod stiff retired Air Force colonel were trying to match answers with a panel of Hollywood "stars," half of whom were burnt out has-beens, the other half doped up hopefuls. The results had struck me as mildly hilarious.

I lingered in front of the set for a couple minutes more, then wandered out through the kitchen to see if I could lend a hand carrying stuff from the car. Since neither Lori nor The Bomber had come in yet, I figured that's what they were waiting for. I pulled back the door that opened onto the attached garage and started through.

I caught only a fleeting glimpse of The Bomber sprawled motionless beside Lori's station wagon and had absolutely no time to react before something exploded against the right side of my head. I fell away from the blow, bounced off the door frame, crumpled into cold, hard blackness.

•   •   •

"Damn it to hell," Bomber groaned. "We let them snatch her right out from under our noses."

"At least you two were there and took your lumps," Tommy McGurk lamented. "I was tucked away safe in bed—napping, for Christ's sake, like some idiot without a worry in the world."

"So let's stand around blaming ourselves and feeling sorry for our bruised egos," I said. "That'll help a bunch."

The two of them glared at me.

I ignored them and, for the umpteenth time, studied the note that had been left under the windshield wiper of the station wagon. It was made up of words and word fragments clipped from magazine print then cellophane-taped to a sheet of unlined stationery. Its message was contained in one chilling sentence: EL BANDIDO WINS TONIGHT OR THE REAL LOSER IS MRS. McGURK.

A wave of anger washed through me as I read, causing the paper to start to tremble in my hands. I fought it back, forcing myself to keep a cool head.

"All right," I said to The Bomber. "One more time. I want to hear it again."

He sighed heavily. "Hell, Joe. We've been through it—"

"One more time," I repeated. "Try to remember everything, every little detail. The smallest thing could be important."

He heaved another sigh, then once more began to relate how the snatch had gone down.

"They were waiting somewhere inside the garage when we pulled up. You said the back door had been jimmied, I guess that's how they got in. I think there were only two, but there could have been more. I figure one was ducked down behind Tommy's car, the other one probably behind that stuff at the end of the work bench. That would have kept them out of sight while we were pulling in and then placed them on either side of the car once we were inside. When I got out and leaned into the back seat for the bags of groceries, the one on my side clubbed me from behind and, well, I guess you know about as much as I do from there. One of them just have gone over to wait beside the door in case anybody came out of the house and, when you did, Joe, they clobbered you too."

"Did you see or hear anything—anything at all—before you got sapped?"

"Nothing. Whoever they were, they—"

"But wait a minute," I cut in. "You said you thought there were only two. If you didn't see or hear anything, what made you think that?"

Bomber looked genuinely perplexed. "Well, I . . . I'm not sure."

"There must have been something," I prompted. "Something that caused you to draw that conclusion."

The three of us were in the McGurks' kitchen, where we'd gathered after Bomber and I had regained consciousness and alerted Tommy to what had happened. Bomber was seated at the table with a wet washcloth pressed to the spot on the back of his head where he'd been hit, I was leaning against the counter licking my own wounds, Tommy was pacing furiously. He stopped abruptly now and he and I both hovered over The Bomber like expectant fathers, waiting for his reply.

Bomber gnawed his bottom lip and scowled with concentration. "When I went down," he said slowly, "I wasn't completely out. You know how it is sometimes when you take a cheap shot? Well, like that. Everything was blurry and kind of distorted. I only had a couple seconds before I conked out all the way but, yeah, I do remember a couple more things."

"What!" Tommy demanded. "What else can you remember?"

"The way I fell," Bomber went on, "I was facing underneath the car. I couldn't move or speak but I was aware of what was going on around me. I could *feel* the guy standing over me, the one who'd hit me. And on the other side of the car I could see feet—Lori's feet and the feet of the guy who grabbed her. Yeah, and that's what left me with the impression there were just two guys involved."

"What else?" Tommy said.

The Bomber shook his head. "Afraid that's it, kid. That's when I went the rest of the way under. The last thing I remember is seeing Lori's feet and the guy in the white shoes."

"White shoes?" I said. "You mean sneakers?"

"No, not sneakers. There were regular white shoes. Not those dressy, real shiny kind either, these were more like the kind that singer used to wear back in the fifties."

"What singer?"

"Hell, I can't remember his name. That clean cut kid who was popular about the same time Elvis first hit it big. I think he's got a daughter who sings or something now."

"You mean Pat Boone?" Tommy said.

"Yeah, that's the one. Pat Boone. What was it they called those shoes he always wore?"

"White Bucks."

Something darted from a distant corner of my brain, bumped against the edge of my consciousness, darted away again. The fact that one of the abductors wore White Bucks had stirred something in my memory, something that had nearly surfaced but then had ducked away as elusively as an eel in murky water. What the hell was it? I tried to concentrate, to dredge it back up, but that only made it dive deeper into the murkiness.

"So we've established that one of the kidnappers wore white shoes," Tommy said with undisguised bitterness. "Big fucking deal. What does that gain us?"

"It's more than we had a few minutes ago," I told him.

"Yeah, but it's nowheres near enough, is it? What are you going to do—drive all around the city looking for guys wearing white shoes?"

"There are some more logical steps we could take. We could check with your neighbors, for instance. Maybe somebody saw the kidnappers going in or out the back of your garage and could furnish a physical description to go with the shoes."

Tommy shook his head firmly. "No. In the first place, it's too late for any of that. It's five o'clock now, I have to leave for the arena in another hour. In the second place, we do nothing—I repeat, *nothing*—to endanger Lori. I'll dump the match like they want and then just hope to God they return her unharmed."

"He's right, Joe," The Bomber said. "We gave it our best shot and we blew it. The only thing we can do now—for Lori's sake—is exactly what they want us to do."

When it was time, we drove to the arena in my old Mustang. Bomber sat up front with me, Tommy McGurk sat alone with his thoughts in the back seat. Before leaving the house, I'd made a final check with my office answering machine. Still nothing. I'd even contacted a couple of my better snitches direct, but the results were the same. As I drove, the significance of the White Bucks again nibbled at a corner of my brain, but with all the other thoughts churning around in there I couldn't bring anything into focus.

Outside the arena, it was painful to watch Tommy forced to put on a confident act for a throng of autograph seekers, most of them young boys with hero worship gleaming in their eyes. Once inside, in the dressing room, he asked to be left alone to get suited up and go through his warm-up exercises. He assured us he'd be okay. Bomber and I went looking for the beer stand, to take some of the edge off our tension.

It was there that Alex Mekapolis caught up with us. The little promoter was dressed to the nines and wielding a cigar that looked at least a foot long.

"Look at this crowd," he crowed. "The prelim matches haven't even started yet and we're already turning people away. I could have filled Madison Square Garden with this card, and ninety percent of the credit goes to Tommy McGurk. The young fella has a ton of loyal fans out there."

"Yeah, and he's not going to let a single one of them down," The Bomber replied, putting on an act of his own. We'd agreed that, to help ensure Lori's safety as well as protect Tommy's integrity, absolutely no one else need know the truth about what had to happen in that ring tonight.

Mekapolis studied the both of us shrewdly for a minute. "Then that problem we talked about the other day is all taken care of?" he wanted to know.

"We can't discuss any of the details," I said, trying to sound officious. "But yeah, it's all taken care of."

Mekapolis looked genuinely relieved. "Hey, that's great. It really is. I guess I owe you a bonus, Hannibal. Look me up after the matches, I'll settle with you."

He strutted away, beaming, puffing contentedly on the over-sized stogie and surveying the capacity crowd with dollar signs dancing in his eyes. As I watched the dapper little Greek depart, I spotted another familiar face in the crowd.

" 'Lo, Benny," I said when he drew closer.

"Hannibal and Bomber, two of my mainest. I see you've also

ventured out this evening seeking culture and refinement."
Benny Jewel's smile displayed more gold and ivory than the city
museum's African Resources exhibit. Benny is a gambling man.
He lives to bet money and he bets money to live. Judging from
the fancy threads that hung on his bod and the curvy blonde who
hung on his arm tonight, he'd been making some real smart bets
lately.

"It always does my heart good to see someone expanding
their horizons," The Bomber commented dryly. "Time was,
Benny, I wouldn't have recognized you without a card table under your elbows."

"Hey, you get stale doing the same gig all the time, right?
Don't get me wrong, cards and horses are still my bread and
butter. But doing things like this bit tonight offer some variety,
you know? If I make a little money on it, fine; if I don't, well,
it's kicks. Besides, Glory Jean here gets really worked up watching those big sweaty dudes in action so I come out on top no
matter what—if you get what I mean."

He punctuated the last with a bawdy wink and Glory Jean responded with a bubbly giggle and a slap at his arm.

I frowned. "No, I'm not sure I do get what you mean. How
do you stand to make or not make money on 'this bit tonight'?"

"By betting on it, man, how do you think?"

Even The Bomber had some trouble fielding that one. "You
mean you *bet money* on a pro wrestling match?"

"Yeah," Benny replied somewhat indignantly. "That's what I
do, remember? I bet on things. Don't tell me you two haven't
heard that the main event tonight is going to be a shooting
match? That means it's for real, man. McGurk and El Bandido
head to head, no hanky panky, flat out best man wins. When
one of the local bookies got wind of it, he started offering odds.
Me and plenty of the other guys placed some money with him.
Like I said, you need a little variety, right?"

Something tingled through the short hairs on the back of my
neck. "What were the odds?" I asked.

"Three-to-one on El Bandido. Hell, he was bound to get
action with those numbers. Even your most experienced bettor
will show some sentiment for a hometown hero like McGurk."

"This bookie," I said. "He got a name?"

"Everybody calls him Eddie The Sleeve."

It all came together then, like tumblers falling into place and tripping open a combination lock. I suddenly knew the significance of the White Buck shoes. What's more, I knew who was behind the phone threats and the abduction and I had a pretty good idea why. I clapped The Bomber on the back and let out a whoop, unable to control my excitement. Heads spun to look at us.

"What the hell's with him?" Benny said, stepping back.

I grabbed the gambler by his fancy lapels and stuck my face close to his. "Don't ask questions," I said, talking fast. "Just listen close and do exactly what I say. Get word to Tommy McGurk somehow, I don't care how—just do it. Tell him that if his match starts before we get back, to stall. You got that? Stall! Whatever he has to do, tell him not to let the match end before we return."

"Why!?" Benny sputtered. "What's going on?"

But I'd let go of him and was already sprinting for the exit.

"Just do what he says!" The Bomber's voice boomed as he fell into step behind me.

•   •   •

"Damn!" The Bomber exclaimed after I'd laid it all out for him. "Eddie The Sleeve all this time. Why in hell didn't we tumble to that? And why didn't any of your street contacts sniff it out?"

"That just shows how close to the vest Eddie's been playing this," I explained. "He's strictly a nickel and dime book. Never been able to cover more than a few grand in bets in his life. Anything bigger than that he has to have covered by one of the Syndicate set-ups and then he only gets a cut of the action. Well, this time he thought he saw a chance to get the whole pie. As you implied back there, who the hell ever heard of betting on a wrestling match? The fact that no one would be looking for a betting operation to be connected to it was probably the main reason he figured he could get away with it. So when Eddie somehow learned that the McGurk–El Bandido contest was for real, he saw to it that word got spread to regular bettors like Benny who were willing to try something different. To really hype their interest, he even offered odds *against* the hometown boy."

"And all the while figured he didn't have to sweat the outcome because he had his goons working to wire the match."

"Exactly."

"That could make Eddie a very unpopular fellow," Bomber observed. "Not only with the bettors, but with the Syndicate boys he didn't invite in on the action."

"Yeah, and wouldn't that be a shame," I said with a shark's smile.

We were driving west on State Street, having just crossed the river. I had to keep telling myself not to push it too hard, we sure as hell didn't have time for a speeding ticket. The few minutes it had taken for me to run a phone check on Bucky Reno's current address had seemed like hours.

"And those damn white shoes," The Bomber muttered. "I should have recognized them myself. Bucky Reno has been sporting that crazy footwear almost as long as he's been providing the muscle for Eddie's operation."

"Longer," I corrected. "Where do you think he got the nickname Bucky?"

Reno's digs were in the back unit of a rundown motel just inside the westernmost edge of the city limits. I parked next door in the lot of an auto parts store. It was full dark now and the high mercury vapor lights of the parking lot cast everything in an eerie bluish glow.

I opened the Mustang's trunk and slid back the cover of the special compartment underneath the spare tire.

"This isn't a picnic we're inviting ourselves to." I reminded The Bomber. "Eddie and his boys may be so much gutter slime but it's going to take more than our size and good looks to impress them." I pulled a snub-nosed .38 and a sawed-off pump shotgun from the compartment and held them out to him. "Which'll it be?"

The Bomber raised his two huge fists. "All my life I've been able to handle trouble with these, Joe."

I shook my head. "Don't be a fool. This is different. This could turn out to be a shooting match a hell of a lot more real than the kind Tommy McGurk is involved in."

His jaw muscles worked for several moments, then he reached out and took the sawed-off.

I shoved the .38 in my belt and closed the trunk. The derringer was still in my boot but, like I said before, it's strictly an emergency weapon. The piece I usually resort to when I figure a situation calls for more firepower is a tried and true old .45 automatic. But that was in a desk drawer back at my office and there had been no time to stop for it. So the .38 would have to do.

Bomber and I started across the weedy patch of grass that separated the auto parts lot from the back side of the motel. The latter was an old fashioned set-up with the units being individual little cabins. The one we wanted, the end one, was conveniently segregated by distance as well as by a clump of untrimmed bushes.

We paused in the deep shadow of the bushes to review our hastily formulated plan.

"You're sure you can take out that door on the first try?" I asked.

The Bomber snorted, "Does a bear dump in the woods?"

"Okay. I'll give you about a minute and a half to get in position before I go in through the window. When you hear the glass break, hit the door. I don't know how many there are in there, but we'll have their attention split for a few precious seconds. We have to take advantage of that."

"No sweat," The Bomber said confidently.

"And if you have to use that blunderbuss, make damn sure Lori isn't in your line of fire," I cautioned, "Or me!"

We separated, moving in opposite directions through the darkness. The cabin's rear window was long and narrow, its bottom sill scarcely a foot above the ground. I crouched there a moment, trying to peer inside, but the shade was drawn tight and I could see nothing. Inside, a radio was playing rock music.

I backed off a half dozen steps and crouched again, waiting, giving The Bomber time to get set. Doubts began poking at me. This thing needed a hell of a lot more planning than we'd had time to give it. We weren't even a hundred percent sure that Lori was in there. And now the cabin suddenly looked bigger than it had before. What if it had two rooms, instead of only one like we'd figured? That would mean Bomber and I would still be separated once we were inside. Liz Grimaldi's words came to mind, her concern over Bomber being involved in gunplay. And then, of course, there was the memory of my own disturbing dream . . .

I shook myself out of it. No time for that, damn it. Bomber

knew the risks and he'd dealt himself in willingly. The alternative, letting Eddie The Sleeve and his bunch get away with what they were trying to pull, was something neither of us could stomach.

It was time.

I stood, pulling the .38 from my belt, gripping the cool, reassuring steel tightly. I crossed my arms over my chest, tucked in my chin, ran forward and plunged elbows first through the window.

I came somersaulting out of a tangle of curtains and glass slivers and bumped to a halt against the side of a bed. On top of the bed, directly in front of me, Lori McGurk lay bound and gagged. On the other side of the bed, in the living area of the cabin's single room, Bucky Reno and a tall gangly kid I had never seen before were rising up out of their chairs, reaching for weapons.

The door crashed inward and The Bomber entered with a roar.

The gangly kid brought up a nickel-plated revolver but couldn't decide which way to point it. I put a .38 slug through his forearm and he fell down whimpering.

The Bomber took two measured steps forward and swung the shotgun butt in a short, savage arc that nearly tore the top of Bucky Reno's head off. The gun he'd been trying to bring into play fell from Bucky's suddenly limp fingers. He did a backflip over the chair in which he'd been sitting, his white shoes kicking high in the air, and landed in a motionless heap on the floor.

The Bomber advanced to hover over him—old fighter's habit. After a moment, he looked up and showed me a toothy grin.

"One shooting match down," he said. "One to go."

•   •   •

We got out of there ahead of the cops, though just barely. They'd have to be dealt with sooner or later, of course, but for the time being all three of us had a more pressing matter on our minds.

Lori put it into words when she said, "Just get us to the arena in time to save that match. We've all been through too much to let it slip away now."

Except for where the ropes that bound her had cut into the

flesh of her wrists and ankles, Lori was physically unharmed. And whatever emotional trauma she might have suffered seemed to be offset by her anger.

I sent the Mustang hurtling back down West State, reversing our route of a short time ago. It was just past nine o'clock now. The first match had been scheduled to start at seven-thirty. Figure about twenty minutes for each of the four prelims, with three to five minutes in between. That meant Tommy and El Bandido should be stepping into the ring at any moment. It was going to be close, but we still had a chance.

As I weaved through the traffic, I thought about Eddie the Sleeve. It hadn't surprised me much that he wasn't at the motel. I'd have been more surprised if he *had* been there. I figured him to be either at the arena or somewhere very close by, anxiously awaiting the outcome of the match. And it was doubtlessly more than coincidence that this also kept him well removed from where the kidnap victim was being held—just in case things turned sour.

I would've loved to have gotten my hands on him, of course, but it didn't really matter. His days were already numbered. When word spread—and it would—about what he'd tried to pull, Eddie "The Sleeve" Slevinsky would be a marked man. Not by me or the cops or the bettors he'd cheated—but by the Syndicate boys he hadn't let in on the deal.

I stood on the brakes and brought the Mustang to a screeching halt in the middle of the street out front of the arena. The three of us piled out and went charging up the steps. Horns blared from the blocked traffic behind us. With The Bomber running interference, we plowed past the ticket window, through the lobby security guards, and into the main hall. I had Lori by one arm, half supporting, half dragging her.

Tommy McGurk and El Bandido were battling it out in the middle of the ring. The crowd was going wild on all sides, totally oblivious to the three of us running down the center aisle. A cordon of stone-faced security guards surrounded the ring. Bomber shouldered two of them aside, making a hole for Lori and I, and we rushed to the edge of the mat.

El Bandido had McGurk on his knees in a punishing headlock. Both men were glistening with sweat, their torsos reddened from brutal contact.

"Tommy!" Lori called to her husband. "Tommy, I'm all right. Everything's all right. Don't hold back—*go* for it!"

I couldn't tell whether or not he heard her. Neither could she.

"Tommy!" she called again. "*Tah-mee!*"

The security guards were starting to converge on us now, more than even The Bomber could hold off. And the crowd had taken notice of us. Some of them decided to pick up on Lori's chant. It started with just a nearby handful, but caught on and spread like wildfire. In a matter of seconds, the place was booming with it.

"TAH-MEE! . . . TAH-MEE! . . . TAH-MEE!"

Damned if I didn't get caught up in it myself, stamping my foot and throwing a fist in the air like some wild-eyed revolutionary in a banana republic uprising. Even several of the security men seemed to hesitate, as if they, too, wanted to join in.

And, up in the ring, it began to have an effect. Tommy struggled to his feet. His body trembled with the effort. He threw off El Bandido's confining arm and knocked the masked grappler back with a resounding forearm smash.

The crowd came to its feet as one massive body, applauding thunderously.

In the last glimpse I had of the ring before a phalanx of blue shirts blocked my view and tidal-waved me back, I saw the two wrestlers getting ready to lock up once more.

Tommy McGurk was actually smiling.

He finally had his shooting match, and that's all he'd ever asked for.

THE PIT

Joe R. Lansdale

Six months earlier they had captured him. Tonight Harry went into the pit. He and Big George, right after
the bull terriers got through tearing the guts out of one another.
When that was over, he and George would go down and do their
business. The loser would stay there and be fed to the dogs, each
of which had been starved for the occasion.

When the dogs finished eating, the loser's head would go up
on a pole. Already a dozen poles circled the pit. On each rested a
head, or skull, depending on how long it had been exposed to
the elements, ambitious pole-climbing ants and hungry birds.
And of course how much flesh the terriers ripped off before it
was erected.

Twelve poles. Twelve heads.

Tonight a new pole and a new head went up.

Harry looked about at the congregation. All sixty or so of
them. They were a sight. Like mad creatures out of Lewis Car-
roll. Only they didn't have long rabbit ears or tall silly hats.
They were just backwoods rednecks, not too unlike himself.
With one major difference. They were as loony as waltzing

Joe R. Lansdale *has written so well in so many genres publishers aren't quite sure how
to categorize him, which has probably slowed his career somewhat. His first novel,* ACT
OF LOVE, *is one of the best suspense novels of this decade and is long overdue
for reprint. His story here is every bit as violent and controversial as most of his other
stories.*

mice. Or maybe they weren't crazy and he was. Sometimes he felt as if he had stepped into an alternate universe where the old laws of nature and what was right and wrong did not apply. Just like Alice plunging down the rabbit hole into Wonderland.

The crowd about the pit had been mumbling and talking, but now they grew silent. Out into the glow of the neon lamps stepped a man dressed in a black suit and hat. A massive rattlesnake was coiled about his right arm. It was wriggling from shoulder to wrist. About his left wrist a smaller snake was wrapped, a copperhead. The man held a Bible in his right hand. He was called Preacher.

Draping the monstrous rattlesnake around his neck, Preacher let it hang there. It dangled that way as if drugged. Its tongue would flash out from time to time. It gave Harry the willies. He hated snakes. They always seemed to be smiling. Nothing was that fucking funny, not all the time.

Preacher opened his Bible and read:

"Behold, I give unto you the power to tread on serpents and scorpions, and over all the power of the enemy: and nothing will by any means hurt you."

Preacher paused and looked at the sky. "So God," he said, "we want to thank you for a pretty good potato crop, though you've done better, and we want to thank you for the terriers, even though we had to raise and feed them ourselves, and we want to thank you for sending these outsiders our way, thank you for Harry Joe Stinton and Big George, the nigger."

Preacher paused and looked about the congregation. He lifted the hand with the copperhead in it high above his head. Slowly he lowered it and pointed the snake-filled fist at George. "Three times this here nigger has gone into the pit, and three times he has come out victorious. Couple times against whites, once against another nigger. Some of us think he's cheating.

"Tonight, we bring you another white feller, one of your chosen people, though you might not know it on account of the way you been letting the nigger win here, and we're hoping for a good fight with the nigger being killed at the end. We hope this here business pleases you. We worship you and the snakes in the way we ought to. Amen."

Big George looked over at Harry. "Be ready, sucker. I'm gonna take you apart like a gingerbread man."

Harry didn't say anything. He couldn't understand it. George was a prisoner just as he was. A man degraded and made to lift huge rocks and pull carts and jog mile on miles every day. And just so they could get in shape for this—to go down into that pit and try and beat each other to death for the amusement of these crazies.

And it had to be worse for George. Being black, he was seldom called anything other than "the nigger" by these psychos. Further more, no secret had been made of the fact that they wanted George to lose, and for him to win. The idea of a black pit champion was eating their little honkey hearts out.

Yet, Big George had developed a sort of perverse pride in being the longest lived pit fighter yet.

"It's something I can do right," George had once said. "On the outside I wasn't nothing but a nigger, an uneducated nigger working in rose fields, mowing big lawns for rich white folks. Here I'm still the nigger, but I'm THE NIGGER, the bad ass nigger, and no matter what these peckerwoods call me, they know it, and they know I'm the best at what I do. I'm the king here. And they may hate me for it, keep me in a cell and make me run and lift stuff, but for that time in the pit, they know I'm the one that can do what they can't do, and they're afraid of me. I like it."

Glancing at George, Harry saw that the big man was not nervous. Or at least not showing it. He looked as if he were ready to go on holiday. Nothing to it. He was about to go down into that pit and try and beat a man to death with his fists and it was nothing. All in a days work. A job well done for an odd sort of respect that beat what he had had on the outside.

The outside. It was strange how much he and Big George used that term. *The outside.* As if they were enclosed in some small bubble like cosmos that perched on the edge of the world they had known; a cosmos invisible to *the outsiders*, a spectral place with new mathematics and nebulous laws of mind and physics.

Maybe he was in hell. Perhaps he had been wiped out on the highway and had gone to the dark place. Just maybe his memory of how he had arrived here was a false dream inspired by demonic powers. The whole thing about him taking a wrong turn through Big Thicket country and having his truck break down just outside of Morganstown was an illusion, and stepping onto

the Main Street of Morganstown, population 66, was his crossing the River Styx and landing smack dab in the middle of a hell
designed for good old boys.

God, had it been six months ago?

He had been on his way to visit his mother in Woodville, and
he had taken a shortcut through the Thicket. Or so he thought.
But he soon realized that he had looked at the map wrong. The
short cut listed on the paper was not the one he had taken. He
had mistaken that road for the one he wanted. This one had not
been marked. And then he had reached Morganstown and his
truck had broken down. He had been forced into six months
hard labor alongside George, the champion pit fighter, and now
the moment for which he had been groomed had arrived.

They were bringing the terriers out now. One, the champion,
was named Old Codger. He was getting on in years. He had
won many a pit fight. Tonight, win or lose, this would be his last
battle. The other dog, Muncher, was young and inexperienced,
but he was strong and eager for blood.

A ramp was lowered into the pit. Preacher and two men, the
owners of the dogs, went down into the pit with Codger and
Muncher. When they reached the bottom a dozen bright spot
lights were thrown on them. They seemed to wade through the
light.

The bleachers arranged about the pit began to fill. People
mumbled and passed popcorn. Bets were placed and a little, fat
man wearing a bowler hat copied them down in a note pad as
fast as they were shouted. The ramp was removed.

In the pit, the men took hold of their dogs by the scruff of the
neck and removed their collars. They turned the dogs so they
were facing the walls of the pit and could not see one another.
The terriers were about six feet apart, butts facing.

Preacher said, "A living dog is better than a dead lion."

Harry wasn't sure what that had to do with anything.

"Ready yourselves," Preacher said. "Gentlemen, face your
dogs."

The owners slapped their dogs across the muzzle and whirled
them to face one another. They immediately began to leap and
strain at their masters' grips.

"Gentlemen, release your dogs."

The dogs did not bark. For some reason, that was what Harry

noted the most. They did not even growl. They were quick little engines of silence.

Their first lunge was a miss and they snapped air. But the second time they hit head on with the impact of .45 slugs. Codger was knocked on his back and Muncher dove for his throat. But the experienced dog popped up its head and grabbed Muncher by the nose. Codger's teeth met through Muncher's flesh.

Bets were called from the bleachers.

The little man in the bowler was writing furiously.

Muncher, the challenger, was dragging Codger, the champion, around the pit, trying to make the old dog let go of his nose. Finally, by shaking his head violently and relinquishing a hunk of his muzzle, he succeeded.

Codger rolled to his feet and jumped Muncher. Muncher turned his head just out of the path of Codger's jaws. The older dog's teeth snapped together like a spring-loaded bear trap, saliva popped out of his mouth in a fine spray.

Muncher grabbed Codger by the right ear. The grip was strong and Codger was shook like a used condom about to be tied and tossed. Muncher bit the champ's ear completely off.

Harry felt sick. He thought he was going to throw up. He saw that Big George was looking at him. "You think this is bad, motherfucker," George said, "this ain't nothing but a cake walk. Wait till I get you in that pit."

"You sure run hot and cold, don't you?" Harry said.

"Nothing personal," George said sharply and turned back to look at the fight in the pit.

Nothing personal, Harry thought. God, what could be more personal? Just yesterday, as they trained, jogged along together, a pickup loaded with gun bearing crazies driving alongside of them, he had felt close to George. They had shared many personal things these six months, and he knew that George liked him. But when it came to the pit, George was a different man. The concept of friendship became alien to him. When Harry had tried to talk to him about it yesterday, he had said much the same thing. "Ain't nothing personal, Harry my man, but when we get in that pit don't look to me for nothing besides pain, cause I got plenty of that to give you, a lifetime of it, and I'll just keep it coming."

Down in the pit Codger screamed. It could be described no

other way. Muncher had him on his back and was biting him on the belly. Codger was trying to double forward and get hold of Muncher's head, but his tired jaws kept slipping off of the sweaty neck fur. Blood was starting to pump out of Codger's belly.

"Bite him, boy," someone yelled from the bleachers, "tear his ass up son."

Harry noted that every man, woman and child was leaning forward in their seat, straining for a view. Their faces full of lust, like lovers approaching vicious climax. For a few moments they were in that pit and they were the dogs. Vicarious thrills without the pain.

Codger's legs began to flap.

"Kill him! Kill him!" the crowd began to chant.

Codger had quit moving. Muncher was burrowing his muzzle deeper into the old dog's guts. Preacher called for a pickup. Muncher's owner pried the dog's jaws loose of Codger's guts. Muncher's muzzle looked as if it had been dipped in red ink.

"This sonofabitch is still alive," Muncher's owner said of Codger.

Codger's owner walked over to the dog and said, "You little fucker!" He pulled a Saturday Night Special from his coat pocket and shot Codger twice in the head. Codger didn't even kick. He just evacuated his bowels right there.

Muncher came over and sniffed Codger's corpse, then, lifting his leg, he took a leak on the dead dog's head. The stream of piss was bright red.

The ramp was lowered. The dead dog was dragged out and tossed behind the bleachers. Muncher walked up the ramp beside his owner. The little dog strutted like he had just been crowned King of Creation. Codger's owner walked out last. He was not a happy man. Preacher stayed in the pit. A big man known as Sheriff Jimmy went down the ramp to join him. Sheriff Jimmy had a big pistol on his hip and a toy badge on his chest. The badge looked like the sort of thing that had come in a plastic bag with a capgun and whistle. But it was his sign of office and his word was iron.

A man next to Harry prodded him with the barrel of a shotgun. Walking close behind George, Harry went down the ramp and into the pit. The man with the shotgun went back up. In the bleachers the betting had started again, the little, fat man with the bowler was busy.

Preacher's rattlesnake was still lying serenely about his neck, and the little copperhead had been placed in Preacher's coat pocket. It poked its head out from time to time and looked around.

Harry glanced up. The heads and skulls on the poles—in spite of the fact they were all eyeless, and due to the strong light nothing but bulbous shapes on shafts—seemed to look down, taking as much amusement in the situation as the crowd on the bleachers.

Preacher had his Bible out again. He was reading a verse. ". . . when thou walkest through the fire, thou shalt not be burned; neither shall the flame kindle upon thee . . ."

Harry had no idea what that or the snakes had to do with anything. Certainly he could not see the relationship with the pit. These people's minds seemed to click and grind to a different set of internal gears than those on *the outside*.

The reality of the situation settled on Harry like a heavy, woolen coat. He was about to kill or be killed, right here in this dog-smelling pit, and there was nothing he could do that would change that.

He thought perhaps his life should flash before his eyes or something, but it did not. Maybe he should try to think of something wonderful, a last fine thought of what used to be. First he summoned up the image of his wife. That did nothing for him. Though his wife had once been pretty and bright, he could not remember her that way. The image that came to mind was quite different. A dumpy, lazy woman with constant back pains and her hair pulled up into an eternal topknot of greasy, brown hair. There was never a smile on her face or a word of encouragement for him. He always felt that she expected him to entertain her and that he was not doing a very good job of it. There was not even a moment of sexual ecstasy that he could recall. After their daughter had been born she had given up screwing as a wasted exercise. Why waste energy on sex when she could spend it complaining.

He flipped his mental card file to his daughter. What he saw was an ugly, potato-nosed girl of twelve. She had no personality. Her mother was Miss Congeniality compared to her. Potato Nose spent all of her time pining over thin, blond heartthrobs on television. It wasn't bad enough that they glared at Harry via the tube, they were also pinned to her walls and hiding in magazines she had cast throughout the house.

These were the last thoughts of a man about to face death?

There was just nothing there.

His job had sucked. His wife hadn't.

He clutched at straws. There had been Melva, a fine looking little cheerleader from high school. She had had the brain of a dried black-eyed pea, but God-All-Mighty, did she know how to hide a weenie. And there had always been that strange smell about her, like bananas. It was especially strong about her thatch, which was thick enough for a bald eagle to nest in.

But thinking about her didn't provide much pleasure either. She had gotten hit by a drunk in a Mack truck while parked offside of a dark road with that Pulver boy.

Damn that Pulver. At least he had died in ecstasy. Had never known what hit him. When that Mack went up his ass he probably thought for a split second he was having the greatest orgasm of his life.

Damn that Melva. What had she seen in Pulver anyway?

He was skinny and stupid and had a face like a peanut pattie.

God, he was beat at every turn. Frustrated at every corner. No good thoughts or beautiful visions before the moment of truth. Only blackness, a life of dull, planned movements as consistent and boring as a bran-conscious geriatric's bowel movement. For a moment he thought he might cry.

Sheriff Jimmy took out his revolver. Unlike the badge it was not a toy. "Find your corner, boys."

George turned and strode to one side of the pit, took off his shirt and leaned against the wall. His body shined like wet licorice in the spot lights.

After a moment, Harry made his legs work. He walked to a place opposite George and took off his shirt. He could feel the months of hard work rippling beneath his flesh. His mind was suddenly blank. There wasn't even a god he believed in. No one to pray to. Nothing to do but the inevitable.

Sheriff Jimmy walked to the middle of the pit. He yelled out for the crowd to shut up.

Silence reigned.

"In this corner," he said, waving the revolver at Harry, "we have Harry Joe Stinton, family man and pretty good feller for an outsider. He's six two and weighs two hundred and thirty-eight pounds, give or take a pound since my bathroom scales ain't exactly on the money."

A cheer went up.

"Over here," Sheriff Jimmy said, waving the revolver at George, "standing six four tall and weighing two hundred and forty-two pounds, we got the nigger, present champion of this here sport."

No one cheered. Someone made a loud sound with his mouth that sounded like a fart, the greasy kind that goes on and on and on.

George appeared unfazed. He looked like a statue. He knew who he was and what he was. The Champion Of The Pit.

"First off," Sheriff Jimmy said, "you boys come forward and show your hands."

Harry and George walked to the center of the pit, held out their hands, fingers spread wide apart, so that the crowd could see that they were empty.

"Turn and walk to your corners and don't turn around," Sheriff Jimmy said.

George and Harry did as they were told. Sheriff Jimmy followed Harry and put an arm around his shoulders. "I got four hogs riding on you," he said. "And I'll tell you what, you beat the nigger and I'll do you a favor. Elvira, who works over at the cafe has already agreed. You win and you can have her. How's that sound?"

Harry was too numb with the insanity of it all to answer. Sheriff Jimmy was offering him a piece of ass if he won, as if this would be greater incentive than coming out of the pit alive. With this bunch there was just no way to anticipate what might come next. Nothing was static.

"She can do more tricks with a six inch dick than a monkey can with a hundred foot of grapevine, boy. When the going gets rough in there, you remember that. Okay?"

Harry didn't answer. He just looked at the pit wall.

"You ain't gonna get nowhere in life being sullen like that," Sheriff Jimmy said. "Now, you go get him and plow a rut in his black ass."

Sheriff Jimmy grabbed Harry by the shoulders and whirled

him around, slapped him hard across the face in the same way the dogs had been slapped. George had been done the same way by the preacher. Now George and Harry were facing one another. Harry thought George looked like an ebony gargoyle fresh escaped from hell. His bald, bullet-like head gleamed in the harsh lights and his body looked as rough and ragged as stone.

Harry and George raised their hands in classic boxer stance and began to circle one another.

From above someone yelled, "Don't hit the nigger in the head, it'll break your hand. Go for the lips, they got soft lips."

The smell of sweat, dog blood and Old Codger's shit was thick in the air. The lust of the crowd seemed to have an aroma as well. Harry even thought he could smell Preacher's snakes. Once, when a boy, he had been fishing down by the creek bed and had smelled an odor like that, and a water moccasin had wriggled out beneath his legs and splashed in the water. It was as if everything he feared in the world had been put in this pit. The idea of being put deep down in the ground. Irrational people for whom logic did not exist. Rotting skulls on poles about the pit. Living skulls attached to hunched-forward bodies that yelled for blood. Snakes. The stench of death—blood and shit. And every white man's fear, racist or not—a big, black man with a lifetime of hatred in his eyes.

The circle tightened. They could almost touch one another now.

Suddenly George's lip began to tremble. His eyes poked out of his head, seemed to be looking at something just behind and to the right of Harry.

"Sss . . . snake!" George screamed.

God, thought Harry, one of Preacher's snakes has escaped. Harry jerked his head for a look.

And George stepped in and knocked him on his ass and kicked him full in the chest. Harry began scuttling along the ground on his hands and knees, George following along kicking him in the ribs. Harry thought he felt something snap inside, a cracked rib maybe. He finally scuttled to his feet and bicycled around the pit. Goddamn, he thought, I fell for the oldest, silliest trick in the book. Here I am fighting for my life and I fell for it.

"Way to go, stupid fuck!" A voice screamed from the bleachers. "Hey nigger, why don't you try 'hey, your shoe's untied,' he'll go for it."

"Get off the goddamned bicycle," someone else yelled. "Fight."

"You better run" George said. "I catch you I'm gonna punch you so hard in the mouth, gonna knock your fucking teeth out your asshole . . ."

Harry felt dizzy. His head was like a yo-yo doing the Around The World trick. Blood ran down his forehead, dribbled off the tip of his nose and gathered on his upper lip. George was closing the gap again.

I'm going to die right here in this pit, thought Harry. I'm going to die just because my truck broke down outside of town and no one knows where I am. That's why I'm going to die. It's as simple as that.

Popcorn rained down on Harry and a tossed cup of ice hit him in the back. "Wanted to see a fucking foot race," a voice called, "I'd have gone to the fucking track."

"Ten on the nigger," another voice said.

"Five bucks the nigger kills him in five minutes."

When Harry backpedaled past Preacher, the snake man leaned forward and snapped, "You asshole, I got a sawbuck riding on you."

Preacher was holding the big rattler again. He had the snake gripped just below the head, and he was so upset over how the fight had gone so far, he was unconsciously squeezing the snake in a vice-like grip. The rattler was squirming and twisting and flapping about, but Preacher didn't seem to notice. The snake's forked tongue was outside its mouth and it was really working, slapping about like a thin strip of rubber come loose on a whirling tire. The copperhead in Preacher's pocket was still looking out, as if along with Preacher he might have a bet on the outcome of the fight as well. As Harry danced away the rattler opened its mouth so wide its jaws came unhinged. It looked as if it were trying to yell for help.

Harry and George came together again in the center of the pit. Fists like black ball bearings slammed the sides of Harry's head. The pit was like a whirlpool, the walls threatening to close in and suck Harry down into oblivion.

Kneeing with all his might, Harry caught George solidly in

the groin. George grunted, stumbled back, half-bent over.

The crowd went wild.

Harry brought cupped hands down on George's neck, knocked him to his knees. Harry used the opportunity to knock out one of the big man's teeth with the toe of his shoe.

He was about to kick him again when George reached up and clutched the crotch of Harry's khakis, taking a crushing grip on Harry's testicles.

"Got you by the balls," George growled.

Harry bellowed and began to hammer wildly on top of George's head with both fists. He realized with horror that George was pulling him forward. *By God, George was going to bite him on the balls* .

Jerking up his knee he caught George in the nose and broke his grip. He bounded free, skipped and whooped about the pit like an Indian dancing for rain.

He skipped and whooped by Preacher. Preacher's rattler had quit twisting. It hung loosely from Preacher's tight fist. Its eyes were bulging out of its head like the humped backs of grub worms. Its mouth was closed and its forked tongue hung limply from the edge of it.

The copperhead was still watching the show from the safety of Preacher's pocket, its tongue zipping out from time to time to taste the air. The little snake didn't seem to have a care in the world.

George was on his feet again, and Harry could tell that already he was feeling better. Feeling good enough to make Harry feel real bad.

Preacher abruptly realized that his rattler had gone limp. "No, God no!" he cried. He stretched the huge rattler between his hands. "Baby, baby," he bawled, "breathe for me, Sapphire, breathe for me." Preacher shook the snake viciously, trying to jar some life into it, but the snake did not move.

The pain in Harry's groin had subsided and he could think again. George was moving in on him, and there just didn't seem any reason to run. George would catch him, and when he did, it would just be worse because he would be even more tired from all that running. It had to be done. The mating dance was over, now all that was left was the intercourse of violence.

A black fist turned the flesh and cartilage of Harry's nose into smouldering putty. Harry ducked his head and caught another blow to the chin. The stars he had not been able to see above him because of the lights, he could now see below him, spinning constellations on the floor of the pit.

It came to him again, the fact that he was going to die right here without one good, last thought. But then maybe there was one. He envisioned his wife, dumpy and sullen and denying him sex. George became her and she became George and Harry did what he had wanted to do for so long, he hit her in the mouth. Not once, but twice and a third time. He battered her nose and he pounded her ribs. And By God, but she could hit back. He felt something crack in the center of his chest and his left cheekbone collapsed into his face. But Harry did not stop battering her. He looped and punched and pounded her dumpy face until it was George's black face and George's black face turned back to her face and he thought of her now on the bed, naked, on her back, battered, and he was naked and mounting her, and the blow's of his fists were the sexual thrusts of his cock and he was pounding her until—

George screamed. He had fallen to his knees. His right eye was hanging out on the tendons. One of Harry's straight rights had struck George's cheekbone with such power it had shattered it and pressured the eye out of its socket.

Blood ran down Harry's knuckles. Some of it was George's. Much of it was his own. His knuckle bones showed through the rent flesh of his hands, but they did not hurt. They were past hurting.

George wobbled to his feet. The two men stood facing one another, neither moving. The crowd was silent. The only sound in the pit was the harsh breathing of the two fighters, and Preacher who had stretched Sapphire out on the ground on her back and was trying to blow air into her mouth. Occasionally he'd lift his head and say in tearful supplication, "Breathe for me, Sapphire, breathe for me."

Each time Preacher blew a blast into the snake, its white underbelly would swell and then settle down, like a leaky balloon that just wouldn't hold air.

George and Harry came together. Softly. They had their arms on each others shoulders and they leaned against one another, breathed each others breath.

Above, the silence of the crowd was broken when a heckler yelled, "Start some music, the fuckers want to dance."

"It's nothing personal," George said.

"Not at all," Harry said.

They managed to separate, reluctantly, like two lovers who had just copulated to the greatest orgasm of their lives.

George bent slightly and put up his hands. The eye dangling on his cheek looked like some kind of tentacled creature trying to crawl up and into George's socket. Harry knew that he would have to work on that eye.

Preacher screamed. Harry afforded him a sideways glance. Sapphire was awake. And now she was dangling from Preacher's face. She had bitten through his top lip and was hung there by her fangs. Preacher was saying something about the power to tread on serpents and stumbling about the pit. Finally his back struck the pit wall and he slid down to his butt and just sat there, legs sticking out in front of him, Sapphire dangling off his lip like some sort of malignant growth. Gradually, building momentum, the snake began to thrash.

Harry and George met again in the center of the pit. A second wind had washed in on them and they were ready. Harry hurt wonderfully. He was no longer afraid. Both men were smiling, showing the teeth they had left. They began to hit each other.

Harry worked on the eye. Twice he felt it beneath his fists, a grape-like thing that cushioned his knuckles and made them wet. Harry's entire body felt on fire—twin fires, ecstasy and pain.

George and Harry collapsed together, held each other, waltzed about.

"You done good," George said, "make it quick."

The black man's legs went out from under him and he fell to his knees, his head bent. Harry took the man's head in his hands and kneed him in the face with all his might. George went limp. Harry grasped George's chin and the back of his head and gave a violent twist. The neck bone snapped and George fell back, dead.

The copperhead, which had been poking its head out of Preacher's pocket, took this moment to slither away into a crack in the pit's wall.

Out of nowhere came weakness. Harry fell to his knees. He touched George's ruined face with his fingers.

Suddenly hands had him. The ramp was lowered. The crowd

cheered. Preacher—Sapphire dislodged from his lip—came forward to help Sheriff Jimmy with him. They lifted him up.

Harry looked at Preacher. His lip was greenish. His head looked like a sun-swollen watermelon, yet, he seemed well enough. Sapphire was wrapped around his neck again. They were still buddies. The snake looked tired. Harry no longer felt afraid of it. He reached out and touched its head. It did not try to bite him. He felt its feathery tongue brush his bloody hand.

They carried him up the ramp and the crowd took him, lifted him up high above their heads. He could see the moon and the stars now. For some odd reason they did not look familiar. Even the nature of the sky seemed different.

He turned and looked down. The terriers were being herded into the pit. They ran down the ramp like rats. Below, he could hear them begin to feed, to fight for choice morsels. But there were so many dogs, and they were so hungry, this only went on for a few minutes. After a while they came back up the ramp followed by Sheriff Jimmy closing a big lock-bladed knife and by Preacher who held George's head in his outstretched hands. George's eyes were gone. Little of the face remained. Only that slick, bald pate had been left undamaged by the terriers.

A pole came out of the crowd and the head was pushed onto its sharpened end and the pole was dropped into a deep hole in the ground. The pole, like a long neck, rocked its trophy for a moment, then went still. Dirt was kicked into the hole and George joined the others, all those beautiful, wonderful heads and skulls.

They began to carry Harry away. Tomorrow he would have Elvira, who could do more tricks with a six inch dick than a monkey could with a hundred foot of grapevine, then he would heal and a new outsider would come through and they would train together and then they would mate in blood and sweat in the depths of the pit.

The crowd was moving toward the forest trail, toward town. The smell of pines was sweet in the air. And as they carried him away, Harry turned his head so he could look back and see the pit, its maw closing in shadow as the lights were cut, and just before the last one went out Harry saw the heads on the poles, and dead center of his vision, was the shiny, bald pate of his good friend George.

TURN AWAY

Edward Gorman

On Thursday she was there again. (This was on a soap opera he'd picked up by accident looking for a western movie to watch since he was all caught up on his work.) Parnell had seen her Monday but not Tuesday then not Wednesday either. But Thursday she was there again. He didn't know her name, hell it didn't matter, she was just this maybe twenty-two twenty-three year old who looked a lot like a nurse from Enid, Oklahoma he'd dated a couple times (Les Elgart had been playing the Loop) six seven months after returning from WWII.

Now this young look-alike was on a soap opera and he was watching.

A frigging soap opera.

He was getting all dazzled up by her, just as he had on Monday, when the knock came sharp and three times, almost like a code.

He wasn't wearing the slippers he'd gotten recently at K-Mart so he had to find them, and he was drinking straight from a quart of Hamms so he had to put it down. When you were the manager of an apartment building, even one as marginal as The

Ed Gorman *appeared abruptly on the mystery scene (which also happens to be the name of the magazine he co-publishes with Bob Randisi) and has in a few years established himself as an interesting if somewhat off-beat private eye writer. (One reviewer noted, unfondly one assumes, that his books swing between "satire and cold rage, sometime on the same page.") Gorman started out in literary magazines and came late (age 42) to popular fiction.*

Alma, you had to go to the door with at least a little "decorous-ness," the word Sgt. Meister, his boss, had always used back in Parnell's cop days.

It was 11:23 A.M. and most of the Alma's tenants were at work. Except for the ADC mothers who had plenty of work of their own kind what with some of the assholes down at Social Services (Parnell had once gone down there with the Jamaican woman in 201 and threatened to punch out the little bastard who was holding up her check), not to mention the sheer simple bur-den of knowing the sweet innocent little child you loved was someday going to end up just as blown-out and bitter and use-less as you yourself.

He went to the door, shuffling in his new slippers which he'd bought two sizes too big because of his bunions.

The guy who stood there was no resident of the Alma. Not with his razor cut black hair and his three-piece banker's suit and the kind of melancholy in his pale blue eyes that was almost sweet and not at all violent. He had a fancy mustache spoiled by the fact that his pink lips were a woman's.

"Mr. Parnell?"

Parnell nodded.

The man, who was maybe thirty-five, put out a hand. Parnell took it, all the while thinking of the soap opera behind him and the girl who looked like the one from Enid, Oklahoma. (Occa-sionally he bought whack off magazines but the girls either looked too easy or too arrogant so he always had to close his eyes anyway and think of somebody he'd known in the past.) He wanted to see her, fuck this guy. Saturday he would be 61 and about all he had to look forward to was a phone call from his kid up the Oregon coast. His kid, who, God rest her soul, was his mother's son and not Parnell's, always ran a stopwatch while they talked so as to save on the phone bill. Hi Dad Happy Birthday and It's Been Really Nice Talking To You. I-Love-You-Bye.

"What can I do for you?" Parnell said. Then as he stood there watching the traffic go up and down Cortland Boulevard in bak-ing July sunlight, Parnell realized that the guy was somehow fa-miliar to him.

The guy said, "You know my father."

"Jesus H. Christ—"

"—Bud Garrett—"

"—Bud. I'll be god damned." He'd already shaken the kid's hand and he couldn't do that again so he kind of patted him on the shoulder and said, "Come on in."

"I'm Richard Garrett."

"I'm glad to meet you, Richard."

He took the guy inside. Richard looked around at the odds and ends of fuurniture that didn't match and at all the pictures of dead people and immediately put a smile on his face as if he just couldn't remember when he'd been so enchanted with a place before, which meant of course that he saw the place for the dump Parnell knew it to be.

"How about a beer?" Parnell said, hoping he had something besides the generic stuff he'd bought at the 7-11 a few nights ago.

"I'm fine, thanks."

Richard sat on the edge of the couch with the air of somebody waiting for his flight to be announced. He was all ready to jump up. He kept his eyes downcast and he kept fiddling with his wedding ring. Parnell watched him. Sometimes it turned out that way. Richard's old man had been on the force with Parnell. They'd been best friends. Garrett, Sr. was a big man, six three and fleshy but strong, a brawler and occasionally a mean one when the hootch didn't settle in him quite right. But his son . . . Sometimes it turned out that way. He was manly enough, Parnell supposed, but there was an air of being trapped in himself, of petulance that put Parnell off.

Three or four minutes of silence went by. The soap opera ended without Parnell getting another glance of the young lady. Then a "CBS Newsbreak" came on. Then some commercials. Richard didn't seem to notice that neither of them had said anything for a long time. Sunlight made bars through the venetian blinds. The refrigerator thrummed. Upstairs but distantly a kid bawled.

Parnell didn't realize it at first, not until Richard sniffled, that Bud Garrett's son was either crying or doing something damn close to it.

"Hey, Richard, what's the problem?" Parnell said, making sure to keep his voice soft.

"My, my Dad."

"Is something wrong?"

"Yes."

"What?"

Richard looked up with his pale blue eyes. "He's dying."

"Jesus."

Richard cleared his throat. "It's how he's dying that's so bad."

"Cancer?"

Richard said, "Yes. Liver. He's dying by inches."

"Shit."

Richard nodded. Then he fell once more into his own thoughts. Parnell let him stay there awhile, thinking about Bud Garrett. Bud had left the force on a whim that all the cops said would fail. He started a rent-a-car business with a small inheritance he'd come into. That was twenty years ago. Now Bud Garrett lived up in Woodland Hills and drove the big Mercedes and went to Europe once a year. For a time Bud and Parnell had tried to remain friends but beer and champagne didn't mix. When the Mrs. had died Bud had sent a lavish display of flowers to the funeral and a note that Parnell knew to be sincere but they hadn't had any real contact in years.

"Shit," Parnell said again.

Richard looked up, shaking his head as if trying to escape the after-effects of drugs. "I want to hire you."

"Hire me? As what?"

"You're a private investigator aren't you?"

"Not anymore. I mean I kept my ticket—it doesn't cost that much to renew it—but hell I haven't had a job in five years." He waved a beefy hand around the apartment. "I manage these apartments."

From inside his blue pin-striped suit Richard took a sleek wallet. He quickly counted out five one hundred dollar bills and put them on the blond coffee table next to the stack of Luke Short paperbacks. "I really want you to help me."

"Help you do what?"

"Kill my father."

Now Parnell shook his head. "Jesus, kid, are you nuts or what?"

Richard stood up. "Are you busy right now?"

Parnell looked around the room again. "I guess not."

"Then why don't you come with me?"

"Where?"

When the elevator doors opened to let them out on the sixth floor of the hospital, Parnell said, "I want to be sure you understand me."

He took Richard by the sleeve and held him and stared into his pale blue eyes. "You know why I'm coming here, right?"

"Right."

"I'm coming to see your father because we're old friends. Because I cared about him a great deal and because I still do. But that's the only reason."

"Right."

Parnell frowned. "You still think I'm going to help you, don't you?"

"I just want you to see him."

On the way to Bud Garrett's room they passed an especially good looking nurse. Parnell felt guilty about recognizing her beauty. His old friend was dying just down the hall and here Parnell was worrying about some nurse.

Parnell went around the corner of the door. The room was dark. It smelled sweet from flowers and fetid from flesh literally rotting.

Then he looked at the frail yellow man in the bed. Even in the shadows you could see his skin was yellow.

"I'll be damned," the man said.

It was like watching a skeleton talk by some trick of magic.

Parnell went over and tried to smile his ass off but all he could muster was just a little one. He wanted to cry until he collapsed. You sonofabitch, Parnell thought, enraged. He just wasn't sure who he was enraged with. Death or God or himself—or maybe even Bud himself for reminding Parnell of just how terrible and scary it could get near the end.

"I'll be damned," Bud Garrett said again.

He put out his hand and Parnell took it. Held it for a long time.

"He's a good boy, isn't he?" Garrett said, nodding to Richard.

"He sure is."

"I had to raise him after his mother died. I did a good job, if I say so myself."

"A damn good job, Bud."

This was a big private room that more resembled a hotel suite. There was a divan and a console tv and a dry bar. There was a Picasso lithograph and a walk-in closet and a deck to walk out on. There was a double-sized water bed with enough controls to drive a space ship and a big stereo and a bookcase filled with hardcovers. Most people Parnell knew dreamed of living in such a place. Bud Garrett was dying in it.

"He told you," Garrett said.

"What?" Parnell spun around to face Richard, knowing suddenly the worst truth of all.

"He told you."

"Jesus, Bud, you sent him, didn't you?"

"Yes. Yes, I did."

"Why?"

Parnell looked at Garrett again. How could somebody who used to have a weight problem and who could throw around the toughest drunk the barrio ever produced get to be like this. Nearly every time he talked he winced. And all the time he smelled. Bad.

"I sent for you because none of us is perfect," Bud said.

"I don't understand."

"He's afraid."

"Richard?"

"Yes."

"I don't blame him. I'd be afraid too." He paused and stared at Bud. "You asked him to kill you, didn't you?"

"Yes. It's his responsibility to do it."

Richard stepped up to his father's bedside and said, "I agree with that, Mr. Parnell. It is my responsibility. I just need a little help is all."

"Doing what?"

"If I buy cyanide, it will eventually be traced to me and I'll be tried for murder. If you buy it, nobody will ever connect you with my father."

Parnell shook his head. "That's bullshit. That isn't what you want me for. There are a million ways you could get cyanide without having it traced back."

Bud Garrett said, "I told him about you. I told you you could help give him strength."

"I don't agree with any of this, Bud. You should die when it's your time to die. I'm a Catholic."

Bud laughed hoarsely. "So am I, you asshole." He coughed and said, "The pain's bad. I'm beyond any help they can give me. But it could go on for a long time." Then, just as his son had an hour ago, Bud Garrett began crying almost imperceptibly. "I'm scared, Parnell. I don't know what's on the other side but it can't be any worse than this." He reached out his hand and for a long time Parnell just stared at it but then he touched it.

"Jesus," Parnell said. "It's pretty fucking confusing, Bud."

"It's my life. I'm sane, I'm sober. I should be able to decide, shouldn't I?"

But all Parnell could say was, "It's pretty fucking confusing, Bud. It's pretty fucking confusing."

Richard took Parnell out to dinner that night. It was a nice place. The table cloths were starchy white and the waiters all wore shiny shoes. Candles glowed inside red glass.

They'd had four drinks apiece, during which Richard told Parnell about his two sons (six and eight respectively) and about the perils and rewards of the rent-a-car business and about how much he liked windsurfing even though he really wasn't much good at it.

Just after the arrival of the fourth drink, Richard took something from his pocket and laid it on the table.

It was a cold capsule.

"You know how the Tylenol Killer in Chicago operated?" Richard asked.

Parnell nodded.

"Same thing," Richard said. "I took the cynaide and put it in a capsule."

"Christ. I don't want to know about it."

"You're scared, too, arent you?"

"Yeah, I am."

Richard sipped his whiskey-and-soda. With his regimental striped tie he might have been sitting in a country club. "May I ask you something?"

"Maybe."

"Do you believe in God?"

"Sure."

"Then if you believe in God, you must believe in goodness, correct?"

Parnell frowned. "I'm not much an intellectual, Richard."

"But if you believe in God, you must believe in goodness, right?"

"Right."

"Do you think what's happening to my father is good?"

"Of course I don't."

"Then you must also believe that God isn't doing this to him—right?"

"Right."

Richard held up the capsule. Stared at it. "All I want you to do is give me a ride to the hospital. Then just wait in the car down in the parking lot."

"I won't do it."

Richard signaled for another round.

"I won't god damn do it," Parnell said.

By the time they left the restaurant Richard was too drunk to drive. Parnell got behind the wheel of the new Audi. "Why don't you tell me where you live? I'll take you home and take a cab from there."

"I want to go to the hospital."

"No way, Richard."

Richard slammed his fist against the dashboard. "You fucking owe him that, man!" he screamed.

Parnell was shocked, and a bit impressed, with Richard's violent side. If nothing else, he saw how much Richard loved his old man.

"Richard, listen."

Richard sat in a heap against the opposite door. His tears were dry ones, choking ones. "Don't give me any of your speeches." He wiped snot from his nose on his sleeve. "My Dad always told me what a tough guy Parnell was." He turned to Parnell, anger in him again. "Well, I'm not tough, Parnell and so I need to borrow some of your toughness so I can get that man out of his pain and grant him his one last fucking wish. DO YOU GOD DAMN UNDERSTAND ME?"

He smashed his fist on the dashboard again.

Parnell turned on the ignition and drove them away.

When they reached the hospital, Parnell found a parking spot and pulled in. The mercury vapor lights made him feel as though he were on Mars. Bugs smashed against the windshield.

"I'll wait here for you," Parnell said.

Richard looked over at him. "You won't call the cops?"

"No."

"And you won't come up and try to stop me?"

"No."

Richard studied Parnell's face. "Why did you change your mind?"

"Because I'm like him."

"Like my father?"

"Yeah. A coward. I wouldn't want the pain either. I'd be just as afraid."

All Richard said, and this he barely whispered, was "Thanks."

While he sat there Parnell listened to country western music and then a serious political call-in show and then a call-in show where a lady talked about Venusians who wanted to pork her and then some salsa music and then a religious minister who sounded like Foghorn Leghorn in the old Warner Brothers cartoons.

By then Richard came back.

He got in the car and slammed the door shut and said, completely sober now, "Let's go."

Parnell got out of there.

They went ten long blocks before Parnell said, "You didn't do it, did you?"

Richard got hysterical. "You sonofabitch! You sonofabitch!"

Parnell had to pull the car over to the curb. He hit Richard once, a fast clean right hand, not enough to make him unconscious but enough to calm him down.

"You didn't do it, did you?"

"He's my father, Parnell. I don't know what to do. I love him so much I don't want to see him suffer. But I love him so much I don't want to see him die, either."

Parnell let the kid sob. He thought of his old friend Bud Garrett and what a good god damn fun buddy he'd been and then he started crying, too.

When Parnell came down Richard was behind the steering wheel.

Parnell got in the car and looked around at the empty parking lot and said, "Drive."

"Any place especially?"

"Out along the East River road. Your old man and I used to fish off that little bridge there."

Richard drove them. From inside his sportcoat Parnell took the pint of Jim Beam.

When they got to the bridge Parnell said, "Give me five minutes alone then you can come over, ok?"

Richard was starting to sob again.

Parnell got out of the car and went over to the bridge. In the hot night you could hear the hydroelectric dam half a mile downstream and smell the fish and feel the mosquitos feasting their way through the evening.

He thought of what Bud Garrett had said, "Put it in some whiskey for me, will you?"

So Parnell had obliged.

He stood now on the bridge looking up at the yellow circle of moon thinking about dead people, his wife and many of his WWII friends, the rookie cop who'd died of a sudden tumor, his wife with her rosary-wrapped hands. Hell, there was probably even a chance that nurse from Enid, Oklahoma was dead.

"What do you think's on the other side?" Bud Garrett had asked just half an hour ago. He'd almost sounded excited. As if he were a farm kid about to ship out with the Merchant Marines.

"I don't know," Parnell had said.

"It scare you, Parnell?"

"Yeah," Parnell had said. "Yeah it does."

Then Bud Garrett had laughed. "Don't tell the kid that. I always told him nothin' scared you."

Richard came up the bridge after a time. At first he stood maybe a hundred feet away from Parnell. He leaned his elbows on the concrete and looked out at the water and the moon. Parnell watched him, knowing it was all Richard, or anybody, could do.

Look out at the water and the moon and think about dead people and how you yourself would soon enough be dead.

Richard turned to Parnell then and said, his tears gone completely now, sounding for the first time like Parnell's sort of man, "You know, Parnell, my father was right. You're a brave sonofabitch. You really are."

Parnell knew it was important for Richard to believe that—that there were actually people in the world who didn't fear things the way most people did—so Parnell didn't answer him at all.

He just took his pint out and had himself a swig and looked some more at the moon and the water.

THE SECOND COMING

Joe Gores

"*B*ut fix thy eyes upon the valley: for the river of blood draws nigh, in which boils every one who by violence injures other."
            Canto XII, 46-48
            The Inferno of Dante Alighieri

I've thought about it a lot, man; like why Victor and I made that terrible scene out there at San Quentin, putting ourselves on that it was just for kicks. Victor was hung up on kicks; they were a thing with him. He was a sharp dark-haired cat with bright eyes, built lean and hard like a French skin-diver. His old man dug only money, so he'd always had plenty of bread. We got this idea out at his pad on Potrero Hill—a penthouse, of course—one afternoon when we were lying around on the sunporch in swim trunks and drinking gin.

"You know, man," he said, "I have made about every scene in the world. I have balled all the chicks, red and yellow and black and white, and I have gotten high on muggles, bluejays,

When The Second Coming *first appeared,* **Joe Gores** *was unknown. The story, near as one can tell, had a men's magazine appearance then an anthology appearance and then vanished. It should not have, being a powerful and unique look at the early '60s that would later become the social holocaust of a few years hence. Gores, author of* Hammett, *is one of the deans of mystery fiction, and his story here shows why.*

redbirds, and mescaline. I have even tried the white stuff a time or two. But—"

"You're a goddam tiger, dad."

"—but there is one kick I've never had, man."

When he didn't go on I rolled my head off the quart gin bottle I was using for a pillow and looked at him. He was giving me a shot with those hot, wild eyes of his.

"So like what is it?"

"I've never watched an execution."

I thought about it a minute, drowsily. The sun was so hot it was like nailing me right to the air mattress. Watching an execution. Seeing a man go through the wall. A groovy idea for an artist.

"Too much," I murmured. "I'm with you, dad."

The next day, of course, I was back at work on some abstracts for my first one-man show and had forgotten all about it; but that night Victor called me up.

"Did you write to the warden up at San Quentin today, man? He has to contact the San Francisco police chief and make sure you don't have a record and aren't a psycho and are useful to the community."

So I went ahead and wrote the letter, because even sober it still seemed a cool idea for some kicks; I knew they always need twelve witnesses to make sure that the accused isn't sneaked out the back door or something at the last minute like an old Jimmy Cagney movie. Even so, I lay dead for two months before the letter came. The star of our show would be a stud who'd broken into a house trailer near Fort Ord to rape this Army lieutenant's wife, only right in the middle of it she'd started screaming so he'd put a pillow over her face to keep her quiet until he could finish. But she'd quit breathing. There were eight chicks on the jury and I think like three of them got broken ankles in the rush to send him to the gas chamber. Not that I cared. Kicks, man.

Victor picked me up at seven-thirty in the morning, an hour before we were supposed to report to San Quentin. He was wearing this really hip Italian import, and fifty-dollar shoes, and a narrow-brim hat with a little feather in it, so all he needed was a briefcase to be Chairman of the Board. The top was down on the Mercedes, cold as it was, and when he saw my black suit and hand-knit tie he flashed this crazy white-toothed grin you'd never see in any Director's meeting.

"*Too much*, killer! If you'd like comb your hair you could pass for an undertaker coming after the body."

Since I am a very long, thin cat with black hair always hanging in my eyes, who fully dressed weighs as much as a medium-size collie, I guess he wasn't too far off. I put a pint of Jose Cuervo in the side pocket of the car and we split. We were both really turned on: I mean this senseless, breathless hilarity as if we'd just heard the world's funniest joke. Or were just going to.

It was one of those chilly California brights with blue sky and cold sunshine and here and there a cloud like Mr. Big was popping Himself a cap down beyond the horizon. I dug it all: the sail of a lone early yacht out in the Bay like a tossed-away paper cup; the whitecaps flipping around out by Angel Island like they were stoned out of their minds; the top down on the 300-SL so we could smell salt and feel the icy bite of the wind. But beyond the tunnel on U.S. 101, coming down towards Marin City, I felt a sudden sharp chill as if a cloud has passed between me and the sun, but none had; and then I dug for the first time what I was actually doing.

Victor felt it, too, for he turned to me and said, "Must maintain cool, dad."

"I'm with it."

San Quentin Prison, out on the end of its peninsula, looked like a sprawled ugly dragon sunning itself on a rock; we pulled up near the East Gate and there were not even any birds singing. Just a bunch of quiet cats in black, Quakers or Mennonites or something, protesting capital punishment by their silent presence as they'd done ever since Chessman had gotten his out there. I felt dark frightened things move around inside me when I saw them.

"Let's fall out right here, dad," I said in a momentary sort of panic, "and catch the matinee next week."

But Victor was in kicksville, like desperate to put on all those squares in the black suits. When they looked over at us he jumped up on the back of the bucket seat and spread his arms wide like the Sermon on the Mount. With his tortoise-shell shades and his flashing teeth and that suit which had cost three yards, he looked like Christ on his way to Hollywood.

"Whatsoever ye do unto the least of these, my brethren, ye do unto me," he cried in this ringing apocalyptic voice.

I grabbed his arm and dragged him back down off the seat. "For Christ sake, man, cool it!"

But he went into high laughter and punched my arm with feverish exuberance, and then jerked a tiny American flag from his inside jacket pocket and began waving it around above the windshield. I could see the sweat on his forehead.

"It's worth it to live in this country!" he yelled at them.

He put the car in gear and we went on. I looked back and saw one of those cats crossing himself. It put things back in perspective: they were from nowhere. The Middle Ages. Not that I judged them: that was their scene, man. Unto every cat what he digs the most.

The guard on the gate directed us to a small wooden building set against the outside wall, where we found five other witnesses. Three of them were reporters, one was a fat cat smoking a .45-calibre stogy like a politician from Sacramento, and the last was an Army type in lieutenant's bars, his belt buckle and insignia looking as if he'd been up all night with a can of *Brasso*.

A guard came in and told us to surrender everything in our pockets and get a receipt for it. We had to remove our shoes, too; they were too heavy for the fluoroscope. Then they put us through this groovy little room one-by-one to x-ray us for cameras and so on; they don't want anyone making the Kodak scene while they're busy dropping the pellets. We ended up inside the prison with our shoes back on and with our noses full of that old prison detergent-disinfectant stink.

The politician type, who had these cold slitted eyes like a Sherman tank, started coming on with rank jokes: but everyone put him down, hard, even the reporters. I guess nobody but fuzz ever gets used to executions. The Army stud was at parade rest with a face so pale his freckles looked like a charge of shot. He had reddish hair.

After a while five guards came in to make up the twelve required witnesses. They looked rank, as fuzz always do, and got off in a corner in a little huddle, laughing and gassing together like a bunch of kids kicking a dog. Victor and I sidled over to hear what they were saying.

"Who's sniffing the eggs this morning?" asked one.

"I don't know, I haven't been reading the papers." He yawned when he answered.

"Don't you remember?" urged another, "it's the guy who smothered the woman in the house trailer. Down in the Valley by Salinas."

"Yeah. Soldier's wife; he was raping her and . . ."

Like dogs hearing the plate rattle, they turned in unison toward the Army lieutenant; but just then more fuzz came in to march us to the observation room. We went in a column of twos with a guard beside each one, everyone unconsciously in step as if following a cadence call. I caught myself listening for measured mournful drum rolls.

The observation room was built right around the gas chamber, with rising tiers of benches for extras in case business was brisk. The chamber itself was hexagonal; the three walls in our room were of plate glass with a waist-high brass rail around the outside like the rail in an old-time saloon. The other three walls were steel plate, with a heavy door, rivet-studded, in the center one, and a small observation window in each of the others.

Inside the chamber were just these two massive chairs, probably oak, facing the rear walls side-by-side; their backs were high enough to come to the nape of the neck of anyone sitting in them. Under each was like a bucket that I knew contained hydrochloric acid. At a signal the executioner would drop sodium cyanide pellets into a chute; the pellets would roll down into the bucket; hydrocyanic acid gas would form; and the cat in the chair would be wasted.

The politician type, who had this rich fruity baritone like Burl Ives, asked why they had two chairs.

"That's in case there's a double-header, dad," I said.

"You're kidding." But by his voice the idea pleased him. Then he wheezed plaintively: "I don't see why they turn the chairs away—we can't even watch his face while it's happening to him."

He was a true rank genuine creep, right out from under a rock with the slime barely dry on his scales; but I wouldn't have wanted his dreams. I think he was one of those guys who tastes the big draught many times before he swallows it.

We milled around like cattle around the chute, when they smell the blood from inside and know they're somehow involved; then we heard sounds and saw the door in the back of the chamber swing open. A uniformed guard appeared to stand at attention, followed by a priest dressed all in black like Zorro, with his face hanging down to his belly button. He must have been a new man, because he had trouble maintaining his cool: just standing there beside the guard he dropped his little black book on the floor like three times in a row.

The Army cat said to me, as if he'd wig out unless he broke the silence: "They . . . have it arranged like a stage play, don't they?"

"But no encores," said Victor hollowly.

Another guard showed up in the doorway and they walked in the condemned man. He was like sort of a shock. You expect a stud to *act* like a murderer: I mean, cringe at the sight of the chair because he knows this is it, there's finally no place to go, no appeal to make, or else bound in there full of cheap bravado and go-to-hell. But he just seemed mildly interested, nothing more.

He wore a white shirt with the sleeves rolled up, suntans that looked Army issue, and no tie. Under thirty, brown crewcut hair—the terrible thing is that I cannot even remember the features on his face, man. The closest I could come to a description would be that he resembled the Army cat right there beside me with his nose to the glass.

The one thing I'll never forget is that stud's hands. He'd been on Death Row all these months, and here his hands were still red and chapped and knobby, as if he'd still been out picking turnips in the San Joaquin Valley. Then I realized: I was thinking of him in the past tense.

Two fuzz began strapping him down in the chair. A broad leather strap across the chest, narrower belts on the arms and legs. God they were careful about strapping him in. I mean they wanted to make sure he was comfortable. And all the time he was talking with them. Not that we could hear it, but I suppose it went *that's fine, fellows, no, that strap isn't too tight, gee, I hope I'm not making you late for lunch.*

That's what bugged me, he was so damned *apologetic*! While they were fastening him down over that little bucket of oblivion, that poor dead lonely son of a bitch twisted around to look over his shoulder at us, and he *smiled*. I mean if he'd had an arm free he might have *waved*! One of the fuzz, who had white hair and these sad gentle eyes like he was wearing a hair shirt, patted him on the head on the way out. No personal animosity, son, just doing my job.

After that the tempo increased, like your heart beat when you're on a black street at three a.m. and the echo of your own footsteps begins to sound like someone following you. The warden was at one observation window, the priest and the doctor at the other. The blackrobe made the sign of the cross, having a last go at the condemned, but he was digging only Ben Casey. Here was this M.D. cat who'd taken the Hippocratean Oath to preserve life, waving his arms around like a tv director to show that stud the easiest way to *die*.

Hold your breath, then breathe deeply: you won't feel a thing. Of course hydrocyanic acid gas melts your guts into a red-hot soup and burns out every fibre in the lining of your lungs, but you won't be really feeling it as you jerk around: that'll just be raw nerve endings.

Like they should have called *his* the Hypocritical Oath.

So there we were, three yards and half an inch of plate glass apart, with us staring at him and him by just turning his head able to stare right back: but there were a million light years between the two sides of the glass. He didn't turn. He was shrived and strapped in and briefed on how to die, and he was ready for the fumes. I found out afterwards that he had even willed his body to medical research.

I did a quick take around.

Victor was sweating profusely, his eyes glued to the window.

The politician was pop-eyed, nose pressed flat and belly indented by the brass rail, pudgy fingers like plump garlic sausages smearing the glass on either side of his head. A look on his face, already, like that of a stud making it with a chick.

The reporters seemed ashamed, as if someone had caught them peeking over the transom into the ladies' john.

The Army cat just looked sick.

Only the fuzz were unchanged, expending no more emotion on this than on their targets after rapid-fire exercises at the range.

On no face was there hatred.

Suddenly, for the first time in my life, I was part of it. I wanted to yell out *STOP!* We were about to gas this stud and *none of us wanted him to die!* We've created this society and we're all responsible for what it does, but none of us as individuals is willing to take that responsibility. We're like that Nazi cat at Nuremberg who said that everything would have been all right if they'd only given him more ovens.

The warden signalled. I heard gas whoosh up around the chair.

The condemned man didn't move. He was following doctor's orders. Then he took the huge gulping breath the M.D. had pantomimed. All of a sudden he threw this tremendous convulsion, his body straining up against the straps, his head slewed around so I could see his eyes were tight shut and his lips were pulled back from his teeth. Then he started panting like a baby in an oxygen tent, swiftly and shallowly. Only it wasn't oxygen his lungs were trying to work on.

The lieutenant stepped back smartly from the window, blinked, and puked on the glass. His vomit hung there for an instant like a phosphorus bomb burst in a bunker; then two fuzz were supporting him from the room and we were all jerking back from the mess. All except the politician. He hadn't even noticed: he was in Henry Millerville, getting his sex kicks the easy way.

I guess the stud in there had never dug that he was supposed to be gone in two seconds without pain, because his body was still arched up in that terrible bow, and his hands were still claws. I could see the muscles standing out along the sides of his jaws like marbles. Finally he flopped back and just hung there in his straps like a machine-gunned paratrooper.

But that wasn't the end. He took another huge gasp, so I could see his ribs pressing out against his white shirt. After that one, twenty seconds. We decided that he had cut out.

Then another gasp. Then nothing. Half a minute nothing.

Another of those final terrible shuddering racking gasps. At last: all through. All used up. Making it with the angels.

But then he did it *again*. Every fibre of that dead wasted comic thrown-away body strained for air on this one. No air: only hydrocyanic acid gas. Just nerves, like the fish twitching after you whack it on the skull with the back edge of the skinning knife. Except that it wasn't a fish we were seeing die.

His head flopped sideways and his tongue came out slyly like the tongue of a dead deer. Then this gunk ran out of his mouth.

It was just saliva—they said it couldn't be anything else—but it reminded me of the residue after light-line resistors have been melted in an electrical fire. That kind of black. That kind of scorched.

Very softly, almost to himself, Victor murmured: "Later, dad."

That was it. Dig you in the hereafter, dad. Ten little minutes and you're through the wall. Mistah Kurtz, he dead. Mistah Kurtz, he very very goddamn dead.

I believed it. Looking at what was left of that cat was like looking at a chick who's gotten herself bombed on the heavy, so when you hold a match in front of her eyes the pupils don't react and there's no one home, man. No one. Nowhere. End of the lineville.

We split.

But on the way out I kept thinking of that Army stud, and wondering what had made him sick. Was it because the cat in the chair had been the last to enter, no matter how violently, the body of his beloved, and now even that febrile connection had been severed? Whatever the reason, his body had known what perhaps his mind had refused to accept: this ending was no new beginning, this death would not restore his dead chick to him. This death, no matter how just in his eyes, had generated only nausea.

Victor and I sat in the Mercedes for a long time with the top down, looking out over that bright beautiful empty peninsula, not named, as you might think, after a saint, but after some poor dumb Indian they had hanged there a hundred years or so before. Trees and clouds and blue water, and still no birds making the scene. Even the cats in the black suits had vanished, but now I understood why they'd been there. In their silent censure, they had been sounding the right gong, man. *We* were the ones from the Middle Ages.

Victor took a deep shuddering breath as if he could never get enough air. Then he said in a barely audible voice: "How did you dig that action, man?"

I gave a little shrug and, being myself, said the only thing I could say. "It was a gas, dad."

"I dig, man. I'm hip. A gas."

Something was wrong with the way he said it, but I broke the seal on the tequila and we killed it in fifteen minutes, without even a lime to suck in between. Then he started the car and we cut out, and I realized what was wrong. Watching that cat in the gas chamber, Victor had realized for the very first time that life is far, far more than just kicks. We were both partially responsible for what had happened in there, and we had been ineluctably diminished by it.

On U.S. 101 he coked the Mercedes up to 104 m.p.h. through the traffic, and held it there. It was wild: it was the end: but I didn't sound. I was alone without my Guide by the boiling river of blood. When the Highway Patrol finally got us stopped, Victor was coming on so strong and I was coming on so mild that they surrounded us with their holsters flaps unbuckled, and checked our veins for needle marks.

I didn't say a word to them, man, not one. Not even my name. Like they had to look in my wallet to see who I was. And while they were doing that, Victor blew his cool entirely. You know, biting, foaming at the mouth, the whole bit—he gave a very good show until they hit him on the back of the head with a gun butt. I just watched.

They lifted his license for a year, nothing else, because his old man spent a lot of bread on a shrinker who testified that Victor had temporarily wigged out, and who had him put away in the zoo for a time. He's back now, but he still sees that wig picker, three times a week at forty clams a shot.

He needs it. A few days ago I saw him on Upper Grant, stalking lithely through a grey raw February day with the fog in, wearing just a t-shirt and jeans—and no shoes. He seemed agitated, pressed, confined within his own concerns, but I stopped him for a minute.

"Ah . . . how you making it, man? Like, ah, what's the gig?"

He shook his head cautiously. "They will not let us get away with it, you know. Like to them, man, just living is a crime."

"Why no strollers, dad?"

"I cannot wear shoes." He moved closer and glanced up and down the street, and said with tragic earnestness: "I can hear only with the soles of my feet, man."

Then he nodded and padded away through the crowds on silent naked soles like a puzzled panther, drifting through the fruiters and drunken teen-agers and fuzz trying to bust some cat for possession who have inherited North Beach from the true swingers. I guess all Victor wants to listen to now is Mother Earth: all he wants to hear is the comforting sound of the worms, chewing away.

Chewing away, and waiting for Victor; and maybe for the Second Coming.

Watch out for the Black Lizard!